Gabriel.

He could feel flames coming through the floor, looking for him. The sound of wood giving way was deafening. Sparks and ash rained down.

He wasn't going to make it. He was going to fail. *Again.*

Then a hand closed over his wrist and pulled, *hard.*

Gabriel followed—what else could he do?

He burst into fresh air that felt arctic on his cheeks. That hand kept pulling, dragging him.

He stumbled and almost fell, but he caught himself before he dropped the girl.

He felt grass under his feet and slowed.

Someone was jerking the girl out of his arms. "Is she breathing?"

Hunter.

Had Hunter gone into . . . into *that* to drag him the rest of the way out of the darkness?

Also by Brigid Kemmerer

STORM

ELEMENTAL (an e-book)

SPARK * The Elemental Series

BRIGID KEMMERER

KENSINGTON PUBLISHING CORP.
www.kensingtonbooks.com

K TEEN BOOKS are published by

Kensington Publishing Corp.
119 West 40th Street
New York, NY 10018

Copyright © 2012 by Brigid Kemmerer

All Kensington titles, imprints, and distributed lines are available at special quantity discounts for bulk purchases for sales promotion, premiums, fund-raising, educational or institutional use.

Special book excerpts or customized printings can also be created to fit specific needs. For details, write or phone the office of the Kensington Special Sales Manager: Kensington Publishing Corp., 119 West 40th Street, New York, NY 10018. Attn. Special Sales Department. Phone: 1-800-221-2647.

Kensington and KTeen Reg. U.S. Pat. & TM Off.

ISBN-13: 978-0-7582-7282-9
ISBN-10: 0-7582-7282-0

First Kensington Trade Paperback Printing: September 2012

10   9   8   7   6   5   4   3   2

Printed in the United States of America

For Jonathan, Nicholas, and Baby Sam:
I thank my lucky stars every day for each of you.

ACKNOWLEDGMENTS

As always, I have to start with my mother. She's an amazing woman, and if not for her incredible support, you wouldn't be holding this book in your hands. I'm grateful for her presence in my life every single day.

My husband, Michael, makes writing possible. He's my best friend, my support system, the love of my life. And for some reason, he insists on waiting to read a finished book. So here you go, honey. I hope you like it. Thank you for everything.

Alicia Condon and the entire team at Kensington are all incredible. I can't thank you all enough. I'm so glad I've gotten the chance to work with you all.

I have many close friends on this writing journey, but I would be remiss in not thanking Bobbie Goettler, Alison Kemper Beard, and Sarah Fine. You all keep me grounded, you keep me sane, and you keep me writing. You're all amazing women, amazing mothers, and amazing writers, and I'm so lucky to know you.

This book took a tremendous amount of research. It absolutely would not have gotten written without support and assistance from Ed Kiser, Assistant Fire Chief for Riviera Beach Volunteer Fire Department. He already works tirelessly at a thankless job, and he was able to spare a considerable amount of time for me (including immediate response to e-mails at one o'clock in the morning). Ed, I cannot thank you enough.

Additionally, I owe special thanks to Officer James Kalinosky, of the Baltimore County Police Department, and Officer Todd Schwenke, of the Anne Arundel County Police Department, for their information on police investigations, arson, arrest procedures, and anything else I could think to ask. I took all this research and delightfully twisted it to fit my needs. Any inaccuracies are on my part, not theirs.

Special thanks to Thomas Berry for providing every math question included in this book, as well as advice on how to handle teaching situations. If you're his student, say thanks from me.

Special thanks to Layne Berry for letting me use her first name. I hope I did you proud.

Finally, extra special thanks to the Kemmerer boys, Jonathan, Nick, and Sam, for your love and support, especially understanding when I need to just plug in my headphones and write.

CHAPTER 1

Gabriel Merrick stared at the dead leaf in his palm and willed it to burn.

It refused.

He had a lighter in his pocket, but that always felt like cheating. He *should* be able to call flame to something this dry. The damn thing had been stuck in the corner of his window screen since last winter. But the leaf only seemed interested in flaking onto his trigonometry textbook.

He was seriously ready to take the lighter to *that*.

A knock sounded on his bedroom wall.

"Black," he called. Nicky always slept late, always knocked on his wall to ask what color he was wearing. If he didn't, they ended up dressing alike.

Gabriel looked back at the leaf—and it was just that, a dead leaf. No hint of power. Behind the drywall, electricity sang to him. In the lamp on his desk, he could sense the burning filament. Even the weak threads of sunlight that managed to burn through the clouds left some trace of his element. If the power was there, Gabriel could speak to it, ask it to bend to his will.

If the power wasn't, he had nothing.

His door swung open. Nick stood there in a green hoodie and a pair of khaki cargo shorts. A girl on the cheer squad had once asked Gabriel if having a twin was like looking in a mirror all the time. He'd asked her if being a cheerleader was like being an idiot all the time—but really, it was a good question. He and Nick shared the same dark hair, the same blue eyes, the same few freckles across their cheekbones.

Right now, Nick leaned on a crutch, a knee brace strapped around his left leg, evidence of the only thing they didn't share: a formerly broken leg.

Gabriel glanced away from that. "Hey."

"What are you doing?"

Gabriel flicked the leaf into the wastebasket beneath his desk. "Nothing. You ready for school?"

"Is that your trig book?"

"Yeah. Just making sure I told you the right assignment."

Gabriel always attempted his math homework—and then handed it over for Nick to do it *right*. Math had turned into a foreign language somewhere around fifth grade. Then, Gabriel had struggled through, managing Cs when his twin brought home As. But in seventh grade, when their parents died, he'd come close to failing. Nick started covering for him, and he'd been doing it ever since.

Not like it was a big challenge. Math came to Nick like breathing. He was in second-year calculus, earning college credit. Gabriel was stuck in trigonometry with juniors.

He was pretty frigging sick of it.

Gabriel flipped the book closed and shoved it into his backpack. His eyes fell on that knee brace again. Two days ago, his twin's leg had been broken in three places.

"You're not going to make me carry your crap all day, are you?" His voice came out sharp, nowhere near the light ribbing he'd intended.

Nick took it in stride, as usual. "Not if you're going to cry about it." He turned toward the stairs, his voice rising to a mocking falsetto. "I'm the school sports hero, but I can't possibly carry a few extra books—"

"Keep it up," Gabriel called, slinging the backpack over his shoulder to follow his brother. "I'll push you down the stairs."

But he hesitated in the doorway, listening to Nick's hitching steps as he descended the staircase, the creak of the banister as it supported his weight.

Gabriel knew he should help. He should probably be taking the place of that crutch. That's what *Nick* would do for *him*.

But he couldn't force himself through the doorway.

That broken leg had been his fault. Thank god Nick could pull power from the air, an element in abundance. He probably wouldn't even need the brace by the end of the week.

And then Gabriel wouldn't need to stare at the evidence of his own poor judgment.

He and his brothers had always been targeted for their Elemental abilities. Being pure Elementals, they should have been put to death as soon as they came into their powers. Luckily, their parents had struck a deal with the weaker Elementals in town.

A deal that had led to their parents' deaths.

Their oldest brother, Michael, had been able to keep the deal in place—until a few weeks ago, when Tyler and Seth, two of the other Elemental kids in town, had attacked Chris. It started a snowball of events that led to an Elemental Guide coming to town to do away with the Merrick brothers for good.

He'd almost succeeded, too. After the Homecoming dance, they'd been attacked.

They'd fought back the only way they knew how. But Gabriel had let Nick call storms that were too strong. He'd begged his twin for more power. When Nick fell, the accident had practically shattered his leg—if they weren't full Elementals, he probably would have needed surgery.

That night, Gabriel couldn't keep him safe. The Guide had kidnapped Nick and Chris, had held them prisoner.

Becca and Hunter had found them. But Gabriel couldn't do anything. Ineffective and out of control, just like always.

But now they were safe, and things were back to normal. Nick was his usual self. *Life's good. Move on. No use complain-*

ing. He hadn't even said a word about what had happened on the field.

As far as Gabriel was concerned, he didn't need to.

Just like with math, Nick was used to his twin being a failure.

Gabriel pulled onto Becca Chandler's street and glanced in the rearview mirror at his younger brother. Chris was chewing on his thumbnail, leaning against the window.

"Nervous?" said Gabriel.

Chris looked away from the window and glared at him. "No."

Nick turned in his seat. "Make sure you open the door for her. Girls eat that crap up."

"Nah," said Gabriel. "Play it cool. Make her work for it—"

"For god's sake," Chris snapped. "She just broke up with Hunter, like, *yesterday,* so it's not like that. Okay?"

Jesus. Someone was worked up. Gabriel glanced back again. "But she asked you for a ride."

Chris looked back out the window. "I offered."

Nick turned his head to look at his twin. "Very nervous," he whispered.

Gabriel smiled and turned into Becca's driveway. "Very."

"Would you two *shut up?*"

Becca was waiting on the front step, her arms around her knees and her hands drawn up into the sleeves of a fleece pullover, dark hair hanging down her back.

"She looks upset," said Nick.

She did, her eyes dark and shadowed, her shoulders hunched. Or maybe she was just cold. Gabriel wasn't one for figuring out emotion.

Her face brightened when she saw them, and she sprinted for the car almost before Chris had time to jump out and hold the door for her.

She stopped short in front of him, spots of pink on her cheeks. "Hey," she said, tucking her hair behind her ear.

"Hey," Chris said back, his voice soft and low.

Then they just stood there breathing at each other.

Gabriel hit the horn.

They jumped apart—but Chris punched him in the shoulder when he climbed back into the car.

Becca buckled her seat belt. "I'm glad you're all here."

Her voice was full of anxiety. So Nick had been right.

Chris shifted to look at her. "You all right?"

She shook her head. "My dad just called. He wants to meet with me. Tonight."

No one said anything for a moment, leaving her words floating in the warm confines of the car.

Her dad was the Elemental Guide who'd been sent to kill them all.

When they escaped and didn't hear anything for two days, they'd all started to think he'd run off again, the way he had when Becca was eleven.

Chris took a breath, and his voice was careful. "Do you want to meet with *him?*"

Gabriel glanced at her in the rearview mirror. She was practically hunched against the door, staring out the window. "I want him to get the hell *out of here.*"

Chris was still watching her. "He is your father." He paused. "You sure?"

"He might have made a 'contribution,' but that man is *not* my father."

"I want to see him," said Gabriel. His shoulders already felt tight.

She hesitated. "Wait. You'd . . . go with me?"

"Yeah. I owe him a little payback."

"*We,*" said Nick. There was heat in his voice, too.

"Did he say why he wanted to meet?" asked Chris.

"He said he wants to help us. That they'll send another Guide if he doesn't report back that you were . . . um . . ."

"Killed." Gabriel hit the turn signal at the end of her road.

She swallowed. "Yeah. Hey, make a left. We need to pick up Quinn."

Gabriel glanced at her again. He wasn't a big fan of Becca's best friend, so the last thing he wanted to do was pick her up—

especially when there was so much left to talk about. "Anyone else?" he said. "Should I pick up Hunter, too?"

Becca faltered and glanced at Chris. "I'm sorry . . . I should have asked—"

"It's fine," he said, and Gabriel could feel his youngest brother's eyes in the rearview mirror. "I'm sure he's not intentionally being a dick."

Gabriel ignored him. "What time tonight? Did he say where?"

"Annapolis Mall. Eight o'clock. Make a right at the stop sign. She's down at the end of the block."

"He wants to meet at the *mall?*" said Nick.

"Food court," said Becca. "I told him it had to be somewhere public."

"Great," said Gabriel. "More people in the line of fire."

"Do you think the mall was a mistake?" said Becca.

Gabriel shrugged. Her father hadn't hesitated to put normal people in danger last week.

But really, what difference did it make?

They were pulling alongside the curb, and Quinn threw open the door and launched herself inside. Blond hair was caught inside her jacket, and her backpack was barely zipped. Notebooks spilled onto the floorboards before she could get the door shut.

"Jesus, *drive,*" Quinn said, hitting the back of his seat. "God, I hate my mother."

She was just so frigging *overdramatic.* Gabriel pulled the car away from the curb, deliberately moving as slowly as possible.

But Nick turned his head to look at her over his shoulder. "Everything all right?"

Quinn shoved the notebooks back into her bag and yanked the zipper. "I'm stuck living with Satan. When's the car situation going to improve, Bex? I can't keep doing this."

Nick was still looking into the backseat. "We can keep driving you to school, if you need a ride."

Quinn stopped fighting with her things and looked up at him. "Really?"

"We'd love it," said Gabriel, making sure his sarcasm carried an edge. "Maybe we can pick up half the junior class."

"What is *with* you?" said Chris.

"Don't worry," said Quinn. "I already know he's an ass."

"Love you, too," said Gabriel.

But Nick grinned. "You can tell us apart?"

"Please. When you're talking, there's no challenge." She punched the back of Gabriel's seat again.

He glared at her in the rearview mirror. "What are you, six years old?"

"Oh, you don't like that? What about this?" She licked her finger and stuck it in his ear.

He smacked her hand away. He'd never punched a girl, but she might be the first.

Becca laughed. "Quinn has two brothers."

"I know all the ways to irritate a boy," Quinn said.

Gabriel snorted. "I don't doubt that one bit."

CHAPTER 2

The day started with U.S. History and English, two classes Gabriel couldn't give a crap about. He kept thinking about Becca's father, how they were going to sit in the food court and have a conversation with the guy.

Now her father wanted to help. Yeah, *right*.

The Homecoming dance wasn't the first time the Guide had nearly killed them. Gabriel could still remember the explosion that had taken out the bridge two blocks from school—and almost killed Gabriel. The fire hadn't hurt him, but concrete didn't make for a soft landing.

And then there was the way the Guide had attacked them on the soccer field. The way he'd taken Nick, broken leg and all.

The way Gabriel hadn't been able to stop him.

His pencil snapped in his hand.

The fluorescent lights flickered and buzzed, making the teacher pause in her lecture and glance up.

Gabriel took a deep breath. He needed to get a handle on his temper before he set the whole school on fire.

Chris and Nick were lucky. Chris could carry a bottle of water with him and be close to his element. And Nick—hell, air was everywhere. He'd have a harder time getting away from it. Even Michael spent his days playing in the dirt, perfect for an Earth Elemental.

Natural energy was all around. But it was weak. Controlled. Filtered sunlight, electrical wiring contained behind layers of rubber and plastic. All it did was make him crave *more*—and Gabriel couldn't exactly walk around with a candle.

Third period: Trigonometry. Gabriel felt his shoulders tighten as he walked through the doorway. Mr. Riley, their wiry teacher, wasn't at his desk yet, but Gabriel dropped his homework in the basket and made his way to the third seat in his row. He usually spent this hour riding a line of tension to make sure he didn't get called on. This was a junior-level class, but luckily he sat next to that advanced sophomore chick who raised her hand for just about every question. Gabriel pulled his notebook out of his backpack, but he'd snapped his only pencil in English.

Not like it mattered. What was he going to do, doodle?

Taylor Morrissey, another senior stuck in here, sat on the desk in front of him, her feet on the chair. Blond hair swung over her shoulder and perfectly accented her chest. Her skirt was so short it flared around her on the desk and put Gabriel at eye level with just about everything.

He knew she'd be giving the same show to any guy around, but it was tough to look up from *that*. "Hey, Taylor."

"You going out for basketball this week?"

"Don't I always?" Sports were his one saving grace, the only reason he bothered to keep his grades up. Being active took the edge off, let him run down energy that looked for things to burn in other ways.

Taylor leaned forward, resting her hands on her knees and giving him a clear view down her shirt, too. "Me and the other girls are going to think up something special for the seniors this year." She looked at him from under her lashes. "Any ideas?"

Usually, he could do this banter stuff all day. But he was already exhausted from plotting to destroy Becca's father, and he didn't feel like playing. "I'm sure you'll think of something."

She frowned a little, then flipped her hair. "Heather's parents are going away this weekend, and we're thinking of having a little party after the tryouts. They've got that hot tub, and it's just getting cold enough to use the fire pit. . . ."

Fire. The thought was more alluring than anything she was showing off. "Count me in," he said.

Now she smiled, but it looked a little feral, the way a cat might smile at a trapped mouse. "Maybe you could—" She broke off and glanced sideways, her voice sharpening to a point. "Do you mind?"

Gabriel glanced right. That sophomore jerked her eyes back to her paper, her cheeks flushed. "Sorry."

"Ohmigod," Taylor whispered, leaning in conspiratorially. "She was totally staring at me. What a freaking lesbo."

Sharp heels clicked into the classroom, a tall woman in a business suit bustling through the door to drop a briefcase on the desk. Dark hair was pulled into an honest-to-god bun, and it wasn't doing her face any favors.

"Sorry, class," she said. "I'm Ms. Anderson, and I'll be filling in for Mr. Riley. This school is a maze—" Her eyes fell on Taylor, who was practically straddling the desk. "Maybe we could all take our seats?"

Taylor heaved a sigh and climbed off the desk, making a show of sliding into her chair.

Gabriel slouched in his own. At least they'd watch a movie or get a free period or something.

"Since Mr. Riley's mother is ill," Ms. Anderson said, "this might be a long-term solution, so if you're looking forward to a free period . . ."

Now Gabriel heaved a sigh.

"I think we'll start with a pop quiz," said Ms. Anderson. "So I can get a feel for where you all are—"

Gabriel froze.

"We just had a test last week," whined Andy Cunningham, rocking back in his chair.

They had. Gabriel hadn't taken it. He'd traded places with Nick.

"Ms. Anderson?" Taylor raised her hand, her voice dripping with sugar. "I know you're new here and all, but Mr. Riley doesn't give pop quizzes."

"That may be the case, but it's a nice way for me to see where you all stand. These quizzes won't go against you," she said. "It's just for my purposes, so I can see what your strengths are."

Gabriel wiped his palms on his jeans.

He should go to the bathroom and not come back.

Yeah, that would be subtle.

Ms. Anderson stood at the front of each row and started passing out sheets of Xeroxed paper. Two pages, double sided.

Gabriel took a deep breath. He could do this.

He didn't even have a pencil. He shoved his hand into his backpack. Gum. Car keys. A yellow highlighter. His spare lighter—he was tempted to take that to the quiz sitting on his desk.

He glanced up at the sophomore. He'd been sitting next to her for six weeks and had no idea what her name was. She didn't help things by remaining completely nondescript. Mouse brown hair in a loose braid down her back, simple gray turtleneck, and no-brand jeans. Her features were soft and young and makeup-free behind a pair of glasses.

"Hey, Brainiac," he said. "Can you hook me up with a pencil?"

She didn't look up.

"Hey," he said again.

Were her cheeks turning pink? Whatever, she didn't look up.

His irritation flared. "Hey," he said. "Got a pencil, Four-Eyes? What are you, deaf?"

Her head snapped around. "No. And my name isn't 'Four-Eyes' *or* 'Brainiac.'" But she flipped her pencil at him, then bent to get another one from her backpack.

He rolled his eyes and looked at the paper.

Question 1. Change $5\pi/12$ radians to degrees.

He had to wipe his hands on his jeans again. He'd go back to that one.

Question 2. Given that $\sin x = \frac{1}{4}$ and x is in Quadrant II, find the exact values of $\sin 2x$ and $\cos 2x$.

WTF. He looked at this every day, and it was still like reading Chinese.

He heard something snap.

His pencil. He'd broken *another* one in half.

Brainiac whipped her head around. What was her *problem?*

He glared back at his paper. The sub had said it didn't count. But he couldn't exactly hand in a blank test.

He had no idea what they'd do if he failed. What if they asked him to take another one? If they figured out Nick was taking his tests for him, they'd kick him off every team for sure.

They'd tell Michael.

Snap.

Now he had a quarter of a pencil. Other students were looking at him.

Gabriel took a deep breath. He could do this.

He could do this.

He could.

He put the pencil nub against the paper and tried to work through each problem.

It was the longest thirty minutes of his life. He didn't even get to the last three.

"Okay, I think that's enough time," said Ms. Anderson.

Thank god. He didn't feel this worn out after long runs around the soccer field.

"Now exchange papers with the person beside you for grading."

He snapped his head up.

The sophomore was already holding out her paper, not even looking at him. He took it but didn't relinquish his own. The tests sat side by side, one neat and perfectly ordered, one a complete fucking mess.

Brainiac sighed and reached out to grab his test, snatching it back to her desk.

Gabriel chewed on the end of the pencil nub. It hurt his lip. He could pick a fight. Get sent to the office. Alan Hulster sat to his left, and that guy was a tool. Gabriel wouldn't even mind laying into him.

"Hey."

He glanced to his right. That sophomore was staring at him, her brow furrowed. She licked her lips. "These are all wrong," she whispered.

Like he needed her to tell him that. He looked back at her test. Ms. Anderson was reading off the answers, one by one, and of course Brainiac had gotten every one right.

Her name was written in perfect script at the top. *Layne Forrest.*

Why the hell couldn't he remember a name like Layne Forrest?

He should punch Hulster now, before papers were handed forward.

"Hey," Layne whispered again.

He glanced over. *"What?"*

She flinched a little, then whispered, "You got a ninety-two on the test last week. I saw."

Of course he had. He would have gotten a perfect score, but Nick usually answered some wrong on purpose.

He glared at her, hoping it would make her back down. "Yeah? And?"

It worked. She recoiled and looked back at his paper.

But then he saw her slowly turn her pencil around and start erasing.

She did it subtly, artfully, so her pencil was barely moving, and her eyes were intent on the front of the room.

And then she was writing.

What was she doing?

He couldn't figure it out. Then Ms. Anderson was calling for the papers to be passed forward and telling them to use the rest of the time as a free period while she reviewed them.

"Hey," he whispered.

Layne didn't turn her head, just pulled a slim paperback out of her book bag and started reading.

He flicked a broken piece of pencil her way. It hit her on the arm.

She sighed and looked over. "Seriously?"

"What did you do?"

Her cheeks turned pink again. She looked back at the book. Her voice was so small he almost didn't hear her.

"You got an eighty."

She'd fixed his test?

Gabriel couldn't decide whether he was furious or giddy with relief. "Why?" he snapped. "Why would you do that?"

The substitute cleared her throat near the front of the room. "Is there a problem?"

"No." Damn, his voice was breaking. He coughed. "Sorry."

When the bell rang, Layne bolted.

Gabriel wasn't on four sports teams for nothing. He blocked her in the hall, cornering her against the lockers. She was a tiny thing, at least ten inches shorter than he was.

"Why did you do that?" he said.

She looked up at him, her binder clutched protectively against her chest. Her voice was still soft, quiet, somehow carrying over the students in the between-class rush. "Your brother took your test for you, didn't he?"

Gabriel felt hot, flushed, even though it was the truth. For some reason it was humiliating to have her figure it out.

He put a hand against the locker beside her head and leaned in. "Are you going to tell anyone?"

She swallowed. "You bully everyone who helps you?"

He snatched his hand away. Was that what he looked like?

"Hey, man." A voice spoke at his shoulder. "You all right?"

Gabriel jerked back. He'd been so close to her.

Hunter stood there, a navy backpack slung over his shoulder. That white streak interrupted his sandy blond hair and hung across one eye, leaving the other wide and full of scrutiny.

Hunter's father had been a Guide, too, until he'd been killed by a rock slide. Hunter had come to town to kill the Merricks, in retaliation. He'd thought they were responsible for his father's death—until Becca had convinced him otherwise. For the last few days, they'd shared a kind of awkward truce.

"Yeah," said Gabriel. "I'm all right."

Hunter glanced at Layne. "Are *you* all—"

"Fine," she said. Then she turned and dashed into the crowd of students.

Hunter stared after her. "What just happened?"

Gabriel didn't hate this dude the way Chris did, but some

sense of brotherly loyalty insisted he feel irritation at his presence. "None of your business, Mom." He started walking.

Hunter followed him. "All right, then what happened in second period?"

"I slept through English. You?"

"I don't think that was sleeping." Hunter gave a pointed look up, at the lights embedded in the ceiling.

Gabriel sighed and kept walking. Could *everyone* see through him today?

"You know I'm a Fifth," Hunter pressed. "I can sense all the elements. The others might not have noticed, but I did."

"Good for you."

"Does this have something to do with why Becca wants to meet at lunch?"

Gabriel stopped. "She talked to you?"

"She dropped a note on my desk in History. What's going on?"

"We have a dinner date."

"We do?"

"Yeah." Gabriel started walking again. "And you might want to bring your gun."

CHAPTER 3

Layne sat on her bedspread and watched her best friend paint her nails an unflattering shade of purple. Sunset had come and gone, and darkness cloaked her bedroom window.

She couldn't stop thinking of that quiz, the way she'd changed Gabriel Merrick's answers.

God, she could have been caught. What had she been *thinking?*

As if her life weren't already held together by a fraying thread.

"Your hands look like they belong on a corpse," she said.

Kara frowned and waved her hand in the air. "I like it. Are you sure your mom won't care that I'm using it?"

Layne shrugged and looked out the window. Her dad would be home soon, so she should start dinner before too long. Otherwise, her little brother would be raiding the kitchen for Pop-Tarts and potato chips.

"She won't even know," she said.

"You know, this is like, the *good* stuff. They don't even carry this at the salon where my mom goes. It's probably twenty bucks a bottle."

"I wouldn't know."

Kara rolled her eyes. "Of course you wouldn't. I can't believe you're related to that woman."

Layne picked at her own nails, which were short and unpolished. Sometimes she couldn't believe it, either. Her mom lived in labels, the kind splashed all over fashion magazines. More than once, Layne had seen her with the same bag some celebrity was carrying on the cover of *Us Weekly*.

Layne couldn't tell the difference between Gucci and Juicy Couture.

Kara thought this was sacrilege. When they'd first become friends freshman year, Kara would beg to rifle through Layne's mom's closet. Layne would sit on the end of her parents' bed and tolerate it, because a friend was a friend. But Layne finally got Kara to knock it off by saying her mom had found out and was *pissed*.

A complete lie, of course, but there was only so much staring at fabric that she could tolerate.

Kara wasn't as smart as Layne, either—the only classes they shared were gym and lunch—but she was someone to talk to who didn't call her a lesbian or get in her face about changing test scores.

Spending half her classes with students two years ahead didn't leave Layne with a whole lot of friendship options.

Since the first day of school, she'd wondered what it would be like to have a guy like Gabriel Merrick talk to her. She'd noticed him right off—honestly, what girl *wouldn't?*—and when Kara told her he had a twin, she'd wondered how fate could create two guys to look like that.

She'd lucked out with that assignment to sit next to him in trig—or so she'd thought. He sat behind Taylor Morrissey, who seemed to make it her life's goal to humiliate Layne every time she saw her. But it also gave Layne a chance to watch Gabriel check Taylor out.

Every. Frigging. Day.

Really, she couldn't blame him. Some days, Taylor could have worn a bathing suit to school and covered more skin. Layne could barely keep from staring herself.

And it wasn't like Gabriel's eyes ever drifted right. Even today, when he'd been looking for a pencil. She hadn't realized he was actually talking to her until his tone had dissolved into spite.

What are you, deaf?

God, she'd wanted to hit him.

She should have.

Then she'd gotten a look at his test. How could someone get *every* question wrong?

For an instant, she'd felt strangely validated. He'd been a jerk, and he was going to fail that quiz.

Then she'd remembered the A on his test last week.

And she'd put two and two together.

She was tempted to pass him off as just some stupid jock. But his pencil had snapped, twice. He'd been angry. No, frustrated.

No, *embarrassed*. You had to care to be embarrassed, right?

After looking at Gabriel's quiz, where he'd clearly *tried* to work through each problem, she'd felt a flash of pity.

So she'd started fixing.

"You should take an interest in your mom's stuff more," said Kara. "She's going to disown you."

"Too late," said Layne.

Kara glanced up. "What?"

"Nothing." Layne rolled her eyes. "You want to stay for dinner?"

"One day you're going to wake up and realize you missed your prime years, you know."

"My prime years?"

Kara waved a gothic nail her way. "This little ensemble isn't making the boys drool, you know."

"I can't exactly flit around in a camisole and low riders." Layne gave a pointed look at Kara, who was wearing a hot-pink camisole and jeans that sat so low they were making Layne blush.

"Oh, for god's sake, *why not?* Jesus, Layne, save the turtlenecks for your eighties. Come on, I bet your mom has something in her closet you could wear tomorrow."

Then Kara was through the bedroom door, and Layne was scrambling after her.

She beat her friend to her parents' bedroom door and held it shut. "Forget it, Kara."

"Layne, I'm doing you a favor, really. Someone needs to."

Layne tightened her grip on the door, feeling her heart start to slam against the inside of her rib cage. "I said, forget it."

"What is your problem?" Kara tried to wrench her hand off the doorknob. "It's not like you've got leprosy or something. Show that body off!" She grabbed the hem of Layne's shirt and started to yank.

"*Stop!*" Layne screeched. The word came out like an assault.

Kara backed off. "Jesus, Layne . . ."

Then they heard the key in the front door and her father was calling out, "Laynie? I'm beat. What's the status on dinner? Layne?"

"Up here!" Her voice sounded strangled. "You'd better go," she said to Kara.

Kara tossed her hair over her shoulder. "Look, I'm just trying to be a friend. I didn't realize you'd go ballistic. I mean, with that brother of yours, you need all the help you can get—"

"Hey." Layne bristled. "Don't talk about Simon."

Kara shrugged. "You know it's true." She ducked into Layne's bedroom to grab her bag. On the way out, she called, "Take my advice. You might be surprised how it works out."

"Maybe," said Layne.

But she knew exactly how it would turn out. If she dressed like Kara or Taylor or any of the other girls at school, she'd be even more of an outcast than she was already.

CHAPTER 4

Gabriel felt the end of his rope coming up quick.

His lighter rolled through his knuckles, making that reassuring click each time it changed direction. Fire at his fingertips—it would be so easy to draw flame from this tiny silver square, to send it straight at Becca's father and let him burn.

He just wasn't entirely sure how that would turn out.

They'd found a free table near the center of the Annapolis Mall food court: Nick sat to Gabriel's left, Chris to his right, fingers loosely intertwined with Becca's. Hunter sat at one end of the table, wearing a denim jacket over a light-colored hoodie, the stones he always strung along his wrist hidden from view. Michael sat at the other end, still sporting the red T-shirt with their last name across the chest that he usually wore on landscaping jobs.

And on the other long side, completely alone, sat Becca's father.

The Guide.

"Call me Bill," he'd said.

Yeah, Gabriel had a few ideas of what to call him.

He looked completely nondescript: just an average guy in his late thirties. Sandy brown hair, a goatee, gray eyes that matched Becca's. He hadn't changed after work, either. He was still wearing a beige button-down with the sleeves rolled up his forearms, patches on each shoulder reading *Department of Natural Resources* and *Wildlife Control Division.*

Not exactly the kind of guy you'd expect to find trying to slaughter a bunch of teenagers.

The tension in the air seemed to be forming a barrier around the table. No other patrons had even come close to sitting nearby.

"So, *Bill,*" said Becca, her eyes hard, "why don't you start with the reason behind this one-eighty."

Her father's expression didn't flicker. "One-eighty?"

"You were trying to kill us all last week. Now you want to help?"

"I wasn't trying to kill *you.*"

"Funny how you blew up my car—"

"When you weren't in it." While his voice was mild, there was a glint of wicked humor in his eye, something not entirely pleasant. "I even offered to replace it."

Becca leaned in against the table. "You could have killed innocent people," she hissed.

"Could have. Didn't." He looked across the table to meet Gabriel's eyes. "I didn't kill anyone, innocent or not. Right?"

Gabriel let the lid of his lighter fall open, flicking the igniter while it rolled.

Nick reached out and snapped it closed before a flame could fully form. He held fast, and Gabriel could almost read his thoughts. *Don't. You'll start a fight we can't win.*

And that . . . *that* made Gabriel look away.

He jerked free of his twin, shoved the lighter into his pocket, and scowled.

"Why *didn't* you kill us?" said Chris. "Why go to all that trouble with the walk-in freezer, and setting Nick's leg—"

"Ever go fishing?" said Bill.

"Sure."

"I only had two of you. In my experience, live bait works better."

"You're avoiding the question," said Becca. Her voice was full of challenge, but her fingers looked like they had a death grip on Chris's. "Why do you want to help us *now?*"

"I'm not avoiding the question." Bill leaned back in the chair and shrugged. "I don't necessarily *want* to help, but the stakes have changed."

Her eyes narrowed. "Meaning *what?*"

Her father hesitated.

Michael jumped on it. "Meaning, *Becca,*" he said. "We're not the only ones hiding anymore. I'm willing to bet that the only people who know Becca's a Fifth are sitting at this very table." He turned dark eyes to Bill. "Am I right?"

A nod. "Yes."

Michael leaned in against the table. "And I'm guessing the other Guides wouldn't be too happy to find out you kept her a secret."

"Probably not."

"So you're protecting yourself," said Becca. She snorted. "Typical."

Her father turned to look at her. "Just what do you think they'd do, Becca? Slap me on the wrist and forget you exist?"

She stared back at him, and Gabriel could see the battle in her expression, that she wanted to know what they'd do—but she was afraid of the answer.

"They'd make you kill her," said Hunter, his voice low. "To prove your loyalty." He was watching Bill, too, his expression shadowed.

Becca's father didn't say anything—and that was obviously answer enough. Her face paled a shade, and she glanced at Hunter. "How did you know that?"

He shrugged a little. "My father used to tell me stories. Of how the Guides wouldn't allow their goals to be compromised. One death is nothing compared to the greater good, right?"

"Yeah?" said Chris, his tone unfriendly. "And where do you fit into that?"

Hunter met his eyes and didn't back down. "I'm sitting here, aren't I?"

"Stop," said Becca. "Don't fight."

Michael cleared his throat. "So what are you proposing?"

"I'm proposing that you lie low. Don't draw attention to yourselves. They'll send another Guide if I don't check in with progress—but I can hold them off for a while. Let them know I'm still investigating. If there aren't continued reports of problems in this area, they'll stay away."

"What about Seth and Tyler?" said Nick. "You know it's not usually us causing the problems."

"I don't think we need to worry too much about them for the time being," said Chris, and for the first time, his voice carried a little satisfaction.

"Yeah," said Becca. "We just came from the police station. Turns out assault and attempted rape are pretty serious charges."

Now Bill looked at her. "Attempted rape?"

Becca's eyes were hard. "Don't even look at me like that. I don't want your concern. You don't *get* to care. Do you understand me? As far as I'm concerned, you're—"

"Easy," said Chris, his voice soft. "Take it easy."

"I want to help you," said Bill, his voice gentler. "You need to let me—"

"We need to lie low," said Becca. "Got it."

Gabriel kept his mouth shut, but this guy was crazy if he thought he had a shot in hell at her trust. Not to mention the rest of them.

"And while we're waiting around," said Nick, "what are you going to be doing?"

Bill glanced at his daughter. "I'll be showing Becca how to protect herself."

Becca sat up straight. "No. No way."

He raised his eyebrows. "You'd rather run on sheer adrenaline and luck? As much as you don't want to believe it, I *am* doing this with the end goal of keeping you safe. You don't even have a clue what you're dealing with."

"I do," said Hunter.

Chris glared at him, but Becca smiled. "Good. Hunter can tell me everything I need to know." She gave her father a dismissive look. "You can go back to ignoring me since it's worked so great for the last five years."

"I haven't been ignoring you, Becca." He glanced at Hunter. "And regardless of who you learn from, I definitely won't be ignoring you now."

"So that's it," said Michael. "You don't turn us in, we don't turn you in."

Bill spread his hands. "For now, that's it."

Gabriel waited for his brothers to scoff, to refuse, to flip this frigging table and start the fight of the century. The Guide was *right here,* like a sitting duck. They could take him down in a heartbeat.

Probably.

Unfortunately, everyone else was nodding, acting like it was a good idea to wait and see.

Gabriel wanted to punch his twin in the shoulder and ask what was wrong with him.

Why the hell are you nodding? he wanted to say. *Don't you remember the way your leg shattered when he attacked us?*

He'd thought they were coming here to finish things, to *fight.*

Not to be placated and reassured.

Gabriel wound his fingers around his lighter again. The potential for fire was *right there,* pulsing under his fingertips.

Mocking him.

"And what about you, Gabe?"

He snapped his head up, the lighter slick against his palm. He *hated* being called Gabe, but correcting this guy for something like that seemed like criticizing a mass murderer for littering.

"What about me?" he said.

Becca's father spread his hands, looking far too patient. Gabriel wanted to hit him.

Unfortunately, everyone else looked like they were on his side.

Her father was still looking at him. "Any thoughts?"

Oh, he had plenty.

"Yeah," he said, leaning in, putting a hand against the table.

"I don't buy it. What if we just save time and take you out to the parking lot to kill you."

"Jesus, Gabriel," said Michael, rubbing at his eyes. "We don't have a lot of choice—"

"I'm in," said Becca.

"No." Nick put both hands flat on the table. "Bill's plan makes sense. For now. Just—"

"It doesn't make sense." Gabriel kept his eyes firmly locked on Becca's father.

Bill didn't make a move, but he very clearly wasn't backing down, either. "Don't push me, kid."

The lighter sat tucked between Gabriel's knuckles. It would take nothing to have fire in the air. He could almost taste smoke on his tongue.

But he kept thinking of the fight on the field, how they'd lost control.

No, how *he'd* lost control.

You'll start a fight we can't win.

He shoved the table away and got to his feet. "Fuck you."

He didn't realize he'd bolted from the mall until cold air slapped him across the face. At least he was outside.

Nick had the car keys, so Gabriel walked along the side of the mall. There weren't many cars out here anyway, in this space between the food court and the nearest department store. He flipped the lighter open and ran fire through his fingers, snapping the flame off the wick to cradle it in his palm.

Dead leaves were caught against the curb here, and Gabriel scooped a few into his palm, feeding them to the fire one by one, the way you'd sneak scraps to a dog under the table. Each sent sparks curling into the night air.

He felt calmer already.

"Got a light?"

Gabriel whirled, feeling the flame blaze between his fingers— just not with his own power. Hunter stood there, close enough to touch, as still as the night was dark.

"Go away." Gabriel crushed the flame to nothing and shook

the ash from his palm. He turned to walk toward the far corner of the mall, where all the delivery bays were. "Shouldn't you be back there macking on Becca, anyway?"

Hunter followed him. "You don't want to provoke him."

"Actually, that's exactly what I want to do."

"He'll kill you," Hunter said. "He's trying to play nice, to help because of Becca, but if you push him to it, he'll—"

"Oh, how do you know?" Gabriel rounded on him, his breath clouding in the air. "You don't know shit, Hunter. You don't know—"

"I knew my father." Hunter's voice was low. It felt colder suddenly, and Gabriel wondered if Hunter was responsible. The change felt different, subtler than when Nick affected the air.

"Don't cry to me about Daddy. I'm not in the mood."

Hunter moved closer. "Becca's father is stronger than you are. If you push him, he'll retaliate."

Gabriel craved that, a knock-down, drag-out rematch. It was almost enough to send him back into the mall, throw caution to the wind, and *fight*.

Almost.

He ducked his head and started walking. "Go away."

"I don't know why I was worried," Hunter said from behind him. "Considering you only seem to know how to run and hide."

Gabriel swung around and hit him.

Or he tried to. Hunter had some serious military training, and he deflected the blow easily.

But Gabriel was no stranger to fighting dirty. He caught Hunter with a solid punch to the stomach.

Hunter got him in the jaw.

And then they were fighting in earnest.

Christ, it felt fantastic to drive his fist into something. Especially when Hunter fought back with enough force to really make it worth it. Enough force that Gabriel started to wonder if this would turn into a test of endurance.

Enough force that Gabriel started to wonder if he could *win*.

His back slammed into the concrete wall of the mall. Breath

rushed out of his lungs. He braced against the wall to throw Hunter off, getting enough leverage to shove the other boy to the ground. He followed him down to pin him there.

"Whoa, hold up," Hunter said, breathless. He made his hands into a T. "If I tear my clothes, my grandmother will shit a brick."

Gabriel stared down at him, unsure whether to let him go. Then he caught the glint of light on steel under Hunter's jacket. "You are one crazy bastard. You really did come armed."

"Sure."

"You had a gun and you still fought me like that?"

Hunter grinned. "Wait—you were fighting for *real?*"

Yeah, he had been—but suddenly it didn't seem so important. Gabriel let him go.

Hunter rolled to his feet and dusted bits of grass from his hair. "You want a ride home?"

His brothers were still here. Gabriel could see their red SUV across the parking lot. But getting a ride home with his brothers meant going back into the mall and facing the Guide.

"Yeah," he said. "I do."

The fight had loosened something in him. Not permanently— Gabriel was too smart for that. But something about it felt good. Reassuring. Steadying, in a way.

It had been so long that Gabriel almost didn't recognize it for what it was, until after they'd driven home, not talking, just listening to the music pouring from Hunter's radio. Until after he'd let himself into an empty house, a luxury he didn't experience very often.

It felt like the beginning of friendship.

CHAPTER 5

M ath class.
Hell.

Ms. Anderson was ten times more annoying than old Riley. If Gabriel had to put up with her asking students to come up to the whiteboard and struggle through problems in front of the class, at least she should have legs to write home about.

He worried about getting called, but she seemed to be going in alphabetical order and the class was almost over. *Merrick* was safely stationed in the second half of the alphabet.

He glanced to his right. Layne looked equally bored. Then again, she could probably do these equations in her head.

And what was with her and the old turtlenecks?

Gabriel watched her a moment too long, hoping she'd feel the weight of his eyes and turn her head. But she didn't, and he finally felt like a freak and turned back to the front of the class with a sigh.

Taylor Morrissey turned around in her seat and flicked a piece of paper his way.

He caught it and unfolded it under his notebook.

Pink gel pen, scripty letters.

Why are you staring at lesbo?

Because Layne had helped him. Because he was intrigued. Because he'd learned when his parents died that it wasn't human nature to help, not really. It was human nature to seek out vulnerability and squash it.

That's why he didn't buy this bullshit with the Guide.

Taylor glanced over her shoulder, hair and lip gloss equally shiny.

Gabriel gave her a confused look and shrugged, like he didn't know what she was talking about.

"Gabriel Merrick."

Oh, *shit*.

He snapped his eyes forward, surprised at how fast his palms went damp. "What?"

Ms. Anderson gestured to the board. "Do you care to tackle the next problem?"

He gave her half a smile. "Not really, no."

Three girls near him giggled. Ms. Anderson didn't even crack a smile. "Humor me."

He stared at the board. There was a triangle there, numbers written along two of the three sides, another number tucked into one of the angles.

"Solve for the missing side," said Ms. Anderson. "We've been doing this the whole period."

That didn't mean he'd been *listening* for the whole period.

"Just look at the previous one," Layne hissed under her breath. "It's the exact same formula."

He glanced at the problem to the left. Jake Bryerly had found the answer. A completely different triangle, with lengthy equations laid out in rows beneath it.

He'd never be able to do this.

"Mr. Merrick?"

Gabriel slid from behind his desk and approached the board.

He wished he had his lighter.

Instead, he picked up a dry-erase marker and stared at the triangle. He'd never known a simple shape could be so intimidating.

Alan Hulster snorted from the middle of the classroom. "I think reading a scoreboard is about the most advanced math Merrick is capable of."

Half the class laughed. Gabriel looked back at him. "Keep it up and you'll find out what else I'm capable of."

Now the class did that *ooooh* sound that predicated a fight or a trip to the principal's office. Hulster laughed again, but it sounded a little strangled. He didn't hold Gabriel's eyes. "Whatever, man."

"That's enough." Ms. Anderson gestured back to the board, her expression patient. "Go ahead."

Gabriel put his pen against the whiteboard. Christ, his hand was shaking.

The lights in the classroom flickered, the fluorescent bulbs buzzing with power.

Get it together. He took a deep breath.

"Maybe you should start with something easier," called Hulster, fed by Gabriel's obvious hesitation. "Maybe line up some cheerleaders and he can count them—"

"Shut *up*." Another flicker.

Hulster laughed. "Look, man, I can't help it if you're too stupid to—"

Half the lights in the classroom exploded.

Mayhem. Girls screamed and students bolted for the doors. Ms. Anderson was trying to assume some kind of control.

Gabriel felt the power in the air, the way the electricity wanted to arc onto paper, to clothing, to find something consumable and burn. He stood there in front of the board, the stupid marker clenched in his fist, trying to keep the electricity right where it was supposed to be.

The end-of-class bell rang, flooding the hallways with people. Ms. Anderson raced after students who'd already made it out of the classroom.

If anyone was hurt, it was his fault.

"Are you all right?"

His eyes flicked open. He didn't even remember closing them.

Layne stood there in front of him, her backpack hanging loose over one shoulder. They were the only people left in the darkened classroom.

Gabriel swallowed. "No."

She frowned. "Do you need me to get the nurse—"

He shook his head quickly. "No . . . yeah . . . I'm fine." He paused. "Why do you keep trying to help me?"

"Because you look like you need it."

He studied her, the dark-framed glasses, the length of braid that fell down along one shoulder. He'd dismissed her as being nondescript, but she really wasn't. Her hair shined in the braid, and her eyes were bright and intelligent. No freckles, just soft, clear skin. Being smart wasn't always easy, not in high school, anyway. Maybe she dressed this way on purpose, to avoid attention. It made him think of that note Taylor had tossed onto his desk, the comments from that dickhead Hulster. Everyone was so quick to pounce on weakness.

"Hold still," he said, reaching out. "You have glass in your hair."

He could swear she stopped breathing. He picked two pieces free and then had to use both hands to work loose a third that had gotten trapped.

"I could help you," she said.

"Nah," he said. "I think this is the last piece." He picked at a shard caught by her ear.

"No, I meant . . ." Her voice almost squeaked. "I meant with the trig stuff."

Gabriel shook his head. "Nick—my brother—he's tried. It's a waste of time."

"So you're just going to keep switching?" She frowned up at him. "Ms. Anderson isn't an idiot like Riley. I think she'll catch on."

"No one has caught on for four years," he said, brushing past her to get his backpack. His feet crunched on broken glass. "I'm a senior. People like to look the other way. "

"I'd still like to try. Maybe at lunch—"

"We don't have lunch at the same time."

"Oh," she said, thrown. Then she seemed to realize he was brushing her off. "Okay. Sorry. Forget it." She turned away.

Gabriel sighed. "Wait."

His free period was right after lunch. It was supposed to be for study hall, but they weren't required to study. Most kids went to the library or the computer center; he usually went to the weight room.

Why was he even considering this?

Because he hated hearing Hulster heckle him.

Even more, he hated that Hulster was right.

"I do have a free period," he said. "Fifth period. Your lunch hour, right?"

Layne looked up at him. "Meet you in the library?"

He hefted his backpack onto his shoulder. "Can't wait."

Gabriel broke off half a protein bar inside his backpack. They weren't allowed to eat in here, but he was bored and Layne hadn't shown up yet.

Some kids at the next table glared at him, and he glared back.

He checked the time on his phone. Her lunch period had started ten minutes ago.

Maybe she was grabbing a quick bite to eat.

He fidgeted and ate the second half of his protein bar.

Now she was fifteen minutes late. The period was only forty-five minutes long.

Gabriel slammed his trig book back into his backpack. He was being stood up for a study date? To study something he *hated?*

Maybe this had been a joke. Like Hulster's heckling, only meaner.

He imagined Taylor's voice. *OMG, you really thought I would help an idiot like you?*

But Layne wasn't anything like Taylor. She wouldn't do that. Would she?

He should have gone to the gym.

He still had time. He even had to walk down the freshman/

sophomore wing to get there, so if he passed Layne in the hall, he could brush her off and make it seem like he was the one ditching *her*.

The halls in this half of the school were empty. He could hear some sort of squeaking or scuffling up around the next corner, and he hoped two kids weren't trying to get it on right in the middle of the hallway.

No, but he found Layne. And three boys. Half her hair had come loose from the braid, and her face was red and tear streaked. The shortest of the boys stood by her side, also red-faced, but with fury, not tears.

The other two kids had their backpacks and they were dumping the contents in the middle of the aisle. Binders split open and papers went everywhere.

One laughed. Red hair, freckles, face and hands still soft. "Oops," he said. "Hate when that happens."

The boy beside Layne rushed forward to shove him, saying something unintelligible.

The other kid grabbed him by the shoulder and flung him away, sending him to the ground to skid on the papers. Some tore.

They hadn't even noticed Gabriel yet.

"Knock it off!" cried Layne. "I'm going to get—"

"You're going to shut up," said the other kid. "We're sick of you and that retard."

Then he shoved her to the ground.

Gabriel didn't even remember moving. He just had the kid by the front of the shirt and he'd slammed him up against the lockers. "What the hell do you think you're doing?"

The boy wilted. His mouth worked for a moment, no sound coming out.

Gabriel slammed him again, a little harder, a little rougher. "Talk."

He didn't, just hung there shaking.

The other bully bolted down the hallway. Didn't matter— Gabriel would find him later.

He looked back at the one he had pinned and clapped him on

the side of the head. Not hard enough to hurt, but hard enough to make the kid flinch. "Want me to knock some sense into you?"

The boy shook his head quickly. "No—we were just—we were—it's—they're—"

"Shut it," said Gabriel. "I catch you screwing with them again and you won't be around to talk about it. Get it?"

The kid nodded, his head bobbing hard.

Gabriel let him go. He slipped and skidded and almost fell in the stream of papers, but he found his footing and bolted after his friend.

Layne and the younger boy were staring after them. The boy had a grin on his face now. He poked Layne in the arm and made a bunch of complicated hand gestures, then pointed to Gabriel.

Sign language.

Now Gabriel understood the unintelligible scream of rage when things were being strewn about the hallway. He remembered the bully's comment about someone being a *retard*.

Layne sighed. "Thanks." She bent to start sorting the papers.

The boy poked her arm again, more aggressively this time. He had to be a younger brother—Gabriel could read that dynamic like a book. But the boy signed again, and then pointed at Gabriel.

Layne rolled her eyes and didn't look at him.

"What's he saying?" said Gabriel.

"He said thanks," said Layne.

The boy punched her in the shoulder and said something emphatically. It took Gabriel a moment to work out the words.

"Tell him, Layne."

Layne sighed again and looked up. Her voice was flat. "He said that was fucking awesome."

Gabriel grinned. "You can take them next time, buddy."

He'd spoken without thinking, but before he could glance at Layne to translate, the boy grinned back and held out a fist. Gabriel bumped it with his own.

"This is my little brother," said Layne. Her hands signed while she talked. "His name is Simon."

Gabriel bent and began helping them catch the loose papers. "Freshman?"

"Yeah." She paused, and then signed while she spoke. "It's Simon's first year at a real school." She stopped signing and covered her mouth. "In case you couldn't tell, it's not going well."

Simon punched her in the shoulder again.

Layne dropped her hand. "And he hates it when I don't let him see what I'm saying."

Simon was signing again, so fast that Gabriel had no idea how anyone would be able to make sense of it.

But Layne did. "He wants to know if you're going out for basketball again this year. He just made the JV team. He made me take him to every basketball game last year, so he saw you play."

Everyone made JV, but Gabriel didn't say that. "Yeah," he said, "varsity tryouts are Friday." He probably didn't have to show up.

"I'm sorry I didn't make it to the library." Layne gestured to the mess around them. "I was busy."

"It's cool," he said, feeling a flash of guilt that he'd assumed she was standing him up. "Let me know if those dicks mess with you again."

"Why?" she said, her voice flat again. "You gonna rumble under the bleachers?"

"What does that mean?"

"Nothing. Forget it." She shoved the last of her papers into her backpack. She tapped her brother on the arm, and then signed while speaking, "Come on, Simon."

Gabriel studied her, nonplussed. "You're *mad* at me?"

"Maybe if you thought with something other than your fists, you'd be passing math on your own."

Gabriel stared, having no idea what to say.

And in that moment of silence, she picked up her backpack and rounded the corner, without once looking back.

CHAPTER 6

Gabriel took a third processed chicken patty from the pan on the stove and another scoop of macaroni and cheese, then joined his brothers at the table. Nick had cooked, which usually worked out best all around. Not that mac and cheese was haute cuisine, but their older brother's cooking skills topped out at pressing buttons on the microwave. After their parents died, Michael had been all they had left, so they'd spent the latter half of middle school living entirely on frozen dinners.

The table was quiet for a change. Michael was absently eating, his laptop open on the table in front of him. He made an effort to sit at the table with them, but he might as well have been sitting in the garage. Chris was glowering at his plate. Gabriel wondered what was up with that, but he couldn't stop rolling Layne's words around in his head.

Maybe if you thought with something other than your fists, you'd be passing math.

Nick jabbed him in the arm with his fork. "What's up with you? Usually you don't shut up about my crap cooking."

"Maybe I don't want to hurt your feelings."

Chris snorted, finally looking up from his plate. "That'll be the day."

Gabriel kicked him under the table. "What's up with *you?*"

"Nothing's *up* with me."

"Becca's with Hunter," said Nick.

Chris rolled his eyes and stabbed a piece of chicken.

Gabriel smiled. "Want to come out with me and Nicky and blow stuff up on the beach?"

Michael's hands went still and he looked up over the laptop. "You'd better be kidding."

He wasn't, but Michael didn't need to know that. "Don't worry. Go back to your 'work.'" Gabriel made little air quotes with his hands.

"You're supposed to be lying low," said Michael. "Do you have any understanding of what that means?"

Gabriel ignored him.

"I'm *talking* to you," said Michael.

Gabriel's fork clinked against his plate and he leaned in against the table. "Don't start this shit with me, Michael."

Nick put a hand on his arm. "Stop. It's fine."

Gabriel didn't say anything, just glared across the table at his older brother.

But Chris was staring across the table at Nick, his eyes telegraphing something Gabriel couldn't figure out.

He drew back. "What? What's with the look?"

Nick pulled his hand back. "Chris is going out with Becca later."

"I'll alert the media. So what?"

"So . . ." Nick pushed the macaroni around on his plate. "Quinn was giving her a hard time about leaving her sitting at home, and I made some comment that we should make it a double date, and she said yes."

"You like her?"

"Maybe." Nick shrugged and looked at his plate, pushing the macaroni noodles with his fork. "It's something to do."

The *only* time Nick hedged like this was when he really liked a girl. Gabriel smiled. "Don't you mean some*one*?"

Now Nick snapped his eyes up. "It's not like that."

Oh, this was *fantastic*. "You know she had her tongue down Rafe Gutierrez's throat, like, three days ago."

"I said it's not like that." The temperature in the room dropped ten degrees.

Michael was looking over the top of the laptop again. "Easy."

Nick's eyes were like ice. "Maybe we should talk about what happened in third period today. I didn't even ask if you were *okay*."

What a bastard. "Shut up."

"What happened?" said Michael.

"Nothing," said Chris. He glared at Nick across the table.

Good little brother. "Yeah," said Gabriel. "Nothing."

"It was all over school," said Nick. "Lights exploded for no reason at all. They're getting experts in to check all the wiring."

Michael slapped the laptop shut. *"What?"*

Gabriel wanted to knock his twin upside the head—his hand was already tight at his side. But he kept hearing Layne's parting comment, and he kept his hands to himself.

He sighed and looked back at his plate. "It was an accident."

"An accident." Michael looked like he was going to have an aneurysm, right here at the table. "Are. You. Crazy."

"Yeah, Michael, I'm crazy." Gabriel shoved away from the table. He couldn't help it: He smacked Nick on the back of the head. "And *you're* an asshole."

Gabriel flung his plate into the sink and stormed through the back door.

Michael caught up to him before he made it off the porch. "Wait a minute. Tell me what happened."

"Forget it. Go back to work. I'm going for a walk."

"Please tell me you're not really having a tantrum because Nick decided to do something without you."

Oh, for god's sake.

Wait. Was he?

"Jesus, Michael, we're almost eighteen years old. Nick does stuff without me all day."

Like asking out girls without even mentioning that he *liked* them.

Michael didn't say anything, so Gabriel stepped off the porch into the twilit darkness of the yard.

He almost made it to the tree line before Michael called after him, "Let me grab my jacket. I'll walk with you."

Gabriel hesitated, a bare pause at the edge of the woods. "Whatever. Don't play the brother card now." Then he stepped into the crunching leaves.

He half expected Michael to follow him anyway, but a moment later, Gabriel heard the back door close. He was alone, surrounded by chilled air and the cloak of night.

And it *was* cold. He probably should have grabbed a jacket himself. But that would have ruined the effect of a perfectly good storming out.

A tantrum. It made him think of Layne's comment. Again.

He wondered what she looked like with her hair out of that silly braid.

The leaves were loud beneath his feet. Early stars flashed between the nearly bare trees overhead. Next week, his evenings would be crammed with practice and games, but for now, his time belonged to him alone.

Michael would have loved this, walking in his element, nothing between him and the ground. He probably would have walked barefoot. Even Nick would like the crispness in the air. Chris would want to walk down to the water, but that was one element that carried no draw for Gabriel, so he stayed deep in the trees.

No fire for him.

He picked up a leaf and spun it by the stem. "Burn," he said.

It didn't.

God, he *hated* this. He was confined to blowing out light-bulbs and praying he didn't accidentally kill anyone. Even with that, he was so powerless he couldn't draw on his element without help.

The leaf broke off at the stem and fell, so Gabriel scooped up another one. *"Burn."*

Nothing.

Why hadn't Nick said anything about Quinn? It's not like Nick had never dated anyone before. Hell, they usually double-dated *together*. He could go out with Chris. Gabriel didn't give a crap.

Much.

Another leaf. Nothing.

Gabriel crushed it and picked up another. "Damn it!" he snapped. "Burn!"

It didn't.

But the hundreds of leaves surrounding him *did*.

Layne spooned mashed potatoes onto her father's plate, careful to avoid the edge of the *Wall Street Journal* he was reading. While she had the spoon in her hand, she dumped some on Simon's plate, too.

I don't want any more, he signed.

Eat, she signed back.

He glared at her, scooped up as much as he could on his fork, and flung it back into the bowl.

You're. Not. Mom, he signed emphatically.

"How was school?" said her father, oblivious, his eyes on his paper.

"Fine," she said. "We have a new math teacher. She's better than the old guy."

"And how's Simon doing?"

Layne glanced at her brother. *He wants to know how you're doing.*

I know. I can read his lips. Simon jabbed his fork into his chicken, making a loud clink when it connected with the plate. *He can ask me himself.*

Do you want me to tell him about what happened in the hall-way?

NO.

Their father glanced up from the paper. "What's going on?"

"Simon just made the JV basketball team," she said smoothly, used to covering for her brother's hostile signing. Their father knew enough ASL to get by, but he'd never put the time in that Layne and her mother had. Most of what Simon said went right over his head.

Something that irritated Simon to no end.

Her brother could talk, though. He just refused to do it, since the first day of high school when half the freshman class had decided his affected speech meant Simon was a retard. She'd just about fallen over when he'd spoken in front of Gabriel Merrick.

Especially since their father had tried no shortage of threats to get Simon to speak at home.

"Basketball?" said their father. "Is that possible?"

Simon flung his fork against the plate and shoved away from the table.

"Get back here," their father snapped. The paper dropped to the table. They had his full attention now—but Simon's back was turned, and he was already going through the doorway.

"He played all through middle school," she whispered—unnecessarily, since Simon couldn't hear her.

"That was different," said her father.

She thought of those bullies in the hallway and agreed with him.

Though she'd never say that to Simon, of course.

"How's the chicken?" she asked.

"It's fine," said her father, spearing another piece before picking up the newspaper again.

She'd burned two pieces before figuring out the timing, but she'd made sure to give her father one of the good ones.

She'd already failed one parent.

She couldn't afford to let it happen again.

CHAPTER 7

Fire surrounded him.

Gabriel dropped to his knees and ran a hand through the flames. It reached for him, licking along his palm.

A blanket of flame—no, bigger than that. A carpet of flame, the size of his bedroom. The fire singed the edge of his jeans, and he told it to find something else to burn. It wouldn't hurt him, but it could definitely burn his clothes off.

The flames flicked higher than his head, now that he was sitting. One of the trees at the edge of the circle caught and started to burn.

Then another.

"Easy," he breathed, feeding it his own energy, trying to pull it back, to keep it contained. Usually when he played with fire, Nick was with him, choking oxygen from the air if the flames got to be too much.

The fire listened, waiting for guidance.

Curious, Gabriel gave a little *push*.

For an instant, it felt incredible, the strength—no, the *potential*—in the flames surrounding him. He could level this whole forest with a thought. So much power, right at his fingertips, awaiting his direction. True control.

And then he lost it.

Seven trees caught and blazed. Eight. Nine. Fire suddenly

stretched as far as he could see. Gabriel tried to rein it in, to pull the fire back to his area, but now it had fuel to burn and it didn't care what he wanted.

The flames mocked him, each crack and snap a taunt. *Burn. Destroy. Consume.*

The smoke turned thick, blinding, black against the red of the flames. Fire completely surrounded him, and he lost track of which direction was home.

A tree fell, crashing through the leaves right beside him.

Gabriel skittered sideways. Another danger: The fire wouldn't hurt him, but a tree to the head sure would. Flames curled along the trunk, obscuring it from view almost immediately.

"Stop!" he said. Jesus, he needed Nick.

And he hadn't even grabbed his cell phone on the way out of the house.

He couldn't see how far the flames reached, and he hadn't been out walking too long. Their house backed up to the woods along with a dozen others. Would the fire leap onto porches and roofs? Would he end up taking out half the neighborhood because he'd wanted one leaf to burn?

He knew what it was like to cause destruction. He'd started the fire that killed his parents.

Don't think about that.

But he couldn't think of anything else. He had to make it to the house. He had to get his brothers out.

Another tree fell. Gabriel bolted, praying he was going the right way.

He ran through fire forever. It felt incredible, and he hated it.

Then he heard men shouting, and before he could process that, someone tackled him and sent him to the ground.

Wet leaves were in his mouth; red lights flashed through the trees above him. Hands were hitting him everywhere. He smelled wet wool. His arms were trapped somehow; he couldn't even find his hands to fight them off.

What. The. Fuck.

He spat leaves, but didn't get them all. "Stop!" he yelled. He didn't even know who he was *talking* to. "Stop it!"

"Medic!" A woman's voice, right close to him. "He's conscious!"

People crouched over him. Firemen, with hats and gear and everything. Gabriel couldn't even tell which was the woman. Sirens and radios and diesel engines created a racket behind them.

"I'm okay," he croaked around the crap in his mouth. "I'm okay. I don't need a medic."

He needed to get off this ground. He needed to make sure the fire hadn't made it back to the house.

They were pulling a blanket away from him. His clothes had to be ruined; he could smell the singed fabric, feel the rough edges against his skin.

He coughed, and then someone was pressing an oxygen mask to his face.

God, he didn't need a damn mask. He needed to get to the house. His brothers would be trapped. He needed to stop the fire. He needed—

Cold steel touched his wrists. What were they *doing?*

Cutting his clothes off.

Gabriel fought. Hard.

Then hands were pinning him down, men yelling that "whoa, whoa, *whoa*" they did when someone was absolutely out of control.

"Take it easy." A fireman was kneeling over him, adjusting the oxygen mask now that he was pinned to the ground. The woman's voice again, but he couldn't see anything but her eyes. "We're trying to help you. Is anyone else out there?"

He shook his head fiercely. "Let me up. Let me up. I need to get my brothers."

She glanced up at the woods, where fire still raged. "In there?"

"No. Home." He fought again, but there must have been a lot of guys holding him down. He couldn't get purchase. "Please. The fire . . . spreading—"

"We've got it," she said. She put a hand against his face. He could smell smoke on her palm, but it felt nice and reminded him of his mother for half an instant. "Just settle down and let us see how bad the burns are."

"They're not," said a guy near his feet.

"What?" She turned her head.

"They're not," the guy said. "Hannah, this kid doesn't have a mark on him."

"Please," said Gabriel. He sounded pathetic, his voice croaking like an old smoker. "Please let me up. I'm okay."

She was staring down at him with something like disbelief.

"Sit him in the back of the bus," said another guy. "Let him get some more oxygen in there and we'll reassess."

"The bus" turned out to be an ambulance. Gabriel sat, wrapped in a blanket, breathing oxygen he probably didn't need, watching his flames turn to smoke, flashing lights from the fire trucks bouncing off the billowing darkness.

They'd taken his name and address, and then left him alone so they could deal with more important things.

But then that girl firefighter was back, her helmet off, a spill of blond hair tucked into her reflective coat. She was younger than he'd thought, early twenties maybe. Her expression was all business, no compassion now that he wasn't dying.

"What happened?" she said.

I started a fire. Gabriel shook his head, looking at anything but her face.

"They found a lighter in your pocket," she said. "Were you smoking out there?"

He coughed. "No."

"Did you start a fire on purpose?"

He shook his head again and felt his throat tighten. His eyes burned. He had to swallow twice. No way he could lie right now; she'd see right through it. He couldn't even think straight to come up with a story. "I was just walking."

"Did you see anyone?"

He shook his head. At least that was the truth. "The leaves were on fire." He coughed again, and it hurt. Maybe he did need the oxygen. "It spread fast."

She took the mask out of his hands and pressed it to his face again. That compassion was back. "No kidding."

"Gabriel."

He jerked his head up. Michael stood a few feet behind her, the emergency lights flickering off his hair and clothes, turning his eyes red and his expression frightening. It was an intense look, a fierce look. A grown-up look.

Gabriel couldn't cut through the guilt to snap at him. He wanted to wilt like that stupid kid had when Gabriel pulled him away from Layne.

He could already hear Michael's voice. *We're supposed to be lying low. You could have burned down the house. You're such a disappointment.*

Or maybe that was his own voice.

Gabriel swiped at his eyes. "I'm sorry, Michael. I'm sorry. I'm sorry. Please—"

But then his brother grabbed him by the back of the neck.

And just when Gabriel thought Michael was going to haul off and take a swing at him, he pulled Gabriel forward and wrapped him up in a hug.

Michael held him for a long time, and Gabriel let him.

Finally, Michael pushed him back by the shoulders and looked at him. "Are you all right?"

Gabriel nodded.

Michael ran a hand through his hair and sighed. "I swear to god, you guys are going to give me gray hair before I hit twenty-five."

He wasn't mad. Gabriel stared at him.

"Just some smoke inhalation," said Hannah. "We can run him to the hospital to be sure."

Gabriel shook his head. "No way."

"You're one lucky kid," she said.

Gabriel snorted and looked at the woods, the smoke pouring into the night sky. *Lucky.*

"Are Chris and Nick all right?" he said.

Michael nodded. "They aren't even home. They left right after you did."

So they'd never been in danger at all. That loosened something in Gabriel's chest.

Michael was looking at Hannah. "Is he all right to go home?"

She looked doubtful. Gabriel stepped closer to his brother, putting some distance between himself and the ambulance, suddenly worried they were going to make him go to the hospital, anyway. "Michael, I'm fine."

"Just chill out and let her be the judge, okay?"

Hannah was staring now. "Michael," she said. "Mike Merrick."

"Yeah?"

Her cheeks looked pink, but it might have been the strobe lights from the fire truck. "Hannah Faulkner." She paused. "We went to school together."

Michael was staring back at her blankly. "Hey."

His brother, the master of conversation.

"You don't remember me." Her expression evened out. "I was a year behind you."

"Oh." Now Michael looked flustered. "Yeah. Sorry. It's been a while."

Then they just stood there looking at each other.

Gabriel cleared his throat. "So can I go home or what?"

She blinked and looked back at him. "Yes. Let me get one of the EMTs so your brother can sign for you to go."

It took twenty minutes, but eventually he was sitting beside Michael in the front seat of the work truck. Now that they were alone, Gabriel wondered if his brother's relief would morph into that anger Michael always carried around. Normally Gabriel would poke at him, provoke him into a fight.

Right now he just wanted Michael to yell, to slice into some of this guilt that had Gabriel in a choke hold.

But his brother didn't say anything.

After they'd pulled into the driveway, Gabriel moved to slide out of the cab, but Michael caught his arm.

Gabriel braced himself.

Michael said, "Take your clothes off in the garage, and put them in the bin. Don't touch anything until you take a shower."

That was it?

Gabriel stared at him for a moment. It felt like he needed to clear his throat again. "Why?"

"You'll see why when you look in a mirror."

Michael went into the house and left him to strip down to his shorts. Here in the light of the garage, Gabriel could see his hands and forearms were blackened with soot. His clothes were practically unrecognizable. Even his shoes wouldn't be salvageable.

They all went in the trash.

Gabriel paused with his hand on the door. The air was cold and he didn't want to stand out here too long, but he wondered if this was it, if Michael would be waiting to lay into him now.

But his brother was just cleaning up the dinner dishes, so Gabriel went upstairs to take a shower.

Michael had been right: Soot lined his face, and his hair was full of charred bits of leaves and bark. His hands left prints all over everything. After he toweled off, he took one of those Lysol wipes to the sink and the light switch. Oh, and the door.

Destroying the evidence.

He couldn't stop thinking about his parents.

The summer of Michael's senior year, Seth and Tyler and the other Elementals in town had gotten serious. They'd tried to kill Michael. Their parents had taken the whole family over to Seth's house to talk.

It had turned into a full-scale battle.

Gabriel's anger had started a fire. At twelve, he'd had no control of his abilities.

His parents hadn't made it out of that house alive.

And tonight, he could have caused that kind of damage again.

Michael wasn't in the kitchen or the living room now, but Gabriel didn't go looking for him. He just walked out the back door and dropped into one of the Adirondack chairs on the porch. The smell of smoke hung thick in the air, but he didn't feel any fire nearby. The firemen had been thorough.

He usually told Nick everything, but this, right on the tail of their dinner argument . . . Gabriel suddenly couldn't stand the thought of telling his twin. Just the thought had him fidgeting, reaching for the lighter in his pocket.

But he didn't have it. The EMTs must have kept the one in his jeans, and he hadn't grabbed another from his bedroom.

Gabriel sighed.

The sliding door opened, and then Michael was clomping across the porch. Gabriel didn't look at him, just kept his gaze on the tree line.

Michael dropped into the chair beside him. "Here."

Gabriel looked over. His brother was holding out a bottle of Corona.

Shock almost knocked him out of the chair. They *never* had alcohol of any kind in the house. When Michael had turned twenty-one, they'd all spent about thirty seconds entertaining thoughts of wild parties supplied by their older brother.

Then they'd remembered it was *Michael,* a guy who said if he ever caught them drinking, he'd call the cops himself. Really, he'd driven the point home so thoroughly that by the time he and Nick started going to parties, they rarely touched the stuff.

Gabriel took the bottle from his hand. "Who are you, and what have you done with my brother?"

Michael tilted the bottle back and took a long draw. "I thought you could use one. I sure can."

Gabriel took a sip, but tentatively, like Michael was going to slap it out of his hand and say, *Just kidding.* "Where did this even come from?"

"Liquor store."

Well, that was typical Michael. "No, jackass, I meant—"

"I know what you meant." Michael paused to take another drink. "There's a mini-fridge in the back corner of the garage, under the old tool bench." His voice was careful, as if he wasn't sure he wanted to share this secret.

Gabriel didn't look at him, hiding his own surprise. "You hid a fridge?"

"I didn't. Dad did." Another drink. "I found it after he died."

They both fell silent for a while, Michael probably reliving it, Gabriel imagining it, his brother at eighteen, finding their father's stash of beer. Gabriel wondered if Dad had only been hiding it from his sons, or if he'd kept it a secret from their mother, too.

Not like it mattered.

"Please tell me this beer isn't five years old," he said.

"It's not." Michael smiled.

And that, too, was almost enough to knock Gabriel out of the chair.

He stared out into the darkness for a moment, and then took another sip. "You're not mad?"

Michael didn't say anything, just took another drink.

Gabriel felt his shoulders tighten. The cold of the bottle bit at his fingertips.

"You remember that summer Chris got mono?" said Michael.

The question came out of left field. But Gabriel did remember. Right after their parents died, Chris had gotten really sick. A pediatrician had diagnosed him with mononucleosis and given him antibiotics, but his "illness" had probably been more due to the fact that none of them were sleeping, and it was the driest summer Maryland had seen in years. Chris suffered without water.

"You and Nick got into it with Seth and Tyler that week," said Michael. "At the mall, of all places. You remember that, too?"

"Yeah." Gabriel remembered the security guards pulling them apart.

"The custody stuff still wasn't straight," said Michael. "Chris was sick, and I didn't know how insurance worked, if we even *had it,* what with Mom and Dad . . . and then you two got in all that trouble at the mall. The social worker started saying it was too much for me, and she was going to recommend foster care—"

"I didn't know that." Gabriel looked at him.

Michael shrugged. "It doesn't matter now, does it?" He took another long sip and shook his head. "Anyway, I thought I was going to lose it. I was so angry. Angry at you two for not keeping out of trouble, angry at Chris for getting sick, angry at stupid stuff like missing graduation. I was worried she was right, that I couldn't do it. And what was worse, I was angry at Mom and Dad for leaving me with such a frigging *mess*."

Gabriel almost held his breath. Michael had never talked like this before. Especially not to *him*.

"I was so mad," said Michael. "I hated them. I actually went to the cemetery and started swearing at the headstones. Punching them. I almost broke my hand. I looked like a lunatic."

Another drink.

Gabriel stared.

"But I wanted them back so badly," said Michael. "I would have done anything . . . well." He took a breath and turned his head, meeting his brother's eyes. "You know."

"Yeah." Gabriel paused. "I know."

Michael turned and looked out at the night again. "So I'm kneeling there in the grass, wanting them back, feeding fury into the ground." Another drink, this time a long one. He finished off the bottle. "The ground opened up and pushed their coffins to the surface." He paused. "And not just theirs. Like twenty of them."

Gabriel almost dropped his beer. He was horrified—but also a little fascinated.

"Were they open?" he asked, his voice hushed.

Michael shook his head. "It scared the crap out of me. I mean, aside from the obvious, it was the middle of the afternoon—"

"What did you do?"

"What do you mean, what did I do?" Michael swung his head around. "I *put them back*."

"Holy shit."

"No kidding." He made a face and added, "I don't even know if I put them back *right*."

"You mean, Mom and Dad—"

"No, they're right. Just . . . everyone else." Michael paused. "Jesus. What a week that was."

"I'm surprised you came home," said Gabriel, and he meant it. He'd never thought about what would have happened if he and his brothers had been thrown into foster care. If he and Nick had been split up.

"I did," said Michael. "And that night was when I found the fridge. Fully stocked and all. I don't even remember what made me go into that corner of the garage, but I swear to god, it was like Dad was standing right there, saying, 'Here, kid, you look like you need a drink.'"

He stopped talking, and Gabriel let silence fill up the space between them for a moment.

Then he looked over. "Thanks." He paused. "Does anyone else know?"

"No. Just you."

That meant something. The beer, the story—Michael was saying he trusted him. Gabriel wasn't sure he deserved it.

"You're not alone, you know." Michael hesitated, as if he wasn't sure Gabriel would keep listening. "Fire's not my thing, but the pull, the power . . . I understand it. Nick and Chris do, too."

Gabriel didn't say anything.

Michael sighed. "I'm just saying. You're friends with half the school, but you don't have any real *friends*. You're with a different girl every week, but you've never had a *girlfriend,* you don't—"

"Wait a minute. Are you seriously trying to talk *girls* with me?"

"No—Gabriel." Michael sounded frustrated. "I'm trying to talk about being alone—"

Gabriel couldn't decide if he was pissed or amused. "When was the last time you *spoke* to a girl? Are you even aware the firefighter chick was checking you out?"

His brother faltered. "She's just a girl from school."

"You should call her up. Ask her out."

"Please."

"God knows getting some would probably improve your mood."

"I think that's enough."

Gabriel didn't often think of Michael in terms other than *overbearing* and *pain in the ass,* but the secret beer had him wondering what else he didn't know.

"Have you gone out with anyone since Mom and Dad died?"

Michael didn't move, and Gabriel didn't think he was going to answer. But he finally nodded. "Yeah," he said, his voice low. "Once, when I was twenty-one. She said I had too much baggage."

"What a bitch."

Michael rolled his eyes. "Yeah, I'm a real catch. I'm shocked they're not lined up at the door."

Gabriel reached out and gave his ponytail a yank. "Maybe if you didn't look like Charles Manson, they would be."

"I do not look like Charles Manson."

Gabriel gestured at the door. "Go *tap-tap* on your laptop and look him up. Dead ringer."

Michael laughed. It was a good sound, one Gabriel couldn't remember hearing since . . . forever.

But then Michael stood up, and Gabriel lost the smile. He shouldn't have mentioned the laptop. Their landscaping business was probably on the brink of collapse since Michael had spent ten minutes not being an asshole. That familiar wall was going to fall back into place between them; Gabriel could feel it.

Michael stopped and turned. "I won't tell Chris and Nick."

Gabriel glanced up, surprised. "Thanks." He paused. "I won't either. About . . . the other stuff."

And then Michael was sliding the door open, pushing through, leaving Gabriel alone on the porch. Game over.

But Michael stopped before sliding it closed. "You know, they won't be home for a while. You want another beer?"

Gabriel smiled. "Yeah," he said. "I do."

CHAPTER 8

Gabriel dribbled the basketball a few times and threw, making the basket for an easy three-pointer. He was alone on the court, killing time until Nick was done with whatever after-school do-gooder activity he'd signed up for.

Layne hadn't said a word to him in class.

Gabriel hadn't known what to say to her, either.

Dribble, dribble. Shoot.

Basket.

If Nick hadn't broken his leg, Gabriel would be finishing the soccer season this week. He'd played under his twin brother's name so he could get around the school's stupid rule limiting students to playing on two varsity teams per year. Gabriel missed the team, the camaraderie, the physical exertion fed by a common goal.

He didn't really miss any of the guys.

It made him think of Michael's comments.

Stupid. He didn't need friends. He had his twin brother.

His phone chimed. Speaking of Nick.

Go ahead without me. I'm going home with Quinn.

Of course. Gabriel shoved the phone back in his pocket.

Nick hadn't even talked to him last night. Usually they did

the postmortem when one went out without the other. But maybe Nick didn't feel like he had to. He'd been with Chris, after all.

Whatever.

Dribble. Shoot.

The ball hit the rim and ricocheted sideways, toward the bleachers.

Gabriel swore and jogged to retrieve it—but Layne's brother stepped out of the shadowed corner by the door and picked it up.

Simon wore basketball shorts and a loose T-shirt, the clothes making him look smaller than he really was. Sweat darkened his shirt and matted his hair at the temples—he'd probably been out running. The JV coach always made them run at the end of a practice, Gabriel remembered.

If Simon had stayed late for practice, did that mean Layne was still around?

She'd said her little brother dragged her to all the basketball games last year, so Simon had seen him play. It hadn't occurred to him until now that it meant *Layne* had seen him play, too.

He should have apologized. In class. He should have said something.

Yeah, and how would that go? *I'm sorry I stopped those douchebags.*

He scanned the bleachers, as if he could have missed a lone girl sitting there while he shot baskets.

Empty.

Gabriel shook it off. " 'Sup, Simon."

The kid grinned and held out a fist like he had yesterday.

Gabriel hit it. "How was practice?"

Simon lost the smile. His face was flushed from the run, and with the sudden darkness in his eyes, it made him look angry.

"Not good, huh?" said Gabriel.

Simon signed something furiously.

Gabriel frowned. "Dude. I'm sorry, I—"

Simon made a frustrated noise, then a gesture that didn't

need much translation. *Forget it.* He tossed the ball to Gabriel and turned away.

"Hey," said Gabriel. Simon kept walking, and it took Gabriel a moment to realize that the other boy couldn't hear him.

He jogged a few steps and caught him by the arm.

Simon swung around. His eyes were red.

Gabriel fished his cell out of his pocket and held it out. "Here. Text it."

Simon's eyes widened. He took the phone and worked the buttons like his thumbs were on fire.

Then he held it out. Gabriel read.

I can practice, but can't play. Coach says liability.

Gabriel frowned, but he understood. If Simon couldn't hear, how could the coach call plays? How could the other kids get his attention on the court? He wouldn't hear a whistle or the buzzer.

Simon took the phone from him again.

I'm good. Not a liability.

Gabriel smiled.

Simon took the phone a third time.

I just want to play.

Gabriel lost the smile. He understood *that.*

"You're good?" he said.

Simon clenched his teeth and nodded.

Gabriel slid the phone into his pocket and tossed the ball back at Simon. "Prove it."

The kid was faster than Gabriel expected, light on his feet and agile. Fit, too—he was all over the court despite just finishing practice. His ball control sucked; Gabriel could tell he was used to getting by with speed. He missed half the shots he took.

At first Gabriel tried calling out pointers—but then he remembered *again* that Simon couldn't hear him.

Yeah, he saw where the coach was coming from.

Finally, he caught the ball and held his hands in a T. He'd been playing in jeans and a hoodie, and his own hair felt damp.

"You need to slow it down, buddy."

Simon was breathing hard. He nodded.

"He needs to remember the bus schedule," said a voice from the bleachers. "We've already missed the late one."

Gabriel turned. Simon didn't. Layne sat there, a textbook open on the bench beside her, a notebook in her lap.

"How long have you been sitting there?" he said.

She glanced at the watch on her wrist. "Like twenty minutes."

God, he was baking in this sweatshirt. He swiped a hand across his forehead. "Why didn't you say something?"

She glanced away, tucking a loose piece of hair back into her braid. "Because Simon never gets to play."

"So you missed the—hey!"

Simon had smacked the ball out from under his arm and was tearing off across the court.

Layne laughed, but then she caught herself and sobered.

They stared at each other across twenty feet of gym floor. Gabriel pushed the hair back from his face. "You need to go?"

She clicked her pen. "I've got nowhere to be."

Gabriel wasn't entirely sure what that meant. He couldn't figure out her tone. It certainly wasn't friendly.

The ball hit him in the arm. Simon was back, dribbling beside him.

His expression said, *We playing or what?*

"Go," said Layne. "Play."

It sounded like a challenge.

Gabriel grabbed the edge of his sweatshirt and dragged it over his head. Half his T-shirt came with it, but he yanked it down.

When he flung the hoodie onto the bench, Layne was staring at her textbook, the edge of her lip between her teeth.

Her cheeks were bright pink.

Interesting.

Then Simon was throwing him a pass, and the ball was in play.

Gabriel had never been so *aware* of an audience before. He played harder, feeling her watching him. But when he looked up, her head was always bent over her notebook, her pen moving along the paper.

Oof. The ball hit him in the stomach, hard. Gabriel caught it automatically and glared at Simon. "Dude, what the hell?"

Simon grinned. He pointed at him, then Layne, then signed something.

Layne shot off the bench. "Simon!" She came across the court and smacked him in the arm.

"What did you say?" said Gabriel.

Simon was just laughing silently.

Gabriel glanced at Layne. "What did he say?"

"Nothing." Her cheeks were red for sure. She grabbed Simon's arm and tugged, then signed as she walked. "Come on. We'll call Dad to pick us up on his way home."

"I can give you a ride," said Gabriel.

"Don't be silly. He won't be more than an hour or so."

An *hour?* "That's stupid. And your brother seriously needs a shower. Let me give you a ride home."

Simon nodded emphatically, and then signed something.

Layne gave a huge sigh and turned for the bleachers. "Fine. Whatever."

While she was packing her things, Gabriel grabbed Simon's arm and turned to face him. "What did you say?"

Simon grinned and gestured for his phone.

I said you'd play a lot better if you weren't staring at my sister.

Gabriel fiddled with the dials when they pulled onto the main road, trying to get some heat going. Layne was curled into the front seat, her backpack on the floor. Her eyes were locked forward, her hands in her lap. Lights from oncoming cars flickered off her glasses.

"You warm enough?" Gabriel said, just to break the silence.

"I'm fine." Her voice seemed very small in the confines of the car.

"You'll have to give directions."

She cleared her throat and shifted in her seat. "We live in Compass Pointe. You know where that is?"

"Yeah." Compass Pointe was the rich neighborhood at the north end of town, the kind with eight-bedroom houses and servant quarters over the garage—though he didn't know any that actually *had* servants. Michael did the landscaping for three houses out there, and they were three of his highest-paying customers.

"Shouldn't you be in a private school or something?" he asked.

"My father says he got by on a public education, and that should be good enough for anybody." She paused. "He's a defense attorney. A good one."

"I'm surprised you're not driving a BMW to school."

She bristled. "First of all, my parents have the money, not me, and second of all, I don't have a *license* yet. I didn't think you'd be the kind of guy to get all weird about where I live—"

"Whoa!" God, it was like he couldn't avoid colliding with the chip on her shoulder. "I'm just saying. Heather Castelline lives out here and no one can get her to shut up about crap like how much her manicure costs."

Layne made a face. Her arms were folded across her chest now. "I'm not Heather Castelline."

Gabriel snorted. "Obviously."

Layne didn't say anything, just turned her head and looked out the window. Her sudden silence smacked him across the face as effectively as a hand would have.

He sighed and ran a hand through his hair. He couldn't figure her out at all.

And it was making him *crazy*.

Then he noticed the little sniffing sounds, the way her fingers had a death grip on her biceps.

"Layne?" He glanced over. "Are you *crying?*" Simon was silent, oblivious in the backseat.

She didn't turn her head. "Forget it."

What had he said? He wished he could pull the car over, but they were in the middle of three lanes of traffic on Ritchie Highway. He didn't even know how to play this. "I don't . . . what's—"

"I don't know why you have to be so mean all the time," she said, turning her head just far enough that he could see there were definitely tears on her cheeks. "Do you have any idea what it feels like, the way you treat people?"

"What the hell did I say?" he demanded.

She sniffed. "Obviously."

Jesus, this was so *infuriating*. "Obviously *what?*"

"You said *obviously*. Obviously I'm not Heather Castelline. Well, you know what? Not everyone is a hot blond cheerleader, Gabriel Merrick. I'm sure in your world, every girl should have a perfect rack and great legs and flaunt them for your benefit, but we aren't all such paragons of perfection."

Wow.

Gabriel stared out the windshield at the traffic. The ridges in the steering wheel were biting into his palms. "I guess you told me."

This was worse than fighting with Michael. At least he could haul off and hit his brother and tell him he was being an asshole.

But Layne was still crying silently, staring out the window, her shoulders shaking almost imperceptibly.

When he came to a red light, he looked over. "Hey."

She didn't look. "I said, *forget it.*"

"I know what you said. Look at me."

"If I look at you, Simon will know I'm crying."

The light turned, and he had to look back at the road anyway.

He spoke into the silence, hearing his voice come out rough. "When I said 'obviously,' it was because Heather Castelline is a total bitch who'll only give you the time of day if she needs something from you. Nicky went out with her *once,* and he spent two days swearing he'd rather cut his balls off than date a girl like her again."

Layne didn't say anything.

"She's the last person who'd criticize me for getting into it with some sophomore tool in the hallway, and she'd be more likely to copy my quiz than to fix the wrong answers. She sure as hell wouldn't stay after school because her brother was having a good time."

Layne didn't speak, but he could swear she was looking at him now.

Gabriel kept his eyes on the road. "It had nothing to do with what you look like."

She swallowed. "Okay. Whatever."

"Besides, you could totally have a perfect rack and great legs. I just can't tell. If you want to flaunt them so I can make final judgment—"

She punched him in the arm.

But now she was smiling.

And blushing.

He had to stop for the next light, and he looked over. Dampness still clung to her cheeks, but she didn't look like she was plotting to kill him.

When he made the turn into her development, she said, "I can still help you with math." She paused, her tone nonchalant. "If you want."

"What, you mean now?"

"Did you understand tonight's assignment?"

He hadn't understood an assignment in about five years. His shoulders were already tense. "I'll be all right."

"You planning to go home and have your brother do it for you?"

He wasn't even sure if Nick *was* home. Gabriel didn't say anything. He didn't like that Nick did the work for him, but Layne knowing . . . *That,* he hated.

He pulled into her driveway and sat there, putting the car in park but not killing the engine. He stared at the pattern his headlights made on the garage, wide circles of light bouncing off the stone façade of her house.

"What's wrong?" she said. "Tough guy can't be good at math?"

"Hey." He swung his head around, his jaw tight.

She didn't back away, her eyes gleaming in the darkness. "How can you sit there in class every day, pretending to follow along?"

"That's the easy part."

She stared back at him. "I don't think it is."

He looked back at the garage and didn't say anything. She was right. It was killing him, but she was right.

Simon reached between the seats and tapped Layne on the shoulder. Gabriel didn't need to understand sign language to figure out the message.

What's going on?

Gabriel turned the key and yanked it out of the ignition, reaching over the center console to grab his backpack. "All right," he said with a sigh. "Let's give it a shot."

CHAPTER 9

Layne's house looked like something that should have been featured in a decorating magazine. His own house wasn't small—they each had their own room, and no one had to fight for a bathroom or anything like that—but this was crazy.

The front hall featured rich hardwood flooring, but just beyond that, every inch of carpeting he could see was white—and it was a lot of inches. Dark wooden furniture, mahogany or something he didn't know, sat against the walls in a forbidding way. Framed paintings that looked original hung on the walls. The kinds of sofas adults kept for show, not for sitting, sat at angles to the walls. Everything was accented with white: throw pillows, coasters, even a vase of white roses on the hall table.

The place was dead silent.

Simon flashed a quick sign, flung his backpack on the floor, and bolted up the hardwood staircase.

Gabriel wanted to pick up Simon's backpack and shove it in the front closet. The décor was *that* intimidating.

"He says he'll be down in a while," said Layne. "Come on, we can go in the kitchen."

Gabriel hesitated at the juncture of hardwood and carpeting before following her. Should he take off his shoes? But she hadn't.

"Does your mom work, too?" he said. The house had obviously been empty prior to their arrival.

"Well, *work* is a little strong." Layne led him around a corner into a huge white kitchen with stainless-steel appliances. Even the granite countertop was white with flecks of silver.

The white was getting a little creepy.

"I know," said Layne. "It looks like a serial killer should live here, right?"

"I wouldn't go that far," said Gabriel. But, really, he would. "What do you mean, *work* is a little strong?"

"She volunteers. For everything. AIDS benefits, Children's Hospital in DC, Johns Hopkins, that women's center downtown—"

"You don't sound impressed." He gingerly set his backpack on one of the white chairs, but he wasn't ready to sit down yet.

"It would be impressive if she actually volunteered in a way that helped people. She helps with benefit functions. She likes to throw big parties where she can look *perfect*." Layne flicked an invisible speck of dust off the counter. "Get it?"

Not really. But he nodded.

She pulled the trig book out of her backpack.

Gabriel stared at it, hating that a rectangle of pages glued together could cause such stress. "You're not going to give me the tour?"

She raised an eyebrow. "You *want* the tour?"

He shrugged and tried to look expectant.

She shrugged and pushed out of the chair.

The entire house looked like they'd broken into a museum exhibit. Doors whispered open against the carpeting. He only spotted one television, a huge big screen that took up half the wall of one room—but even there, it wasn't the kind of place where you'd want to kick back and watch the game. It felt like someone had put a TV in there according to a mansion instruction manual. *Living room: bay window, white carpeting, white sofa, silver big screen.* Even Layne's dad's "office" didn't have a piece of paper out of place.

No photographs on the first floor. Anywhere.

Layne narrated the room titles like a bored tour guide, her voice dispassionate.

"You don't like your house?" he finally said.

"I'm trying to figure out why you care." She glanced over her shoulder at him as they started up the stairs. "Or are you just stalling?"

"Yes."

She stopped halfway up, turning to look at him. "At least you admitted it."

Gabriel was one step behind her, and it put them on eye level. "I'm trying to figure out how a girl like you could come out of a house like this."

He watched the fire spark in her eyes, and he held a hand up. "That's not an insult."

It cut her anger off at the knees; he could tell. She shut her mouth and looked past him. "Maybe I don't like perfect."

"Yeah?" They were almost close enough to share breath. "What do you like, Layne?"

She sure didn't like being kept off balance; that was clear enough from the way she faltered and fought for words. He wondered if her cheeks would feel warm, if he could gather the nerve to touch her. She'd been so assertive in school when she'd told him off for fighting. If he touched her now, she'd probably push him down the stairs.

Then again, maybe not. Her expression was just vulnerable enough, her breathing soft and rapid. Gabriel shifted his weight, ever so slightly.

And she spun, striding up the steps. "Come on. If I let you stall too long, I'm no better than your brother."

He'd been moving to follow her, but that made him stop on the staircase. "What does that mean?"

"It means he's not doing you any favors by doing your homework."

"I told you—"

"Yeah, yeah, he's tried to help you. Screw it, turn to cheating. Did you ever ask a teacher to help you? You know, they have special classes—"

"Are you for real?" Special classes. As *if*.

"Was it all about sports? Did he start helping you just so you could play on a stupid team?"

"No. It wasn't—" He gritted his teeth and looked at the wall. "You don't even know what you're talking about."

"I know it would be easier to do everything for Simon, but sometimes I have to let him figure out how to handle things on his own."

Now he snapped his head around to look up at her. "Like getting beat up in the hallway?"

"Oh, so I should tell him to fight? Just what do you think would happen to a kid like Simon if he took a swing at someone?"

Gabriel took the last few steps until he was on equal ground, looking down at her. "Right now? He'd get his ass kicked."

"Great." She turned away, the sarcasm thick. "That's *totally* the goal we should be shooting for."

Gabriel caught her arm. "He'd figure out how to fight back. They'd figure out he was *willing* to fight back. Then they'd leave him alone."

"Is that what worked for you?"

"That's what works for *everyone,* Layne." He gave her a pretty clear up-and-down, hearing his voice turn cruel before he could stop it. "And I might be wrong, but I think you've learned that particular life lesson already."

Her face went pale. She jerked her arm free and spun away from him.

Then she opened one of the hall doors, went through, and slammed it shut.

Shit.

God, he didn't need this. He should grab his stuff from the kitchen and *go.*

But he stopped in front of the door. He put his hand against the white wood.

She saw him as a cheater. A jock thug who picked fights in the hallway.

Maybe that's all there was to see.

He inhaled, to call her name, to apologize, to try to figure out how she'd managed to wedge herself into his thoughts until he couldn't work her loose.

But she flung the door open, and he was left there with his hand in the air. Her eyes held the remnants of anger.

She glanced at his hand. "I'm sorry."

She was sorry? He pulled his hand back.

She looked at the molding around the doorway, rubbing at an invisible spot with her finger. "I shouldn't have come off like that. Sometimes you just—you cut right to the quick, you know?"

"You too," he said.

"I shouldn't have slammed the door in your face."

"I much prefer it to getting hit." He looked up, past her, at the bedroom. Finally, a break to the white—but this wasn't much better. Pink carpeting, princess border along the ceiling, white walls, and a gold canopy bed.

"What," he said, "no Barbie dream castle?"

Layne flushed. "Shut up."

She moved to push past him and shut the door, but he slid into her room instead. She had a bookcase, white trimmed with pink, packed double and triple with paperbacks. No shocker there. It looked like she still had every book she'd ever read. Her bedspread wasn't childish, though, just a simple pink, white, and yellow checked quilt. More books threatened to fall from a pile on the nightstand.

He'd been kidding about the Barbie dolls, but a row of model horses marched across the top of the bookcase, with a framed picture of a girl on a horse at the corner.

He touched a gray horse on the nose, and she was beside him immediately.

"Horses, Layne?" he said.

"Isn't that what rich little girls do?" she said, her voice vaguely mocking. "Ride horses?"

The girl in the photo wore a helmet, so he couldn't be sure who it was. "Is that you?"

"Yeah. Last year." She hesitated, and something about it felt personal.

He withdrew his hand and made his own voice vaguely mocking. "I didn't mean to make you talk about it."

She bit at her lip. "No one knows I do it anymore." Then she blushed and rubbed the gray horse on the nose where he'd touched it. "I mean, my parents know. They pay the bills and all. Just . . . no one at school."

"What a crazy thing to keep secret." He leaned closer to the picture. The horse was clearing a jump, with Layne crouched close to the animal's neck. "That's a big jump."

"Nah. Only three and a half feet."

He glanced back at her. "Aren't you afraid you'll fall?"

A little shrug. "Sometimes. I think that's why I like it. No matter how good you are, you're never completely in control. The horse has a mind of its own. You can't force it."

"So how good are you?"

She met his eyes, and he liked the spark of challenge he found there. "Good enough." She paused. "When I was younger, I used to compete all the time. We went to New York, Devon, Washington, all the big ones. My mother loved it. She couldn't wait to have another blue ribbon to hang on the wall, to brag about at the next benefit. Her perfect daughter."

Like flipping a switch, Layne's voice went from tentative to furious. "I hated the competition, I hated the pressure, I hated how something I loved had turned into something else my mother could use against me."

She reminded him of the fire in the woods, under control one minute, then blazing.

"But still you do it," he said.

"I don't compete," she said. "I just ride. Horses don't care that I have—" Her voice broke off suddenly, and he studied her, waiting. But she didn't say anything else, and she was staring at that picture, her shoulders tense.

The horses didn't care that she had *what?*

She didn't want him to ask—that much was clear from her posture. "You ride after school?"

She shook her head. "In the mornings. If I cut through the woods, I can walk to the farm in ten minutes."

They had to be at school by seven forty-five. "You must get up early."

She shrugged. "I like being the first one up. I can forget every-one else exists, and it's just me and the elements."

Gabriel smiled. "I know what you mean."

She gave him a wry glance. "Please. I bet your alarm goes off at seven-forty."

"You'd lose that bet." He looked at the horses again, touch-ing the next one in the row. It wasn't his first time in a girl's bed-room, but usually, the only talking they did was to shut him up before a parent heard. Here, alone with Layne, simply talking suddenly felt more intimate than anything he'd ever done with any random girl.

"I wouldn't figure you for a morning person," she said.

He brought his eyes back to hers. "I usually go for a run be-fore the sun comes up."

He liked running in the dark, before sunrise, when the sun couldn't feed him energy. That always felt like cheating. It was one of the few things he did without Nick.

She tucked a strand of hair behind one ear. He wanted to reach out and undo the elastic at the end of her braid, to let her hair come loose, to see what she looked like when she wasn't hiding behind this wall of *I don't care*.

Layne was looking at him expectantly.

Crap. She'd said something.

This was ridiculous. He cleared his throat. "What?"

Her cheeks sparked with pink. "I . . . ah . . . asked if you wanted to go back to the kitchen to work on the trig stuff."

He really wanted to stay right here and figure her out.

But this wasn't why she'd asked him in. She wasn't flirting with him. She hadn't even asked him up here—he'd asked for the tour and had practically strong-armed his way into her bed-room.

He was being an idiot, standing here thinking about her hair.

Gabriel stepped back. "Sure. Whatever."

The air in the hallway felt cooler, fed by the new distance be-tween them. It reminded him of Nick.

He didn't like that.

Gabriel touched her arm. "Hey." He paused. "Thanks. For trying to help."

She looked up at him, her eyes shadowed in the darkened hallway. "Thanks for helping Simon."

He could hear her breath, as quick as his own.

Then he could hear a key in the front door.

He instinctively jerked back—not like he'd been doing anything.

Layne's eyes went wide. "Crap. It's my dad. Come on." She grabbed Gabriel's hand and tugged.

He jogged down the steps behind her, but there was no way they'd make it to the kitchen before her dad came through the door.

"Layne," he said. "Christ, just *relax*. We weren't—"

"You don't understand." The door started to open and she stopped short, turning, like maybe they should run back upstairs.

God, it was like being dragged by a panicked bird. Gabriel almost ran into *her*. One hand caught the banister, and he grabbed Layne around the waist to keep from knocking her down the stairs.

And that's exactly how her father found them.

If Layne hadn't told Gabriel that her dad was a lawyer, he would have guessed. The guy could have played one on television, what with the long camel coat over a black suit, the dark hair threaded with gray, the calculating eyes and angled jawline.

Eyes that narrowed on seeing them.

Gabriel let go of Layne and straightened. Nick was way better at doing the parent thing, and this guy didn't look like the kind of dad to ignore their predicament, crack open a beer, and ask how Gabriel felt about the Ravens' defensive line.

Layne's face was bright red. "Dad. Look. It's not—"

"Not what I think?" Her dad had a handful of mail that he tossed on the hall table. Those eyes leveled on Gabriel. "I certainly hope not."

Gabriel stared back at him. "We were studying."

"Studying. Really." Mr. Forrest glanced around. "Here on the staircase? And where are your books?"

"Don't talk," whispered Layne.

"In the kitchen," said Gabriel. With his keys. The only thing keeping him trapped here was twenty feet of white carpeting, blocked by her father.

"Yet you were upstairs." Her father still hadn't broken eye contact. "Taking the tour, I assume?"

Gabriel smiled, though it wasn't really funny. "Actually, yeah."

"Shut up," hissed Layne.

Her dad's eyes narrowed. "How old are you?"

Gabriel already didn't like this guy. He gritted his teeth and wondered if he could shove past him. "Seventeen."

"Do you know what the age of consent is?"

"Dad! *Oh my god.*" Layne took a step forward. Her face was even redder. "We weren't doing anything!"

"I asked you a question, son."

"I'm not your son." Now Gabriel just wanted to shove him, period. He stepped into the foyer, feeling his shoulders tighten. "And I didn't know there was an age of consent for standing in a hallway."

"Don't get smart with me, kid."

"Stop it," said Layne, putting her hands up like they were going to take a swing at each other. "Look, it's a misunderstanding—"

"Layne." Mr. Forrest didn't even glance at her. "Get his things. Right now."

"I can get my things," said Gabriel.

"I'm not letting you out of my sight."

Layne was caught between them, flustered. She was nearly wringing her hands. "Dad, it's not—"

His eyes cut right. "Now, Layne."

She swallowed and slinked past him into the living room.

"Don't forget my box of condoms," called Gabriel.

Now her dad looked like he wished he had a shotgun. "If I find out you laid a hand on my daughter—"

"What?" said Gabriel. "You'll stand here and bitch about it?"

"Stop it!" cried Layne, dragging his coat and backpack from the kitchen.

Her dad took a step forward. "I'll have you arrested and charged with trespassing and statutory rape."

"Then I'm going to need another fifteen minutes."

"Shut *up*." Layne flung the coat at his chest, then barely gave him time to grab it before she shoved the backpack at him. Her eyes were red. Was she ready to cry?

He felt something inside his chest loosen. "Layne—"

"Get out of my house," said Mr. Forrest. His words could cut ice.

Gabriel didn't move. He couldn't tear his eyes away from Layne. "Hey, I'm—"

"Go." She wasn't looking at him. "Just go."

Her dad opened the door. *"Now."*

Gabriel dug his keys out of his backpack and pushed past him. But on the front walk he stopped and turned.

Before he could say a word, her father slammed the door and locked it shut, leaving Gabriel out in the cold.

CHAPTER 10

For the first time, Gabriel was glad Nick would be out with Quinn. Chris would probably be out with Becca, Michael would be working, and Gabriel could just hole up in his room, blast loud music, and set his math book on fire.

But Hunter's jeep was in the driveway, along with a little four-door sedan he didn't recognize.

And when Gabriel opened the front door, he was hit with the smell of a home-cooked meal. And the animated sounds of a good conversation.

He almost stepped back on the porch to check the house number.

Nick's efforts notwithstanding, Gabriel couldn't remember the last time he'd walked through the door and felt like he was walking into a home.

It practically sounded like a dinner party was going on in the kitchen. Gabriel dropped his backpack in the foyer and headed back.

His brothers were seated around the table, plus Hunter, Becca, and Quinn. Michael didn't have a laptop in front of him for once. They were all laughing about something; he'd walked in too late to pick up the story. A mostly eaten lasagna was in a pan in the center of the table, plus a platter of garlic bread, the remnants of a tossed salad in a bowl, and assorted side dishes.

His stomach was making a pretty clear case that he hadn't eaten dinner yet.

But he stopped in the doorway, feeling very far removed from the good times.

"Hey," said Nick. "Where've you been?"

"Out." Gabriel still didn't move. "What's all this?"

"Becca and Quinn made dinner," said Chris. He gave Gabriel a funny look. "That all right?"

"Out where?" said Michael.

Gabriel ignored him. He looked at his twin. "I thought you were going home with Quinn."

Nick frowned. "Yeah, and?"

"Home meaning *here,* dumbass," said Quinn. "I've got my mom's car."

Gabriel really couldn't stand her.

"And I drove Becca over," said Hunter.

"No one asked you to stay," said Chris. But even his remark lacked the usual acidity.

Becca smacked him in the shoulder. "I did."

Gabriel didn't move from the doorway. Everyone seemed to be getting along just fine.

Without him.

"You hungry?" said Michael. His voice was careful—but then maybe he was picking up on Gabriel's mood. "There's plenty left."

"Not for long," said Quinn, and she reached out to pick up a piece of garlic bread.

"I thought you were trying out for the cheer squad," said Gabriel.

Quinn took a bite. "That's tomorrow. I didn't know you cared."

"I don't." He gave her a significant look. "But maybe you want to lay off the carbs."

She stopped chewing. "What the hell is wrong with you?"

God, what *was* wrong with him?

Nick's expression lost any shred of good humor, but he wasn't angry—yet. "Come on. Back off."

Gabriel shrugged. "Hey, I guess they could put you at the bottom of the pyramid with the sturdy girls—"

"Knock it off," said Becca.

"Leave her alone," said Nick. Now they were getting closer to anger.

"You're an asshole," said Quinn. She flung the bread onto the plate. Her eyes looked red.

Great. He could make two girls cry in the span of fifteen minutes.

"So I've heard," said Gabriel. Then he turned and headed back down the hallway, hoping to god there was a protein bar in his backpack.

A chair scraped the floor in the kitchen, the sound full of fury. Gabriel didn't wait to see who was coming after him.

But he felt the air change even before his twin caught him by the arm and jerked him around.

Nick looked pissed—but puzzled, too. "What is *with* you?"

"Nothing." Gabriel shrugged out of his grip and reached to open the front door. "Jesus, Nicky, it's not my fault she can't take a—"

Nick grabbed him again and shoved him against the doorjamb. The air temperature dropped another five degrees.

Then he leaned in. *"Stop."*

Gabriel glared back at him. "Don't start this, Nick."

"I didn't start anything." His brother's voice was low. "What is it? Do you like her or something?"

Gabriel snorted. "Please." Then he jerked free and shoved Nick away.

Nick shoved him back.

Gabriel went still. He could count on one hand the number of times he and Nick had gotten into it—seriously gotten into it. They were more likely to gang up on Chris than fight each other.

"Don't start this," he said again.

"Leave Quinn alone," said Nick.

"Yeah, whatever." Gabriel made to move away.

"I'm serious." His twin shoved him again, a little harder, a little rougher. "Or are you too stupid to realize that?"

Stupid.

Gabriel shoved him back, putting some real strength behind it. His brother half stumbled into the banister of the staircase.

But Nick hesitated before retaliating. Gabriel could feel it, that moment of indecision before a fight turned into a *fight.* That moment when you could back down and lose nothing.

"You know," said Gabriel, hearing his voice turn cruel, "you can tell me to leave her alone, but I don't know what you're going to do about the guys at school. It's not like she was the type to say no before, if you catch my drift—"

Nick punched him in the face.

And then they were fighting for real.

This wasn't like when he'd fought with Hunter. Nick wasn't a fighter, not really. He got some solid hits in, but he wouldn't fight dirty. Gabriel drove him back until he hit the wall, and he knew it wasn't going to last long.

But then they were being dragged apart. Someone was yelling; someone else had him by the arms, pulling him back.

Nick had blood on his lip, and he jerked his arm free from Chris to wipe at his mouth. "Jesus, Gabriel, *what?* You can't let someone else be happy for five minutes?"

Gabriel tried to pull free from whoever had him—had to be Michael. "Sorry, Nicky. Guess everyone can't be as perfect as you."

The girls were in the dining room doorway. Becca had her hands up, her expression placating. "Look, guys, just chill out."

"Don't bother," said Quinn. Her eyes weren't red anymore, and she leveled an icy glare at Gabriel. "If he wants to act like an animal, just take him out back and shoot him."

"The only animal I see," said Gabriel, "is the dog in the front hall—"

"Cut it out!" said Michael from behind him.

But then Gabriel couldn't breathe.

He didn't quite get it at first. Was Michael holding him too tightly? Was he winded from the fight? His lungs were trying to inhale, but it was like there was nothing there.

He found Nick's eyes across the foyer, grim and determined and just a bit satisfied.

Gabriel had a string of insults ready. He just couldn't talk.

He couldn't inhale. This wasn't funny anymore.

This *wasn't fucking funny*.

His lungs were burning. He fought the hands holding him.

Outside. He needed to get outside. He was going to drown in the middle of the hallway, without a drop of water around.

Fighting made it worse. His vision turned spotty. Nick's power choked the air around him, flicking at his skin, mocking him.

His own power flared without direction, seeking fire, energy, anything it could find to draw strength and retaliate.

The lights in the foyer exploded.

Then the lights in the dining room.

The girls shrieked, clinging to each other, ducking into the hallway where there weren't lights.

"Stop it," yelled Michael. "Both of you. Stop!"

Fire was in the air, fed by electricity in the walls. Nick was trying to choke it off, to steal the oxygen the fire craved. Gabriel pulled more power without trying—his element was taking over. He had to get it under control before he burned the house down.

But he needed to *breathe*.

The front porch light exploded. Glass tinkled against the front door.

"No!" Hunter's voice. He leapt around Michael and hit the switches on the wall, killing most of the flow of electricity to the foyer. "Where's the breaker box?"

"Got it," said Chris. He let go of Nick and bolted for the basement door.

Gabriel felt his knees hit the floor. He couldn't figure out whether things were still exploding or if that was his oxygen-starved brain giving him his own personal light show.

Then Hunter was there in front of him, hands clasping him around the neck.

Like he needed another barrier to breathing.

"*Breathe,*" said Hunter, and Gabriel felt his power in the space around them, different from his brothers, different from anything he'd ever felt before. "Please. Breathe."

Gabriel caught a breath—but that was it. It was enough to steady his control, to stop feeling like the house would explode at any minute.

He could feel Hunter fighting Nick now, as if contact let him feel the five-pointed star that connected them all.

Gabriel got another breath.

He was *so* going to beat the shit out of Nick.

He felt the moment Chris threw the master switch on the circuit breaker box. The power to the house just . . . died. His own power searched farther, to the lines on the street, cars on the road.

"Don't look for it," said Hunter. He hadn't let go, and Gabriel could feel his tension through his hands.

And just like flipping that switch, Gabriel could breathe again.

At first that's all he could do. He jerked free of Hunter's hands and coughed, sucking in great lungfuls of air, his forehead pressing against the floor.

But after a while, he realized how silent the house was without power. He could hear his heartbeat, still pounding. The soft grit of glass on wood, when someone shifted their weight.

He could hear them waiting.

Finally, he lifted his head. He didn't want to look at his twin, but he couldn't help it. He expected to see his brother look smug, to find righteous vindication on his face.

But Nick looked stricken.

Suddenly the house felt too small, too enclosed. Each breath tasted stale. He could smell the faint odor of burned electrical wiring.

Gabriel felt trapped.

"Open the door," he said, hearing his voice come out hoarse.

No one moved.

So he fought to his feet and grabbed the knob. October night air coursed through the doorway and cooled his face. He ran a hand across his forehead and found it damp with sweat.

"You all right?" said Michael.

Gabriel nodded and didn't look at him.

"Nick?"

Gabriel didn't want to hear his brother's answer. He reached down and grabbed his backpack, slung it over his shoulder, and stepped out onto the porch.

"Where are you going?" called Michael from the doorway.

"Out," said Gabriel. Thank god he still had his car keys. He flung his backpack onto the passenger seat and started the engine.

Michael was halfway down the walk to stop him, but Gabriel hit the accelerator to power down the driveway. He couldn't deal with them now. Just another perfect night, ruined by the resident fuckup.

But at the end of their street, he stopped. He had no idea where to go.

The sad thing was that he wanted to light things on fire. Despite nearly torching the house, his element was riding high, calling to him.

This was so unfair! The rest of them could practically bask in their element. No wonder Nick had such control.

Gabriel hadn't even known his twin could *do* something like that.

He pulled out from the stop sign, heading left, though he didn't really have a destination in mind.

Almost immediately, flashing red and white lights strobed from behind him, and Gabriel swore, moving to the shoulder. This would be the perfect end to his night.

But it was just a fire truck, roaring past with a blazing siren.

A fire truck.

A *fire truck*.

Maybe he didn't have to *start* a fire to feel his element.

Maybe he could just follow those flashing lights and find one.

Layne pulled her blankets up to her chin and stared at the ceiling.

She'd been trying to sleep for twenty minutes, but her body

wasn't tired and her mind wouldn't stop raging. The sun was barely down, but she couldn't bear the thought of sitting in the living room, pretending to watch a movie while her dad sat *right there*.

Damn Gabriel Merrick. She should have slapped him. No, punched him.

Then I'm going to need another fifteen minutes.

To her father, of all people. Her *father*.

Her door creaked open, a whisper of wood against carpeting. The hall light was off, but she could make out her father's silhouette.

He probably thought she was asleep. He didn't say anything.

"I'm still awake," she said.

"Are you all right?" He didn't move from the door. "You didn't say much at dinner."

God, what could she say? Her cheeks felt warm again, just remembering that little drama in the hallway. She knew better than to invite some meathead sports junkie into the house. She probably should have offered to teach him manners before math.

At least she didn't have to worry about Simon rambling about Gabriel. Her brother spent dinnertime glaring at their father, refusing to communicate.

"Are you mad at me?" her father said.

She swung her head around. "At you? No, of course not."

He came the rest of the way into the room, but he hesitated by the side of her bed. Early moonlight streamed through the window and caught the strands of gray in his hair, making him look older than he was. "I thought I might have embarrassed you."

Layne gritted her teeth. "Well, I was embarrassed, but it wasn't your fault."

"You sure?"

She scooted back in bed, sitting up to lean against the wall. "He really did come over to study, you know." Her cheeks flamed again. "No matter what he *said*."

"May I sit down?"

Her father usually wasn't this distant. Not once she had his attention, anyway. "Dad. Yes. I'm not mad."

He sat on the edge of the bed. "I know you're growing up, Layne, and I know you're going to be interested in boys. I wish your mother—"

"Stand up. I changed my mind."

He smiled, but it was grim. "You're under a lot of stress," he said. "If it's too much, I want you to talk to me. We can find—"

"We're all under a lot of stress, Dad." She gave him a dark look. "I'm fine."

He didn't flinch from the look, but then again, he sat across a table from alleged murderers every other day. "I know what high school boys are like, Layne. I don't want you getting hurt because you're looking for an outlet."

Her eyebrows went way up. "An *outlet?*"

"I know you know what I mean."

Her cheeks were hot again. "Gabriel Merrick isn't going to hurt me, Dad. He's a dumb jock who can't pass math. He's not *interested* in me." She rolled her eyes. "And I'm not looking for an *outlet.*"

"You sure? Because he's the first boy you've ever brought home." He gave her a very level look, his voice taking on the first shadow of anger. "And I find it interesting that you went for someone older, someone who acts like a future *felon,* not two weeks after—"

"To *study,*" she snapped. "He gave us a ride because we missed the late bus."

"If he came over to study, I would have found you in the kitchen."

She folded her arms across her chest, but before she could say anything else, he put a hand on her shoulder.

His voice was gentler. "Layne, I'm not accusing *you* of anything."

"Sounds like it."

"I just want you to be safe. I know you've been dealing with a lot." He paused. "I'm sorry I haven't been home much lately."

She looked up at him, feeling a flash of guilt. "It's not your fault. We all have to do our part."

He took her face in his hands and kissed her on the forehead. "Thanks for taking on so much."

She nodded.

He stood and moved toward the doorway. She slid back under the covers.

But then he stopped before closing the door. "Layne?"

"Yeah?"

"Don't bring him over here when I'm not home."

Like there was much chance of that. But *still.* Anger made her sit straight up again. "You don't *trust* me?"

He laughed like she'd said something truly funny. "Oh, Layne, I trust *you* plenty. Good night, sweetheart."

Then he shut the door.

And all she could think about was Gabriel Merrick.

About how much she wanted to hit him. Really hard. Right where it would count.

But worse, about how much she'd liked, just for an instant, the way his arms felt when he'd caught her on the staircase.

Chapter 11

Following a fire truck was harder than he expected. Gabriel couldn't blow through red lights, and people sure as hell weren't pulling over to give *him* the right of way. Once, he thought he'd lost the truck, but then he heard the wail of a siren and caught a flash of lights through the trees. Two turns and he found them.

He parked half a mile down the road, part of a line of cars along the curb. He cracked the window and sat for a minute. He'd worried this might be a false alarm, like a sparking outlet or a cat in a tree or some crap like that.

But something was burning—he could feel fire calling him even from here.

Come play.

He took a deep breath. In it, he tasted smoke.

Like his own community, the houses here were widely spaced, with lots of trees to provide plenty of shade. People were already wandering down the street to gawk at the destruction. Better than TV.

Like he was in a position to judge.

He thought about walking down the street with everyone else. But there was a chance he might be recognized. Kids from school lived in this neighborhood, and he'd helped Michael with a few jobs over here. One of his favorite running trails ran right through the woods behind the houses.

He walked up a driveway nonchalantly, like he was going to head up the front walk. No cars sat in front of the garage, and the drapes were all drawn, so he walked right past the front door, around the corner, and into the woods.

The trees here weren't quite as dense as behind his own house, but the sun had set and his clothes were dark. He slipped between the trunks, following the call of his element until his eyes could take over.

Gabriel stopped short at the tree line. Smoke poured through every window of the two-story home. Fire blazed through what was left of the roof. Smoke detectors were definitely working— they screeched into the darkness and gave Gabriel a shot of adrenaline he *so* didn't need.

Firefighters had smashed most of the windows on the first level, but they were working toward the back. Gabriel felt the flames cheer at the presence of more oxygen. Radios crackled with static and commands. People were yelling incoherently in the front yard. He could barely make out the words over those damned smoke detectors. *Flashover . . . stairs unstable . . . pull out . . .*

Then a woman screamed in the front yard, a sound full of anguish that twisted something in his chest. He'd heard a sound like that once.

Gabriel had to put a hand against a tree. He shouldn't have come here.

Come play.

Smoke was everywhere. He clenched his eyes shut. It felt like he couldn't breathe again.

The fire thought it was a game. A sick, twisted, cruel game of destruction.

Come. Play.

The worst part was that he *wanted* to.

"You all right?"

The voice spoke from his shoulder. Gabriel almost came out

of his frigging skin. He actually staggered into the tree before his heart would slow down enough to let him talk.

"Hunter," he choked.

"Yeah?"

Gabriel got it together and pushed off the tree to punch him in the chest. "What the hell is *wrong* with you? Jesus."

"I didn't mean to scare you."

His heart still wasn't too sure about that. "What are you doing here? Go home."

Hunter shrugged and looked past him at the house. "I followed you. What are *you* doing here?"

He'd *followed* him?

"Dude, I'm not playing." Gabriel stepped close and pointed up the street. *"Get out of here."*

Hunter didn't move. "You want to go in, don't you?"

Yes.

Gabriel sighed and ran a hand through his hair. "Go home, Hunter."

"Did you hear them? The firemen have been ordered out. There's still someone inside, but there was something called a flashover. Do you know what that means?"

A flashover meant the fire had gotten too hot, and with nowhere else for that heat to go, the interior of the house was being consumed. The heat would be enough to kill anyone before the fire even got to them. No wonder they weren't hitting the house with hose trucks—nothing to do now but let it burn to the ground.

Someone inside.

Gabriel bit the inside of his cheek. "Yeah. It's bad."

From the front yard, that woman screamed again. His heart kicked.

"What if they're still alive?" said Hunter. His breathing sounded quick.

"What if they are?" Gabriel snapped. "You think thirty firemen are just going to let me walk in the front door? Do you have *any idea* how hot it must be inside that house?"

"Look." Hunter pointed at an ambulance parked on the grass along the side of the house.

Gabriel looked. A fireman was on a stretcher, not moving. Someone held one of those breathing bags over his face. Other people were doing . . . something. Fast and rapid and almost panicked. He had no idea.

Hunter grabbed his arm and shook him. "No, *there*. His gear is lying in the grass." He started untying one of the twine bracelets at his wrist. "Take this. Tie it against your skin—"

"Dude, I don't know *what* you think I'm going to—"

Hunter jerked his head up. "Don't you *want* to help?"

Gabriel stared back at him. He gritted his teeth and didn't say anything.

He hadn't been able to help his parents.

That thought tightened his throat, and it took him three tries to speak. "They might be dead already."

Hunter shook his head. "I don't think so. I'd feel it."

"What? How do you—"

"Because *he's* dead." Hunter pointed at the fireman on the stretcher. His voice was strong, but his breath shook. "And I feel *that*."

Gabriel stared back at him. His breath was shaking, too.

"All right. Give me the stupid rock."

Getting the gear wasn't hard. Gabriel slipped through the darkness and grabbed the coat and helmet, pulling into the shadows under the back porch to slide his arms into the sleeves. He'd left the oxygen tanks—it was going to be hard enough to move in this coat. It had to weigh twenty-five pounds. The helmet felt damp with sweat. Gabriel tried not to think about the fact that the last guy to wear this stuff had just died.

Hunter's rock was tied to his wrist.

If you get hurt or need help, I'll know.

Cheerful.

The basement was a walkout, onto a concrete patio. The sliding glass door had been smashed out, but most of the firefighters had retreated to the trucks at the front of the house. He should be able to walk in without anyone noticing, especially with those smoke detectors still screeching a warning to anyone smart enough to listen.

Not him.

Gabriel wasn't ready for the darkness. He knew the sounds of a fire; he spoke its language. The pop of contained liquids exploding, the roar of flames, the crackle of a fire making progress. But the basement was a well of pure blackness, a claustrophobic blanket of smoke and nighttime. Stairs would probably be along the wall, right? He strode forward.

Only to run into a pole. The metal beam came out of nowhere to crack him in the forehead. It almost pushed the helmet clean off his head.

Now he could see stars.

He wished he had a flashlight. In the house thirty seconds, and he'd practically given himself a concussion.

He moved more slowly now, hands outstretched, waving in front of him, ready for obstacles.

His feet found the next one. He didn't even know *what* he fell over, it just cracked into his shins and sent him sprawling. He rolled and whacked his head on something.

The smoke detectors kept screeching, pounding into his head. The blackness in the basement was absolute.

Now he had no idea which way to go.

He crawled.

It felt like he spent hours looking. He actually found the back door again, glass and splinters rough under his palms. Somewhere near the wall his hands found something he couldn't identify—something small. Something soft and pliable. Fur?

Holy crap. A dead cat.

He gritted his teeth and kept crawling, trying not to think what it'd be like to put his hand down on a dead body.

The thought almost made him turn back, but he didn't.

Finally his hands found a raised surface, then another.

Up he went.

Fire everywhere. It welcomed him onto the main level with a streak of flame across the ceiling.

You've come. Come to play.

No one could be alive in here. He could barely recognize the normal shapes of furniture. Everything was ablaze. Another staircase across the room was so fully consumed that he could no longer see steps. The heat seared his lungs with every breath. Gabriel tried to rein in the fire, to force it to his will, but it fought him.

The fire was effectively giving him the finger.

The house was still standing. There was still more to burn. If he pushed hard, the fire would push back.

Like in the woods, the fire wouldn't hurt him, but if the whole place came crashing down—well, it would hurt like a bitch. If he stayed alive to hurt at all.

"Easy," he said. Maybe he could try this another way. He held his hands out, placating, feeding it a little of his own energy. "Look. We can play."

He felt a pause, like the fire was considering it.

Gabriel fed it a little more, sharing a bit more. "I'll play, too."

At first, he thought it was going to backfire. Flames curled closer, spiraling around his feet.

But then he realized the fire along the walls had died down. The flames had calmed, except those near his feet.

He reached down and scooped up a palm full of fire, feeding it energy until it burned like a torch without a base. The fire liked this, tasting his energy, rolling like a cat in the sunshine.

The thought of the dead cat turned his stomach, and he forced the image out of his mind.

"Someone else is here," he said. "Show me where."

You. You play.

Gabriel closed his fist, killing the flame in his palm. "If I play your game, you play mine."

The fire hesitated, and Gabriel worried he'd lose what little control he'd gained.

But then a streak of flame started off across what must have been carpeting, reminding him of those old Looney Tunes cartoons when he was a kid. The kind where there'd be a stick of dynamite with a really long wick, so the flame could race along until *boom*.

He probably shouldn't think about explosions.

The fire led him toward that destroyed staircase, and he swallowed. If there were people upstairs, he had no idea how he'd get to them.

But the fire veered left, into a room that had been a kitchen.

A little kitchen, too. The walls weren't as badly burned, but the linoleum was warped and cracked from the heat.

Play.

"I'm not playing," he snapped, feeding his anger to the fire. "Where are they?"

Here. Here. Here. Play!

Jesus, he was having an argument with fire. Maybe he should have kept the oxygen tanks.

The line of flame ran straight up the center of the kitchen. No one was here. The sink, the oven, the dishwasher—yeah, that was a hell of a lot of help. A pantry door hung open; smoke billowed out. Unidentifiable boxes of food were on fire.

Here.

The fire sounded desperate and excited, like it wanted to please him—it just wasn't sure how.

God, he couldn't *think* with these wailing smoke detectors.

Here!

He gave an aggravated sigh and started throwing open cabinets.

Nothing. Nothing. Nothing.

The fire started another imaginary wick and ran to the back wall of the kitchen again.

The refrigerator? The door was hanging half off—the seal would have melted in this kind of heat. Gabriel yanked it anyway.

Nothing.

The cabinets under the sink.

Nothing.

The dishwasher, maybe?

Nothing.

The oven. Would someone climb in an oven?

He checked. No. Not in this house, anyway.

Another imaginary wick. Fire caught at the pantry door.

The *open* pantry. Why would the door be open? From the flames, it looked like the shelves started three feet above the ground. The pantry wasn't that deep; even with the smoke, he'd be able to see someone under the shelving.

And they wouldn't be alive anyway.

But when he stepped closer, the fire blazed around him, dancing excitedly.

Gabriel stuck out a hand. He felt the frame of the pantry, the inner walls, spongy and fragile from the damage.

And on the back wall, his hand found a handle.

Without thinking, he pulled. The wall seemed to swing forward on a hinge. He couldn't figure it out. A hidden trash can?

He stuck a hand into the opening. Metal sides, some kind of vertical tunnel.

You idiot. A laundry chute.

The upstairs was completely consumed by fire. This level wasn't much better. Would someone go down a laundry chute? He could never fit. It would have to be someone tiny.

He thought of that anguished scream from the front lawn.

A child.

Holy shit. He needed to get back to the basement.

The stairs were on fire now, almost giving way beneath his weight. The basement was still a pit of blackness; he had no idea how he'd find a small kid. Based on the location of the kitchen, he slid away from the stairs, on hands and knees again.

He found the dead cat again.

Thank god he hadn't eaten dinner.

But here was a door, the knob cool. He threw it wide.

More darkness. He'd kill for a light.

And just like that, fire swept down the stairs, slithering around his feet and into the opening, gorging on the fresh oxygen. A laundry room. Fire raced up the bare insulation that lined the walls, tearing into a rack of shirts hanging by the ironing board.

Raging toward a pile of sheets and towels.

He almost couldn't make out the crumpled figure on top of them.

He dashed through the flames and grabbed hold of what felt like an arm, yanking the body into his arms. Someone small, fragile, all slim legs and knobby joints. Long hair—a girl. He felt satin, like a nightgown. She weighed nothing and hung limply against his chest.

Was she breathing? He couldn't tell. It was too hot to tell.

Fire grabbed the nightgown. He crushed it in his fist. More leapt from the wall to make another attempt.

He had to get her out.

But he had to get low, under the smoke. He clutched her to his chest with one arm and crawled with the other. Once he got out of the laundry room, the fire followed him. Flaming ash began to fall from the ceiling, sparking in his hair and on her face.

If the ceiling fell in, they were done for.

The smoke detectors fell silent.

Gabriel hesitated. He could hear himself breathing. He couldn't hear her.

Then a crash shook the house and sent beams slamming into the floor.

The second level had fallen into the first.

And now it was going to fall into the basement.

He ran. Shoulder first, sliding his feet along the floor as fast as he could. He hit walls. Beams. Something cracked against his helmet, but he kept going.

He could feel flames coming through the floor, looking for him. The sound of wood giving way was deafening. Sparks and ash rained down.

He wasn't going to make it. He was going to fail. *Again.*

Then a hand closed over his wrist and pulled, *hard.*

Gabriel followed—what else could he do?

He burst into fresh air that felt arctic on his cheeks. That hand kept pulling, dragging him.

He stumbled and almost fell, but he caught himself before he dropped the girl.

He felt grass under his feet and slowed.

Someone was jerking the girl out of his arms. "Is she breathing?"

Hunter.

Had Hunter gone into . . . into *that* to drag him the rest of the way out of the darkness?

"Gabriel! Damn it, was she breathing inside?"

Hunter had her on the ground, his cheek over the girl's mouth.

"No," said Gabriel. "No, she wasn't breathing."

Hunter wasn't even listening. He'd put his mouth over the girl's and was now blowing into hers.

"Call the medics!" he yelled between breaths.

Gabriel ran around the side of the house and waved his arms. "One got out the back! We need a medic over here!"

He'd never seen people move so fast. EMTs and firemen were just *there,* swarming the girl, treating her. Gabriel lost track of Hunter.

He needed to lose track of himself before someone figured out he wasn't a real fireman.

Someone caught his sleeves and turned him.

A woman, her face tear streaked through lines of soot, her clothes damp and filthy. She wasn't a fireman or an EMT.

But she *was* hugging him, her arms around his neck before he knew what she was doing, her slim hands full of a surprising amount of strength.

"Thank you," she sobbed into his jacket. "Oh my god, they said they couldn't get to her—*Thank you.*"

He didn't know how to respond.

But then the girl was coughing, then crying, then huge racking sobs and cries for her mommy.

The woman let him go.

Gabriel stepped out of the crowd and walked off into the night.

CHAPTER 12

Hunter was waiting in the woods. Far back, but still within sight of the house. When Gabriel caught up, Hunter didn't say anything, just turned and fell into step beside him.

Thank god, because Gabriel didn't know what to say, either.

He yanked the fireman's helmet off his head, dragging a hand through his damp hair. He felt like he couldn't catch his breath, and only part of it was from the smoke and the exertion.

A pair of headlights cut through the woods, catching the reflective stripes on the coat. Gabriel swore and shrugged out of it, rolling it up inside out to carry under his arm.

But the headlights continued on. No one saw them.

"I can stash those in the jeep," said Hunter.

His voice sounded raw. Gabriel stopped at the tree line and looked at him, holding out the helmet and then the coat. Hunter had soot across one cheek, and his hair was every bit as damp as Gabriel's.

He took the stuff, but then he didn't move.

Gabriel wondered if he also looked this . . . stricken. What was the right thing to say? Thanks? That was terrible? That was awesome? They'd just pulled a girl out of a blazing house. Could he really just climb in his car and drive home?

Hunter cleared his throat. "So."

"Yeah."

Hunter shifted the rolled up coat under one arm, hunching his shoulders. "Want to come over and play Xbox?"

Gabriel stared at him for a minute, wondering if he was serious.

Then he realized he didn't care.

"Yeah," he said. "I do."

Hunter lived in an old farmhouse set back from the road, practically in the middle of nowhere. The windows were dark when they pulled up, and stayed that way despite two sets of tires crunching along the gravel driveway. Only an old gas lamp at the end of the front walk threw any light into the yard, revealing a split-board fence stretching back into the darkness.

A dog burst through the doorway when Hunter turned the key, the large German shepherd practically knocking his master down.

Hunter laughed softly and rubbed his dog behind the ears. "Casper's pissed I left him home."

Gabriel picked up on his hushed tone. It seemed early, but the dark house spoke volumes. "Your mom asleep?"

Hunter lost the smile. "Probably." He gave the dog one last scratch along his neck, then sent Casper out into the yard. "My grandparents definitely are. Come on."

Gabriel scrubbed his hands and face in the kitchen sink, grateful for the coat and helmet that had kept him a lot cleaner than the last time he'd ventured into a fire. His jeans were sooty from the knees down, but they'd wash. He smacked his shoes against the porch to get out the worst of the soot, then followed Hunter.

The gaming system was in the basement, hooked up to a newish flat screen that looked completely out of place among the wood-paneled walls, the mustard-yellow carpet, and wooden mallards accenting the end tables. Even the sofa was plaid, a red and orange number that had seen better days.

But Hunter's bedroom was down here, too, and from what Gabriel could see, it was huge.

"Do you really have a refrigerator and a microwave in your room?" he said, peering through the doorway.

Hunter was sliding a disk into the Xbox. "It wasn't always my bedroom. But yeah." He glanced up. "My grandparents only come down here to do laundry. It's like having my own apartment."

No mention of his mother, making Gabriel wonder about Hunter's tone in the driveway, when he'd said *probably*. Even now, he wasn't bragging. He sounded self-deprecating.

Then he said, "Grab a soda if you want."

Gabriel did.

And then they were killing pixelated zombies.

It was surreal, sitting here doing something completely mundane, when they'd been pulling a body out of a burning house an hour ago.

Especially since Hunter had put a gun in his face last week.

When the game changed landscapes, Gabriel watched him, thinking of the moment in the hallway when Hunter had broken Nick's hold. "Just how much control do you have?"

A shrug. "Not enough. I couldn't have gone into that fire alone."

Gabriel untied the translucent white stone from his wrist and set it on the coffee table. He suspected he wouldn't have been as effective alone, either. Their powers had a way of improving when combined. "Thanks," he said. "For dragging me out."

"Sure."

"And thanks for . . . whatever you did back at my house."

Hunter shrugged. "I didn't really *do* anything. I just had to block his focus." He took the stone, twisting the twine between his fingers while they waited for the game to load.

It made Gabriel think of Becca, who used to wear Hunter's rocks strung along her wrist. "You're not screwing with my little brother, are you?"

Raised eyebrows. "With Chris?"

"What are you really doing with Becca?"

Hunter shrugged and looked back at the twine, letting the

rock untwist itself. "Nothing. She asked for my help. I'm giving it."

"This *help* wouldn't be the naked kind, would it?"

A smirk. "No. Just talking." Hunter lost the smile. "I'm not messing with Chris. Or Becca. I wouldn't. After . . . you know."

Gabriel nodded. Then the screen loaded, and they were slaughtering zombies again.

"You know," said Hunter, not looking away from the apocalypse on the screen, "I could tie that rock into the coat."

"For what?"

"For next time."

Gabriel didn't look at him, just took another swig of his soda, keeping his eyes on the screen so Hunter wouldn't kick his ass at Xbox.

But he kept thinking about those words. *Next time.*

There couldn't be a next time. This time had been all about sheer luck. Luck and power. So much power Gabriel could feel it sparking under his skin, even now.

He gave a short laugh. "What happened to 'lying low'?"

Hunter shrugged. "We don't have to *tell* anyone . . ."

Gabriel hadn't been planning on telling anyone, anyway. Accidentally lighting the woods on fire was one thing. Willfully walking into a burning building—Michael would definitely have a problem with that.

"I have my uncle's old police radio," Hunter said. "We could do this again. On purpose."

Gabriel gave him a look. "You mean, instead of by accident?"

"I don't believe in accidents."

His tone caught Gabriel by surprise.

Hunter shrugged a little, keeping his eyes on the controller in his hands. "I just mean, sometimes things happen for a reason. Think about it."

He'd said something similar when he'd been accusing Michael of killing his father and his uncle. Gabriel wondered if Hunter still thought that wasn't an accident, that maybe there had been more to the car crash than bad weather and poor timing. He opened his mouth to ask.

But then the zombies attacked, and their focus was back on the screen.

Gabriel pulled into his driveway well after midnight. The house was dark.

Then again, he'd destroyed the porch lights.

He hadn't wanted to come home, but Hunter's grandfather had come downstairs and made some bleary-eyed comments about it being a school night, and maybe it was time for friends to *go*.

Michael would probably be sitting in the kitchen, waiting. He'd sent half a dozen texts asking where Gabriel had gone, whether he was all right. He hadn't shut up until Gabriel texted back that he was at Hunter's.

Gabriel steeled his shoulders and let himself into the house.

But the lower level was dark and silent. Chris's window had been dark, and Gabriel didn't see a light under Michael's door. Maybe his brothers had all gone to sleep.

Figured.

But then he saw the line of light under Nick's door. His twin was still awake.

Gabriel hesitated in the hallway. He'd fought with Nick before, but this . . . this felt different. He lifted a hand to knock.

But he heard a girl giggle. Then the creak of a bedspring.

Gabriel snatched his hand away.

Holy shit. Quinn was still *here*.

His breathing sounded loud in the quiet hallway, so he took a step back.

Nick had *never* let a girl spend the night.

It wasn't allowed, for one thing, and Nick wasn't a rule-breaker. Michael always said if he could get them to eighteen without going to jail or getting a girl pregnant, he'd consider it a success.

For an instant, Gabriel entertained calling Nick on it. Walking in on them, creating enough ruckus to wake the house. He remembered Nick trapping him in the hallway, stealing his breath.

Humiliating him.

Stupid.

Gabriel gritted his teeth. What an asshole.

But when he reached out to grab the knob, to throw the door wide, he thought of Layne, the intensity in her eyes when she stood up to him.

Sometimes you cut right to the quick, you know?

It made him think of the hurt on Nick's face when he'd laid into Quinn.

He'd been the one to fuck this up. Not Nick.

So he turned and locked himself in his room, burying his head under his pillow when he heard Quinn's giggle through the wall.

CHAPTER 13

This frigging substitute had to go. Gabriel hadn't even done the previous night's assignment, and now she wanted to start every class with a six-question warm-up that she would collect and grade each day.

He might as well just kill himself right now.

It wasn't like he could wrangle his thoughts into submission, anyway. He kept thinking about the fire.

Last night had been a fluke. Too many things could have gone wrong. Sure, he'd held the flames for a few minutes—but he could have lost it. He could have killed that kid. Hunter. Himself.

He'd felt that kind of potential before.

But this had been different. Working with Hunter was like finding another level of control. It was nothing like calling elements with Nick, who always backed away from risk.

Gabriel scowled. He didn't want to think about his twin.

Because thinking about the fight with Nick just made him think about the fight beforehand, with Layne's father.

At least Layne wasn't here yet. Gabriel wasn't sure what to say once she showed up.

Taylor Morrissey swung onto the desk in front of him. Low-slung jeans revealed a solid six inches of tanned midsection despite the fact that temperatures had been in the low fifties every morning. Her hair spilled over one shoulder, but it just felt like such an *act.*

He kept his expression uninterested. "Hey, Taylor."

She leaned forward, until he could see clear down the V-neck of her top. "Gary Ackerman said he saw you take the bus to school. What's up with that?"

What was *up with that* was Nick being an asshole. He'd taken the car while Gabriel was in the shower.

He shrugged and looked at the doorway. Still no sign of Layne, so he dragged his eyes back to Taylor. "My brother had to get here early. I didn't feel like it."

He caught movement from the corner of his eye and saw Layne push through the doorway, her head down. Turtleneck, jeans, hair in a braid. She didn't look at him.

"Your brother, huh?" said Taylor. She smirked.

He couldn't figure out her tone—and he didn't really care. He frowned at her. "What?"

Layne slipped into the chair beside him. It took everything he had not to look at her.

Taylor shrugged one shoulder. "You're looking kind of, you know, *tired* today."

She was implying something, but he had no idea what. He probably did look tired. It went right along with *being* tired. "Yeah, well, we can't all be paragons of perfection like you, Taylor."

From the corner of his eye, he saw Layne stiffen beside him. Hadn't she said something similar last night? But then she was moving again, pulling things from her backpack.

Taylor leaned in, showing more of what she had to offer. Her voice was almost taunting. "Did you sleep at someone else's house?"

Layne suddenly went very still.

Gabriel wanted to glare at her. Did Layne seriously think he'd leave her house like that, then go find some mindless girl to hook up with?

"Jesus, Taylor, scope your gossip with someone else. I was home all night."

"Whatever you say." She swung her legs against the desk, not at all bothered. "Did you hear about Alan Hulster?"

He glanced at the empty seat on the other side of his chair. "What, did someone finally kick his ass?"

"No, his house burned down."

Gabriel snapped his head around. "What?"

"Yeah, like, *to the ground.*" Taylor pulled a piece of gum out of her purse and rolled it across her tongue suggestively, as if this news was just a sideline to her flirtation. "His little sister was trapped. They thought she was dead, but some fireman got her out just before the whole place collapsed. That dude is a hero. Isn't that *intense?*"

Gabriel could feel his heart smacking his rib cage. He'd never thought about that house belonging to someone he *knew.*

Layne cleared her throat, and her voice came out small. "Is his sister okay?"

Taylor rolled her eyes and pushed her hair over one shoulder. "I'm sorry, were you a part of this conversation?"

"God, Taylor." Gabriel kicked the leg of her chair. It was a miracle his voice wasn't shaking. "Is his sister okay?"

"Jeez." Taylor frowned. "Yeah . . . I think so—"

Ms. Anderson chose that moment to slide into the room. Taylor swung around and dropped into her chair.

Gabriel couldn't think through the six questions on the board—not like it would matter. He scribbled random numbers, his mind spinning through the events of last night.

That dude is a hero.

He sure didn't feel like it.

He'd gone there to be close to a fire. Not to save someone.

Thoughts gripped his mind so tightly that he couldn't say a word to Layne—but she had her head down over her work, anyway.

He passed his paper forward with everyone else, and he didn't even care what he got. The substitute was lecturing, but he didn't hear a word. His ears were full of Hunter's words from last night.

We could do this again. Think about it.

When the bell rang, Layne bolted from her seat without looking at him.

Gabriel bolted after her, intending to catch her in the hallway.

But Ms. Anderson's voice stopped him before he got out of the room. "Mr. Merrick, I'd like to speak with you."

Mr. Merrick. He hated when teachers called him that, like he was an old man stopping by to learn a few math tricks.

He stopped beside her desk and glanced at the door. "Yeah?"

"You didn't turn in last night's homework. Or the day before."

He shrugged his backpack higher on his shoulder and looked at the door again. "I forgot it. I'll bring it tomorrow."

"And I was reviewing the quizzes from the other day."

That got his attention. "I thought they didn't count."

She leaned back in the chair. "They don't. I was concerned about how you answered the questions."

Who gave a crap how he answered the questions? "So?"

"Some were right, and some were wrong. I'm having a hard time with the fact that nothing was wrong the same way."

He could hear his own breathing. "I don't understand."

"I think you do." She paused. "And in class the other day, when I called you to the board, you struggled with the formula."

"Look, could we get to the point?"

She raised her eyebrows. "My point is that someone with an A average shouldn't be struggling with anything at this point in the year."

"Well, if I've got an A average, two homeworks shouldn't matter too much."

"Maybe not." She leaned forward and looked up at him. In a creepy way, it reminded him of Taylor, though she was hot, and Ms. Anderson was . . . *not.* "Do I understand that you have a twin brother?"

God, it was hot in here. "Yeah?"

She gave him a level look. "He's in AP Calculus, so he's presumably taken this class before?"

Gabriel stared at her. He sure as hell wasn't going to volunteer anything now.

"Look," she said. "I'm not trying to hassle you. But you need a math credit to graduate. And you need to earn it yourself. If you need help, I'll give it to you. But you can't expect me to turn a blind eye to blatant cheating. You'll need to work harder, apply yourself . . ."

He glanced at the door again. Layne was probably on to her next class by now, and he'd missed the first five minutes of lunch.

". . . the coach will let you back on the team," Ms. Anderson finished.

Gabriel snapped his head back around. "Wait." He put a hand on the desk and leaned in. His backpack slid off his shoulder to hit the floor. "What did you just say?"

She didn't flinch from his tone. "I said you have a week and a half to prove that you're doing the work yourself. You can't play sports if you can't pass your classes. I'll let you retake the last unit test that Monday, and if you can show that you're putting the time in, I'll speak to the basketball coach, and he'll let you on the team."

His fists clenched. "But that's *bull*—"

The lights flickered, and his breath caught. The sub glanced up.

Gabriel swallowed his words. "Tryouts are tomorrow." He kept his voice low, even. If he blew the lights again, Michael would flip out.

"And Coach Kanner agreed to hold a spot for you. *If* you can prove you're doing the work."

He wanted to punch something. He'd never wanted to hit a girl, much less a teacher, but right now—

"You don't have to get an A," she said evenly. "You just have to pass."

He gritted his teeth and fought to keep his hands at his sides. "You can't do that."

"Actually, you're right. I should follow procedure and report you to the principal. Then you could sit in his office, take an exam in front of him, and see how you do. Want to handle it that way?"

Fury had his chest in a vise grip. He ground the word out. "No."

Her voice softened. "I'm trying to help you here. I can give you some extra time after class, if you'd like—"

"No, thanks." He slung the backpack over his shoulder again and turned for the door. "I think you've done enough."

After school, Gabriel stood on the free throw line in the empty gym and shot an easy basket. Twice.

He kept thinking of what Michael had said the other night, about being surrounded by people, yet not having any true friends. The first few weeks of the season were everything. Figuring out positions, how to work as a team. He'd probably miss the first game. The other guys wouldn't want him walking onto the team late. He sure wouldn't.

He'd already been to talk to the coach. He'd done that instead of going to lunch—what was he going to do, sit by himself? Pretty clear where Nick stood. But then the coach hadn't been too encouraging.

And the one person who'd offered to help him—well, he'd done a pretty good job of chasing her off last night.

He was so fucked.

The halogen lights buzzed more loudly for an instant, and Gabriel closed his eyes. *Breathe.*

He wanted to pull the lighter out of his pocket, to spin the flame through his knuckles—but getting caught with a lighter could be an automatic suspension. Like he didn't have enough problems.

Still. He felt like a junkie looking for a fix.

"You all right?"

Gabriel opened his eyes. Hunter stood there, almost directly beneath the basket.

"Dude. You're starting to freak me out with this showing up out of nowhere."

"You weren't at lunch."

Gabriel shrugged and threw at the basket. It bounced off the rim.

Hunter's hand shot out to catch it, and he passed it back, lightning quick.

Gabriel raised an eyebrow and bounced the ball against the court. "You play?"

"Nah." A shrug. But then he dropped his backpack against the wall and put his hands up. Gabriel tossed him the ball, and Hunter sank a basket from the line. "Team sports aren't really my thing. You know."

Hunter's abilities drew other people to him—but just because they were drawn to him didn't mean they were nice about it. Gabriel knew that from Becca.

He thought about what Hunter had said: *You weren't at lunch*.

Maybe Hunter was every bit as lonely as he was.

"I'm avoiding Nick," he offered.

Hunter caught the ball again and threw it back to Gabriel. "I get it."

Gabriel caught it and dribbled, each smack of the ball echoing in the gym, then passed it back, hard. "You never told me why you followed me last night."

Hunter caught it and returned with equal force. "Maybe you're not the only one who wants to use his powers."

"You know that was Alan Hulster's house. He goes to school here."

"So?"

"So we could have been caught."

Hunter scoffed. "Please. You don't give a crap about getting caught."

"I give a crap about killing people."

Hunter frowned. "You didn't start that fire."

Gabriel didn't say anything, just tossed the ball at the basket again. It swished through.

Hunter caught it and passed it back. "They were going to *leave* that girl in there. If she had died, it still wouldn't have been your fault."

"Keep your goddamn voice down." Gabriel cast a glance at the doors, but they were still alone.

"You saved her life! I can't believe you—"

Gabriel got in his face and hit him in the chest with the ball. *"Leave it."*

Hunter stared at him, and for half a second, Gabriel wondered if he was going to back down, the way Nick or Chris would.

Or if he was going to fight back, the way he had behind the mall.

But then Hunter smiled and took the ball. "You're afraid."

"Of you?" Gabriel raised his eyebrows. "Fat chance, you—"

"No." Hunter backed off, dribbling the ball as he went. "Of yourself. You pick a fight every time someone might figure you out." He threw the ball at the basket from some distance down the court—a solid three-pointer. It went right in. "You think I don't wonder if I could have saved my dad and my uncle, if I'd been stronger?"

Gabriel didn't look at him. That vise grip had his chest again, but it was an entirely different feeling from math class. "You didn't kill them, Hunter."

"We can talk blame all day. What difference does it make?"

It shouldn't make a difference. But it did.

Hunter threw another basket. "My dad used to say, 'If you can't fix what you did wrong, at least try to make something else right.'"

He was talking about house fires.

But Gabriel thought of Layne.

He fished his cell phone out of his pocket to check the time. JV basketball practice would still be going on, so she was probably in the school somewhere.

"Got a date?" said Hunter.

"Maybe." He shoved the phone into his pocket and grabbed his bag.

"That's it? No comment?"

"No comment." Gabriel swung around and hit him in the chest. "And I am not afraid."

"Liar."

Gabriel made a disgusted sound and turned for the door.

"So, later," Hunter called. "If there's a fire—you in or out?"

Out. Out, out, out.

Gabriel pressed his forehead against the cold steel of the door and sighed.

"In."

CHAPTER 14

Layne pulled another yearbook off the stack and sighed. They'd been in the library for an hour, but there were still another thirty minutes left to Simon's practice. "This is the dumbest research project ever."

Kara rolled her eyes without looking up from her notebook. "You'd probably be happier writing about the history of physics, or Marie Antoinette's biography, or—"

"You know who Marie Antoinette *is?*"

"Shut up."

"Researching something from the school's past? That's just lame. There's no challenge."

"God, you are such a nerd." Kara fished lip gloss out of her purse and dabbed it on. "I don't know why I hang out with you sometimes."

Me neither. But if Layne didn't have Kara, she'd be sitting in the library by herself, waiting for her deaf brother to finish basketball practice—for a game the coach wouldn't even let him play.

God, it just sounded *pathetic.*

"*Layne,*" Kara hissed. Her nails—bright fuchsia today—dug into Layne's wrist.

Layne snapped her head up. "What?"

Kara was staring at the entrance to the library. One of the

Merrick twins had just pushed through the doors and was strolling toward the stacks.

Layne sighed. She wanted it to be Nick.

But she'd sat next to Gabriel in class. She'd seen that faded blue henley clinging to his chest and shoulders four hours ago.

"Great," she muttered.

"He is insanely hot," whispered Kara. She dabbed more lip gloss on her mouth, to the point where it started to look a little comical. "How do I look?"

"Don't even bother. He's a jerk."

"Maybe to you." They watched him disappear between the stacks on the opposite side of the library. "Do you know which one it is?"

"Gabriel. I sit next to him in trig."

"That's a waste. You are so lucky. I wish I were better at math."

"Don't worry. You're probably right at his level." Layne hoped he didn't notice them sitting here.

Mostly. Some butterflies were kicking up a fit in her stomach, and they were totally in favor of him heading this way.

That was stupid. He hadn't even looked at her in class.

She had no idea how one boy could inspire such warring emotions, like she wanted to punch the crap out of him but then hide in the circle of his arms.

"You're all red," said Kara.

Ugh. Was she? "It's hot in here."

"Oh my god." Kara snorted. "You've got a *crush* on him."

Layne bent over her notebook again. "Please."

Kara began to sing. "Layne and Gabriel sitting in a tree. K-I-S-S-I—"

"Layne?"

God, this could *not* be happening. Her face bright red, Kara singing that *stupid* song, and Gabriel Merrick appearing around the corner.

Kara dissolved into giggles. Yeah, this was so hilarious.

Layne couldn't look at him. She felt like her entire body

might burst into flame. She stacked the yearbooks on the table, then shoved her notebook into her backpack.

Gabriel cleared his throat. It sounded like he'd moved closer. "Can I talk to you?"

This made Kara giggle harder. "Oh. Maybe I should give you two a moment alone."

"That'd be awesome," he said absently. "Thanks."

The giggles stopped like someone had flipped a switch. "Seriously?" said Kara.

Now Layne looked up. Kara was staring at Gabriel, dismayed, like she couldn't believe he'd want to talk to *Layne,* when Kara was fully available, boobs perked out and everything.

"Don't bother," Layne said.

Gabriel put a hand on her bag, preventing her from slinging it over a shoulder. He was just suddenly *there,* in her space, close enough to touch.

"You won't even give me a chance to apologize?"

"Like you'd mean it." She jerked the bag out from under his hand and started walking. She didn't even bother to zip it all the way.

"Apologize for what?" called Kara.

Gabriel was right behind her. "Of course I'd mean it. What the hell are you trying to say?"

"*Shhh.*" Mrs. Beard, the librarian, poked her head out from where she was shelving.

"Sorry," Layne whispered, hustling for the exit.

Gabriel followed her straight out the doors. "You won't even hear me out?"

"No." If she stopped to turn around, he'd see how red her cheeks were. Had he heard Kara's little chant?

"Why not?" He sounded honestly perplexed.

"Because you're the kind of guy who apologizes because you're *supposed* to, not because you truly give a crap."

"All right, look." He caught her arm and spun her around.

She gasped and stared up at him—and the dim school hallway seemed to collapse around her. She had to take a step back, and her shoulders ran into a row of lockers.

The hallway was empty. Kara hadn't followed them.

Just her and Gabriel. She had to stop staring into his eyes or she was going to forgive him for everything, always.

"What?" she demanded.

"I'm not sorry for what I said to your father."

"Well, you should be." She bit the words out, and it helped. "Mentioning *condoms*? Are you insane?"

"He was a dick to start with." Gabriel's blue eyes were intense and almost frightening. "And I'm not real crazy about getting accused of rape in the first thirty seconds I meet someone."

"Wow, you're really good at this apology stuff."

He took a long breath and didn't look away—like he was gathering his temper, or his mettle, or . . . something.

"I am sorry," he said, "for upsetting you."

He meant it. She could feel it. It cost him something to say it, and the little tugs in her chest were begging her to nod, to forgive him, to acknowledge that there were many things unsaid, on both sides of this conversation.

She didn't move.

Gabriel moved a bit closer. "I'm sorry, Layne. Really."

His voice was low and rough, and this close, she could make out each individual eyelash, the line of his cheekbone, the bare start of shadow across his jaw. She felt ready to slide down the lockers and melt into a puddle at his feet.

But she couldn't stop thinking about her father's warnings last night, about an *outlet*. Her dad was right. Falling for a guy like Gabriel would end up with her hurt and her secrets all over school.

"So," she said, feeling her throat close up, "is this when girls usually fall all over you and forgive you for everything?"

He jerked back like she'd hit him.

God, she regretted it immediately. His eyes went dark, walled off. Closed. A second ago, the distance between them had felt like an inch; now it felt like a mile.

But then he glanced down the hallway and back at her. He almost had a small smile on his face. "A friend just told me I pick a fight every time someone gets close to figuring me out."

She swallowed.

Gabriel leaned in again, putting a hand on the locker beside her head. "What're your secrets, Layne?"

She couldn't speak. She couldn't breathe.

He held there for a moment.

Then he reached around her and jerked a yellow notebook out of her open backpack—the one she used to keep assignments in order. A pen was still attached to the spiral, and he pulled it loose.

That was so unexpected that she faltered. "My . . . what . . . why . . ."

He'd flipped to the middle and was already writing.

Before her heart could catch up, he shoved it back into her bag. He didn't even smile, just stepped back. "Call me when you're ready to cut through the bullshit."

He'd turned the corner before she could get it together to pull the notebook out of her backpack, to see what he'd written.

There in the middle, scrawled across the page, was a phone number.

And right under it, in his handwriting, even and blocky:

I'm not perfect either.

CHAPTER 15

Gabriel poured Cheerios in a bowl and chased them with milk. Not much of a dinner, but food was food, and he was the only one home.

He had no idea where Nick was. Probably out somewhere with Chris, doing something with Quinn and Becca. Or maybe just out somewhere, doing Quinn. Like Gabriel gave a crap.

He dropped into the kitchen chair and set the bowl beside his textbook. The house was so silent that the sound echoed in the kitchen. Gabriel had his cell on the table, sitting next to the trig book, taunting him by remaining completely silent.

He'd never given a girl his number and walked off. At the time, it seemed like a great idea—put the ball in her court, leave her with a line and ten digits scrawled in her notebook.

Now it was like water torture, knowing she had it, knowing she was making the deliberate decision *not* to call.

Christ, was this how girls felt?

His pencil had dug trenches in his notebook. One page of questions had been assigned for homework, and he was stuck on the first one.

Find the focal diameter of a parabola with focus (2,4) and directrix y = –1.

It was almost enough to make him call Nick.

And he hated to admit it, but there was a small part of him that wished Nick would call. Or text. Something. Almost twenty-four hours had passed since they'd last spoken. That hadn't happened . . . ever.

The front door slammed, and his older brother's work boots clomped down the hallway. When Michael stopped in the kitchen doorway, Gabriel looked up.

Michael was filthy, covered in sweat and dust. Stains streaked across his T-shirt. His expression was puzzled. "What are you doing?"

Gabriel half shrugged. "Homework."

An eyebrow raised. "Homework? Should I call a doctor?"

Gabriel took a spoonful of Cheerios and gave him the finger.

"That's better." Michael walked to the fridge and pulled out a bottle of water. "You all right?"

I made my twin brother hate me.

I can't try out for basketball.

I gave my number to some girl who thinks I'm a thug.

Gabriel looked back at his textbook. "Yeah. Fine."

Michael turned and walked back down the hall. "Cheerios? Order a pizza or something. I'm starving."

Since his phone wasn't doing anything better, Gabriel dialed for pizza. A minute later, he heard the upstairs shower turn on.

He went back to staring at the math problem. Maybe he could Google it.

Victory! He was right in the middle of the fourth question when the doorbell rang. He glanced at his watch. Twenty minutes was record time for pizza.

He had cash in his hand, but there wasn't a pizza guy on the porch. A young woman stood there, wearing jeans and a canvas jacket, blond hair spilling across her shoulders. Her eyes looked vaguely familiar, and Gabriel tried to place where he knew her from.

"Hi." She gave him a gentle smile. "You look a lot better than the last time I saw you."

His brain engaged. The chick firefighter! She looked smaller without all the gear.

Then he froze, feeling the doorknob go slick under his hand. This had to be about last night. She would have been there, right? She must have recognized him.

But wouldn't she be here with cops or something?

A little frown creased her mouth. "I'm Hannah. Hannah Faulkner."

"Yeah." His breath rattled around in his chest.

"Are you all right?"

He peered past her. No cop cars in the driveway, nothing other than a late-model Jeep Cherokee that was beat to hell, like she'd driven through the outback to get here. "What are you doing here?"

She looked a bit taken aback. "I hoped to talk to you about the other night. The fire in the woods."

God, it was like he couldn't breathe. "Yeah, and?"

Her fingers fidgeted with the edge of her jacket. "I probably shouldn't have stopped by without calling, but I was in the neighborhood, and I thought maybe I could say hi to your brother, too." She shrugged a little, a touch of pink on her cheeks. "You know. If he's around."

Wait. A. Minute.

"Sure," said Gabriel, feeling his heartbeat settle. He stood back and held the door open. "Come on in the kitchen. Mike's in the shower. You want a soda or something?"

He practically shoved her into a chair with a can of Pepsi, then left her there with the reasoning that he should warn Michael a girl was in the house, before he came down the stairs in his boxers or something.

That would really make her blush.

Gabriel took the steps two at a time, just as Michael was coming out of his bedroom. His hair was wet and trailed over his shoulders, and he was wearing a pair of faded sweatpants and an ancient T-shirt that looked like he might have stolen it off a homeless guy.

Gabriel shoved him in the shoulder. "Go hit your face with a razor or something. God, would it kill you to shave more than once a week?"

Michael pushed past him. "I'm not sure the pizza guy will give a crap—"

"No, idiot," Gabriel hissed. "That Hannah chick is here. Put some decent clothes on. Here"—he stepped around Michael, into his bedroom—"I'll help you."

He started yanking open drawers to Michael's dresser. Worn jeans, old T-shirts, faded sweatshirts.

"This is pathetic," he said.

Michael hadn't moved from the doorway, his expression bemused. "You know what I do for a living."

"And why aren't you shaving yet? Don't you *care* that a girl is here to see you?"

His brother hesitated. "Look. Gabriel. I'm not—"

"Forget it. You can wear one of my shirts."

Now Michael gave him a look. "Like your shirt will fit me."

Gabriel stopped in the doorway. "First, jackass, don't flatter yourself. And second, don't you know *anything* about girls?"

Michael just stared at him.

"For god's sake." Gabriel walked down the hallway to his own room, grabbed a slate-gray crewneck T-shirt, and brought it back. He flung it at Michael. "That's the whole point."

Gabriel had plates on the table and was serving Hannah a slice of pizza by the time Michael appeared in the doorway. He'd shaved and pulled his hair back, and he was wearing the gray T-shirt with jeans that didn't look *too* beat up. And yeah, maybe the shirt was a little too tight across the chest, but his brother didn't look like a freak or anything.

It was better than looking like an angry serial killer.

Hannah seemed to appreciate it, anyway. She gave him a small smile.

"Hey," Michael said from the doorway. He barely stepped into the kitchen, looking awkward.

So they were off to a rousing start.

"Hi," she said. "I'm sorry to interrupt your dinner and everything—"

"There's plenty," said Michael. He still hadn't sat down.

This was ridiculous. Gabriel shoved a plate in his direction. "Hannah said she wanted to talk about the other night."

At least that got Michael's attention. He pulled a chair back and dropped into it. "Yeah?" Only now he sounded pissed. "Is Gabriel in trouble?"

"No!" Hannah looked startled. "I just—"

"You just what?"

God, it was like his brother had a time limit before he had to start acting like an asshole. Gabriel gave him a look over the top of her head. *Shut up,* he mouthed. *Be nice.*

Hannah pushed her hair back from her face and sighed. She hadn't even touched her pizza. "Look, I shouldn't be here. It's unofficial, okay? I just wanted to ask if you'd seen anything the other night, in the woods."

Gabriel dropped into his own chair, wondering how careful he needed to be. "No. Like I said, just fire."

"No people?"

He shook his head and picked up his slice of pizza.

"Why?" asked Michael.

"Because there have been a lot of fires lately." She paused. "And the fire marshal suspects arson. Did you hear about the fire over on Linden Park Lane last night?"

Gabriel shrugged and picked up his slice. "I go to school with the guy who lives there."

"He's lucky to be alive. They all are. A girl was trapped, but someone got her out."

Gabriel raised an eyebrow and tried to sound skeptical. "'Someone'?"

Jesus. He sounded guilty as hell. He shoved more pizza into his mouth. It tasted like cardboard.

He should have kept his mouth shut. Michael was staring at him now.

Hannah shook her head. "We were all in the front yard, and whoever got her out, went in through the back." She scowled. "The press is having a great time with this. We would have kept it out of the papers, but the mom talked. Now it's all out there—the unusual burn patterns, the way the girl escaped down the laundry chute, the mysterious 'hero.'"

Her voice was full of disdain, but Gabriel was stuck on the mom. He could still remember the way she'd grabbed him around the neck, the way she'd sobbed her thanks.

He dropped his pizza onto the plate and cleared his throat. "So you think someone is starting the fires just to save people?"

"No." She paused for a long moment, and her voice dropped. "Yesterday one of the other firehouses lost a fireman. We're just trying to stop this guy before he kills anyone else."

Gabriel's appetite was entirely gone.

He wished he'd gotten there fifteen minutes earlier. Maybe he could have saved that guy, too.

At the same time, he wished he'd never gotten involved.

"I told you," he said woodenly. "I didn't see anyone."

He could still feel Michael watching him.

His cell phone chimed. Gabriel grabbed it, glad for an excuse to look away.

Layne. Please be Layne.

No. Hunter.

Fire at 116 Winterbourne. In?

Gabriel stared at the display. Then he texted back.

Don't have the car.

Hunter's reply was lightning quick.

Pick U up in 5.

Gabriel shoved the phone into his pocket and realized Hannah and Michael were both staring at him now. He scraped his chair back. "I'm going out." He glanced at Hannah. "Sorry I couldn't help you."

"Where?" said Michael.

"With Hunter," he said, going through the doorway.

"*Where?*"

"Out," he called back. He grabbed his backpack. "Remember, you told me to make friends."

CHAPTER 16

Last night's fire had wanted to play. This one was a raging wall of hot fury. Gabriel stood beside Hunter in the shadows of the neighbor's storage shed and felt the power wash over him.

The entire upstairs of the split-level was consumed, flames blazing through shattered windowpanes. Winterbourne Way was one of those residential neighborhoods that took two weeks to build, where each house had exactly a quarter of an acre of land and everything looked identical.

Except this one would look like a charred mess in the morning.

Three fire trucks lined the road out front, firefighters and EMTs scurrying around in the front yard.

No one was screaming tonight. He couldn't even hear smoke detectors.

The fire was making him jittery, like the fury was seeping into his skin and begging him to throw a punch or something.

Gabriel jammed his hands into the pockets of his hoodie, wishing for his lighter. He'd left everything in the jeep, not wanting to take the chance of losing something and being tracked back here. Knowing someone was investigating these fires made him cautious.

"What do you think?" he said.

Hunter shifted the reflective coat under his arm. The helmet sat at his feet, reminding Gabriel that he hadn't saved everyone last night. "There's a lot of power to this one."

"No shit. Is anyone trapped?"

Hunter looked at him sideways. "Don't know. Want to go see?"

Gabriel kept thinking of what Hannah had said about an arsonist. Did that mean someone else could be here, watching this same fire from the shadows, pouring his own desire for destruction into the flames? Another Elemental, maybe?

It felt odd, to consider that he might be sharing the darkness with another guy who shared his affinity for fire.

"There *are* firefighters in there," said Hunter.

Gabriel knew that. The fire practically screamed with rage when the water from the hoses hit it. With the amount of fury pouring from the house, he had a strong suspicion that the fire wanted to kill them.

He put out a hand. "Give me the jacket."

This time, Gabriel was glad for the cloak of smoke and darkness. The girl he'd rescued last night didn't know he wasn't a firefighter, but *real* firemen probably would. He could hear them talking to each other, yelling orders about checking the walls.

He didn't know what that meant, but he knew to stay the hell out of their way.

He snuck through a back window on the lower level. Not too much fire on this floor, but the smoke was dense. He dropped to his knees so the smoke would stop burning his lungs. Trails of fire came to him right away, proud of the destruction, bragging like those idiots at school who left stink bombs in lockers.

Look. Look what we did.

Gabriel ran a hand through the flames. He'd never felt power like this. Fire always wanted to consume, to destroy, but this . . . this was different. This fire wanted to level the entire house. To kill everyone in it.

And it wanted Gabriel to help.

Maybe someone else *had* started this fire, lit a match or poured gasoline. Before last night, he'd never been around a fire set with the sole purpose to cause harm. Flames in a fireplace never carried this kind of anger. When he lit the grill on the back porch, it never showed a desire to do anything more than burn fuel and oxygen. Even his flames in the woods weren't full of anger, just curiosity gone overboard. Did this fire know the arsonist's intent? Would it act on it?

He had no idea.

The floors creaked above him, and Gabriel flinched sideways. He could feel the heat through the ceiling, knew the firemen were trying to clear the house and put out the flames.

The fire didn't want them here.

It raced away from him, burning up the walls to the ceiling.

"No!" he called.

The fire laughed at him. *Don't just stand there. Help.*

He reached up and swiped a band of fire off the ceiling, pulling the flames into his hands to blow them into nothingness.

More fire replaced them immediately.

This would be so much easier with Nick.

The floors creaked again, and he heard the firemen shout to each other. He couldn't hear the words, but they carried a tone of panic. Gabriel had no idea how long these floors would hold.

Then he heard what they were shouting. "Out! Everybody out!"

Good. They were going. They'd be safe.

The fire raged. Flames tore at the walls, eating at the ceiling. He had no idea where the flames were coming from, but Gabriel knew they were going to bring the house down with everyone inside.

So he called the fire to him.

It took everything he had—and then some. Hunter had to be just outside, feeding him power, because he'd never been able to control a fire of this magnitude on his own. But he appealed to the rage and fury, promising the fire it could bring the house down if those firemen escaped. Promising to help. Promising it would be fucking *spectacular.*

The flames encircled him the way they had in the woods that night—and they were still coming, burning through the walls and throwing choking smoke into the air until Gabriel couldn't see *anything*.

But the firefighters were escaping. He could feel the fire's regret as they poured out the door upstairs.

Gabriel smiled. This fire could bring down the building in a minute. For now, he held the control.

Then he heard the crack. The creak of splitting wood.

And a firefighter was coming through the floor.

Gabriel couldn't move for a moment. At first he lost the man in the smoke, but then he darted forward, feeling burning splinters slice his palm. Then he hit something solid—a body. The guy had to have broken a leg or something—bodies just didn't lie like that naturally. His helmet had come off, lost somewhere in the fire, and he was cursing a blue streak. Gabriel almost couldn't hear him over the roar of flames.

Especially when the fire abandoned Gabriel and attacked the man on the ground.

Gabriel had once watched this documentary in science class or something, where there'd been a dead animal lying in the woods, and they sped up the film to show the insects attacking and devouring the animal.

That's what this fire looked like.

He swiped at the man's coat, flinging fire away. He smacked hard to kill the flames, trying to use his ability to drive the fire off into the darkness. He had no idea if these coats could really burn, but this didn't seem like the time to find out.

The guy was shouting. It took Gabriel a minute to realize he was yelling at *him*.

"The floor's gonna fall! Get to a doorway!"

Gabriel looked up. The ceiling was a blanket of flame.

Shit. He hooked his arms under the fireman's and started to pull. His jeans were on fire; flames bit against his leg.

Christ, this guy weighed a ton, what with the gear and the oxygen tanks. He was trying to help, though, pushing with his good leg, but it was slow going.

"Tell them," the guy gasped. "Tell them we're coming through the back."

Gabriel gave another good yank that bought them three feet. Maybe the guy had hit his head. Tell them? Tell who?

"Tell them!"

Gabriel could see blisters on the guy's face. Just how hot was it down here?

"Damn it, man, get on the radio before they send more guys in here."

The radio.

"Not working," Gabriel said, coughing through the smoke. "Come on. Almost there."

Sure, Hunter could help when there was a forty-pound kid to carry. Three hundred pounds of firefighter and equipment, not so much.

Fire was raining from the ceiling now. It stung Gabriel's cheeks, protesting their escape. He wasn't entirely sure he was dragging the guy in the right direction, but he was pretty sure the door was straight back.

"Just get out," the guy coughed. His efforts to help were lacking strength now. "Get out of here before the floor falls."

Gabriel grunted and dragged. Sweat was streaking down his face, and he was terrified the back door wouldn't be there when they hit the wall. The flames were too thick to see anything. "How about less talking and more pushing."

The fireman gave a solid shove, and Gabriel had to adjust his grip. He almost dropped him, and the guy cried out.

Gabriel thought of Nick breaking his leg last weekend. "I'm sorry," he said. "I'm—"

"Just *go!*"

Gabriel pulled.

And then he had help. He didn't know where they'd come from, but two firefighters were beside him, dragging them through the door that must have been *right there,* pulling them out of the smoke and flames, getting them into the fresh air.

Someone had a blanket around his shoulders, smacking at the flames on his coat and his legs. Someone else was in his face yelling something about a medic—making Gabriel remember that he had only a helmet and a coat. No pants, no oxygen mask, no tanks.

He probably had about fifteen seconds before all these guys realized he wasn't who he was pretending to be.

"Yeah," he coughed. "Medic."

And when the guy turned his head to speak into a radio, Gabriel ran.

CHAPTER 17

Gabriel sat beside Hunter in the front of his jeep, eating a Big Mac and wondering how he was going to go home looking like this. He couldn't even walk into a store. If the cops and firemen were looking for an arsonist, a kid walking around with burned clothes might draw a little attention.

"So we need to bring a change of clothes," said Hunter.

Gabriel gave him a look. "You think?"

"You said they got a good look at you?"

Gabriel shrugged. "I don't know. I had the helmet on. There was a lot of smoke."

But he'd bet good money they'd figure it out.

"Did you delete the text I sent you?"

Gabriel nodded. "I'm not an idiot."

He wondered if Hannah would put it together that he'd run out of the house on the same night a stranger showed up at a fire. She hadn't come to their house suspecting *him* of arson—she'd just been looking for information.

Right?

He set half the burger on the wrapper. "I need to tell you something."

Hunter was eating a grilled chicken sandwich. He didn't even look over. "This is so sudden."

"Shut up. They think someone is starting these fires."

Hunter shrugged. "An arsonist. I know."

Gabriel blinked. "You *do?*"

"Sure. It was in the paper. My grandfather mentioned it at dinner. Something about that guy at school having his house targeted."

Gabriel picked up his soda and took a sip. "He's a tool."

Hunter looked over. "You regret pulling his little sister out of that fire?"

"No." Gabriel hesitated. "I need to tell you something else."

"Shoot."

Gabriel told him about the night he'd started the fire in the woods, how he'd lost control. He told him about Hannah, how she'd come to the house tonight, fishing for information.

Hunter didn't say anything when he was done, just polished off the rest of his sandwich and shoved the wrapper into the bag.

"I couldn't control it tonight," said Gabriel. "There was too much. I lost it. That guy could have died."

"That guy *would* have died." Hunter started the ignition. "If we hadn't been there, he still would have fallen through the ceiling, and he still would have broken his leg, but he would have been dead before anyone could get to him—not to mention the rest of them. You want to stop?"

Gabriel hesitated. He did—and he didn't. It was addictive, drowning in fire every night.

And it was helping his control. He was getting stronger; he could *feel* it. But he eventually *would* kill someone if he couldn't manage his element better than this. He was going to get caught.

He looked out the window. "I don't know," he ground out.

Hunter fell silent again, pulling his jeep onto the main road. But after a while, he glanced over. "Maybe we're going about this all wrong."

"What does that mean?"

"You're a sports guy. You don't just go out and play a game—you practice, right?"

"This isn't a game, Hunter."

"Still. Practice makes perfect."

Perfect. It made Gabriel think of Layne. He pulled his phone out of the center console.

No messages.

He sighed. "So what are you saying? We should go set a house on fire for *practice?*"

"No, not a house. We'd start smaller than that." Hunter glanced away from the road. "My grandparents have an old barn at the back of their property. It's full of old hay bales, the lawnmower, stuff like that."

Gabriel stared out at the road. He and Nick used to go down to the beach to set things on fire. Gabriel would always try to drive the fire as high as he could, to incite the flames to burn as much as possible.

He'd never tried to draw flames back, to convince them to settle.

Hunter hit him in the arm. "Come on. Do I really need to convince you to play with fire?"

Gabriel smiled. "No. You don't." He paused, noticing they were pulling into the Target parking lot. "Where are we going?"

"You sure can't go home looking like that. I'll go in and get you another pair of jeans. You have any cash?"

Gabriel pulled out his wallet and found a twenty.

Hunter shoved it into his pocket and jumped out of the jeep. He left it running. "Don't steal the car," he called.

Gabriel smiled.

He missed his twin—almost to the point it hurt.

But it wasn't so bad having a friend either.

Michael was waiting on the front porch when Hunter pulled his jeep up the driveway.

Gabriel swore under his breath. He'd killed time at Hunter's house, splattering zombies on Xbox again after grabbing a shower. It was after eleven now, and he'd hoped his older brother would be in bed.

"Problem?" said Hunter.

"Stick around. I might need a getaway car."

"Want backup instead?"

Tempting. Gabriel hesitated.

Michael stood up from the porch chair and came to the top step. The light by the door had been replaced, making his hair shine and keeping his face in darkness. "Get out of the car, Gabriel."

Hunter hadn't even put the jeep in park. "Your call."

Gabriel heaved a sigh and grabbed the door handle. "Go home. I'm sure as hell not bringing you down with me."

But when Hunter was backing down the driveway, Gabriel felt very alone facing his brother from the sidewalk.

He set his shoulders and tried to play it easy. "Why'd you wait up? Think Hunter was going to get fresh with me?"

"Where were you?"

Gabriel shrugged. "Grabbed a burger. Hung out."

Michael was looking at him a little too intensely. "And what did you do last night?"

For a second, Gabriel wondered what his brother would think if he told him the truth.

He wondered how much Michael had guessed already.

"Cut the crap, Michael. What do you want?"

"I want to know if you're starting these fires."

The words hit Gabriel like a fist to the face.

That's what his brother thought? That Gabriel was out *deliberately* setting fires, purposely killing people?

He almost couldn't breathe for a second, the feeling of betrayal hit so hard. Just like last night, when Nick had stolen his air. Only Nick hadn't been accusing him of murder.

That moment of brotherly camaraderie earlier in the evening was completely gone. He'd been so stupid to think Michael could ever be a *friend*. Gabriel clenched his jaw and moved to walk past him up the steps. "Fuck you."

His brother caught his arm. "Are you doing this to get back at Becca's father? Do you *want* the Guides coming here? Tell me."

Not just a murderer, but someone who would turn on his family. Gabriel jerked free and shoved him away in one motion.

Michael caught him and spun him around before he could make it through the door. "You were pretty upset when you ran out of here last night. Where did you go?"

Gabriel tried to yank his arm free again, but Michael was working a death grip.

"Let go of me."

"Damn it, I can't help you if you won't *talk* to me."

"Help me? *Help* me?" Gabriel hit him with his free hand, getting in a solid punch before Michael wrestled him against the siding of the house to pin him there.

"Yeah," Michael said, and his voice was tired. "Help you."

Gabriel glared at him, struggling, but his brother had six years and a good twenty pounds on him, plus leverage to boot. Gabriel ground words out. "I'm not doing anything."

"You don't sound like you're not doing anything."

Life would be so much easier if Michael was an idiot.

Michael narrowed his eyes. "Why are you hanging out with Hunter all of a sudden?"

"What difference does it make?" Gabriel heaved against his brother's hands, throwing his weight into it.

Michael slammed him back into the house. His head cracked against the siding. Hard.

The porch light sizzled and flared for a brief moment. Gabriel heard his brother's breath catch.

The sound filled Gabriel with shame and pride all at the same time, a sickening euphoric feeling that gripped his chest and churned his stomach, but let him meet his brother's eyes.

He gave the electricity a tiny *push,* making it flare again. "Don't screw with me, Michael."

Michael didn't move. They stood frozen for an eternal second, until the front door flew open.

Nick, his eyes a little wide, his face a little pale. "Michael. Let him go."

"Go back in the house," said Michael. But his hands were already loosening.

Gabriel wrenched free, scraping along the siding until he had some distance from his brothers.

But not enough distance that he couldn't feel their judgment.

All of a sudden, he didn't want to stay here. He didn't want to have to walk past them, to go upstairs and do normal things like brush his teeth and wash his face, knowing that his brothers thought he was out of control. Not just out of control, but a *murderer*.

He couldn't look at his twin, didn't want to find accusation or condemnation or, hell, even *pity* on his face.

He wanted out of here.

But he had nowhere else to go.

Gabriel took a step forward, throwing the door wide again. He half expected one of them to stop him, to catch his arm or call his name or *something*. He was ready to argue, to fight, but silence followed him to the top of the stairs.

He'd never felt so isolated. Christ, by the time he shut his bedroom door and locked it, his throat felt tight.

God, he missed Nick.

Knock, he thought. *Knock. I'll apologize. I'll explain. Knock.*

Nothing. *Nothing.*

He wanted to burn this whole house to the ground.

Gabriel sat on the floor under his window and pressed his forehead against his knees.

If Layne called now, he'd be such a mess that he'd tell her everything.

He fished the phone out of his pocket, staring at it. Praying for exactly that.

But just like everyone else around him, the phone remained silent.

All night long.

CHAPTER 18

L ayne cantered her horse along the path in the woods, the breeze in her face stealing tendrils of hair from under her helmet. The sun had barely risen, streamers of red and yellow filtering through the trees to light the trail.

She wasn't supposed to be riding out here alone, especially when no one was at the farm. Especially bareback. Especially when she'd left her phone sitting on the tack trunk, and if she had a bad fall, she'd have no way to call for help.

Reckless. She didn't care.

Looking at her phone reminded her of Gabriel's note, his handwriting in her notebook.

She'd stared at it last night.

She'd even dialed, but never found the courage to actually *call*.

The trail started downhill, a gentle slope, but at a canter, Layne had to shift her weight and focus. This was why she'd come out here. Stupid circles in a stupid ring would have done nothing to take her mind off Gabriel.

What had Kara said? *He is insanely hot.*

He was. And he knew it, too. He probably saw Layne as a conquest. He was the kind of guy who'd keep a list of all the girls in school and check each one off when he was done with her. God, she watched him check out Taylor every day.

I'm not perfect either.

Oh, that had sent her heart tripping in her chest for a long while.

Until she remembered that he probably had a whole cache of one-liners.

The cool air made her horse fresh, and he skittered sideways when a bird flew across the trail. She gave him a quick pat on the neck, checking the rein to remind him that she was up here, in control.

Ha. In control.

This was just about the only place she ever felt in control. Of anything.

But at least the horse was fooled. He settled, relaxing into a rolling stride that she could sit all day. The trail was open ahead, the sunlight painting dapples across the grass. Peaceful. She closed her eyes and inhaled.

And then she was in the air, no horse beneath her.

And then she was hitting the ground.

Her fingers still had a firm grip of the reins, one of those things they teach you early. Presumably so the horse wouldn't get away.

But not only was he getting away, he was also dragging her.

It hurt.

Let go. Let go. Let go. Her fingers wouldn't work.

Then they did. Layne crumpled into a heap on the path. She wished her helmet could protect her whole body. She hadn't even hit her head, so a fat lot of good that did. Her hip was making a good case that it would be protesting this venture to-morrow.

The horse must have spooked. The fall had been one of those hard ones where the animal is suddenly gone from underneath you, leaving nothing to catch you but dirt. *Stupid,* to close her eyes like that. God, what kind of idiot closes her eyes while can-tering on the trail?

The same kind of idiot who takes a full ten seconds to realize you should let go of the reins.

Thank god no one was at the farm, though she didn't have

much time. If her horse made it back without her . . . well, there'd be hell to pay. They'd call her father.

Like he needed one more disappointment in his life.

Layne sat up on the trail, dusting off her breeches, assessing damages. Nothing hurt too badly. She looked back to see what could have frightened the animal—though sometimes it didn't take much.

But there was someone sitting in the middle of the trail. Sitting up, dusting himself off, doing the same things she was doing.

Holy crap, she'd run into a *man*.

She'd left her glasses on her tack trunk next to her phone, so she wasn't able to make out features, but the filtered sunlight let her identify shorts, a sweatshirt. Athletic shoes.

For a second, she considered the implications of being alone in the woods with a man, but she'd just plowed into him with her horse, and a little courtesy probably wasn't out of line.

Layne stood up and started walking toward him. Her knees weren't a big fan of this activity, and her head wasn't feeling much better. She unsnapped her helmet and clipped the strap through a belt loop, shaking her hair free so it wouldn't be matted with sweat across her forehead.

"You all right?" she called. "God, I'm sorry. I wasn't paying attention—" She broke off the apology, hearing her father's voice in her head. *If you're ever in an accident, don't apologize. It immediately implies guilt. . . .*

But how could she *not* apologize?

He was staring at her now, and she was relieved to see that he wasn't a *man* man, but a teenager, with dark hair and features that were slowly coming into focus as she got closer.

Features that shifted into something like surprise. "Layne?"

She stopped short on the path. "Gabriel?" Then she hesitated. "Or Nick? I'm sorry—"

"It's me." His voice was rough. "Gabriel."

And just then, all her rationalizing went straight out the window. He looked . . . overwrought. Rumpled sweatshirt, disheveled hair. That shadow across his jaw had turned into true stubble overnight.

Regret twisted her gut. She should have called. He'd apologized and left his number, and then she'd as good as smacked him in the face.

No, she'd trampled him with her horse.

Get over yourself, Layne. He's probably hungover.

She straightened, folding her arms. "Are you hurt?"

He must have heard her voice turn flat, because his expression hardened. "I'm all right. You?"

"I'm great."

And then he was standing, looming over her, an abrupt shift from vulnerable and wounded to vaguely threatening. "What are you doing out here?"

She always had to battle with her emotions when he looked like that. One part of her wanted to back away to get a little more air. The other part wanted to step into him, just to see what it felt like to share his warmth.

"Riding," she said. "What are *you* doing out here?"

"Running," he said, like it should have been obvious—and really, it kind of was. His eyes flicked down her form, and she wished riding breeches weren't quite so formfitting. "I guess I should be glad you weren't driving a car."

"Shut up." Then she realized what he'd said. "Wait. You live around here?"

He lifted one shoulder and looked around—though they were surrounded by trees, so she had no idea what he was looking for. "Nah. I've been running for a while." He pulled an iPod out of the pocket of his hoodie and glanced at it. "Four miles, maybe."

Layne blinked. "You ran . . . four . . . *miles?*"

"Yeah. I didn't realize my morning run could get fucked up, too, but maybe that's just my week."

His voice was sharp enough for her to feel an edge against her skin. But somehow it didn't seem directed at *her*. He'd reacted the way an animal would lash out if it was in pain. Layne frowned, afraid to dig at an open wound—but kind of afraid not to.

She opened her mouth to ask, but her words died at his expression. Eyes hard, jaw set. His hands were in his pockets, but it didn't make him look relaxed. It made him look like he was trying not to hit something.

Layne let the air out of her lungs. She smoothed her jacket against her hips. "I need to walk back . . . catch my horse—"

"How far?"

"What?" Her eyebrows went up. "Oh, he probably ran back to the barn. Half a mile, I guess. The trail's a loop. I just don't want someone to find him and call my dad. If they knew I was out here alone . . ."

Her voice trailed off again. Gabriel was simply *looking* at her with that inscrutable expression, so Layne turned and started walking, calling over her shoulder. "Hey, I'm really sorry about running into you. I guess I'll see you around school."

He didn't say anything. Sneakers ground against dirt behind her, and she knew he was taking off, running for home or wherever.

Then he drew up beside her, falling into step.

Her breath caught. "What are you doing?"

"You think I'm going to leave you alone in the middle of the woods? What the hell kind of guy do you think I am?"

She glanced up at him. A streak of dirt ran across his face, and it took everything she had not to reach up and rub it off. She wondered what his cheek would feel like.

She swallowed. "I have no idea."

Gabriel snorted. "I don't think that's true."

She hunched her shoulders, feeling the muscles pull. Having a conversation with him was like navigating a minefield. She bit the inside of her lip and concentrated on keeping her mouth shut.

But after a while, he said, "I should have heard you."

His voice was cautious. She didn't look at him, worried this was just another mine waiting to explode.

"I had the music too loud," he said. "I don't usually run like that—it's a good way to get hit by a car. I didn't even look when I came out onto the main trail. I just . . ." He hesitated.

Layne held her breath. Her dad once told her the best way to get the truth out of a witness was to be patient enough to wait for them to tell you. *Everyone likes to talk,* he'd said. *The trick is letting them talk long enough.*

Gabriel glanced over, making a frustrated noise. "You ever just have to do *something* to get all the thoughts out of your head?"

Layne nodded. That, she understood. "So you ran four miles?"

He shrugged and stared out at the trees around them. "I had to get out of the house."

The words rolled around in her head for a moment, and she could practically see a construction worker throwing a flag in her path. *Proceed with caution.*

She went with something safe. "I'm surprised you're not saving all that energy for tryouts. They're after school, right?"

He shook his head. "Not for me. You were right. Anderson caught on."

Layne almost stumbled on the trail. "What do you mean, she *caught on?*" God, if her dad knew she'd fixed some kid's test—especially the *future felon's*—he'd have her off to an all-girls' boarding school before she could explain herself.

Yeah, and what explanation would you give? Sorry, Dad. He was hot.

"Not you." Gabriel's voice was flat. "She just figured out I was cheating."

"So you're off the team? Are you suspended? Are you—"

"A week and a half. She gave me a week and a half to hand in perfect homework and take a unit test—myself. Then I can try out for the team, if I can pass."

She stared at him. "But . . . that's great! You can just do the work, and—"

"It's not *great.*" His words could cut ice again. "I can't even do the goddamn homework; I'm not going to pass the test."

"But I can still help you—"

He put out a hand to stop her. "Yeah? Why?"

Breath fought its way into her lungs. "Because—because—"

His eyes were fierce. "What, you want to put some do-gooder activity on your transcript? Helped the resident fuckup pass a math test? Why do you even *give a shit*, Layne?"

She jerked back. His chest was rising and falling quickly, and she had a suspicion that if she put a hand against the front of his sweatshirt, she'd find his heart beating every bit as rapidly as hers. Sunlight was pouring through the trees now, and sweat crept along her neck.

Abruptly, he turned away, blowing out a long breath and running his hands back through his hair. "I'm sorry. This isn't about you."

Layne wanted to put a hand on his shoulder, but she wasn't sure how he'd take it. What had he said? *I had to get out of the house.*

She kept her voice careful. "So your parents are pissed?"

"No." His hands dropped, falling into his pockets again. He had to have a cell phone or something there; she could see him fiddling with something. He started walking again, saying nothing, so she hustled to catch up.

"My parents died when I was twelve," he said.

"I'm sorry," she whispered.

"My older brother is twenty-three, so he has custody."

She had no idea what to say.

He glanced her way. "It's been five years," he said flatly. "I'm over it."

She didn't believe that for a minute. "So . . . your older brother . . . is *he* pissed?"

"He would be, if he knew. We had a big fight last night about . . . other stuff."

She had arguments with Simon, but she imagined Gabriel wasn't one to fight with words and tears and threats to tell a parent. "No sense adding fuel to the fire, huh?"

"Something like that."

"Are you going to get Nick to help you?"

Gabriel hesitated. "I don't think that's going to happen." Another pause. "Nick and I aren't speaking."

Wow, pain hid behind *those* words. She only had bits and pieces of this story, like reading the first sentence of every chapter in a book. Something powerful had happened—she just couldn't piece it together.

He'd been banned from the team, from a sport she knew he loved—God, even Simon practically worshipped Gabriel's athletic ability. He was fighting with his twin brother, and they *had* to be close, the way they seamlessly switched places in front of teachers and other students.

And then he'd searched for her in the library. He'd wanted to talk to her in private. He'd *apologized,* and she'd known how much it cost him to do it. He'd seen right through her defenses, leaving that perfectly charming sentence in her notebook.

No, not charming. *Honest.*

Desperate?

It hadn't been a game. He'd wanted her to call.

Gabriel ran a hand through his hair again. "Sorry," he said, his blue eyes dark and full of emotion. "I'll shut up. It's been a shitty week."

Layne took a deep breath.

Then she stepped forward to throw her arms around his neck and hug him.

CHAPTER 19

Gabriel stiffened when Layne's arms went around his neck. With the way his life was going, he wouldn't have been surprised to find her goal was to choke him.

But then she was just holding him, her slender arms full of strength, their height difference putting her head against his shoulder.

He couldn't remember the last time he'd been held like this.

Yes, he could. That mother, after the fire. But hers had been a motion of gratitude and desperation. It hadn't been about *him*.

He should be pushing Layne away. He could slice right through her offer of comfort and make her as miserable as he'd been last night. He'd made himself vulnerable once; he wouldn't make that mistake again.

But the warmth of her body made it all the way through his sweatshirt, and the scent of her hair was in his nose, one of those fruity shampoos like raspberries or apricots. Beneath that, something natural and fresh and outdoorsy, like cut grass or— no, hay. Had to be hay, from the farm.

It felt nice.

Push her away.

He should. He would. The last thing he needed in his life was something else to screw up.

But right now, this second, when the thought of being at home or at school made him feel like a caged, rabid animal, standing in the middle of the woods being held wasn't all that bad.

"Thanks," he said, dropping his head to speak against her hair. Her cheek was right *there*, if she'd just lift her head. Her cheek, the slope of her jaw, the curve of her ear. He wondered what her skin would feel like, what her lips would taste like. He let his hands find her waist.

She stiffened.

Gabriel froze. Maybe he was reading this wrong. She hadn't called last night. Maybe a hug-without-pretense just meant she felt pity for him.

Christ, even his thoughts wanted to screw with him.

There was a tree right here. He wanted to bang his head against it.

No, he wanted to push the hair back from her face and kiss her, to cut this cord of tension between them.

But maybe that cord was the only thing holding him together.

He slid his thumbs along the jacket, just below her ribs, barely a motion, half an inch, if that. But he heard her quick intake of breath, felt the minute shift of her body as she drew back.

Damn.

He couldn't take another rejection. Especially from Layne. She wasn't like other girls. She saw *him*. Every single weakness.

And that was the reason for the hug. She wasn't interested. She felt *sorry* for him.

He let go of her waist. He kept his voice flat, uninterested, like her hanging off him was a random inconvenience. "Come on. I don't have all morning to play escort."

She yanked her hands free, stepping back to stare up at him.

Jesus, he sounded like such a *dick*.

"Don't do that," she said.

"Do what?" He pulled the iPod from his pocket and unwound the cord. He could see buildings through the trees from here, and he nodded down the trail. "You've got to be close, right?"

"Yeah, but—"

But he didn't hear the rest of what she said. He plugged the headphones into his ears, turned his back, and ran.

Gabriel hoped Michael would be gone by the time he got home, but his brother's red pickup truck was still sitting in the driveway when Gabriel stepped out of the woods behind the house.

He had half a mind to fall back into the trees.

He couldn't stop thinking about Layne.

Gabriel hadn't even recognized her at first. Her hair had been down, a spill of chestnut brown that fell almost all the way to her waist, with a few damp tendrils curling around her face. No glasses. Skintight gray pants that left *nothing* to the imagination, with knee-high leather boots. Hell, if she wore that getup to school, she'd have half the male population trailing her in the halls. Even her maroon jacket had an athletic cut, fitting snugly along the curve of her waist. The black ribbed turtleneck had pretty much been the only familiar thing about her.

So what? She pities you.

He walked around to unlock the front door quietly, hoping Michael would be in the shower, or even better, still sleeping. At the very least, in the kitchen, hidden from view.

Nope. Michael was sitting on the staircase, a cup of coffee on the step beside him.

Gabriel couldn't make himself shut the door. The sunshine was a welcome weight against his back.

"Don't run," said Michael. His voice was even.

Gabriel scowled—but he didn't take his hand off the door. "I'm not running from you."

"You look like you're ready to bolt."

"Yeah, well, you look like a—"

"All right, stop." Michael held up a hand. "I didn't wait here to pick a fight with you."

"So what do you want?"

"That girl Hannah—the firefighter?"

"What about her?"

"Her father is the county fire marshal."

He must have looked blank, because Michael added, "That means her 'unofficial' visit might have been pretty damn official."

Gabriel waited, unsure what response would be safe. Really, saying *anything* could be a mistake. Michael had almost seen through him last night. He kept hearing his brother's accusation on the porch. *I want to know if you're starting these fires?*

Michael picked up the coffee mug and stood, gesturing toward the kitchen. "Come here. I want to show you something."

Gabriel kept his hand on the doorknob, as if letting go would leave him trapped, a prisoner to half-accurate accusations. "Look, I've got school—"

"This will only take a second."

Gabriel sighed, but followed.

Michael's laptop was open on the kitchen table, and he slid his fingers across the trackpad to wake the screen. At first, Gabriel had no idea what he was supposed to be looking at. He recognized the local newspaper's Web site; he'd been reading about the Ravens' defensive line all week. The main story was something about a neighborhood dispute in Federal Hill. Big whoop.

Then he saw the headline just below it, in slightly smaller print.

ALLEGED ARSON SUSPECT IMPERSONATES FIREMAN
AT LAKE SHORE BLAZE

Shit.

Gabriel clicked on the link.

"That was last night," said Michael.

"Thanks. I can read." Gabriel's eyes were locked on the article.

A fire broke out in the Lake Shore community last night, injuring three firefighters, one critically. Preliminary investigations have deter-

mined that this fire may have been started by
the same arsonist who allegedly initiated fires at
Magothy Beach Road and Kinder Farm Lane.

Blah, blah. Gabriel skimmed farther.

Firefighters on the scene report an unidenti-
fied man wearing protective gear that matched
that of local volunteer fire companies. No de-
scription of the suspect is available. Fire Marshal Jack Faulkner would not comment on the
investigation, but an anonymous caller who
claims to have been on duty at the scene stated,
"This guy's got a hero complex, starting fires
just to play fireman. We lost a guy this week.
We're going to catch him before he kills someone else."

A hero complex. Were they fucking kidding?

Not only did his brothers think he was setting fires to kill
people, but the firefighters did, too.

Michael was still standing there watching him. "You want to
tell me what's going on?"

Gabriel slapped the laptop shut and turned for the hallway.

"Hey," said Michael. "Let's talk about this."

"What do you want me to say?" Gabriel called over his
shoulder. His throat felt tight, and if he stopped, if Michael kept
up this let's-work-through-it-together crap any longer, he was
going to seriously lose it. "Congratulations, Detective, you
solved the case."

"Goddamn it, Gabriel, this puts all of us at risk. Do you understand me?"

"So turn me in."

"Keep acting like this, and I'll be forced to."

That made Gabriel stop short on the steps, but he didn't turn.
He could barely breathe through his anger. Michael wouldn't.
He couldn't.

Gabriel didn't even know who he'd turn him in *to*. The cops, the Guides?

Did it really matter which? He wasn't starting the fires. If he and Hunter stopped, nothing would change.

Except more people might die.

"Please," said Michael. "I don't want to think you're doing this, but—"

"But what? You can't help it? I'm such a frigging screwup that it has to be—"

"Cut the crap. It's obvious you're involved somehow. Would you just *tell me* what's going on?"

Gabriel started walking again. "Why bother? You sound like you've made up your mind already."

"I can't help you if you won't—"

Gabriel slammed his bedroom door. Then leaned against it, hands in fists at his sides.

He could just shower at school. He didn't even have to wait for his brothers; he could cut through the woods and be there in half an hour. Plenty of time. He grabbed a duffel bag from his closet and shoved some clothes inside.

Then he paused, his hand on a T-shirt. Maybe he should pack some extra clothes, in case there was a fire tonight.

Then he remembered the line from the article: *We're going to catch him before he kills someone else.*

Michael could kiss his ass. But real firefighters—they'd be *looking* for him now. They knew he had the jacket, the helmet.

He needed to stop. He'd talk to Hunter. Seriously, they should *stop*.

But last night's fire had been *raging*. Whoever started that fire wanted people to die. That fireman had come through the floor. He wouldn't have survived.

Neither would that little girl.

Christ, his head hurt. Gabriel kept shoving clothes in the bag. Either way, maybe he could just crash at Hunter's. Hell, he'd sleep in the woods.

Whatever, he didn't have to come back here.

Where he wasn't wanted.

CHAPTER 20

The locker rooms were deserted. No shocker there; school wasn't supposed to start for another half hour, and first period was always saved for freshman health. Gabriel turned the water as hot as he could tolerate and just stood there, letting it blaze into his skin. He'd run far and hard this morning, and he'd hoped the pain would steal his focus and force his brain to think of something other than the fight with his brother.

No luck.

Keep acting like this, and I'll be forced to.

Goddamn Michael.

A door slammed farther out toward the gym. One of the coaches maybe, or someone grabbing a quick half hour in the weight room.

It probably meant he should get moving. Gabriel slapped the faucet to kill the stream of water.

When he was rubbing his hair with the towel, he heard a locker open somewhere out of sight. Then voices, too far away to make out. Laughter. Gabriel pulled his cell phone out of his bag to check the time. Still early.

Whatever. He yanked jeans out of the bag to pull on.

Then he heard a shout, a scuffle, and the crash of metal on metal as something hit a locker.

Okay, WTF?

He dragged a shirt over his head and walked down the aisle of lockers barefoot.

Six guys, sophomores and juniors, stood in the open area at the back corner of the locker room. Gabriel only recognized them vaguely. JV guys, he thought.

They froze when he came around the corner. Exchanged nervous glances, like they weren't sure whether they should be relieved he wasn't a teacher. He knew that look. He'd practically *invented* that look.

Gabriel gave half a smile. "Come on. What's up?"

Then he heard the faint shifting sound inside the locker, and one of the guys hit the face of it with his fist. "Shut up, retard."

One of the other ones laughed. "Stacey, you dumbass. Like he can hear you."

Stacey. What an idiot name for a guy—and Gabriel hoped to god it was a last name. No wonder this prick was slamming people in lockers. He couldn't even be *original.*

Then he realized what the other kid had said.

Like he can hear you.

"Oh yeah." Stacey struck the locker again, harder. He laughed and raised his voice, until he was practically shouting into the locker vents. "Shut up, you fucking ret—"

Gabriel slammed a fist into his shoulder. The kid staggered back into the other lockers.

One of the other guys got in Gabriel's face. "What the fuck, man. It's just a *joke.*"

"Hilarious. Let him out."

Stacey recovered and stepped up beside his friend. His hands were balled at his sides. "This isn't your business."

Gabriel shoved him again. "I'm making it my business."

Stacey shoved back—and he wasn't like those freshmen from the other day. He carried some solid mass, and he drove Gabriel back a step.

Another one shifted forward, a dark-haired thug who looked like he needed to spend more time in the gym and less at Taco Bell. He shoved Gabriel in the chest, too. "Get the hell out of here."

"Open it," said Gabriel. Electricity sizzled in the lights overhead, ready to ignite with his temper.

Stacey snorted. "What if we don't want to?"

"I'll make you want to."

Another one stepped up beside them. "You and what army?"

"This one."

A new voice. Gabriel turned his head. So did the jerks surrounding him.

Chris stood there at the edge of the line of lockers, a backpack slung over one shoulder, his arms folded across his chest.

The other kids exchanged glances again. Chris had a bit of a rep after beating the crap out of some seniors after homecoming—guys who'd been trying to assault Becca.

"Or," Chris said with a shrug, "maybe I should just let you all settle it. I'll get the coach to come unlock the locker."

"Go ahead, Chris." Gabriel gave Stacey a quick shove in the chest. "I don't like fighting girls, but I think I can hold my own until you get back—"

"Shut up," Stacey snapped. He glanced at Chris again. "Whatever. Come on, guys. Forget it."

They all started to move away.

Gabriel grabbed Stacey by the arm and slammed him back into the locker doors. "Let him out first."

Stacey swore, but he worked the combination until the lock popped open. Then he jerked his arm out of Gabriel's grip and started to follow his friends.

Any other day, Gabriel would have followed him and made his morning miserable. But now he just wanted to make sure Simon was okay.

Layne had said her little brother was having a hard time. Gabriel wondered if she knew just how hard.

He eased the locker door open. Simon was wearing jeans and a decent pair of running shoes, but no shirt. His arms were shoved up tight against his chest. His face was furious, guarded, wary—and humiliated at finding Gabriel standing outside the locker.

"It's okay," said Gabriel. "They're gone."

Simon's eyes flicked left, to Chris. He made no move to climb out of the locker.

"He's all right," said Gabriel. "He's my brother. Chris."

Chris lifted a hand. "'Sup."

Simon still didn't move.

"This is Simon," said Gabriel. "I know his sister." He paused. "He's deaf."

"Got it."

Gabriel lifted a hand to gesture. "Come on. You can't stay in there all day."

Simon looked away, at the gray sidewall of the locker. His jaw was set, his shoulders tight. He didn't move for a long moment.

Just when Gabriel was about to ask if they'd superglued him in there or something, Simon extricated himself from the narrow box, then dropped his arms from his chest.

Chris blew out a breath. "Jesus Christ."

Words were scrawled across Simon's chest in what looked like permanent marker.

Most were some variation of *Retard* or *Loser*.

Simon's breath was shaking. His fists were still tight at his sides. Gabriel knew that feeling, that if you let go, just a little, everything would unravel.

"Look," he said, pointing. "Idiots can't even frigging spell."

Simon glanced down, where one of those thugs had scrawled *Rettard*.

Then he *almost* smiled.

"That's actually kind of ironic," said Chris.

Simon took a deep breath and his shoulders loosened. Then he held out a hand and mimed a phone.

Gabriel patted his pockets, but he must have left his phone in his bag. "Chris, give him your phone."

Chris did. Simon tapped out a text.

Thanks.

Chris glanced up. "I hate guys like that."

Simon tapped a few more letters on the screen and handed the phone back to Chris.

Me too.

Gabriel pointed toward the showers. "If you want to go scrub at it, I'll loan you a shirt when you're done."

Simon nodded and turned to walk—then stopped short. He took the phone again and typed out another line.

Don't tell Layne.

Gabriel stared at the words, then glanced up at Simon, who was watching him with pleading eyes.

"All right," he said.

When Simon was safely in the shower, Gabriel dug through his bag for an extra shirt for Simon and a pair of socks for himself. Chris had followed him back to the bench and now just sat there watching him.

Gabriel sighed.

"You know," said Chris, "that's probably not going to come off with soap and water."

Gabriel didn't look at him. "That antiseptic crap in there will practically take your skin off, so maybe . . ." He shrugged. At least it was Friday, and JV wouldn't practice again until Monday. Simon wouldn't have to shower with the rest of the team until then.

And hopefully the words would have faded.

"Ryan Stacey is in my English class," said Chris. "He's an asshole."

"I got that, thanks. He pulls this again, I'm going to light him on fire."

No response, but Gabriel could feel his brother watching him.

"Damn it, Chris. What?" He looked up. "What are you even doing here?"

"Wow. No 'Thanks, Chris, for saving my ass—'"

"You *did not* save my ass."

"Yeah, well, I probably saved you from a suspension. You think Mike's on your case now—"

Gabriel glared at him. "I think you need to stay out of it."

Chris didn't back down, but then he wasn't that type. "What happened with Nick?"

Gabriel looked back at his bag. The worst part was, he had no idea what had happened with Nick. He couldn't even remember why he'd picked that fight.

"You know," said Chris, "I had to listen to a raft of crap from Becca about the things you said to Quinn, but I know you—"

"Boo-hoo." Gabriel yanked the zipper closed. "I'm sorry I interfered in your love life."

Chris sighed and shrugged his backpack onto his shoulder. "All right. Forget it. Sorry for *caring*."

"Oh, is that what you're doing?"

"Not anymore." Chris rounded the bank of lockers.

Gabriel wanted to punch something.

Maybe he could go find Ryan Stacey.

But then Chris reappeared. He threw a glance at the wall that separated the lockers from the shower room. "Who's his sister?"

Gabriel looked back in his bag and kept his voice nonchalant. "Just a girl in my math class."

"Just a girl, huh?"

Gabriel glared at him. "Just a girl."

Chris smiled. "So was Becca."

Layne sat at her desk, waiting for class to begin. She'd started working through the problems at the end of the next unit, desperate for something that would make her look busy.

Unfortunately, her brain wouldn't think about numbers. It was all too content to replay the feel of Gabriel's hands at her waist. His breath against her hair. He wasn't even sitting beside her yet, and her mind was already scripting PG-13 fantasies.

No, probably just PG. She'd never even kissed a boy, much less anything else.

Thank god she'd been wearing that jacket.

And he'd pushed her away, anyway. She might as well scrap the fantasies.

Layne knew the instant he walked into the room. She could feel his eyes find her, so she kept her own on the paper.

Write. Look busy.

But out of the corner of her eye, she watched him drop a piece of paper in the homework basket.

He'd done it. Had he found someone else to help him cheat?

Someone snickered to her left. "Working ahead, lesbo?"

Taylor, sitting backward on her desk, probably waiting for Gabriel. Layne sighed and ignored her.

"You know," said Taylor, "maybe if you spent five minutes looking in a mirror, you wouldn't look like such a loser nerd."

Layne looked up. "Maybe if you spent five minutes *less* looking in a mirror, you wouldn't look like such a prostitute."

Half the class caught its breath. Layne could hear it, the anticipation, the eagerness for Taylor to snap.

Part of her wanted to suck the words back, to reverse time ten seconds.

The other part wanted to finish up the comment by stabbing Taylor with her pencil.

"Aw," said Taylor, giving her a mock pout. "You're jealous. So sweet."

"I'm not jealous of you."

Gabriel stepped through the tension to drop into his seat. He still looked tired. If anything, he looked more drawn than he had at six o'clock this morning. He'd showered and changed at some point, but he'd never bothered to find a razor. It made him look immeasurably rakish and sexy—and overwhelmingly sad, too.

He didn't even glance at Layne.

He didn't look at Taylor, either, just dragged a textbook from his backpack.

Layne sighed and turned back to her work.

"What's wrong, lesbo?" said Taylor. "Run out of insults?"

Gabriel lifted his head. "Leave her alone, Taylor."

"You're defending her? She just called me a prostitute."

He raised his eyebrows and looked at Layne. "Really?"

God, her cheeks felt like they were on fire. "Well . . . I said she *looked* like one . . ."

Gabriel looked back at Taylor, taking in the black fishnets, the tiny little skirt, the top that left three inches of midriff bare. "I can see it."

Perfectly arched eyebrows shot up, then narrowed. "I don't remember you complaining last spring."

Layne couldn't breathe around the sudden lump in her throat.

Get it together. Like it was a shock he'd been with a girl like Taylor.

"Just back off," said Gabriel.

"God, you are so sensitive lately." Taylor uncrossed her legs to lean forward. Layne had a pretty clear view down that top, and she wasn't sitting anywhere near as close as Gabriel. She had to look back at her math work.

"You coming to Heather's after tryouts?" said Taylor.

Gabriel looked away. "I don't think so."

"Come on. Everyone knows about the math thing. That just means you could get there early." Her hand moved, and Layne kept her eyes fixed on her work so she wouldn't have to watch Taylor touch him.

"How do they know about that?" His voice had a sudden edge.

"Please. The whole cheer squad knows. They're working out a schedule to get you the homework."

"Look. Forget it. I don't need their help."

"Sure sounds like you need *someone*'s help." Taylor pulled lip gloss out of her bag and recrossed her legs, throwing her hair back over a shoulder. "Maybe you'd like a personal tutor."

She said *tutor* like she was offering something completely different.

Layne told her brain to stop supplying images of Taylor and Gabriel making out while textbooks and papers fell to the floor.

Her pencil was ready to dig right through her notebook.

"Maybe," said Taylor, her voice suggestive, "we could get to work tonight."

Gabriel laughed a little, his tone equally suggestive. "Maybe I already have a tutor," he said.

Layne's pencil snapped against the paper.

"Who?" said Taylor.

"Layne." He still wasn't looking at her.

Layne felt like the end of that pencil had lodged in her throat.

"Layne," said Taylor, putting a finger to her lips. "Layne. I don't think I know anyone named . . ."

"Me," snapped Layne. "*My* name is Layne."

"But wait," said Taylor in that sickly sweet tone. "Everyone here knows your name is butchy dykey les—"

"Hey." Gabriel came halfway out of his chair.

"Excuse me." Ms. Anderson was standing *right there,* almost next to Layne's desk.

Layne flushed again and looked back at her math book.

"Sorry, Ms. Anderson," said Taylor, her voice still sweet. "We were just talking about how much we love this class since you took over."

The teacher pursed her lips. "Let's settle down so we can begin."

When the teacher went back to the front of the room, Layne tried to get her *heart* to settle down. What did he mean? He wanted her help now?

A folded piece of notebook paper landed on the edge of her desk.

She unfolded it to find Gabriel's handwriting.

> **You don't have to. I just needed
> her to shut up.**

Layne swallowed. He was so hard to read sometimes. Like with his phone number. Did this note mean he wanted her to help, or did it mean he wanted her to give him an out?

When she'd hugged him in the woods, his entire body had

been tight, like he wasn't sure how to react. She hadn't imagined the emotion, the pain in his voice.

And then he'd pushed her away.

No. Wait. *She'd* pulled away.

This was so confusing—and her life was already full up on *confusing*.

Another note appeared on the corner of her desk. She unfolded it slowly.

> **I'm sorry about this morning. There's a lot going on. I shouldn't have been such a jerk.**

He'd apologized to her twice now. She didn't get the impression Gabriel Merrick apologized for very much.

Layne carefully pulled a piece of paper free.

I'll help you, she wrote. She folded it up.

And then she stared at it for the whole period, deliberating. If she was reading this wrong, it was just another opportunity for him to reject her. He could roll his eyes and ignore her.

He could hurt her. Again.

Thank god she'd started the questions for the next unit, because she didn't hear a word the teacher said.

When the bell rang, she shoved her books into her bag quickly.

And before she could change her mind, she dropped the note on his desk.

Then, without waiting to see his reaction, she walked out of class.

CHAPTER 21

Layne flipped through an old yearbook in the library, trying to tune out Kara's whining.

"I just don't understand why you're wasting so much time on one stupid project. Aren't you *hungry?*"

"I brought my lunch." A lie. But her stomach was in knots from the drama with Gabriel, and food seemed like a bad idea. "If you're so hungry, go hang out in the cafeteria."

"And leave you by yourself? God, Layne, do you know how that would look?"

Layne rolled her eyes, hoping yet not hoping that Kara wouldn't see it. "Thanks for your concern."

"Layne! We've been looking everywhere for you."

The bright voice had Layne jerking her head up.

There stood Taylor Morrissey and Heather Castelline. Glossy hair, glossy lips, formfitting clothes. Paragons of perfection.

Layne wondered if she should be running—but they were on the cheer squad and could probably catch her. Would they beat the crap out of her right here in the library?

Kara's mouth was hanging open.

"Hi?" Layne offered.

Taylor was smiling at her. "We were wondering if you were coming tonight. See, everyone is bringing something, and we're trying to plan."

"Coming where?" said Layne.

Heather giggled. "The party, silly."

Kara punched her leg under the table.

Layne folded her arms across her chest. "The party. You want *me* to come to your party."

"Well, Gabriel said you guys are friends, and it's *so* obvious he's got a thing for you, so—"

Kara punched her leg again. Layne was ready to hit her back. She narrowed her eyes at Taylor. "Funny. In class you said I was a . . . wait, let me get this straight . . . a butchy dykey—"

"Please," said Heather, rolling her eyes. "We call each other that all the time. Taylor's a total whore."

Taylor flipped her hair. "Totally. So are you coming or what?"

Layne stared at her.

"Yes," said Kara. "Yes, we're coming."

Layne studied them. "I don't buy it."

She blocked her leg before Kara could punch her again.

"Look." Taylor pulled out the chair and dropped into it. "I know we're not always nice. But that's how we have to be, or we'd be surrounded by losers." She shrugged. "If Gabriel Merrick says you're in, you're in."

"Come a little early," said Heather. She stepped around the table and picked up the end of Layne's braid. "We'll do your hair. I bet you have *awesome* hair."

Layne couldn't move.

"She does," said Kara. "It's, like, all the way to her *waist*."

"If you don't want to come," Taylor said, "I totally get it. I mean, Gabriel wasn't going to come until I told him we'd be inviting you . . ."

Layne tried to imagine it, Taylor confronting him in the hallway, Gabriel brushing her off until hearing Layne would be there.

No way.

Then she thought of those two notes on her desk.

Maybe?

"Here's my address." Heather slid a piece of paper across the table. "Come at seven. Everyone else will show up around eight."

Layne glanced down at the paper—not like she needed to. It figured that Heather wouldn't even remember that Layne lived right down the street. But it meant she wouldn't be trapped at the party. If the girls started acting bitchy, she could walk home.

"Okay," she said, *hating* that part of her was a little eager. She hated these girls. *Hated* them.

But sometimes she desperately wished she were more like them.

Especially lately.

"I'll come," she said. "Seven?"

"We'll come," said Kara.

"Great," said Taylor. "Bring something sweet, 'kay?"

Layne ticked down the minutes until her father would walk in the door. Another late night, as usual. She'd called to tell him that she and Kara were going to a friend's house down the street, and he'd promised to be home before they left.

She and Kara had baked chocolate chip cookies, and they sat on a plate, covered in saran wrap. Kara was actually being *nice* for a change, and for the first time, Layne wondered if this was what a friendship was supposed to feel like: laughter and teasing and baking cookies.

Simon was upstairs, locked in his room. He'd worn a different shirt home from school, and when she'd tried to ask what his problem was, he'd given her a pretty universal sign of displeasure.

Kara was licking the spatula. "Are you seriously going to wear jeans and a turtleneck? To a *party*?"

Layne shrugged. "I think you're showing enough skin for both of us."

Kara was, in a spaghetti-strap top and skintight denim capris. The pants were a little *too* tight, but Layne didn't feel like opening that can of worms.

Kara dropped the spatula into the sink. "I have no idea how you got one of the Merrick brothers' attention."

"Me neither."

"You don't have to show skin to look sexy, for god's sake. What if you wore tights and a skirt? You could even keep the turtleneck."

Layne hesitated.

Kara grabbed Layne's hand and started dragging her toward the stairs. "At least *try*."

Kara fished through Layne's closet with abandon. Most of the clothes were older, grade-school stuff.

"Here!" She yanked out a pleated black and red plaid skirt.

Layne made a face. "Please. I used to wear that in fifth grade. To *church*."

She had. With her parents. They'd gone as a family, sitting together. Then they'd all go out for brunch. Everyone would smile and look happy.

What a joke.

"That means it's perfect now," said Kara. "Do you have black tights?"

Layne did. She wore them under her riding breeches in the winter.

She took a breath. "I don't think—"

"Just *try* it. You don't have to wear it if you don't like it."

So she tried it, in the bathroom, where Kara couldn't see her change. The black tights were opaque; not even a hint of flesh peeking through. The skirt was short, almost indecently so. The pleats barely covered her backside. But the black tights made it less hooker and more . . . playful.

Even so, the black turtleneck made her look like she was going to a funeral.

A slutty funeral.

She could never wear this.

A knock at the door shocked her out of her thoughts. "Layne! Look what I found!"

Layne pulled the door open, and Kara gasped. "Oh, you are so wearing that."

"No way."

"Did you *see* what those other girls were wearing? For *once* in your life would you try to fit in?"

She remembered that feeling from the library. It would probably be dark at the party, right? Layne swallowed. "Maybe."

"With these." Kara held up black boots. Matte leather, a stacked two-inch heel, and laces that went all the way up.

Layne remembered those boots. She knew kids whose whole *outfits* didn't cost as much as those boots. Her mom had bought them for her right before high school started. "Please, Laynie," she'd said. "Wear *something* that doesn't look like it came from the Goodwill."

Layne had buried them in the back of her closet.

She reached out and touched the leather. Smooth as butter.

"All right," she whispered.

The boots, when combined with the tights and skirt, made her legs look twenty miles long.

Kara started digging through her dresser. "Too much black. You need something—here!"

She was holding out a red turtleneck. Layne rarely wore it; the fabric was thin and it clung to her body.

Not to mention, it screamed with color and demanded attention.

"Wear it," snapped Kara.

Layne heard her father's keys in the door.

"Now," said Kara. She backed out the door, pulling it closed behind her. "It's almost time to go."

Layne yanked the shirt over her head and didn't look in the mirror. If she did, she'd never have the courage to walk out of this house. She just threw open the door and went downstairs.

Her father took one look at her and dropped all the mail he was carrying. He coughed. "I thought you said it was a girls' night."

"It is!" cried Kara. "Heather is going to do Layne's hair, and we're going to stuff ourselves with cookies—"

"Kara, I hope you don't think I'm a fool."

Kara rolled her eyes. "Mr. Forrest, no offense, but I don't think you know much about girls' nights."

He looked at her, then back at Layne. "Maybe I should drive you."

"Sure," said Layne easily. Thank *god* they were going early. "Then you can meet the other girls."

It actually worked out better than she expected. Taylor and Heather were full of charm at the door, assuring her dad that Heather's mom was going to be home from the store any minute, and did he want a cup of espresso? Taylor leaned on Layne's shoulder and whispered loudly about never realizing she had such a sexy dad.

It was probably the first time Layne had *ever* seen her father blush.

"All right," he said, jingling his keys in his pocket. "I should probably get back to Simon."

Yeah, like he could get Simon to come out of his room. Layne stood on tiptoe and kissed him on the cheek. "Thanks, Daddy."

When he was out the door, Taylor giggled. "Dads are *so* easy."

"Please," said Heather. "All I have to do is wiggle my ass and my dad hands me his platinum card."

Layne almost choked. She wiggled her ass for her *father*?

"Your house is amazing," Kara breathed.

It was, too. Layne never wanted for anything, but her own house was traditional, all polished wood and marble. The back wall of Heather's house was entirely glass, looking out over an expansive pool deck, with a view of the Severn River beyond. Torches were lit along the patio, and the sound system was on low, one of those top-forty songs that sounded like every other.

Heather shrugged. "It's all right."

Taylor pulled a wine cooler out of the fridge. "Want one?" she asked, holding out something peach colored.

Kara took it immediately.

Layne shook her head. But then she didn't want to seem boring, so she said, "Not yet."

"I hear you," said Heather, who didn't take one either. "I hate being trashed before everyone gets here."

"I say what's the difference," said Taylor. She pointed a manicured nail at Layne. "Now you," she said, her voice sharp, almost challenging.

Layne flinched, suddenly ready for the worst. "Me?"

"Yeah. You. Hot rollers. Now."

CHAPTER 22

Layne sat in a darkened corner of the pool deck, wondering when she could go home.

She'd entertained thoughts of some massive prank where they'd cut off her hair or throw her in the pool fully dressed. But Taylor and Heather had wrapped her hair in hot rollers for a while, then brushed makeup across her cheeks until she didn't recognize herself in the mirror. When the hot rollers were pulled free, her hair fell in thick curls down her back, dark tendrils that looked like they belonged to someone else.

And then the party started, and they seemed to forget she existed.

The night was pitch-black now, the torches blazing against the sky. It was too cold to brave the pool, but a dozen students were crowded into the hot tub—including Kara, who had to be on her fourth wine cooler by now. Layne had tried to talk her out of the second one, but Kara had screeched to stop being such a goody-goody.

Everyone had laughed.

That's when Layne had found a place in the dark.

She'd tried mingling, but she didn't know anyone here, and every time she approached a group, they stared at her in this confused way, like she was a random stranger who'd just wandered in off the street. At first she tried to join their conversations, hoping the awkwardness would dissipate. But she didn't know much about sports, she didn't go to parties every weekend, and she wasn't on any of the committees these girls seemed to care about. Fall formal? Yearbook? Yeah, right.

Hey, guys, want to talk about the social dynamics in the Brontë sisters' novels?

She might as well throw herself into the pool.

Taylor was staggering around somewhere. Layne had already seen her puke into the bushes at the edge of the property once.

Not like Layne really wanted her company. Despite the curls, despite the rah-rah-sisterhood shtick, she still didn't trust Taylor.

Especially since Gabriel hadn't even shown up.

Maybe this was the joke. Maybe the older girls had strung her along with empty words. But . . . if this was a joke, there didn't seem to be any punch line. It wasn't like Taylor was mocking her for sitting alone.

And Layne would be lying if she said her head didn't turn every time a new person stepped out onto the pool deck. She thought she'd seen Gabriel at one point, but his face wore an easy smile, and he was laughing with the athletic blonde attached to his arm.

Nick. No way Gabriel had gone from sullen and brooding to easy laughter in one afternoon. No way he'd show up with some other girl, when Taylor had said he was coming for *her.*

Unless *that* was the joke?

Layne's thoughts were giving way to traitorous doubts when some other guy by the grill called out, "Nick! Hey, man." And then they did that whole guy high-five-handshake-shoulder-hug thing.

Relief.

Until she reminded herself that Gabriel still wasn't here.

And she was still alone.

Layne stared up at the tiki torches lining the pool deck. Small flickers of flame snapped within each. Some boy across the pool had pulled one out of the holder and was using it as a fiery lance to jab at his friends.

"Idiot," she muttered.

"He is an idiot," said a voice behind her. "He still thinks he's in middle school."

Her head snapped around, her heart begging for it to be Gabriel, though her brain knew that wasn't his voice.

It was a guy, though, someone she vaguely recognized, though she couldn't place him. Not cute, but good-looking in that stocky jock way, the kind of guy who'd probably be smashing beer cans into his forehead in college. Dark hair, close cropped, with rounded features. It was too dark to make out the color of his eyes.

He nodded at the kid across the pool, who was now swinging the tiki torch like a sword. "I'd bet money he's quoting one of the Star Wars movies right now."

That made her smile. "'*Luke*,'" she intoned. "'*I am your father.*'"

He grinned back. The firelight caught his eyes and made them shine. "A girl who knows her Lucas."

She shrugged, feeling her cheeks warm. "I have a brother. That's the only line I know."

He gestured at the chaise lounge beside her. "Is anyone sitting here?"

Her cheeks burned hotter, and she hoped he couldn't tell. "No. Plenty of room."

Ugh. Why did she say *that*?

But he sat, and he didn't smell like alcohol or smoke like most of the people at the party. "Who's your brother?" he said, casting a look around. "Is he here?"

She snorted with laughter before covering it with a cough. The only thing more awkward than herself at a party would be *Simon* at one. "No. He's a freshman. He plays basketball, but he's on JV."

"Yeah?" His expression brightened. "I'm on JV. What's his name?"

She hesitated, wondering how this would play out. "Simon Forrest."

His eyebrows shot up. "Simon is *your* brother?"

"What is that supposed to mean?"

He smiled and looked away. "Nothing. Simon's all right." Then he glanced back, a wolfish look on his face. His voice was kind of dark, kind of intriguing. "I'm just surprised he has a hot sister."

Yeah, her face was on fire. "I'm sure he'd be surprised to hear that, too."

"Enough about him. What's your name?"

He seemed closer suddenly, and she could feel sweat on her neck under the spill of hair. He hadn't mocked Simon, and she'd been prepared for it. *Simon's all right.* He'd dropped the words easily. Maybe her brother was starting to build a niche for himself.

Maybe it was okay that Gabriel hadn't shown up.

"I'm Layne," she said.

"Layne," he repeated softly. "I like that. Are you here with anyone?"

It was a testament to Kara's and Taylor's efforts that he actually thought she *would* be here with someone. She shook her head, feeling the curls slide across her shoulder.

He shifted even closer, running a finger from her left shoulder down to her elbow. It was her good side, the *safe* side, so she let him.

"Hey," he said in surprise, his voice a bit teasing. "You've got a little muscle on you for being so tiny."

She flushed. "Yeah, well . . ."

"Don't tell me." He gave her a quick up-and-down. "Yoga?"

She laughed. "No." Then she paused. She never talked about horses at school, but she remembered Gabriel's comment about how it was a silly thing to keep secret—especially from a guy who seemed into her.

"I ride horses," she explained. She turned her head to point. "The farm is just outside the neighborhood. I walk to the barn every morning to ride."

"I know those woods. I live over there, on the other side." He paused, and she felt him move even closer. "You ride before school? That's dedicated."

She shrugged and turned back—to find his lips brushing against hers.

Layne sucked in a breath and pulled away.

He didn't pursue her, but his hand kept up the stroking of her upper arm. "You okay?"

She nodded quickly, without thinking. He'd tasted sweet, like peppermint.

He reached up to brush a thumb against her lips and her breath caught.

"I'm glad you came," he murmured.

It softened something inside her. "Me too."

Then he kissed her again, and she let him, just for the sheer experience of it. His mouth was heavier than she was ready for—but it wasn't bad. Just . . . unexpected.

When his lips moved to part hers, she put a hand against his chest.

Again, he stopped, and Layne tried to catch her breath.

His eyes searched her face. "You're very pretty."

She had the same thought she'd had a moment ago. *Maybe it's okay that Gabriel hasn't shown up.*

"Thanks," she whispered.

His mouth found hers again, heavy and warm and wet.

So this was what kissing felt like.

Nice, but she didn't get the big appeal.

She put a hand against his chest a final time. He lifted his head, barely breaking contact. "What is it?"

"I don't even know your name."

He smiled, and she felt his lips move against hers. "It's Ryan," he said. "Ryan Stacey."

Gabriel stared at the dashboard of Hunter's jeep and made no move to get out of the vehicle.

"I don't know what the hell we're doing here," he said.

"Well," said Hunter, "we could always go back to the and watch *Mamma Mia!* with my grandparents. Or could stare at the police scanner for *another* hou nothing to happen. Or maybe—"

"I just don't feel like being at a party." At *this* party. Full of guys who'd know he wasn't allowed on the team. Full of girls who'd tease him about being an idiot.

Hunter's dog stuck his head between the seats, and Gabriel reached up to scratch him behind his ears. "I'll just stay here with the dog."

Hunter sighed and gave him a look. "Come on, baby, don't be like that. Did you pack your Midol?"

"All right, all right." Gabriel climbed out of the car, slamming the door behind him. "I don't even know why I like you."

Heather's place was packed—but then her parties always drew a crowd. There had to be a dozen kids crammed into the hot tub, though no one was braving the pool. Music blared from a sound system on the far side of the pool deck, loud enough that it was a miracle no one had called the cops already.

Gabriel kept thinking of Layne's house down the road. She'd dropped that note on his desk this afternoon. *I'll help you.* That's it. No phone number, nothing.

And she still hadn't called. Lucky him, it was Friday, and he could wonder about it all weekend.

For about two seconds, he had a fleeting hope that she might be here. Taylor had mocked him at lunch, some crap about inviting Layne so they could all "study together," but Gabriel had ignored her until she went away.

Layne *hated* Taylor. She hated Heather Castelline. And this wasn't exactly her crowd.

"Your brother's here," said Hunter, handing him a soda from somewhere.

"I know." He'd figured Nick would be here, had already spotted him across the pool with Quinn.

Nick had spotted him, too, staring at Gabriel for exactly one second before looking away to laugh at something Quinn said. And then he never looked back.

Fine.

"Hey, aren't you the new kid in my American lit class?"

Gabriel turned—but the girl standing there was talking to Hunter. Calla Dean, tall and lithe and probably on as many sports teams as he himself was—though they rarely ran in the same circles. She'd gotten the school volleyball team to the state championships last year as a sophomore. The only reason he knew her was because she'd caught his eye once: Blond hair streaked with blue was chopped off right at her shoulders, and tattooed flames encircled her wrists and crawled up the insides of her forearms.

He would have hit on her, but she was blunt and aggressive and rumor said she played for the other team—in a way that decidedly did *not* mean sports.

Then again, she was looking at Hunter like he was something to eat.

"Yeah," said Hunter. "Aren't you the girl who told Mrs. Harrison you were intimidated by the 'length' of *Moby Dick*?"

"Who isn't?" said Calla, deadpan.

"I don't think I've ever seen you at a party," said Gabriel.

Calla shrugged. "You never know when something interesting might happen." She reached out a hand to touch Hunter's arm, tracing the small tattoo by his elbow. "I like this. It's not Arabic, is it?"

"Farsi."

Her eyes lit with intrigue.

And that was enough for Gabriel. "I'm going to get some food," he said, turning for the grill.

Usually he'd get stopped half a dozen times when crossing ground at a party. Game recaps, plans for the next weekend, practice strategies.

Tonight? Conversation died when he approached.

He grabbed some burgers and dropped onto an empty chaise lounge by the pool, straddling the cushion to set his plate in front of him. The tiki torches flickered in his direction.

Welcome.

'Sup, he thought.

Some kid across the way was swinging a torch with abandon, and Gabriel could feel the flame's excitement at the potential for danger. Cloth, paper, whatever. As soon as the fire found fuel, it would flare.

What an idiot.

Despite the music, the air was quiet here by the pool. Gabriel could feel people looking at him, talking about him, but it was easier to ignore them when he wasn't standing directly in their midst.

And not *everyone* was talking about him. Some kids by the back door were playing cards. The people in the hot tub had a lively interaction going on—the kind that didn't exactly involve a lot of talking. Hunter was still talking to Calla, following her into the house now. *Interesting.* And another couple was going at it hot and heavy at the opposite end of the pool deck. Probably drunk, or they'd never be out here in the open.

He wondered what Layne would do if he walked to her house and started throwing stones at her window.

Gabriel polished off his food and set the plate below his chair, dropping back to stare up at the stars.

A breeze caught the flames and made them flicker.

Play?

He shook his head. *Not now.*

Then a stronger gust of wind whipped across the pool to sprinkle him with water and blow out the three torches surrounding him.

Nick.

Gabriel flung a surge of power into the torch by his twin, making flames shoot high and spray sparks. Girls shrieked and scattered, including Quinn.

Gabriel smiled.

"That wasn't very nice."

He craned his head back. Becca stood there in the darkness. He couldn't make out her expression, but the displeasure in her voice said enough.

Gabriel looked back at the pool. "Maybe *I'm* not very nice."

"Can I sit down?"

He shrugged. "Go ahead. I already lost my wingman."

She moved forward between the lounges, and he expected her to drop onto the one next to him, but she sat on his. She faced him, her hip against his, the warmth in her body carrying through the gauzy skirt she wore.

His eyes flicked up to hers. "Trying to make Chris jealous?"

"No. I'm trying to figure out what's up with you."

"Don't bother."

"Nick doesn't know what he did wrong. You know, he's beating himself up trying to figure it—"

"Becca, stop." He glared out at the pool. "Nick did nothing wrong."

That was the whole problem. Nick never did *anything* wrong.

"He misses you."

Gabriel snorted and gestured to the dark tiki torches. "Yeah, he's got a funny way of showing it." He fished the lighter out of his pocket and stood to relight them.

Really, he couldn't take her closeness right now.

He pulled down the first torch and flicked his lighter. Becca stood next to him, and he watched the firelight dance across her cheeks. She looked worried.

He sighed. "Please stop looking at me like that."

"Are you really starting these fires?" she whispered.

He pulled down the next torch. If he said no, would it make a difference? He could already hear the plea in her tone, the fear behind her whisper.

But then he flicked his lighter, and something beyond Becca caught his eye.

Taylor and Heather had cell phones in their hands, and they were taking pictures—or maybe video—of the couple writhing on the lounge. The girls were giggling, but he couldn't make out everything they were saying.

He let the flame die and nodded in their direction. "What do you think is going on over there?"

Becca turned and her whole body stiffened. "Hey!" she called. She started storming across the pool deck. "Hey!"

God, she was a ballsy chick. Gabriel followed her.

Taylor and Heather were making wolf whistles, egging the couple on. Some big kid was on top of a much smaller girl in boots and a miniskirt. He couldn't see her face behind the guy, but he'd worked her skirt up to her waist and her shirt up to her chest, revealing the edge of a bra. Thank god she had tights on, or she'd be giving quite a show.

The guy's arm was on her shoulder, pinning her there, his hand over her mouth.

The other hand was trying to force the shirt higher. The girl squealed and struggled.

Becca walked right up and punched him in the kidney. "Get off of her, you asshole!"

He barely grunted. Becca was tiny.

Gabriel was not. He slammed the guy into the concrete pool deck.

Ryan Stacey.

"Jesus," said Gabriel. "You really *are* an asshole."

Chris was suddenly there beside him. He must have seen Becca go flying across the pool deck. "Yeah. He is."

"Ohmigod," said Taylor, almost breathless with laughter. "I got all of that. Hey, Ryan, that was the best hundred dollars I ever spent. Who's the prostitute now, bitch?"

Gabriel snapped his head up. The girl was curled against Becca now, and he couldn't see her face.

Ryan was laughing—he didn't even seem to care that his head had cracked on the pavement. Obviously hammered. "No wonder her brother is a deaf retard. She's all deformed under there."

Layne. Gabriel grabbed the front of Ryan Stacey's shirt and punched him in the face. And again. And—

"Gabriel. *Gabriel.*" Someone had his arms. Nick. And Chris. The torches were blazing now, pouring smoke into the sky, illuminating the pool deck like a bonfire. Ryan Stacey's face was a mess. Gabriel wasn't even sure he was still conscious. They'd drawn a small crowd, but Gabriel had his eyes locked on the trembling figure in Becca's arms.

Layne, definitely Layne.

God, he'd been sitting *right over there.*

Gabriel was frozen, torn between going to Layne or breaking every bone in Ryan's body. Followed by Taylor's. Fire was whipping higher into the air, fed by his temper, looking for something more to burn.

"Take their phones," said Becca. "Break them."

"Please," scoffed Taylor. "Like it's not already online."

But Chris snatched them anyway, snapping the cases and throwing the pieces into the pool. The girls didn't look concerned. They looked satisfied.

"And, Gabriel," said Taylor, "your part in this was too perfect. I didn't think you'd show up."

Layne made a choked noise and lifted her head. Her cheeks were red and tear streaked.

Gabriel wanted to break every bone in his own body. He could have stopped this. He'd been *right here*.

"I'm so sorry," he said.

She made that strangled noise again and pushed free of Becca. And then she was running, shoving past people, fighting her way toward the road.

Gabriel went after her.

But a hand caught his arm and pulled him back. Nick.

Gabriel shoved him, hard. "What?" he yelled, hearing his voice break. "What the fuck, Nick, *what?*"

"Here." Nick was staring back at him, his hand out, his eyes almost haunted. "Here. Take the car. Get her out of here."

There was too much to say. Gabriel couldn't speak past the emotion in his throat.

So he closed his fingers around the keys and ran after Layne.

CHAPTER 23

Gabriel caught up to her in Heather's front yard. Layne was stumbling, her hands at her face, her sobbing almost uncontrollable.

He caught her by the arms. Christ, his voice was still breaking. "Layne. Layne, please. Let me—"

She spun, her fists slamming into his chest. For her size, she hit with surprising force, driving her rage into him.

"How *could* you?" she yelled, her voice thick with tears. "How could you do this?"

"Please. I didn't know—"

She hit him again. "How could you hate me so much—"

"I don't hate you." He caught her arms. "I didn't know you were there. I would never—"

"Oh my god, please just let me go. Please."

She was struggling against him, and it made him sick to think of her fighting Ryan Stacey. He let her go.

She staggered across the lawn. "I need to get out of here."

"Let me take you. I can drive you home—"

"I can't go home. Just go away. You did this—"

"Goddamn it, Layne." He caught her again, looking down at her streaked face, her tangled hair. God, she was killing him, with every word, every step. "I did *not* do this. I would *never* do this. And I swear to Christ if you don't let me drive you *some-*

where, I'm going to go back down there and break that guy's *neck*."

Heather's front porch light exploded.

Layne jumped and gave a little cry. She was shaking, and Gabriel had no idea whether it was from what Ryan had done—or from what he was doing right now.

But at least she was looking at him, her eyes wide, searching his face.

"Come on," he said.

She took a deep breath, then nodded.

Gabriel found the car down the road a ways. Layne had her belt buckled and her arms folded tightly across her chest before he even got in, and her eyes were focused out the window. It reminded him of the first night he'd driven her home, when she'd declared so vehemently *I'm not Heather Castelline.*

Obviously.

Gabriel started the engine and drove toward town. He didn't have a clear destination in mind, but she'd said she couldn't go home, and he sure as hell couldn't take her to his.

At the first stop sign he glanced over. "Did he hurt you?"

Her eyes didn't leave the window. "No."

A thousand questions burned his lips, but she was so closed off. She might bolt from the car if he pushed.

He could kill Taylor. He should have told Chris to throw *her* in the pool.

The air felt sharp, sparking with tension. Gabriel reached out and flicked on the radio, keeping the volume low. One of those guitar ballads rolled through the car, something that felt like it should have been a slow song, but really wasn't.

Finally, her arms loosened, just a little. "I'm such an idiot. I should have known."

Her voice had lost the wild emotion and now carried that core of strength he knew lived inside her.

"It's not your fault," he said.

"I know," she said. "Believe me, I've seen all the after-school specials. That girl who helped me—she kept telling me, too."

"Becca. She's my little brother's girlfriend."

Layne swiped at her eyes, looking more angry than tragic now. "Yeah, well, that guy can't take all the blame. I was the moron who showed up."

"What were you doing there, anyway?" he said. "I thought you hated Taylor and Heather and all those girls."

"Oh, I do. Don't worry." She paused, biting at her lip. "They tricked me into going."

"They *tricked* you? How?"

She looked out the window again. "It's not important."

Gabriel let the car drift to a stop at a red light on Ritchie Highway. He turned to look at her.

Layne very obviously did not want to look at him.

"You want a coffee?" he said.

She didn't answer for a moment. "Sure."

So he left her in the car in front of Starbucks, coming back with two steaming cups, a wad of napkins, and a few wet packs the barista had fished from behind the counter at his request.

Layne took them in surprise, ripping one open to wipe at her cheeks. "Thanks."

He drove down to the end of Fort Smallwood Road, to where the pavement turned to crap and a sign announced a county park—though the county seemed to have forgotten about this one long ago. The parking lot wasn't maintained, and the entrance, once gated, was always open. A shame, really, because the property sported a long stretch of beach, though this passageway to the Chesapeake Bay wasn't anywhere you'd want to swim. Sometimes, during the day, there'd be kids on the old swing set, but there were newer ones in nicer parts of the county, so that was rare.

He and Nick came out here to set things on fire all the time.

Gabriel parked the SUV. As usual, the lot was deserted. "There are chairs in the back," he said, "if you want to go sit by the water. Or we can open up the back and sit on the tailgate."

She licked her lips, staring out the window. "Won't we get in trouble for being here?"

"This whole peninsula is a public park, but no one comes down this way anymore." Then he figured out her tone. "We don't have to stay here," he said. "But it's quiet, and no one will bother us."

Layne took a sip of her coffee, wrapping both hands around the cup like a little girl. "Okay." She paused. "The tailgate."

He killed the engine, but left the radio on, the speakers pouring music into the night. The only light came from the dome in the center of the car and the distant industrial plants across the water. Sitting on the tailgate left her face shadowed, almost a silhouette. Crickets and tree frogs sang in the distance, and if he listened carefully, he could pick up the water smacking the rocky breakers.

She perched on the edge of the tailgate, pulling her skirt against her thighs, though there wasn't enough material to cover much at all.

It made him think of Ryan Stacey again, and Gabriel felt his grip tightening on the coffee cup. He gritted his teeth and looked out at the darkness. "I didn't know it was you," he said. "I was sitting like fifteen feet away, and I saw two people making out—"

"We were *not* making out."

"But I could have stopped him—"

"You did. I let him kiss me."

She let him—she let that guy—she—

Layne glanced over. "You stopped him before he could get much farther than that." She picked at the lid of her coffee cup, her voice bitter. No, *rueful*. "I should have known better."

Gabriel needed to get a handle on his thoughts before the car caught on fire. "What on earth made you go to that party?"

"It's stupid." She pushed a curled strand of hair back from her face. "My mother has always wanted me to be like those girls. She became friends with all their moms and begged me to spend time with their daughters. She used to buy me expensive clothes. Every other day, she'd come home from the mall with another bag from some hot new store. I never wore them. Some I threw in the charity bin behind the school. Some I shoved in the back of my closet. I hated them. I hated *her*."

He remembered the tentative conversation in her bedroom. "You didn't want to be perfect."

"Sort of." She hesitated. "No, I could never be perfect, and she knew it. I think that was the point. It was all this big cover-up. The clothes, the horses, it was all one big sham. Her perfect, *im*perfect daughter."

Gabriel remembered Ryan's little comment before he'd punched the shit out of him. *She's all deformed under there.*

It made him think of that moment in the woods, when he would have kissed her. His hands on her ribs, and she'd pulled away.

Had he misread that entirely?

Layne turned and looked at him, her eyes piercing and sharp. "How much did you see? When he was . . . you know. How much did you see?"

Gabriel sighed and ran a hand through his hair. "It was dark," he said truthfully. "Not much of anything."

"Come on." Her voice was hard.

Gabriel shifted to look at her. The light at her back made the red turtleneck almost glow. "Really. He didn't get the shirt over your bra. Honestly, with the light, I bet Taylor couldn't catch much of anything on her phone."

"God, she is such a bitch." Layne made a disgusted sound. "I can't believe you slept with her."

Gabriel almost dropped his cup. "*What*? Who the hell said I slept with her?"

"No one. But . . . in class . . ." She faltered. Even in the dim light, he could see Layne's cheeks turn pink. "She said—"

"I have never slept with Taylor. Jesus, there's a locker room joke that—" He shook his head. "Never mind."

"That *what*?"

He took a quick sip of coffee. "You know that stupid saying in sex ed about how when you sleep with someone, you're sleeping with everyone that person has had sex with?"

"Yeah?"

"Let's just say I have no desire to sleep with the entire team."

Layne didn't look entirely convinced. "Today. In class. She mentioned *last year*."

This girl was too smart for her own good. He sighed. "All right, look. I was at this *one* party, and I was sitting on a couch, and she came over and climbed in my lap. I didn't exactly shove her away. But I did *not* sleep with her, and we barely spent ten minutes together. She's on the cheer squad. I play a lot of sports. She flirts with any guy she sees, including half the faculty."

Layne settled back onto the tailgate, staring out at the night again.

"Come on," he said. "She just says those things to get a reaction."

"It works."

"I still don't understand how she tricked you."

"Maybe I'm just an idiot."

"Oh, I know that's not true," he said. "Tell me. Did that loser just walk over and start assaulting you?"

"No." Her voice was very small. "He was nice. I liked him. He didn't even assault me. I told you: It didn't *start* like that."

Gabriel snorted. "Couldn't you tell he was drunk off his ass?"

"No!" Sudden anger swung her around. "How am I supposed to know when someone is drunk?"

"Layne—"

"He didn't *smell* like beer. He wasn't slurring his words. Or do you mean, he had to be drunk off his ass to be into someone like—"

"Hey." His voice was sharper than he intended, but it got her to shut up. God, she was crazy if she thought someone would have to be drunk to take a second glance at her. The way she was sitting had the skirt splayed across her lap, leaving a long expanse of spandexed leg stretching into the darkness. Anger flushed her cheeks, and curls of hair fell along one shoulder. Her eyes caught the starlight, making him want to—

"What?" she demanded.

Gabriel jerked his eyes away. He wanted to tell her everything he was thinking, how she looked striking right now, beautiful in the darkness. How he wished he'd known she would be at the party. How he would have been dragging Hunter out of the car instead of the other way around.

He brought his cup to his lips. "Nothing."

She scowled out at the parking lot. "So is this like your *place*?"

"My *place*?"

"Where you bring girls."

"Yes. I bring girls to this run-down parking lot all the time." He gestured with his cup. "I have a sign-up sheet nailed to that tree. Now that you mention it"—he glanced at his watch—"we should probably wrap this up."

Her eyes were intense, challenging, fixed on his. "Do you have a five-minute limit before you start getting mean?"

"I don't know, Layne. Do you have a five-minute limit before you start getting defensive?"

She clamped her mouth shut and turned to face the darkness.

As usual, he didn't know if he owed her an apology—or deserved one.

He picked at the lid of his cup. "Nicky and I come out here sometimes," he said. "I've never brought a girl here."

"Never?" Her voice was some combination of skeptical and hopeful.

"What do you think, that I'm some kind of thug player who'll screw anything in a skirt?"

She didn't answer, and that was answer enough.

"Wow," he said. "I can't believe you think I'd beat the shit out of Ryan Stacey just to drag you to the middle of nowhere so I could—"

"Hey." Her eyes flashed up to his. "Now who's defensive?"

"Touché."

They sat in silence for a while, until the crickets were deafening, and Gabriel began to wonder if he should just offer to drive her home.

"It's funny," she said quietly. "You were the first person I talked to this morning, and you'll probably be the last I talk to tonight."

This morning. It felt like a lifetime ago. He wondered if she had any idea that Ryan Stacey had been trapping her little brother inside a locker after scrawling insults all over his chest.

I let him kiss me.

No. She couldn't possibly know.

"Tell me your secrets," she said.

He looked up. "My secrets?"

Layne drew her legs up to sit cross-legged on the tailgate, her hands in her lap. It put half her face in light, half in shadow, like a challenging angel trying to decide between good and evil. "You said yesterday that any time someone comes close to figuring you out, you pick a fight. You did it this morning in the woods, and you're doing it now. If you're not this thug player who can't pass math, then what are you hiding?"

"What are *you* hiding?"

"I asked first."

He looked out at the night again—but his heart was running a marathon in his chest. "You already know Nick was taking my tests for me."

She cocked her head to the side and gave a little shrug. "That's not even a secret. That's like me saying, *I have a deaf little brother.*"

Gabriel shrugged. Truths were clawing at his lips, begging to escape. God, to tell *someone.*

No way. Like he could sit here, trapped on the tailgate, and spill everything. *Gee, well, I can control fire. Oh, and those articles in the paper? They're talking about me. And maybe I should mention that I've been thinking about your arms around me all day. Or how I've wanted to kiss you for days, but right now that would make me no better than Ryan Stacey . . .*

Yeah, that would be great. He drew a choking breath and fought for words.

"How about," she said, her voice careful, "I get a question, then you get a question."

That made him smile. "Like truth or dare?"

She blushed and her eyes dropped. "I've never played that."

"Come on, Layne, kids play that when they're *ten*."

"Not *all* kids."

She could be so fierce one minute, yet so innocent the next, and it was seriously *making him crazy*. "All right, go. Truth."

"I told you I don't know how to play."

Gabriel leaned in and whispered, "The name of the game *might* be a giveaway."

Her eyes flicked up, sparking with defiance, and for a breathless moment he regretted not choosing *dare*.

"Truth," she said. "Why did you start cheating in math?"

At least that slammed the brakes on his train of thought. "Because I stopped passing. In seventh grade."

"When your parents died." Her voice was tentative, but it wasn't a question.

"Yeah. I'd never been an A student or anything, but after that . . . I didn't even want to be at school, much less do any work." He shrugged and leaned against the side of the tailgate to look at her. "I was in danger of being held back, and things were already so messed up. Nick started doing it for me, just to get us through the year."

But Gabriel remembered that first week of eighth grade, when he'd decided he was done cheating, that he didn't need his brother's help. He'd struggled to figure out how to solve every problem. Losing three months to his family mess, then another three to summer hadn't exactly set him up to start pre-algebra. But he'd been ready to put his brain to a task, to do something *normal*, something routine, when so much of his life wasn't.

Then Nick had come into his room with an identical paper. "Here," he'd said, and his voice had been almost proud. "I did your math."

Gabriel glanced across at Layne, who was still waiting, still listening. "Nick wasn't into sports or anything. He needed to be doing something, to be helping. To have a purpose. I didn't want to take it away from him." He snorted. "Christ, that sounds lame."

"No," she said. "No, I think I get it."

"At first I would do the work and throw it away. But I hated lying to him, so I stopped. Then I hit high school and made varsity freshman year, and it was just one less class to worry about. Now I'm so far behind that I don't think I'll ever make up the difference."

"I'll help you," she said.

"You can try." He almost reached out to push the hair back from her face. "Your turn."

She held his eyes. "Truth."

"How did Taylor get you to that party, really?" He gave her a quick once-over. "Especially looking like that."

She shifted to look out at the darkness. "I changed my mind. Dare."

Gabriel slid his cell phone out of his pocket and held it out. "Okay. Here. I dare you to call your father and tell him you're sitting in a dark parking lot with me."

"Ooooh." She glared up at him without any real malice. "I don't think I like this game."

He smiled. "Come on, pony up."

She folded her arms across her stomach and sighed. Her voice came out very small, warring with the crickets and water. "Taylor told me that she'd talked to you and that you hoped to see me there. My friend Kara picked my clothes."

Oh.

Suddenly he felt like he'd had a hand in this, though he hadn't known anything about it. "Layne," he said. "Taylor never talked to me. I swear—"

"I know! I figured it out, okay? That's why I feel like such an idiot."

Navigating this conversation made controlling fire seem easy. "But I would have—"

"Don't. Please don't."

"Layne, let me—"

"Your turn!"

He drew back and sighed. "Truth."

"How did your parents die?"

The words felt like a weapon, as if she were trying to hurt him for asking her something that obviously left her off balance. But his parents' deaths were just another bolt of guilt that struck him on a daily basis.

"In a fire," he said flatly. "They were arguing with the parents of some kids who used to hassle us. The house burned down. Not everyone got out."

She stared at him for the longest moment. "Really?"

"Yeah, *really*. Why would I make that up?"

Her mouth worked like she wanted to say something, but the words couldn't quite make it out. He knew that expression, and he couldn't take one more ounce of pity. So he made his voice hard. "*Your* turn."

She licked her lips. "Okay," she said slowly. "Truth."

He wanted to fire an arrow back, something to make her flinch, too. "Why did Ryan Stacey say you were *deformed*?"

Of course it did make her flinch, but it made him feel like an ass.

She didn't look at him, but she answered. "Because I have scars all the way up the right side of my body."

"Yeah? From what?"

"From a house fire," she said. "My house burned down when I was five."

Shit.

Now he was the one staring. "Layne," he ground out. "Layne, I'm—"

"I really don't like this game." Her legs swung off the tailgate, and her feet crunched on the rough pavement.

"Stop," he said. "Layne—"

"See, Gabriel?" she called over her shoulder. "I'm not perfect either, right?"

Then she was running, and the darkness swallowed her up.

CHAPTER 24

The short skirt made for easy running. The scent of grass and water was in Layne's nose, and she really had no idea where she was going, except *away*. The sound of her breath filled her ears, ragged and almost sobbing. Thank god the parking lot was empty, because she couldn't see a thing except for the industrial plants across the water. Pavement gritted beneath her boots, then grass as she stumbled and almost missed a curb.

She couldn't believe she'd told Gabriel about the fire.

Really, like it mattered. Her scars would be all over the Internet tomorrow.

She'd kept a secret for ten years, and now *everyone* knew.

"Layne. Stop."

Of course he'd follow. He didn't even sound breathless. "Go away," she yelled. "I'll call my dad to come get me. Just—"

The ground went out from under her. She sucked in a breath, flailing for balance. Arms came around her waist from behind, jerking her back, keeping her feet in the air.

She fought, feeling his chest at her back, but he was too strong.

"Damn it," he said, his voice strained. "Do you *want* to go in the water?"

That forced her still. Red and white lights still hung in the distance, warring with the stars. Now that she wasn't running, the sound of waves hitting the rocks was unmistakable.

And right in front of her.

"The water?" she said numbly.

He put her feet on the ground, but he didn't let her go. "Yeah. Water. Did you miss the part where I said we're parked on a peninsula?"

"Wow," she whispered. Talk about a night going from bad to worse.

"If I let you go, are you going to take off again?"

She shook her head. But she didn't want him to let her go, either.

He did anyway. "You're lucky you didn't break an ankle."

"Thanks." She still hadn't turned to face him. "For catching me." Then she added, "And for punching Ryan. I should have thanked you for that before."

"Oh, you don't have to thank me for that. He's lucky I left the party to run after you."

The heat in his voice made her shiver. She'd seen blood on Ryan's face.

But she couldn't summon the righteous indignation she'd felt in the hallway when Gabriel had hassled those bullies. The only things at risk that day had been school papers and hurt feelings. She had no idea what Ryan had planned—or what else Taylor had paid him for—but she wasn't naïve enough to think he would have stopped there.

"Are you cold?" said Gabriel. He hadn't stepped back, but he wasn't close enough to touch anymore. "There's a fleece blanket in the car."

Layne shook her head and turned away, keeping her eyes on the lights across the water. She wondered if he was thinking about her scars. For the first time, she understood that expression about the gorilla in the corner of the room. She'd always thought being burned in a house fire was one of the worst possible things that could ever happen. Then he went and yanked the rug out from under her, saying his parents had *died* in one. For some reason it made her feel ridiculous and furious all at once.

"You know," he said quietly, "you don't have to keep running from me."

"I don't know what you're talking about." But she did.

"I might pick fights, but *you* run."

Layne whirled. Starlight traced shadows across his features, and she was glad for the darkness.

"You're wrong." She stepped up and poked him in the chest. "*You* ran from *me* on the trail."

He knocked her hand away. "Yeah, after *you* pulled away."

He was so close, almost stealing her breath. She fumbled for words. "Well, I didn't know what *you*—"

Gabriel kissed her.

Thank god his hands were there, catching her arms, because her knees didn't feel up to the job of keeping her on her feet. He tasted like coffee and caramel and sugar. She'd always imagined he would be rough, but he wasn't. He was gentle, cautious, drawing at her lips in a way that pulled a sound from her throat and made her want to press up against him.

Oh. This was what all the fuss was about.

His hands slid up her arms to find her face, his fingers tangling in her hair. His kiss grew more insistent, parting her lips. At the first brush of his tongue, she gasped and knew her knees were going to give out.

But then Gabriel stepped back, his hands braced on her shoulders. She was left shaking there in the middle of the path, wind coming off the water to whip through the space between them.

"I'm sorry." His voice was rough, almost ashamed. "I didn't think . . . after the way that asshole treated you—"

She shook her head fiercely. "No—it's fine—"

"I should have waited."

"I'm glad you didn't."

Her breath stumbled when the words escaped, and she felt her cheeks burn.

But he smiled. "Yeah?"

She couldn't move. Right then, she realized he'd been right, about the running. She *wanted* to run, before his hold on her heart got any tighter.

He leaned closer, until she could see his eyes. The smile was gone. "Do you want me to let you go?"

No. Never. She closed her eyes and nodded.

A hesitation, then, "I think you're lying."

She was. But in what freakish world would a guy like Gabriel Merrick be standing with her in the dark, at the water's edge, sharing kisses and secrets?

He closed that space between them again, until the line of his body just brushed hers. She couldn't breathe.

"Do you want me to let you go?" he said again.

She swallowed. "No."

He dropped his head and ran his lips along the edge of her jaw, and the warmth of his breath made her shiver and lean into him. His hands slid down her arms to catch her waist.

She froze and grabbed his wrists.

He went still and spoke against her skin. "Does it hurt?"

Layne shook her head, feeling fire on her cheeks for an entirely different reason. She kept hearing Ryan's voice. *She's all deformed under there.*

God, she hated him. Them. Everyone.

Don't cry. Don't.

But her emotions were all over the place, and she could barely keep them contained. She didn't even realize Gabriel had pulled her along the path until she felt wood planks against the backs of her knees and he was saying, "Sit."

A bench. She sat. The wood felt rough through her tights, but sturdy. The tears had held back so far, and she said a quick prayer of thanks.

"You should probably take me home," she said.

He leaned in to brush the hair back from her face, and it felt so good that she wanted to catch his hand and hold it there. But she didn't.

"Do you really want me to?" he said.

No, she didn't. She shook her head and looked out at the inky water.

He leaned closer. "Want to play more truth or dare?"

I dare you to kiss me like that again.

"Truth," she whispered.

"Truth. Hmm." He stroked his thumb against her mouth, then brushed his lips against her cheek, moving to kiss the curve of her ear. "Who's a better kisser? Me or jerkoff Stacey?"

It was so unexpected that she burst out laughing. "You," she said. "Ugh, he was all slobbery and—"

"Okay, okay, don't need the visual." He paused. "Truth."

She sobered. "Do you think I'm a freak?"

"No." He was playing with the edge of her turtleneck now, running his finger along her neck in a way that made her wish she'd said to hell with the scars and had worn a tank top.

But then she caught his hand again. "Don't you *care*?"

"Care?"

Anger had her shifting on the bench, ready to unleash the rage she should have poured into that idiot by the pool. "That I'm all *deformed*?"

"I think you're beautiful," he said. "I've wanted to kiss you since the day you fixed my test, when you stood up to me in the hallway."

She brushed his hand away. "You have not."

"Yes. I have. I didn't even tell Nicky about you, and I tell him everything." He paused, and his voice found an edge. "Almost everything."

Layne studied his profile in the darkness. He'd told her this morning that he and his twin weren't speaking. She wondered what had happened there.

But that edge in his voice warned her to tread carefully. If she asked, he might not tell her, and this tentative trust would be shot to hell. They'd be back at square one.

She didn't want to turn back. Not now.

"I've never told anyone everything." She took a deep breath. "I've never told anyone *any* of it."

Everything felt fragile again. She stared at him in the darkness, wanting to take that final leap, unsure whether he'd catch her.

And then, just like when she was bolting blindly for the water, he did.

"I'll keep your secrets," he said softly.

She looked back at the water. "The fire was a retaliation against my father. He's a good attorney, but he doesn't win everything. Some guy went to jail, and his friends were mad. I don't know all the details, because I was five, and my dad doesn't like to talk about it. Because Simon is deaf, he can't hear smoke detectors. There was fire everywhere—they'd thrown glass jars of gasoline into the house. When it all started, my mother went looking for Simon. She didn't know my father had already gotten him out. And she was so busy searching his room that she didn't even think to check mine. The firemen pulled me out, but it was too late. I'd climbed into my closet, and the wall burned through the back—"

Her voice broke, and she told herself to knock it off. It's not like she hadn't lived with this for *years*. "I remember waking up in the hospital, and my mom was crying. She kept asking me, 'Why didn't you get out, Layne? Why didn't you get out?' For *years*, I felt so guilty, like I'd done something wrong. I did everything I could to please her, like wearing the perfect little clothes she'd buy me, or with the horseback riding, going to every perfect little show she wanted. It wasn't until I was twelve, when everyone was wearing those stupid shirts with the shoulder cut out, you know? I wanted to wear one. I begged for one, and she finally snapped, 'But, Layne, people will see your scars. What will they *think*?'

"I felt like such an idiot. All those boots and long-sleeved dresses. Horseback riding, for god's sake! One of the only sports you have to do *fully clothed*! I'd been so desperate to please her that I never realized she was trying to hide *her* mistake. But by then I'd been hiding the scars for so many years that I had to keep them a secret. What eighth grader wants to walk into school and declare she has scars all over her body? But people noticed anyway. I mean, when you wear long sleeves in May, people start thinking you're weird. But I stopped wearing her fancy clothes. Every time she bought me something, I knew it was a cover-up for the scars."

Gabriel was quiet for a moment. "How the hell do you live with her?"

"I don't." Layne paused, unsure whether to keep going. This next part was fresh, and the hardest. "She walked out the week after school started. Moved in with some guy she'd met at the country club. She told our father she was sick of trying to make a silk purse out of a sow's ear. Get it? She was sick of trying to make a perfect family out of a bunch of *freaks*."

"So now you're stuck with your father."

She swung her head around, hearing the derision in his voice. "My dad's not usually like . . . like he was with you. He's going through a lot. My mom was a bitch to him, too, but I don't think he ever thought she'd cheat on him. She always blamed him for the fire. She wanted him to quit his job—and he'd counter that she loved spending the money. She was the one who put Simon in a private school, saying it was better for him, but I finally figured out that he was just one more imperfection she was trying to hide . . ."

Gabriel reached out and ran a finger along her cheekbone, and she didn't realize until then that she was crying. "I'm sorry," he said. "I didn't know."

"No one does." She sniffed. "Until now, and Taylor's going to put that stupid video all over the Internet."

"It's Friday night. People will forget all about it by Monday." He paused, running a finger across her cheek again. "And I'll be surprised if people even believe it's you."

She looked up at him. "You will? Why?"

He picked up a curl of hair from her shoulder. "Because you haven't just been keeping the scars hidden; you've been keeping sexy Layne hidden."

"I am *not* sexy."

"You're lucky I didn't jump you when we were sitting on the tailgate."

"Shut up."

His hand found her knee, and he leaned in to kiss her neck. "Really, you're lucky I'm not jumping you right now."

His hand slid along the outside of her thigh, not too high, just inside the hemline of her skirt. The touch stole every thought from her head. "And you're not . . . you're not freaked out . . . by the . . . um . . ."

"No. I think you're beautiful. And I'm no stranger to fucked-up families."

And then he was kissing her again. The addictive pull of his mouth almost had her crawling into his lap. Her hands bunched in his shirt, pulling him closer. His fingers didn't venture higher, but teased along the edge of her skirt, brushing against her so lightly that she almost couldn't stand it. She'd never thought anyone would touch her this way—she'd never *wanted* anyone to touch her this way. But now that he was being so careful, the building heat in her body made her want to rip all her clothes off.

Layne always rolled her eyes in health class when they talked about hormones getting out of control. But right now, she could barely remember her name. She totally got how someone could forget something like a silly little condom.

Suddenly Gabriel was laughing. "How someone could forget *what*?"

She almost fell off the bench. "I said that out *loud*?"

"Yeah." He leaned closer, his breath against her jaw. "Just what were you thinking about?"

"Health class," she squeaked.

His cell phone chimed. Thank god.

Gabriel sat back to fish it out of his pocket. It threw light on his face, but she couldn't figure out his expression.

"What's wrong?" she said.

He shook his head. "Nothing." He held up the phone so she could read the text. "Nick wants to make sure you're all right."

She read the screen.

All OK w the girl?

She took it out of his hands, oddly touched. "But he doesn't even know me."

"Nick's like that. Always does the right thing."

She glanced up from the phone, hearing the tension in his voice. "You still owe me a secret."

"One is enough for tonight." He took the phone back and tapped out a quick text. The phone chimed almost immediately, and he sighed and shoved it into his pocket before she could see what his brother had said.

She tried to figure out his expression. "You all right?"

His voice was closed off now. "I should probably take you home, before your dad sends out a search party."

So that was that. She bit at her lip, wondering how to fix this.

He stood. "It's late."

Oh. Loud and clear. She nodded. "Okay."

But when they were walking, he reached down and took her hand. "You doing anything tomorrow?"

His fingers were sending bolts of electricity up her arm, and she shook her head. "I don't think so."

He leaned down and brushed a kiss against her temple. "Maybe if you actually use that number I wrote in your notebook, we could figure something out."

Gabriel sat in the car, staring up at his house for the second night in a row. The porch lights were on, but the lower level lights weren't. The front step: empty. Both front windows on the second level were dark, but one was Chris's and one was his, so that didn't mean much.

He'd been tempted to drive to Hunter's, but that would probably give Michael an excuse to report him for auto theft or something.

And then there was the subtle accusation in Nick's second text message.

Gabriel pulled the phone out of his pocket and looked at it again, like he couldn't remember three words.

You coming home?

Simple enough, but full of subtext. Did Nick expect him to be out all night? Was this a challenge? A warning that Nick would be waiting to hash things out?

And then there was Layne.

Christ, Gabriel could have sat in that parking lot with her all night. He'd never been with a girl so perfectly . . . imperfect. She got it. She got *him*. He'd been ready to tell her. About the fires, about everything. He'd warmed up to it, telling her about his parents' deaths.

But then she'd told him about her scars. What was he supposed to say to that?

Funny thing: I actually started *the fire that killed my parents.*

Gabriel punched the steering wheel.

His cell phone chimed. Nick again.

You can come in. Mike is out.

What? Seriously? It was almost midnight. Curiosity was enough to shove Gabriel out of the car.

But when he made it to the second floor, he looked at Nick's door sitting a few inches open. Alt rock music was on low, sneaking into the hallway. No feminine laughter. No Quinn.

Nick was waiting for him.

Gabriel hesitated. He wished those text messages had come with some kind of sign, whether Nick was pissed or exasperated or just completely done with him. Hell, a freaking *emoticon* would have been helpful.

His own room sat pitch-dark at the opposite end of the hall-way. A black hole. Gabriel eased around the creaky spot in the floor and slid past his twin's room. Once in his own, he flung his duffel bag onto the ground and shut the door, closing the dark around himself. He sighed and kicked his shoes into the well of blackness under the bed. Maybe Nick hadn't heard him. Maybe he thought he was still out in the car.

"You are so predictable."

Gabriel swore and fumbled for the light switch.

Nick was straddling his desk chair backward, his arms folded on the backrest.

"What the hell is *wrong* with you?" Gabriel snapped. "Why are you sitting here in the dark?"

His twin shrugged. "Because I knew you'd walk right past my room."

This would be easier if Nick wanted to start throwing punches. Gabriel sighed. "Look. It's late—"

"Did you get the girl home all right?"

"Layne. Her name is Layne. And yes." Though he'd had to park three houses down to watch her walk up the sidewalk. He hesitated. "Thanks for letting me take the car."

"You're welcome."

Silence clung to the air. Nick could read a lot from a silence, Gabriel knew. The air would whisper to him as strongly as fire did to Gabriel. That didn't make gaps in strained conversation any easier to fill.

He fought not to fidget. "Where's Michael?"

"He was meeting someone for coffee." Nick shook his watch straight on his wrist. "That was at seven."

Gabriel picked up on the note in his voice. "Someone?"

"He said it was an old friend from school."

"A girl?"

"He didn't say."

Gabriel had a pretty good idea, anyway.

Then Nick offered, "He spent a long time getting ready. Said, and I quote, 'Don't wait up.'"

"That sneaky bastard." Gabriel dropped onto the corner of his bed, bemused. "He's going out with Hannah."

Nick raised an eyebrow. "Who's Hannah?"

Gabriel snapped his eyes up. That comment hammered home just how disconnected he'd been from Nick over the last few days.

If his twin didn't know about Hannah, that meant Michael had kept his promise about the night Gabriel accidentally set the woods on fire.

But Gabriel couldn't explain Hannah without revealing it himself.

Could he tell Nick about the fires?

No. Nick wouldn't approve. He wouldn't understand.

He'd tell Michael. They'd make him stop.

"Hannah is just a girl." Gabriel couldn't meet his brother's eyes. He focused on the joints of the chair. "She used to go to school with Michael."

Nick sighed, obviously not convinced. "All right, forget about Hannah. Forget about Layne, even. Keep your secrets, since you obviously can't talk to me anymore."

The last bit wasn't said with spite or contempt—which Gabriel had been expecting. Just furious resignation, which was a hundred times worse.

"Look. Nicky—"

"I'm surprised you came home. Chris said you had a bag full of clothes." Nick's gaze went to the duffel bag Gabriel had dropped by the door.

"That's not about you." The words almost hurt to say.

"What's it about, then?"

Every question was another tick toward an explosion, like a bomb counting down. It didn't help that Nick was sitting there, completely implacable. "It's about Michael."

"You mean, because he thinks you're starting fires?"

Gabriel flinched. But what could he say?

"It might help," said Nick, "if you would *deny* it."

"I shouldn't *have to* deny it." The lights flickered.

But that's all. The power waited for direction. Gabriel held his breath.

Nick glanced up, and some of the anger leaked out of his voice. "You want to talk about it?"

Gabriel tried to dial back the power. *Chill out.*

It flickered again, almost a refusal—but then settled, easing back into a normal rhythm. Gabriel let a breath out. "No."

"Fine." Nick's voice sharpened right back up. "You want to talk about why you couldn't give me a heads up that we'd been accused of *cheating*?"

Oh. *Damn.*

"They said something to you?"

"Of course!" Nick straightened in the chair. Wind whipped through the screen to ruffle his hair. "Damn it, Gabriel, you might not give a crap if you graduate, but I sure do."

Of course he cared. What did Nick think, that he was too stupid to bother? It took three tries to speak, and even then, it came out strangled. "When they asked you . . . what did you say?"

"I said I'd stop! What the hell do you think I said? You know, she asked if I was taking your tests in other classes. She said cheating was grounds for expulsion. She said this could go on my transcript—"

"Oh, who cares." Gabriel snorted. "You think the people who hire us to plant perennials are going to check your high school transcript?"

"No, but colleges might."

College? Shock almost shoved Gabriel off the bed. Nick had never said one word about doing anything more after high school than helping Michael with the family business. "You want to go to *college?*"

Now Nick looked sheepish. "Well. I knew you weren't interested—"

"Where the hell are you going to get *money* for college?"

"I don't know. There's aid, and . . . look, I haven't even applied yet. It's just something I'm thinking about."

When Nick *thought about* something, it wasn't a whim. Nick would have schools in mind. He might be thinking about moving *away.*

Away.

Gabriel had spent two days barely saying a word to his twin, and it felt like water torture. He couldn't imagine weeks passing. Months.

When they were little, they'd shared a room, a bed on each wall. For years, Gabriel had thought a twin bed meant only *twins* slept in them. If they dressed in the same pajamas—which had been almost every night—Mom would say they looked like a pair of bookends. Half the time, Gabriel would wake up in the morning to find Nick had climbed into bed with him sometime in the night.

Nick had grown out of that sometime in elementary school.

Only to start back up again when their parents died.

He didn't do that anymore, of course. But now he was just one room down the hall.

Not down the road.

Or in another state.

Gabriel glared at him. His voice was tight, and probably sounded angry. "Why didn't you say something?"

More wind streaked through the room, a good ten degrees colder than the last gust. "Yeah? When should I have said something? When you were insulting Quinn? Or maybe when you tried to burn the house down—"

"I did not *try to burn the house down*." Gabriel was off the bed now, his hands curled into fists. Electricity pulsed in the walls, ready to flare.

The air turned cold enough to bite bare skin, thin and hard to breathe. "That's right," said Nick. "You don't have to try, do you? You're pretty good at destroying things all by your—"

"*Enough.*"

Gabriel jumped. Michael stood in the doorway, a hand braced on each side of the frame. His breath fogged in the air.

"Nick"—he sighed—"would you give us a minute?"

Nick disentangled himself from the chair, but he did it slowly, and the room didn't get any warmer until he'd pushed past Michael to step into the hallway.

He didn't glance back once. Not like Gabriel was looking.

Michael remained in the doorway. Gabriel didn't want to look at him, either.

"You're home," said Michael.

"Yeah." Gabriel picked at a thread on the cuff of his jeans. "Not out destroying any lives tonight."

"Very funny."

"How was your *date*?"

"It wasn't a date." Michael paused. "I was trying to make sure they're not still investigating you."

For some reason, that was infuriating. "So you're just stringing her along to find out what she knows? Christ, Michael, that's kind of a dickhead move—"

"You want to tell me what's really going on?"

"There's *nothing* going on." At least this was a brother he could *fight* with. Gabriel stood. Got close. "I'm home. Go spend your worry on someone else."

Michael didn't move.

Gabriel shoved him. "*Go.*"

He watched Michael draw himself up, ready to hit back. But then his brother just shifted toward the door. "Thanks."

Nonplussed, Gabriel stared after him. "For what?"

His brother paused with the door halfway closed. "For coming home. I'm glad you did."

Then the door clicked shut, closing Gabriel in.

And closing his brothers out.

CHAPTER 25

Saturdays usually meant landscaping work with Michael. The hell with that.

Since he had the car keys, Gabriel was out the door before anyone else was up. He threw the duffel bag in the backseat, just in case. Nick could use those college-bound brains to figure out a way to get around.

Gabriel grabbed a cup of coffee and a breakfast sandwich from Dunkin' Donuts, but that didn't kill any more than fifteen minutes. He decided to test the bounds of friendship.

Do you want to practice today?

Hunter's return text took a minute.

Are you seriously texting me at 6 am?

Gabriel smiled.

Thought you might be up for a 10 mile run before we light hay bales on fire. Go back to bed, slacker.

He set the phone down and took another sip of coffee.

His phone chimed almost immediately. Gabriel glanced at the display and nearly choked on that sip.

Sounds good. Give me 15 mins.

They ran on the B&A Trail, a paved track that stretched from Annapolis nearly to Baltimore. This early in the morning, it was mostly deserted aside from a few lone cyclists and joggers out to take advantage of the chill in the air.

After the fourth mile, Gabriel glanced over. Hunter had looked a little bleary eyed when he'd picked him up, and he hadn't said much in the car, but he was keeping up without any trouble.

Then again, they weren't breaking any records. "You know, I was kidding," said Gabriel. "We don't have to run ten miles."

Hunter didn't slow. "What, you're tired already?"

Gabriel was, a little. He'd run hard yesterday, and he was going on his third restless night.

"Just making sure you can keep up. Thought you might have had a late night with Calla Dean."

A wry glance. "Don't worry." Then Hunter stepped up the pace.

Bastard. Gabriel pushed to keep up. He was fit. He could do this, no problem.

"You know," he said, "Becca tried to talk to me last night." He glanced over. "About the fires."

"She tries to talk to me, too." A pause to catch his breath. "She wants to know if I *know what you're doing.*"

"What do you tell her?"

"I tell her you suck at Xbox." Another pause, another break for breath. "I think her dad's putting pressure on her."

"Because of the Guides?"

"Yeah. But we're being careful."

"Are you worried?"

"Does it matter? I can't sit around doing *nothing*. Could you?"

Gabriel thought about that for a minute. "No. I couldn't." Then he had to shut up, because Hunter stepped up the pace *again*.

Beyond the seventh mile, Gabriel was really starting to feel it.

They were holding a seven-minute-mile pace, and his legs ached. His lungs burned. That stitch in his side that had been a minor irritant at mile three now felt like a red-hot iron poker.

The one time he wanted to pull energy from the sun, and the sky was overcast.

"If you want to stop," said Hunter, with zero strain in his voice, "I can swing back for you when I'm done."

"We'll see who's lying in a pile at the end of the trail."

"Race you to the car?"

"Yeah, I'll *wait* for you at the car."

And then, though his legs screamed in protest, Gabriel leapt forward into a sprint.

Damn, it felt good to compete, to do something he could *control*. He hadn't realized how much he'd miss the easy camaraderie of a team, the physical strain of working toward one common purpose. On the field or on the course, or hell, here on the trail, the objective was clear. Make a basket. Put the ball in the goal. Win the race.

Pass the test?

Gabriel wondered if that's why this guy was starting these fires. It was so much easier to send things on a path toward destruction.

At the turnoff for the parking lot at the trailhead, Gabriel didn't slow. Hunter was right there, not letting up. They veered around a couple with bikes, almost trampled a mother navigating a jogging stroller, and shot onto the parking lot, spraying pea gravel with every step.

He stretched out a hand to slap the tailgate of the SUV.

Right at the same time as Hunter.

"Damn it," he gasped.

At least Hunter was breathing as hard as he was, his hands braced on his knees. "All right. Another five miles?"

"Shut up." Gabriel smiled.

They dug for change in the center console and bought bottles of water from the machine at the ranger station by the trailhead. Then they collapsed in the grass under an oak tree. The sun was starting to break free of the clouds, and Gabriel pushed damp strands of hair off his face.

"Figures," he said. "Now the sun comes out."

Hunter took a long pull of water. "Do you usually run with Nick?"

"Nah. He'll go if I drag him out of the house, but not for any kind of distance. Chris will run in the spring, when baseball starts."

Hunter peeled at the label on his bottle. "I used to run with my dad."

"Was he slow, too?"

That earned a smile and a punch in the arm. "No." A pause. "We were going to run the Marine Corps marathon this year."

Gabriel recognized that hollow note in Hunter's voice. Sometimes he had to fight to keep it out of his own.

Hunter shrugged. "Really, I forgot all about it, what with moving here and all." He hesitated. "Last night, I got an e-mail with the details, when to pick up the packets, stuff like that. I deleted it—I mean, you know."

Gabriel nodded and kept his eyes on his own water bottle. "Yeah."

"Then you texted me this morning and asked if I wanted to run ten miles, and—"

"Shit." Gabriel straightened. Another day, off to a raring start with a fuckup. "Man, I'm sorry. I didn't—"

"No!" Hunter looked at him, hard. "I'm glad. It was . . . good."

"All right." Gabriel settled back and stared at the sky. It was almost eight now, and more reasonable runners were starting to pack into the lot. The sun felt heavy on his face, and he let the energy pour into his skin.

"It gets easier," he said.

"Yeah?" Hunter's voice was skeptical. "When?"

"I'll let you know when it happens for me."

Hunter snorted, but there was zero humor behind it.

"You could still run the race," said Gabriel.

"It's a month away. I'm not in shape."

"I didn't say you could *win* the race."

Hunter didn't say anything.

Gabriel spun his water bottle on the ground, watching the fractured sunlight turn the grass different shades of green. "I'm the only one of my brothers who gets up early. My mom did, too. She used to drink coffee and play board games with me until the others woke up." When he'd turned ten, she'd started making him a cup of coffee, too, filling half the mug with milk and two tablespoons of sugar before adding any coffee at all. He still drank it the same way.

"The morning after the funeral, I came down to the kitchen. I don't know what the hell I was thinking, like there'd be coffee in the pot and a game of Sorry! set up on the table or something." He paused. "Nothing. Just an empty kitchen. I think that's when it really hit me."

Hunter still didn't say anything.

Gabriel glanced over. "So I made coffee."

He'd set up the game, too, for whatever reason. Then he'd sobbed into his mug for forty-five minutes, until his coffee went cold and Michael found him sitting there. Gabriel had been worried his brother would bitch about the coffee or the crying or *something*—he rarely needed a reason in those days.

But Michael had just poured himself a cup of coffee and pushed the dice across the table. "You go first."

Gabriel didn't want to talk about any of that. "All I'm saying is"—he shrugged—"if you were going to run the race, maybe you should run the race."

"Maybe," said Hunter. He'd peeled almost the entire label off his water bottle.

This was getting too heavy. Gabriel leaned in. "Dude. Seriously, if you start crying, people are going to think I'm breaking up with you."

Hunter looked up. A smile broke through the emotion. "The way you run, they'd be more likely to think *I'm* breaking up with *you*."

"You can kiss my ass." His phone chimed, and Gabriel didn't even want to look at it. Probably Michael, whining about some job.

No, but a number he didn't recognize.

Were you serious about today? Layne

Layne! Gabriel sat straight up.

"Who's Layne?" asked Hunter, reading over his shoulder. Gabriel shoved him away and typed back.

Absolutely serious.

Her response took fifteen agonizing seconds.

My dad has to work this afternoon, and Simon is going to see our mom.

He smiled.

Are you inviting me over?

Another lengthy pause.

No. My dad said I'm not allowed to have you over.

Her dad probably had snipers on the roof, trained to shoot Gabriel on sight.

His phone chimed again.

But maybe we could go back to your house and work on your math homework.

He scowled. The words were full of highs and lows. His house! She wanted to come back to his house! But . . . math. *Math.*

Another chime.

The faster you learn math, the faster we can do other things.

Well, that set his heart pounding. He typed fast.

Pick you up at 2?

This time, her response was lightning quick.

Make it 3. Don't text back. Gotta go.

"Come on," he said to Hunter. "Let's go set things on fire."

"Got a date?"

"Actually, yes."

But a few minutes later, he looked over at Hunter climbing into the passenger seat. The heady tension of their conversation had dissipated, but it wasn't completely gone.

"Hey, man," he said. "You all right?"

Hunter nodded, his eyes on the windshield. "Yeah."

When he didn't say anything else, Gabriel started the engine and started to back out of his parking space.

And while he wasn't looking, Hunter said, "I don't think I could do it."

Alone. That's what he wasn't saying. He didn't think he could do the race alone. Without his father.

But he wasn't alone. Even if Hunter didn't realize it yet.

Gabriel wished he'd figured that out five years ago. Maybe then he would have *played* that game of Sorry! with Michael.

Instead of flinging the dice in his brother's face and telling him to fuck off.

Gabriel pulled onto Ritchie Highway. He'd never considered that it might have cost Michael something to sit down with *him.*

He had to clear his throat. "I'll run it with you."

A big hesitation. Then Hunter said, "Come on. You don't have to—"

"I know."

"It's twenty-six miles."

"I know what a marathon is."

Hunter was looking out the window again. "I'll think about it."

Gabriel nodded, shut his mouth, and drove.

CHAPTER 26

Gabriel made it home just before two. Plenty of time to grab a shower and clean clothes and to get out the door to pick up Layne.

Or it would have been, if his brothers had still been out.

He didn't see Michael—thank god—but Nick stopped him in the hallway, blocking the path to the bathroom.

"Where were you all morning?"

"Sorry, Mom, I'll leave a note next time." Gabriel went to push past him.

But Nick stood firm. "You smell like fire."

Not surprising, considering he and Hunter had burned a dozen hay bales at the back of Hunter's grandparents' property. Their *practice* experiment ended with mixed results: Gabriel had practically set the entire field on fire.

But he was close. His control was getting better. He could *feel* it.

And they'd been ready this time. A hose hookup was in the old barn. Luckily.

At least he didn't have to lie about where he'd been. "I went over to Hunter's. We went for a run and then set hay bales on fire."

Gabriel watched the surprise flicker on Nick's face and enjoyed it. The almost-betrayal. The almost-guilt, as Gabriel's words registered. *We did something you never want to do. Then we did something you and I used to do.*

And while Nick was standing there trying to think of a retort, Gabriel shoved past him into the bathroom and locked the door.

When he came out, the house was quiet.

Finally. Maybe his brothers had gone on another job. Maybe he'd lucked out and Michael wasn't going to hassle him all day.

Gabriel pulled on a clean shirt in his bedroom. He'd spent the last twenty minutes telling himself that studying math at the kitchen table meant this wasn't a *date*, that he had a greater chance of looking like a moron at this activity than at just about anything else.

Gabriel jogged down the steps and stuck his hand into his backpack for his car keys.

Nothing.

Then he looked out the window beside the front door. No car, either.

"Fuck!" He hit the door frame. It hurt. He did it again.

"Problems?"

Gabriel glanced down the hallway. He'd assumed Michael was out, but he found his older brother sitting in the kitchen. The laptop sat open in front of him, work papers spread across the table.

"Yeah," said Gabriel. "Nick took the car."

Michael didn't even look up from the screen. "Huh. Didn't you do the same thing this morning?"

"Don't talk to me like I'm a little kid."

Now his brother's eyes flicked up. "I'm sorry, was that a mature adult punching the front door?"

Gabriel took a step forward, ready to let loose with something biting and acerbic, something that would start a fight to take the edge off this anger.

But then he realized he might—just *might*—be able to work this out.

He dropped into the chair across from his brother. "Would you let me borrow the truck?"

Michael laughed, but not like it was really funny. "The last time you 'borrowed' the truck, I got a call from the cops at three in the morning."

"Yeah, yeah." Gabriel paused. "Please."

Michael was already looking back at the laptop. "I need the truck this afternoon. I was going to run to Home Depot."

God, like he couldn't do that *later*. "Come on, Michael. *Please*."

Now his brother really looked at him. Gabriel never asked him for anything. Ever.

"Where do you need to go?"

Gabriel warred with telling the truth—but Michael was more likely to say yes if he knew it was for school. "I'm picking up someone from my math class. We're coming back here to study."

"Try again."

Gabriel sighed. "Really." At Michael's raised eyebrows, he emphasized, "*Really*. Why would I make *that* up?"

Michael studied him for an eternal minute. Then he closed the laptop. "Okay."

Gabriel almost fell out of his chair. "Seriously?"

"Seriously." Michael stood. "Let's go."

Wait a minute. "You're not—"

"Driving? Yeah, I am. We'll pick up this *someone*, I'll bring you back here, and then I'll go to Home Depot."

This was some kind of punishment. Or retaliation. Had to be. "Look, if you're just going to grill me about the fires—"

"No grilling. We can't afford for something to happen to the truck." Michael was already heading for the garage. "This is the best you're going to get. Take it or leave it."

Gabriel couldn't believe he had to get a ride from his *brother*. Christ, this was humiliating. They'd always had a car. He'd never needed to beg a ride to pick a girl up.

Especially to *study*.

He felt about thirteen. Maybe Michael would offer to take them for ice cream, after.

"Hey," he said when they were halfway there. "I need you to do me a favor."

"Another one?"

"Please don't be mean to this girl."

"Aha." Michael glanced over. "I knew this had to be a girl."

"Look . . . just . . . she's not like that, okay?"

"So not only do I have to play chauffeur, but I have to be *nice*, too?" Michael's voice was full of sarcasm, but it lacked the usual edge.

Gabriel didn't trust this new niceness—but if he snapped at Michael, his brother might abort the whole operation. "Maybe it would be best if you just didn't talk to her at all."

Michael fell silent for a while, and trees raced by. Finally, he said, "How bad is it?"

"How bad is what?"

"Math."

"It's fine," Gabriel lied. "I just don't want to fall behind."

Michael glanced over. "You think you'll be able to get back on the team?"

"Damn it." Gabriel scowled. "I can't believe Nick told you."

"He didn't. I've been waiting to see if you'd tell me yourself."

Like that would ever happen. "Chris, then?"

Michael shook his head. "Your teacher called."

"She *what*?"

"I don't know why you guys are so surprised when the school calls me."

Gabriel couldn't believe this. "God, I *hate* her."

Michael fell silent again, but this time it was weighted, like he wanted to say something. Gabriel wasn't about to give him an excuse to lecture, so he kept his mouth shut and stared out the window.

"I used to hate it," Michael finally said. "Your teachers would call me all the time. Especially in middle school. I mean, these were people who'd taught *me*, and four years later, they're calling to ask me to control my little brothers. Every frigging day, another hassle. A fight. A missed assignment. Come in and sign this form, come down and fill out this paperwork. It used to make me *nuts*."

Boo-hoo. Gabriel didn't look away from the window.

He wondered if Michael was looking for an apology. He wasn't getting one.

"By the time you and Nick hit freshman year, I thought it would settle down. But then I had middle school teachers *and* high school teachers calling me. I remember that October, I was trying to figure out how the hell to file a tax return for the business, and Vickers called me up to tell me Nick had gotten in a fight in the locker room."

Vickers was the guidance counselor. Gabriel remembered that day, one of the few days *Nick* had actually been involved in a fight, when he wasn't just taking the fall for Gabriel.

It wasn't really a fight at all. Seth and Tyler had cornered Nick after gym class. They'd beaten the crap out of him.

Gabriel had switched places with Nick the next day. Seth and Tyler backed off after that.

He'd had no idea Vickers ever called the house.

"I hated that stupid cow when I went to school there," Michael said. "I used to think she was useless. So when she called up to whine about Nick, I went off on her. Told her I was sick of her and every other teacher always getting on my case, setting me up to fail. I completely lost it. I'm surprised she didn't hang up on me."

Michael hit the turn signal for Compass Pointe. "When I finally shut up, she said something I'll never forget. She said, 'We're not setting you up to fail. We're calling because we want to help you succeed.'"

Gabriel stared at him for a long moment, waiting, hoping there was more. But his brother didn't say anything else.

Gabriel rolled his eyes and looked back out the window. "That is the dumbest story I've ever heard."

"All I'm saying is, I don't think your teacher is trying to hassle you."

"Yes. She is." But Gabriel kept thinking of Nick's comments about graduation.

He kept thinking about Layne's expression when she'd figured out he was cheating.

It made him want to shrink down in the seat.

Michael glanced over. "At least you're doing something about it."

"Whatever."

Michael sighed. "Which house?"

Gabriel pointed. Layne's house was immaculate in the sunshine, all white pillars and stone facing that reminded Gabriel of her comment about a serial killer living there. Perfect landscaping, too, though he'd bet Michael had already spotted twenty areas where the workers had cut corners and used crap plants.

Gabriel was unbuckling his seat belt and trying to figure how to spin the transportation issue, when Layne came flying out the front door.

Jeans. Forest-green turtleneck. Braid. Glasses. After the getup she'd been wearing last night, it reminded him of those superhero cartoons he'd watched when he was a little kid. The ones where only a few select people got to know what hid behind the meek-mannered exterior.

How had he never realized how hot she was?

She hesitated halfway to the truck, noticing that he wasn't alone. Gabriel slid out of the cab.

"Sorry," he called. "I don't have the car, so my brother had to drive." He came around the front of the truck to meet her.

She cast a glance at Michael, looking flighty. "There's a problem."

"Is your dad still home?" Gabriel glanced at the front door, ready for her father to burst out with a shotgun.

"No . . . but Simon is." She hesitated. "Our mom never showed up."

The more he heard about her mother, the more Gabriel wanted to find the woman and shake some sense into her.

"He can't stay home alone," Layne rushed on. "I'd say you could come in, but if my dad came home early—"

"Statutory rape. I remember."

Her cheeks turned pink. "Yeah."

God, this *figured*. Nick taking the car was probably an omen.

Unless . . . could this be an elaborate way for her to back out? Maybe she'd had second thoughts when he'd pulled up the driveway. Maybe she didn't want anything to do with him after all.

"Don't worry," he said. "I get it."

"No! I'm not . . ." Layne licked her lips. "I'm not backing out. I'm wondering . . ."

Some hair was coming loose from her braid, and if Michael wasn't sitting *right there*, Gabriel would have tucked it back into place.

No, he'd be pulling the elastic free, unwinding the plaits . . .

Focus. "Wondering what?"

She took a deep breath. "Would it be okay if Simon came with us?"

CHAPTER 27

Layne sat at the kitchen table and watched Gabriel glare at his trig textbook. He had a fresh piece of notebook paper in front of him, a sharpened pencil clenched between his fingers.

A murderous expression on his face.

"Come on," she said. "You can't hate math *that* much."

"Trust me. I can." He glanced up. "You hungry? Want something to drink?"

"I want you to quit stalling."

"I am *not*—"

"Oh." She raised an eyebrow. "Does it usually take twenty minutes to hook up your PlayStation, or was that just for Simon's benefit?"

His voice dropped. "I was hoping Michael would leave."

His brother? Layne remembered Gabriel mentioning that they fought, but Michael had been perfectly nice to her. He'd barely said a word during the drive over here, and then left them in the kitchen with the excuse that he had work to catch up on.

"He said he had to run to Home Depot," said Gabriel. "But he's probably sticking around to make sure I don't con you into going upstairs."

The words almost made her breath catch. Thank god he couldn't feel her heart rate stutter. "No chance." She tapped the book with her pencil. "I'm here to help you work."

"Hmm." He leaned in and pushed a strand of hair off her face. "Is that a challenge?"

Now she couldn't breathe at all.

She hadn't bothered to look at the Internet last night. This morning, either. Kara hadn't called, and she couldn't bear to check her e-mail. She had no idea whether Taylor had ever followed through on her threat to put everything online, but if she had, what could Layne do about it?

Nothing.

And it was so much nicer to think about the moments with Gabriel, *after* the party. She'd turned his words over in her head all night. Not just the kind ones, when they'd been sitting by the water. The harsh ones, the *really* honest ones, when they'd sat on the tailgate of his car.

What do you think, that I'm some kind of thug player who'll screw anything in a skirt?

"You're blushing." His breath was against her neck, his lips whispering into her skin.

"You're still stalling. We need to—"

She gasped. His teeth grazed her jaw, the sensitive area below her ear. His hands found her waist, shifting her toward him. Everything suddenly felt ten degrees warmer.

"See?" he murmured. "Who needs math?"

That woke her up. She used her pencil to rap him on the forehead. "*You* do."

He sighed disgustedly and drew back.

Then he went right back to glaring at his blank paper.

"It's only ten questions," she said, still feeling a bit breathless. "We'll just work through these, and then . . ." She let the words trail off, but that open ending was just way too . . . open. "Then we'll talk."

He nodded. But he didn't write anything down.

"Look," she said, "I can't help you if you won't even—"

"Jesus." His eyes flared with anger. "I *know*."

Layne almost flinched—then reminded herself that his anger

had nothing to do with her. "Truth," she said softly. "What's wrong?"

His expression was locked down, and she had a strong feeling he wasn't going to answer. Every time he did this, it made her feel vulnerable. More so now that her secrets were all out on the table—and his weren't.

"I need to pass." His voice was low, rough.

"You will," she said. "You'll pass the test, get back on the team—"

"I don't give a crap about the team." He hesitated. "I mean, I do, but . . ."

She waited.

He kept his eyes on the book. "Nick told me last night that he wants to go to college. If I can't pass math, I can't even graduate from high school."

She studied him. "Do you want to go to college with your brother?"

"No—yes—I don't—" His pencil snapped. "God*damn* it." He dropped the pieces in the spine of the book.

Again, Layne waited.

Gabriel looked up, meeting her eyes. "I never even *thought* about college. The only reason I bother getting halfway decent grades is so I can play sports. I mean, I just figured we'd keep helping Mike with the business."

"What do you want to do?"

He snorted. "I doubt there's money for Nick to go to college, so for me to go *with him* . . . I mean, he'll probably get scholarships, but—"

"No. What do *you* want to do?"

"I don't know." He was looking back at the math book again. "I never really thought I had a choice."

Layne bit at her lip. She didn't know the twins' relationship well enough to judge them, and talking to Gabriel always felt like walking a tightrope. "Obviously Nick thinks he has one."

That brought his eyes back up to hers. "He deserves a choice."

"Why, because he's a good student?"

Gabriel scowled. "He's *good*, period."

It made her think of her mother, volunteering for every charity under the sun—as long as she got to plan a party for it. Most people probably thought she was *good*, too, despite the fact that Layne's father had worked himself to the bone to afford the lifestyle her mother demanded.

And then she'd left, like it wasn't good enough.

No, because Layne and Simon weren't good enough.

There were different levels of *good*, Layne thought. Had to be.

She tapped the math book with her pencil. "You deserve a choice, too."

Gabriel took a deep breath and blew it out. He picked up the broken half of his pencil, the one with a writing end. "Can I choose to not do this?"

She wanted to hit him on the forehead again. "Don't be such a baby. I can't believe you'll kick the crap out of Ryan Stacey but you're afraid of a few equations."

His eyes flicked up at her. "That's because I don't care what Ryan Stacey thinks of me."

Oh. Her breath caught again. She tried to stop her heart from thundering in her chest and shoved the book toward him. "Maybe your brother *should* help you. You can't sweet-talk him."

Layne helped Gabriel struggle through the second problem of the assignment.

And he was definitely struggling.

The first question had taken thirty minutes to work through. He was missing fundamentals they'd covered in Algebra I. It was like trying to teach abstract equations to someone who'd never learned basic multiplication. And as he got more frustrated, he started transposing numbers. It reminded her of that day she'd fixed his test, when half the solutions were written backward. Or that day at the blackboard, when he'd copied someone's equation—but he'd copied it incorrectly. She had to keep reminding him to slow down.

That night she'd driven him home, she'd made a comment about special classes, and he'd brushed her off. But now she was starting to wonder if he genuinely had a learning disability.

Not like she'd say that out loud. Yet.

The second problem took only twenty-five minutes. Progress.

By the end of two hours, he'd worked through eight problems. He wrote the number 9 on his paper just as a peal of thunder rolled overhead. Layne reached out and closed the textbook.

He looked up. "We're not done."

"I should check on Simon." She stretched her shoulders. "And you should quit while you're ahead. Do the other two tomorrow." They hadn't heard a sound from the living room the entire time they'd been in here. Not like Simon was a noisy kid, but she was surprised he hadn't come looking for a soda. A snack. A bathroom, for goodness' sake.

But when they looked in the living room, the PlayStation was turned off, the television silent and dark. She turned around, but the powder room door was wide open, the lights off.

No one was in the front yard, either, when they leaned out the front door. Overcast sky, prestorm humidity thick in the air. But no Simon.

Then a repetitive smacking echoed from the driveway. Followed by a long pause.

Gabriel smiled. "Come on."

Simon was tossing a basketball at the hoop over the garage. To her utter surprise, Gabriel's older brother was playing with him.

Michael caught the ball Simon passed to him, then pointed at her and Gabriel. "Math done?" he asked.

"Mostly," said Gabriel. He gave Simon a grin. "You've been practicing."

Simon's hair was a little damp, but he grinned in return—the first smile Layne had seen on his face all day. He nodded.

"Coach still won't let you play?" said Gabriel.

The grin vanished. Simon shook his head.

Gabriel nodded at the basket. "Keep playing like that, and he'll be an idiot not to."

The smile was back. Simon held out a fist. Gabriel hit it.

"Thanks for playing with Simon," she said to Michael, signing as she spoke, out of habit. "I'm sorry if you were trying to get work done."

"Nah." He didn't quite smile, but his expression was easy. Amiable. Again, it made her wonder about Gabriel's fights with him. He'd been nice enough to drive her over. And then play basketball with her deaf brother. Kara had an older sister in college who'd barely give Kara the time of day, much less Layne.

Honestly, after the way her mother practically ignored them, it was nice to see a family member act like *family*.

It was funny—all along she'd thought Gabriel was the jock thug, when all he'd ever done was protect her and Simon. And then a charmer like Ryan Stacey turned out to be as bad as Taylor and Heather.

It made her wonder what else she was missing about the people around her. Whether their motives were truly hidden, or whether she just chose not to see.

"What time did you say you needed to be home?" Michael asked her.

She shrugged and glanced away. "I told my dad we'd be back by six."

A complete lie, of course. She hadn't mentioned a word of this to her father. But Michael had caught her off guard when she'd first climbed into his truck, asking if it was okay with her parents. She hadn't expected him to do more than give her a passing glance and roll his eyes about playing chauffer.

Really, considering the guys Kara's older sister hung out with, she wouldn't have been surprised to find Michael passing her a joint and asking if she felt like making brownies.

Thunder rolled through the sky again, sounding like a warning. Layne tapped Simon's arm and signed as she spoke. "We should probably go."

No, he signed back, scowling. *I never get to play.*

She sighed and looked meaningfully at the sky before signing and saying, "It's going to storm."

"Nah," said Gabriel. He looked up at the sky as well. "The lightning is a ways off."

Simon smacked her in the arm, harder than was necessary. *See?*

Layne wanted to snap at him, to make him fall in line—like that ever worked. But she kept remembering the way he'd slammed the door to his room after their mother hadn't shown up.

And the smile on his face when she'd found him playing basketball.

She sighed and sat on the concrete against the garage. "Fifteen minutes."

But Gabriel held out a hand. "No way. We play, you play."

She blushed. "I'm not really athletic—"

He snorted. "Come on."

Then he had her hand, and then she was playing basketball.

Playing might have been a little strong. The boys were patient, letting her take time to make a basket. When *they* had the ball, it was a free-for-all of shoving and good-natured ribbing. But the best part was when she had to shoot, and Gabriel's arms came around her, his voice gentle in her ear. "Like this . . ."

She was having so much fun that she didn't realize their fifteen minutes had passed, didn't even register the crunch of tires on pavement until Michael said to Gabriel, "Expecting more company?"

Layne glanced at the driveway. A black BMW was rolling up the hill.

She actually felt the blood drain from her face.

For a split second, she hoped Gabriel *was* expecting more company. Even a girl. Even Taylor Morrissey herself. Because right this instant, Layne would rather face anyone than the one person she *knew* drove a black BMW.

Her father.

Her palms went slick on the basketball. She didn't even remember catching it.

Simon was there beside her, his breathing as shallow as hers.

"What am I missing?" said Michael.

Layne had to clear her throat to find her voice. "It's my dad." God, how had he known where they were? She shook herself and looked at her watch.

Still early! How . . . what . . .

"Layne!" Her father was already out of the vehicle, standing there in the driveway, the door standing open. His tone could slice through steel. "Both of you. Get in the car. Right now."

Her backpack was still in the kitchen, but she didn't dare say she had to go inside to get it. "Dad." Her voice broke, and she tried again. "Dad, we were just playing—"

"Trust me. I know exactly what's getting played here." Layne had never seen him look so livid.

Yes she had—the night her mom left.

It hurt to breathe. Her voice wouldn't rise above a whisper. "Dad—"

"Leave her alone," said Gabriel, right at her shoulder. *His* voice was even. Steady. "We were just playing ball."

Simon signed the same thing, his gestures full of fury. *We were just playing ball. You were working.*

Her father looked like he was forcing himself to stay behind the car door. He gestured, his words punctuated by fury. "Get. In. The. Car."

Layne swallowed. "Okay."

"Hey." Gabriel caught her wrist, his eyes still fixed on her father, his voice still unrelenting. "They didn't do anything wrong."

"Gabriel," said Michael.

"Nothing wrong?" Her father did close the door now, stepping across the pavement. Layne had to fight to keep from backing up. "I believe we might have a different perspective of *right* and *wrong*. For instance, driving a fifteen-year-old girl across town without her parents' permission. To say nothing of her fourteen-year-old brother."

"Yeah?" said Gabriel, stepping forward, almost putting her behind him. Thunder cracked in the sky again, closer. "What's so right about being—"

"*Gabriel.*" Michael had his brother's arm now, and it must have been a death grip. White showed across his knuckles.

But Michael's eyes were on her father, his tone composed. "I drove. They were just getting together for schoolwork." He paused, and Layne thought for a moment that he was going to sell her out, to say that he'd specifically asked whether she had permission and she'd lied. "Gabriel and Layne studied in the kitchen; we played ball. I've been here the whole time."

If anything, her father's eyes turned darker. "Forgive me if I don't find that too reassuring."

Lightning streaked through the sky behind the houses across the street. Thunder cracked. A drop of water struck her cheek.

She could hear Gabriel's breathing beside her, tight and furious.

Please, she prayed, remembering their exchange in her foyer. *Don't make this worse.*

"Dad," she choked. "It was fine."

"Layne, I'm not an idiot. And I'm not going to worry about you and Simon running around with some worthless teenager who's a phone call away from juvenile detention—"

"Hey." Michael took a step forward, almost toe-to-toe with her father. "He's not worthless, and you're out of line."

"*I'm* out of line? Maybe you should think about your position before you get in my face, kid."

"I'm not a kid. And you don't know anything about my *position.*"

"Please," said Layne. "Just . . . it's my fault. We'll get in the car."

But her father would never back down from anyone, and he was barely paying attention to her anymore. "Oh, you don't think I had time to look you up? All I needed was a neighbor to tell me about the strange vehicle in the driveway. She wondered why my kids were getting in a landscaping truck."

Layne flinched. Her father said *landscaping truck* as if she and Simon had been found scrounging in Dumpsters. Another drop of rain hit her cheek. Her forearm. "Dad—stop it."

"Clearly they survived the experience," said Michael. "Funny how you were so concerned, but you had time to *look me up*."

"You know," said her father, his tone softening, gaining the weight of threat, "everything about you is a matter of public record. I saw the court records, the way you run the risk of being denied custody every spring. I saw the financial condition of your little *company*." He paused, the way he did before delivering a final blow to a jury. She'd seen him rehearse one too many times—and the pause was effective because he meant every word that came after it. "You don't want to mess with me, kid. I can mess with you *much* more effectively."

Thunder cracked, just overhead. Lightning struck a tree beside the driveway with a sound like a gunshot. Layne gave a little shriek. Branches and sparks rained down, just behind her father's car. Some landed on the trunk.

Then real rain took over, stopping any fire before it could start. Layne shivered.

Michael shoved Gabriel back against the garage. "Are you *crazy*? Go in the house."

Gabriel surged forward, but his brother pushed him back, holding him there with one hand as he turned to face her father. Layne could see the muscle twitch in Michael's jaw, the hard set of his shoulders. *Now* she saw it, the way he probably got into it with Gabriel. She held her breath, wondering if he'd throw a punch at her father. And how her father would react.

Considering how her dad was acting, she almost wished Michael would.

But Michael took a ragged breath and seemed to shore up all that anger. "I'm sorry for any misunderstanding. Maybe you should leave before the storm gets too bad."

Gabriel jerked himself out of his brother's grip, shoving damp hair out of his eyes. He looked like *he* might go after her father, but Michael gave him another shove toward the front door. "Go inside. *Go*."

Gabriel took a few steps down the walkway, but stopped there, his hands in fists.

Layne was ready to get dragged to the car, but her father was still staring down Michael, ignoring the rain. She grabbed his arm. "Dad, come on." Her voice was breaking, and she didn't care. "Let's go."

He didn't move. "Get in the car, Layne."

She didn't think that was a very good idea.

Thunder cracked again, and she flinched. But lightning flashed harmlessly behind the trees.

Simon stepped forward and shoved her father with his shoulder, stomping to the BMW. At the door, he turned and gave her father a gesture that didn't need any translation. Then he slid into the backseat and slammed the door.

Layne swallowed. But at least her father's focus was thrown. Michael was already herding Gabriel toward the front door, and she turned on her heel and headed for the car herself. She couldn't bear the thought of sitting next to her father for the drive home, so she slid in beside Simon.

She didn't have the courage to slam the door herself.

A lecture had to be forthcoming, but when her father got in the car, he didn't say anything. Just switched on XM Radio, the classical station.

He only listened to classical when he was furious.

"Dad," she whispered, "I'm really—"

"Not now, Layne."

His voice was a smack across the face, disappointment and disgust and fury all contained in three words. She fell back against the seat.

But Simon tapped her leg. His eyes were red, some combination of fear and anger. With rain on his cheeks, he looked like he was simultaneously ready to cry and put his fist through the car window.

It's okay, she signed. *I'll tell him it was my fault.*

Simon brushed her hands aside, his way of telling her to shut up.

Then he glanced at the front seat of the car, the way her father's hands were practically molding the steering wheel into a new shape.

Simon looked back at her. *I hate him.*

Layne remembered her thoughts from the kitchen, when she'd wondered about what she always saw and what was really there.

After hearing her father denigrate Gabriel and his brother, it made her want to realign everything she knew about her father.

And about herself, too.

CHAPTER 28

Gabriel couldn't get the music loud enough. Maybe if he put a pillow over his head. His eyes were fixed on the white drywall of his bedroom ceiling, his iPod earbuds pressed into his ears so tightly that they were beginning to hurt.

He was trying to block out the sound of Layne's father's voice, which kept replaying in his head like it was on some kind of loop.

His door opened, and Michael filled the doorway.

Gabriel yanked the headphones out of his ears, but music still poured out against his comforter. "Ever hear of knocking?"

He wanted his voice to be sharp, but he couldn't generate the usual anger.

He's not worthless. And you're out of line.

"I did knock," said Michael. "Three times."

Oh. Gabriel pushed PAUSE on the iPod and looked back at the ceiling. "Sorry."

He was ready for the lecture about the lightning, about *lying*, but Michael just stood there, keys jingling in his hand. "I still need to go to Home Depot. Want to come?"

He didn't want to. But the alternative was sitting alone in his bedroom, feeling lightning in the air. Regretting the afternoon.

So again, they headed out in the truck, Michael mostly quiet, the wipers snicking back and forth against the windshield.

Gabriel couldn't take it. He looked over. "I'm sorry."

Michael didn't look away from the road. "Did you know?"

"Did I know what?"

"That she wasn't allowed over?"

Gabriel looked back out the window and picked at the weather stripping along the glass. "Mostly. I drove her home last week and her father told me off."

"He *told you off*?"

Michael sounded pissed, but Gabriel couldn't tell if it was directed at him or Mr. Forrest. "Yeah. Said he was going to charge me with trespassing and statutory rape."

"What an *asshole*."

Gabriel smiled tentatively, as if Michael might start on him next. "Yeah. He is." He hesitated. "Thanks. For what you said."

Michael nodded. "Thanks for not setting his car on fire."

Silence streamed through the truck again, but there wasn't any strain to it this time. Gabriel glanced over again. "What did he mean, about the custody stuff? And about the company?"

Michael sighed. "He's not a judge, is he?"

"No. A lawyer."

"I should have figured. You don't have to worry about the custody stuff. It comes up for review every spring. You know that. You and Nick will be eighteen anyway, so . . ." Michael shrugged.

"But Chris?"

"Chris will be fine."

"But—"

"Seriously." Michael looked away from the road now. "He'll be fine. That's the last thing you need to worry about." He paused. "As long as you can stay out of trouble, I can scrape one more year out of the juvenile system."

As long as you can stay out of trouble. He was talking about the fires. Gabriel swallowed.

"What about the stuff with the company?"

"Something else you don't need to worry about."

Gabriel was on the verge of peeling the weather stripping right out of the window. "Come on."

"Really. He's bluffing."

But Gabriel kept remembering Michael's comment in the kitchen earlier. *We can't afford for anything to happen to the truck.*

"You know," said Michael, his voice careful, "when you told me we were picking up a girl, she's not quite what I was expecting."

Layne. Gabriel wished he could have picked her up and carried her into the house, all the while telling her father to fuck off. "I don't think it matters anymore."

"Just saying."

Gabriel snorted. "I'm surprised you're not *just saying* I need to stay away from her."

"Yeah, well"—Michael rolled his eyes—"I already tried that with Chris and Becca, and look where it got me."

Gabriel skipped dinner. Things were all right with Michael—for now—but he didn't feel like putting on the same show for Chris and Nick, especially since Quinn and Becca were here. He holed up in his room again, iPod blaring in his ears.

He rolled his lighter across his knuckles, striking flame in time with the beat of the song.

His cell phone was in his other hand. Silent.

Not that he wasn't checking it every fifteen seconds.

Surrounded by people, and he still felt so alone.

Then his phone chimed. Gabriel was so startled that he dropped the lit lighter in the middle of his chest.

Out, he thought.

The fire went out.

Nice. His control *was* getting better.

He checked the phone. Hunter.

Four alarm fire at Tanyard Springs. U in?

Gabriel slid his fingers across the keys to respond, then froze. *As long as you can stay out of trouble . . .*

But a four-alarm fire would be big. And Tanyard Springs was a townhome community. This could be more than one family.

He paused his iPod and slipped out of bed to crack the door. His brothers were in the kitchen, cleaning up and goofing off from the sound of it. The rain had long since stopped. He could sneak out and be gone before they noticed.

But things weren't terrible right now. Spending the day with Michael had actually been nice, in a bizarre way. He couldn't remember the last time he'd played ball with his older brother. Even the trip to Home Depot had been peaceful.

If he snuck out, it could unravel everything.

But a four-alarm fire. There would be a *lot* of firemen. It would be easy to stay hidden.

Then again, Michael would know. Hell, he'd probably check the news first thing tomorrow morning. And Michael seemed to be offering him some . . . trust.

Gabriel considered going downstairs, joining them. It might be awkward at first, but maybe it would be okay.

Then he caught Nick's voice. "So how was your afternoon of babysitting?"

Gabriel started to ease the door closed, sure his twin was talking to Quinn or Becca—but Michael responded. "Fine. We ran to Home Depot to pick up supplies for that gazebo job tomorrow."

Gabriel jerked back.

Babysitting. *Babysitting.*

Michael wasn't being *nice.* He wasn't being brotherly. He was sitting around, making sure Gabriel didn't go out and start any fires.

No wonder he'd been in the kitchen this afternoon, working on paperwork. No wonder he'd practically dragged Gabriel to Home Depot. And what was he going to do, sit around all weekend?

Gabriel almost put his fist through the wall. Babysitting!
His phone chimed again.

You there?

Fury almost made it impossible to type. But he managed.

Yeah. I'm in.

CHAPTER 29

Monday morning, Layne dug the currycomb into her horse's coat, rubbing in circular motions until her biceps ached. Brisk morning air nipped at her cheeks, but she didn't care. She'd already done this twice and could see the shine on her horse's coat under the dust and hair she was bringing up. But she'd do it a fourth time, and a fifth, too, if she could get away with it.

Anything to stay out of the house until her father left for work. Even if she had to wear this getup to school.

Even if she had to skip school.

Saturday night, the house had felt like a war zone. At first, they'd gone to different rooms, doors closed, only silence beyond. She'd finally crept out at seven to make dinner, hoping baked chicken and mashed potatoes—her father's favorite—would be enough to pull him out of his study.

But she'd knocked, and he'd answered, and he'd told her to feed Simon and go to bed.

Then he'd come back out, for one reason only: to confiscate her cell phone.

Sunday was worse, only because her father showed his face. Every word was clipped, every motion sharp. Layne expected him to yell, to ground her, to issue restrictions. But he didn't mention Gabriel. He barely spoke to Simon—not like there was any change there.

She'd been relieved when a client called with an emergency, and her father had to leave.

But the tension in the house had made her completely forget the events of Friday night. Since she didn't have her backpack, she turned on the computer and loaded her e-mail, hoping to e-mail a classmate to get the weekend assignment for Honors English.

And then she'd been shocked by the onslaught.

At first, she thought her account had been hacked. She had over fifty e-mails.

Then she'd started recognizing the names of fellow students. Taylor. Heather. A few others, all from that crowd.

Her throat still felt tight, thinking about it. She'd clicked on one.

It was a picture of her, pinned on that chaise lounge, but the photo had been doctored. Now it looked like she was completely naked.

Bad enough. But the next one was from Ryan Stacey. The subject line said, *Bring back memories?*

She expected another dirty picture, but it was a link to a newspaper article about a fire Saturday night, at some town house community across town. Four homes, destroyed. Almost everyone had gotten out without injuries, but a young woman had been trapped and badly burned before she was rescued.

There was a picture.

Layne clicked for the next e-mail, before her brain could register the damage.

The next e-mail had obviously been passed around before coming to her account, because she had to scroll through numerous LOLs before getting to another photo of herself on the chaise lounge. But she was on fire, her face a Photoshopped image of a charred dog's head.

And in the e-mail chain, a message from Kara, saying how hysterical it was.

Layne had yanked the computer plug out of the wall.

And then she'd run to the bathroom to throw up.

The horse sidestepped away from the brush, and Layne snapped back to the present. She'd been pressing too hard.

She abandoned the currycomb for a bristle brush, flicking the dirt and loose hairs into the aisle, making the animal's red coat truly shine.

A knock sounded against the wood planks at the end of the aisle, and she jumped, then placed a hand on her horse's shoulder to steady him when he snorted. No one ever came out this early. It was barely six in the morning.

A figure stood at the other end of the barn, in the wide doorway, backed by sunshine, so she couldn't make out who it was.

She set down the brush. "Hello?" she called. "Can I help you?"

"Layne?"

Her step faltered—and then the clouds shifted, just a little, enough so she could recognize Gabriel standing at the end of the barn.

It sent her heart dancing with a skip and a flutter. She hadn't heard from him since Saturday, of course, because she'd practically been on house arrest. Really, she hadn't been sure how she'd face him, after the things her father had said.

But now, seeing him here, she almost fell over her own feet trying to get down the aisle. He was wearing running shoes again. Shorts and a dark hoodie. His face was a bit flushed, his eyes dark with the sun at his back.

It wasn't just that he was *here*. He'd *run*. How many miles had he said? Four?

But then she realized he wasn't coming toward her. He wasn't smiling. He was just standing there, that tense, inscrutable expression on his face.

She stopped short, trying to get her breath and heartbeat to settle into a steady rhythm. She stared up at him, wondering if he hated her now, if her father's words had ruined everything, if she'd be starting school today without a single ally. Or maybe it was those e-mails.

Maybe he'd seen. Maybe he'd reconsidered.

She was a freak.

An outcast.

Only now, she wasn't hidden. Her secrets were out there, for the whole world to see.

For a horrifying moment, she worried she was going to throw up again.

And then she did something worse.

She started sobbing.

Huge, choking sobs that made her shoulders shake and her body tremble. Her hands were over her eyes, and her legs couldn't carry her weight on top of this onslaught of emotion.

Then his hands caught her shoulders, drawing her in against his chest. "Layne. Layne, please."

"They put it all over the Internet. I knew . . . I knew it would be bad—" She choked again.

"I'm sorry." She felt his breath on her hair. "Layne, I'm sorry."

"Even Kara . . . Kara was e-mailing with them."

"Your friend is a *bitch*. And she doesn't deserve you."

"She was my only friend."

"No. She wasn't."

Her hiccupping breaths abated enough for her to look up at him, but he didn't let her go. His arms were around her back. Strong, supportive, doing the job her knees just couldn't. He smelled like sweat and sunshine and the woods, and she loved it.

She pressed her face against his shoulder. "I was worried you hated me."

"Then we have that in common."

Confused, she lifted her head. His eyes were close, blue sparked with sunlight.

"I was worried you hated *me*," he said. "After what your father said—"

"That was my fault."

"No." His voice hardened. "That was *his* fault." He paused to brush a strand of hair from her forehead.

"I don't hate you," she whispered.

"You sure?" There was no relief in his eyes, just wary exhaustion. "You wouldn't be alone."

"What does that mean?"

"Nothing. I'm being stupid. It's been a long weekend." His hands were stroking along her back.

She gave a choked laugh; it sounded strangled. "Tell me about it."

Gabriel paused, and now he seemed hesitant. "I was worried you wouldn't want to see me."

"Are you kidding?" She looked up at him. "You're the only person I want to see right now."

He leaned in, his expression softer now, more sure. "So crying when you see me is a *good* thing. Got it."

She punched him in the shoulder. "I can't believe you ran all the way here."

"I told Hunter I'd run a marathon with him next month." He paused. "So I'll need to do lots of running in the morning."

She picked up on the wry note in his voice. "Funny how I do lots of riding in the morning."

"That's what I figured." He looked up, past her. "Is it always this deserted?"

"Just me and the horses. Plenty of privacy." She flushed, realizing how that sounded. "I mean—"

His hands found her waist, hard through the thin material of her jacket. "I know exactly what you mean."

She sucked in a breath, but then he was kissing her.

When his lips touched hers, it was like lighting a match: a quick flare of heat, a burst of light, and then a slow burn. Her body melted into his, letting him support her again. His hands slid under the edge of her jacket, and even though there was a turtleneck there, she froze anyway.

His hands stopped—but his kisses didn't. They slowed, his mouth drawing at hers carefully, his tongue brushing hers until he'd coaxed small noises from her throat and the heat in her body was everywhere, not just near his hands or his mouth. This time, when his hands slid under her jacket, she let him, even when she knew he had to be feeling the scars beneath the fabric.

She didn't realize they were moving until her back hit the wall of the stable, until she felt his weight against her. Everything accelerated, a pace of desperation. Her pulse, her breathing. The way her jacket was just suddenly gone before she even felt him pull at the zipper. The way his hoodie was a puddle on the concrete floor, before her hands recognized the bare muscles of his arms. His kisses were wild, crazy, addictive.

Layne reached up to find his face, her thumbs tracing the stubble along his jaw. She took a chance and bit at his lip, feeling raw and animalistic and shy, all at once. But he made a small sound, a good sound, and she did it again, more sure.

Then he did it back, and her body lit like a live wire. She wished he didn't have a T-shirt. She wished she didn't have a turtleneck. When his hands slid along her waist and found an inch of bare skin, she didn't flinch. And her indrawn breath meant nothing bad.

Until she heard the roar of a diesel engine, the crunch of truck tires on the gravel road leading to the barn.

Gabriel snapped back. He looked almost panicked.

"The barn manager," Layne said. "She checks the lower barn first. We have a minute."

"Hmm." He looked rueful. "And she probably shouldn't know I'm here."

Her cheeks flamed. "No. She'd tell—"

"I get it." But he smiled and gave her another quick kiss, before dropping to fish his sweatshirt off the ground. "I'll see you in school."

Her entire body felt flushed. Her lips felt raw, swollen. Anyone would know she'd been making out.

Right?

She didn't want him to leave, but her body felt like gelatin.

Gabriel kissed her again, and she caught his face in her hands, holding him there.

He laughed, softly, gently, a sound just for her. "I don't want you to get banned from the farm," he whispered.

Layne nodded. He drew back.

But then he stopped. "I forgot. I actually came to thank you."

"You mean there's more?"

Now he laughed for real, and she loved how it stole the tension from his eyes. "Later. No, seriously. For this." He dug a piece of folded notebook paper from his sweatshirt pocket, and she took it.

Then he was sprinting out of the barn, yanking his hoodie over his head as he went.

Layne touched a finger to her lips. She unfolded the notebook paper, wondering what he'd written. Her heart fluttered again. A note?

No, better. His math homework. He'd done the last two questions. Struggled, clearly, based on the eraser marks.

But he'd done them.

And he'd gotten them both right.

Gabriel shoveled cafeteria macaroni and cheese into his mouth, but he didn't really taste it.

Hunter was watching him with a disgusted expression. They were the only two people at the table. "I don't know how you can eat that crap."

"I'm hungry."

Hunter sliced into the piece of grilled chicken in front of him. He was the only guy Gabriel had ever seen use a plastic knife in the cafeteria. "And you can slow down. I promise I'm not going to steal it from you."

"Are you going to bitch at me for talking with my mouth full next?"

"I just don't get what the big rush is." Hunter speared a piece of broccoli. Gabriel hadn't even known the cafeteria *sold* broccoli.

"I promised Layne I'd meet her after this period." Theoretically, so they could go to the library and work on today's math assignment. Really, so she could walk through the halls without getting hassled. Gabriel had found her hiding in the back corner of the library this morning, her face pale. Even then, he hadn't realized how bad it was, until trig, when Taylor started in on her.

Gabriel had put a stop to it, real quick.

"That Ryan Stacey guy is in my first period chem class," said Hunter. "I didn't know who he was until he showed up looking like he'd gotten hit in the face by a pickup truck."

Gabriel stabbed at the congealed mass of noodles. "If he lays a hand on her again, that might happen."

Hunter was quiet for a moment. "Does she know?" he asked quietly. "About you?"

"No." Gabriel watched Hunter push at the chicken on his tray and wondered if he was really that transparent. "Did you ever tell anyone?"

"Just Becca, but she already knew." A shrug. "Someone said Layne was caught in a fire when she was young, that she's got scars—"

"She does." Gabriel glared at him. "So what?"

"You don't think there's something . . . *interesting* about a girl with burn scars getting involved with a guy who can control—"

"*Control.*" What a joke. Gabriel snorted and shoveled more food into his mouth. "I'm not sure we can call it control yet."

"We're getting better." Hunter paused. "Do you feel it?"

"Not good enough." They'd almost gotten caught Saturday night. Four homes in a row, fully engulfed. Gabriel was in and out of fire so many times that he'd started to lose track of which house he was in, of how many people were left to save.

By the time he got to the last woman, they'd been there for hours. He'd been exhausted, disoriented from inhaling so much smoke. She'd been unconscious, and he'd nearly dropped her in the middle of her flaming living room.

Michael had shown him her picture in the paper the next morning, bandaged and sedated in some generic hospital. Michael's brown eyes had been rock hard as he demanded answers Gabriel couldn't give.

"I can't believe they're no closer to catching this guy," said Hunter. "We're losing time, waiting for the fires to turn up on the police scanner."

"Mike's been going out with the fire marshal's daughter."

Gabriel still thought it was a dick move. "She says they have no conclusive leads."

"Except you."

Gabriel rolled his eyes. "Yeah, well. We both know I'm not the one starting fires."

"Who's starting fires?" Calla Dean dropped onto the bench beside Hunter. Actually, she straddled it. The blue streaks in her hair were gone, replaced with fluorescent pink ones. She'd braided a small section and tied off the end with a yellow feather.

"We're talking about the ones on the news," Hunter said smoothly.

Calla picked up a piece of Hunter's broccoli and popped it into her mouth. Hunter watched this with a bemused expression on his face, but didn't stop her.

"The arson stuff?" she said. "Someone's got a fire fetish, huh?"

Gabriel reached out and turned her wrist over, exposing the flame tattoos. "Go figure."

She snorted. "I got those to piss off my aunt. Did you know the first fire was right next door to my house?" Without waiting for an answer, she took another piece of broccoli and made a face. "What, you couldn't add some butter?"

"I didn't realize I'd be sharing."

"Mind if I eat with you?" She took a third piece.

"Looks like you're already doing that," said Gabriel.

"I don't mind," said Hunter. He pushed the tray her way.

"Ugh. No way. I need salt. I'll be back."

Then she unfolded from the bench to weave through the tables toward the lunch line.

Hunter pulled his tray back and sliced another piece of chicken.

Gabriel watched him for a moment. "What the hell was that? You two have a *thing* now?"

"No." Hunter paused. "Maybe. I can't get a read."

"A girl doesn't steal your food if she's not into you."

"She's unusual."

"Dude, no offense, but *you're* unusual."

Hunter smiled briefly—but then sobered. "We talked for a long time Friday night. Her father is serving in Afghanistan, so she lives with her aunt and uncle. I think she's lonely."

Gabriel looked for Calla in the lunch line. Punk hair notwithstanding, she had a good six inches on most of the girls around her, and she helped the effect by wearing a shirt that revealed a long stretch of tan midriff. "Calla Dean is the captain of the girls' volleyball team. She could probably snap her fingers and have guys bringing her lunch on their knees. She is *not* lonely."

"I don't think that's the kind of attention she's looking for."

Gabriel shoveled another mouthful of macaroni into his mouth. "Oh, you mean you didn't spend the whole evening showing her your Arabic tattoo collection?"

"Farsi. And I don't have a collection. Just this one." He pointed to the inside of his elbow.

"What's it say?"

"Nothing important." Hunter nodded toward Calla, who must have grabbed something easy, because she was already paying. "What do you want to do about the fires?"

Gabriel scowled. It was easier talking girls. "I don't know."

Hunter's voice was careful. "Do you want to stop?"

"No." Gabriel glanced across the cafeteria, at where his brothers were sitting. Chris and Becca, Nick and Quinn. He hadn't spoken to any of them since he'd spent Sunday sleeping off the effects of Saturday's fire. "For the first time, I feel like I'm doing something right."

CHAPTER 30

Almost by accident, Layne found her days falling into an easy routine.

It shouldn't have been easy, what with the catcalls in the hallway at school, the jokes about scars and burn fetishes. The worst was when she didn't know what they were talking about—then it was embarrassing *and* humiliating.

Then Gabriel would appear at her shoulder and she'd remember she wasn't alone.

Every day, they spent fifth period in the library, going through the day's math assignment. Gabriel was getting better. He wasn't *fast*, but he was trying. She could see it in the classroom, too. Instead of slouching in his seat, scowling at the board, he was actually paying attention. When he dropped his homework in the basket on Ms. Anderson's desk, he did it almost defiantly, like throwing down a gauntlet.

He'd be back on the basketball team in no time.

In a way, it made Layne sad. Because now, after the last bell rang, he sat with her on the bleachers and watched Simon's basketball practice. In a few weeks, he'd be in practice himself, and she'd be sitting here alone.

At first, Gabriel would make little comments to her, about what Simon needed to do to improve. When Simon would glance up at them, Layne would translate Gabriel's remarks into quick signs.

When Gabriel realized what she was doing, he asked her to show him the signs, too.

She'd almost fallen off the bleachers. *No one* had ever asked her to teach sign language.

So she'd shown him some basics, for the most common criticisms he was shouting out, blushing as his eyes held hers while she moved his fingers into the right formation.

But afternoons in the school gym couldn't compare to the mornings at the farm. She'd always loved the cool silence, the easy solitude when it was just her and the horses. But now each moment carried a hint of anticipation.

Gabriel had shown up every morning.

He always looked deliciously sexy, his hair tousled from the run, a night's worth of stubble along his jaw. He told her it took twice as long to get to the farm as it did to get home. When she'd given him a puzzled look, he'd almost blushed and said, "I don't want to be a sweaty mess when I get here." Then he'd kissed her for so long that she'd forgotten her name, and he'd whispered against her cheek, "But it's okay if I'm a sweaty mess when I *leave* . . ."

But he never pushed her, never demanded more than she was ready to give. His hands never ventured outside of those safety zones, never even tried to get past her clothing. If her body stiffened at his touch, he backed off.

But now, after days of being *good*, her imagination was starting to get the worst of her. What if Gabriel felt her scars and thought she was disgusting? Talking about them in theory was a lot different from seeing red, puckered skin running up the side of her abdomen.

Thursday morning, they were lying on a grassy hill some distance behind the barn. Her horse was grazing a few yards away, a rope trailing from his halter. The air was crisp, but the sun warmed her cheeks, making her drowsy. She didn't want to close her eyes, in case there was any chance she'd open them to find out it was still Sunday morning, that this week was just a dream.

The horse snorted at a butterfly, but then went back to grazing.

Gabriel turned his head to look at her. "Why doesn't he run away?"

Layne gave a short laugh. "I keep asking myself the same thing about you."

He rolled up onto one elbow to look down at her. It put the sun behind him and made his hair fall into his eyes. "I'm not going anywhere."

Someone pinch me.

"Seriously," he said, glancing over at where her horse was yanking tufts of grass out of the ground. "Is he trained like a dog?"

Layne giggled. "No. Horses are herd animals. If he ran anywhere, he'd go back to the barn." Though really, if the barn manager caught her lying out here with the horse running loose, the woman would probably have a word or two to say about it.

"Like that day on the trail," said Gabriel.

Layne nodded. "The day *you* ran."

He snorted. "You scared me off with that . . . that *hug*."

She almost laughed at his tone, but then remembered the whole reason she'd thrown her arms around his neck in the first place. He'd looked so stricken, so sad. Even now, she could see shards of emotion in his eyes.

Despite the amount of time they'd spent together, she was still no closer to discovering his secrets.

And he was a master at keeping them hidden.

It had to do with his family; she knew that much. She never saw him with his brothers, but talking about them was just about the only thing to turn his voice sharp. No matter how much she loved his company, she couldn't help wondering if he was spending time with her so he could avoid spending time with *them*. Even in the mornings, he stretched the minutes as long as possible, until she knew he must be practically sprinting home to make it to school in time.

She reached up and pushed the hair out of his eyes. He turned his head to kiss her wrist.

Layne had to remind herself to focus. "What's it like, having a twin?"

He closed his eyes and gave a tight sigh. "I never know how to answer that question." He paused. "I mean, what's it like *not* having one?"

"Come on," she teased, trying to lighten his mood. "Do you finish each other's sentences? Feel each other's pain?"

He snorted, obviously not playing. "No."

"Are you and Nick still not speaking?"

He shrugged a little.

She could feel him distancing himself again. "Why won't you tell me what happened?"

Now his eyes turned hard. "Why do you care?"

She matched his tone. "Why shouldn't I care?"

He was going to fire back; she could tell. She braced herself for words sparked with anger.

But then he just sighed and rolled back to the ground to lie beside her. "I'm not even sure where to start. He brought Quinn home for dinner, and I just . . . I picked a fight. I'm not even sure why."

"Did you like her?"

"No, no, nothing like that. But we hardly ever fight, and this one—it got out of control. I almost . . . it could have been bad. Mike and Chris broke it up. Hunter, too."

There was more—a lot more. She could hear it behind the words.

"What else?" she said.

He was staring at the sky now, almost directly into the sun. It had to be hurting his eyes, but he wasn't even squinting. "It's complicated."

"Try me."

He scowled, and she thought he wasn't going to say anything else. But then he turned his head to look at her. "I wish I could undo it, but . . . I can't. They don't understand. Nick especially. I mean, he's the perfect one. Never in trouble, covering my ass when I screw up—which is all the damn time." He turned back to the sun. "You know, he got hurt right after homecoming? My fault. I couldn't even help him. He doesn't blame me, but I just . . . I just . . ."

"You blame yourself."

"Yeah."

"And you're mad at him for not blaming you."

Now she had his attention. "*Yeah*. How do you know that?"

Layne thought of her mother, of how much she hated the woman for abandoning her family—but how much she blamed herself for not being a more perfect daughter. "Trust me. I can play the blame game all day."

Gabriel didn't say anything. The silence suddenly had a weight to it.

She understood only a fraction of what he was talking about, but details could come later. This was the first time he'd come close to saying anything at all, and she didn't want him to stop.

"Have you tried to talk to Nick?" she said.

Gabriel fidgeted. "Yes. No. It's complicated." He rolled up on one arm again, until the line of his body was almost against hers. She could feel his warmth through the material of her jacket. She wanted to hold her breath, as if one small movement would spook him and send him bolting down the path again.

"I just snapped, I guess," he said. "Sometimes I wish I'd never started that fight, but then it feels like some bizarre turning point." He was closer now, his voice gaining momentum. "You know how you can trace back moments to one action that didn't feel important at the time? But then *later*, you go back and think about it, and you realize one little decision turned your whole life upside down. If I hadn't been so angry, we wouldn't have fought. If we hadn't fought, I never would have driven out of there the way I did. If I hadn't driven out of there, I wouldn't have—" He faltered.

Layne stared up at him. His eyes were wide, his breathing a little quick.

"Tell me," she said. "Just tell me."

He flinched and looked away. "It was the night I drove you

home," he said, his voice rough. "I was furious. I wasn't thinking straight. It wasn't . . . I can't . . ." He swallowed.

"Please," she said.

"I don't want you to hate me."

Hate him? What could it be? He *wouldn't have* what?

He'd been angry. Driving. Layne knew too much from her father's profession, and her imagination was getting carried away
again. "Did you hurt someone?" she whispered.

"No." He made a choked sound. "No. Just the opposite."

Well, there went her theories about hit-and-run accidents. *I
wouldn't have* . . . been with another girl? Her own throat felt
tight. "Is there . . . someone else?"

"What?" His eyes snapped to hers. "*What*? No. No, Layne,
there's no one else." He leaned down to brush his lips against
hers. It brought him even closer, his chest weighing on hers.

"Please," he said, kissing her again. "Please. I would never
hurt you like that."

His kisses felt light but heavy: desperate, as if he worried
she'd pull away any minute.

"Just tell me. I won't—" she started, only to have him trap
her lips for a breathless second. "I won't hate you. No matter
what."

He went still, staring down at her. His blue eyes were full of
hurt and fear and wonder. She'd never thought a guy like
Gabriel could look vulnerable, especially not lying on top of her,
but there it was.

Layne stared up at him. "Do you trust me?"

"Yes," he said. "It's not about trust. I don't want to disappoint you." His hand fell at her waist, securing her there against
him.

She froze. Half an inch of fabric sat between his palm and ruined skin.

Gabriel paused, but he didn't move his hand. "Do *you*
trust *me*?"

She could barely breathe. Her voice came out with a squeak.
"It's not about trust. I don't want to disappoint you."

He laughed softly, and it broke through some of the tension.

All of a sudden, any vulnerability was gone. "You're crazy." His hand tightened on her waist, strong and secure through her jacket. He leaned down again, and she was sure he was going to kiss her, but his mouth landed on her neck. His lips whispered against the skin there, followed by his teeth, right against the edge of her jaw. When his mouth caught her earlobe, she gasped and arched into him, surprised at the flood of heat in her body.

His hand slid up her side, holding her there, and she trembled, warring with how much she liked it—and how much she worried he could *feel*.

Gabriel drew back, just enough to look at her. The sun was behind him again, leaving fiery sparks in his hair. A cool breeze kissed her cheeks and made her long for his warmth.

"You still owe me a secret," she whispered.

"I know." His lips brushed hers, featherlight. "I know."

"Tell me—"

"Shhh." He unzipped her jacket.

She shivered, and it had nothing to do with the chill in the air. But he stroked a hand across her cheek. "Cold?"

She shook her head, but her breathing was shaky.

He kissed her again, and for a moment, it felt like his kiss was electric, like the sunlight was tangible, a blanket of warmth and sensation that smothered her thoughts. His tongue coaxed small sounds from her throat, and she buried her hands in his hair. She lost track of his hands, consumed by the feel of his body against hers.

Then he'd pulled her shirt free of her riding pants, and sunlight stroked her bare stomach.

She gasped and broke the kiss, bracing an arm against his chest, using her other hand to try to yank her shirt back down.

"Hey," he said. "Hey." His eyes were locked on hers, his hand on her face, nowhere dangerous. His voice was soft. "Your scars aren't all you are, Layne." He settled back into the grass a bit, though his face was still close to hers. A smile played on his lips. "And I swear I'm not just saying that to get to second base."

She laughed, but it came out like a sob, and she was terrified she was going to cry.

Gabriel shifted closer again, his thumb brushing along her cheekbone. "Do you really think I'm going to run if I see your scars?"

She turned her head to look at him. "Do you really think I'm going to run if I know your secrets?"

That chased the gentle humor off his face. It reminded her of Friday night, sitting on the tailgate of his car, when they'd played truth or dare. When she'd made a decision to jump, praying he'd be there to catch her.

She reached for his wrist, pulling his hand away from her cheek, drawing it down the front of her body. She held her breath again, sliding his fingers under the edge of her shirt. Her palm flattened over his hand, holding his skin against hers.

"Breathe," he whispered.

She shook her head quickly, and he laughed.

Then he slid his hand out from under hers, stroking the length of her abdomen. His thumb traced the line of her bra. She sucked in a quick breath.

"See?" He leaned in to speak against her ear. "I still think you're beautiful."

She knew exactly what his hands were feeling, exactly where the scars turned smooth skin into something that felt like melted rubber. She waited for him to jerk his fingers away, to make a sound of disgust, to recoil.

Instead, he slid her shirt higher, then bent to kiss his way across her stomach.

Every nerve in her body was firing. She thought she might hyperventilate.

Especially when his teeth found the skin at the base of her rib cage.

At that moment, he could have told her he was a bank robber, and she wouldn't have cared. An arms dealer. A foreign spy.

All she knew was that suddenly clothes were *in the way*.

She started yanking at the shoulders of his sweatshirt, trying to drag it over his head. He laughed again, but this time it was a slow sexy growl of sound as he lifted enough to help her yank the hoodie free.

The contents of his pockets spilled across her bare skin, and she giggled, grabbing for keys and his iPod, tossing them on top of the abandoned sweatshirt. Then her fingers closed on something slick and metal.

She frowned as she held it up. "A lighter?"

Gabriel was staring at it in her hand, that same inscrutable expression on his face. Tousled hair, rumpled T-shirt. Somewhat lost, but defiant at the same time. Those typical defenses were falling into place.

For an instant she wondered if his big secret was that he was a smoker. But she couldn't work that out in her head. She'd never seen him smoke a cigarette, had never smelled cigarettes or pot or *anything* on him or his clothes—and god knew they'd spent enough time together over the last few days.

But why would he be carrying around a lighter if he wasn't a smoker?

He still hadn't said anything.

The horse snorted, lifting his head to look at the barn, his ears pricked. He'd moved down the hill a ways, but not far enough for her to worry.

She looked back at Gabriel. "A lighter?" she said again, bewildered. Intuitively, she knew that the time for easy answers had come and gone. *It's my brother's,* or *I found it in the woods.* Maybe something like, *It's dead, but it used to belong to my father.*

Gabriel sighed and pushed the hair back from his face. "That," he said, "is part of my secret."

The horse snorted again, pawing at the grass. He was probably ready to spook at nothing.

Layne sighed and rolled to her feet, zipping up her jacket as she moved. She caught the horse's lead rope and kept her voice even, trying to figure out the mystery before Gabriel laid it on the line. But she had no idea. "Your secret has to do with a lighter?"

He reached out to take it from her hand. "No. My secret has to do with fire."

And at that precise moment, the roof of the barn burst into flame.

CHAPTER 31

Gabriel stared at the flames shooting through the barn roof, blazing flares of orange and red. Smoke poured into the sky. There was plenty of fuel here—hay and wood and probably dozens of things he couldn't even imagine. This fire didn't rage—it celebrated. The entire building would be consumed in minutes.

Something was banging inside the barn. He heard screams, inhuman cries that made him want to clamp his hands over his ears.

Horses.

He could feel his heart in his throat. He'd been pulling power from the sunlight, his emotions riding high.

Had he done this?

This made his mistake in the woods look like a campfire.

Layne was all action, shoving at his chest. Her horse was dancing at the end of his rope, but Layne held fast. She was yelling, her voice hoarse.

He realized she'd been yelling at him for some time.

"Take him, damn it! Get him in the field!" She punched him in the chest again, shoving the rope at him.

Take him. The horse. Gabriel's fingers closed on the rope automatically, just as the animal reared up, nearly jerking the rope free.

"Just get him through the gate!" Layne cried, pointing behind him.

Like he could do that without getting trampled. The horse had to weigh a thousand pounds, and he was dragging Gabriel in a circle, a snorting, panicked mess of muscle and hooves.

He managed to get to the gate, somehow working the latch before the horse swung around, knocking Gabriel into the fence with his shoulder. Gabriel lost hold of the rope—but before he could panic, the horse bolted through the opening, tearing along the fenceline with a thunder of hooves against turf.

But the animal was trapped in the field. Gabriel latched the gate.

When he turned around, Layne was gone.

He spun full circle. *Gone.*

Smoke poured from the barn doors now. Horses were still screaming, banging on the walls. Trapped. Layne couldn't have . . . she wouldn't—

But he was already running before those thoughts could complete themselves.

He made it to the barn doors just as Layne burst through the wall of smoke, coughing as she ran. She had a rope in each hand, two horses trailing behind her. Her face was streaked with soot already. One of the horses had bits of flaming debris on its back. Both were wide eyed, their steel shoes skidding on the concrete outside the barn.

"Layne!" he said. "Don't—"

"Take them!"

Then she flung the ropes at him, and he was lost in a rush of surging horseflesh.

And she was back in the barn.

He couldn't catch the ropes quickly enough. The horses bolted for the path behind the barn, the path where he'd first met Layne, the path that led to the woods and safety.

He had no idea whether she was right about the whole herd animal thing, but the woods were better than the barn. He let them go, then dove into the cloud of smoke after her.

After the sunlight, the darkness of the barn was almost absolute. Sparks dripped from the ceiling, catching at loose straw and wood shavings to create small fires in his path. But most of the fire was overhead, in the hayloft, a pulsing glow that called to him through the smoke.

You're here! Come play.

"Layne!" he yelled. The roar of the fire was a living thing, muting his voice. Horses were still screaming in the darkness—a sound that had started as panic and now carried mostly pain.

He shouted her name again, dropping to his knees where the smoke was less dense—though it didn't help. The fire had found something new to burn, and metal cans were bursting somewhere to his left. He could smell chemicals.

Settle, he pleaded.

He hadn't realized how much Hunter's presence helped, how much another Elemental let him focus his power.

This was too much for him to handle alone.

"Layne!"

Nothing.

How could he have done this? His control was no better than when he'd killed his parents. *And it was going to happen again.*

He swept the aisle, going from side to side, using his hands to learn if she'd collapsed in here somewhere. He found all kinds of items he couldn't identify—no Layne. He heard a crash, and before he could identify the source, something heavy ran into him, knocking him aside. Hooves hit his rib cage; his head hit the wall. Metal horseshoes scrabbled at the concrete flooring, and then the animal was gone, tearing into the sunlight.

Gabriel coughed and rolled back to his knees, ignoring the new pain in his chest, the starbursts flaring in his eyes. He deserved a broken rib or two. A concussion.

He deserved to be trampled. To death.

"Layne!"

Fire rained down more steadily now. Bits of wood struck his back, his cheeks, his hands.

There was only one horse banging now, from what he could tell. Had they all escaped? Or had some died from the smoke, the heat?

Would he find Layne, or just a body?

Stop it.

Larger parts of the ceiling fell behind him, flaming planks of wood crashing into the aisle. Fire leapt onto the walls, into the open stall doors, catching the sawdust bedding and turning it into a carpet of flame.

What if Layne wasn't in the aisle at all, but inside one of the stalls?

Help me, he begged the fire. *Where is she?*

But this fire didn't care about people. It cared about the burn, the destruction, the pure energy.

Metal struck concrete again, and Gabriel scrabbled out of the way. Smoke swelled around the running animal, revealing a white head, soot-covered flanks, and then a tail swallowed up by the smoke.

No more banging.

Someone had let that horse out.

"Layne!" Gabriel dove forward. The horse had come down the center of the aisle, so he didn't know which side to check first.

This new silence was terrifying.

He started left.

Closed door. Closed door. Open door—but no Layne. Maybe it had been pushed open by one of the earlier horses.

The heat was scorching his lungs. He refused to think of what it must be doing to Layne's.

He scurried across the aisle. Closed door. Closed door. Closed—*where the hell was she?*

And then his hand came down on something solid.

A body.

She wasn't moving. Wasn't breathing. When he put his hands on her face, he felt something wet—blood, running from her hairline. Gabriel was choking on smoke, on tears, on saying her *name*. He had her in his arms, but it was like clutching a doll.

Power breathed in the air around him. A fierce contradiction to the lifeless girl in his arms.

He wanted to lie down and die beside her.

But the sheer irony was that he could lie here forever, and the fire would never hurt him.

So much energy, right here for his taking. He could level the woods around them, could destroy the entire city.

But he couldn't save one person.

He slid his hand against her throat, checking for a pulse he knew wasn't there. His fingers slid through blood, and he choked on another sob.

Blood.

He remembered the night Becca's father had tried to kill them all, when they'd been standing in three feet of water, and Chris had been so sure Becca was dead. They'd pulled her broken body from a mangled car. Blood had been everywhere. Chris had cut his hand on glass, and he'd put his blood to hers.

He'd fed his power into her.

She'd been healed.

She'd lived.

But Becca was an Elemental—a Fifth, like Hunter. Had that been part of it? Had her body known to draw from Chris's energy, to heal itself?

Gabriel didn't know. But he was already pounding his knuckles into the rough concrete of the aisle, feeling the skin break. He was already inciting the flames higher, pulling power from the fire, drawing strength from the inferno around him.

Energy coiled inside him, waiting for release. He felt strong, like he could tear this building down. Like he could destroy towns. Cities. Like energy could pour from his fingertips with the power of a hundred suns.

Gabriel coiled his hand into a fist and pressed his knuckles to her forehead, blood to blood.

And then he drove all that energy into *her.*

Layne's body jerked so hard he almost dropped her. But then she didn't move.

"Layne!" He caught her up against his chest. Her head fell against his shoulder. "Layne?"

Nothing.

He choked on another sob.

And then her body jerked again, not quite as violently.

She started coughing.

"Holy shit," he said.

And then he was running, scrambling out of the barn before the raging fire he'd drawn could bring the whole thing down around them.

He got her into the grass, in the bright sunlight, where fifteen minutes ago they'd been lying together. Horses were clustered together along the fenceline, some inside the field, some out. He could see blood on some, could smell burned hair.

But he was more worried about Layne. Her clothes were blackened with soot, her face streaked with blood.

But he didn't see a cut at her hairline. And she wasn't coughing now, just drawing in big gasps of air.

He could hear sirens.

"Talk to me," he said. It sounded like he was crying. "Layne— please. Talk to me."

She coughed then. "Are they . . . are they out?"

He didn't have the heart to tell her some hadn't gotten out. He took a breath, ready to lie.

But she grabbed his arm, her nails digging into his skin. "Truth," she coughed.

He stared down at her. And shook his head.

She started crying.

"I'm sorry," he said, choking on the words. "I'm so sorry."

The sirens were getting closer. Flashing lights strobed through the trees at the end of the property.

He couldn't be here.

"Layne," he said. "I have to go."

She stared back at him. Her eyes were piercing, alert through the tears.

"I'm sorry," he whispered.

"I knew you'd run," she said.

The words hit him like a fist. He fell back.

But she was right: He ran like hell.

CHAPTER 32

Gabriel didn't see the trees, didn't feel the air on his face. He didn't feel the pain in his legs, the way the cool air burned his lungs. He just ran. It took every ounce of focus to keep moving forward, to run *away* from Layne.

He wanted to bolt back to her, to erase that look from her eyes. To hold her hand while the firefighters turned his flames into smoke and bits of cinder.

He kept feeling the way her body had hung in his arms, lifeless.

He'd killed someone *again*.

Did it matter that he'd brought her back?

Emotion gripped his throat and almost made it impossible to run.

He pushed through it. Maybe his ligaments would tear and offer some piercing agony. Maybe his heart would give out and he'd collapse in the middle of the trail.

He had no idea how long it took him to get home. The four miles simultaneously felt like they took all day and no time at all. He was just suddenly at the tree line behind his house, gasping for breath with his forehead braced against the bark of an old maple.

Now he could feel the sun, bleeding through the trees, feeding energy into his skin. It still had to be early: The woods around him were silent, as if even the morning wildlife wouldn't bear witness to his sorrow.

As if he was worth it.

The Guides were right. He should have been killed long before he could cause this kind of damage.

The morning air felt all wrong. Too crisp, too clean, too pure. He could smell the soot on his clothes.

And then he was puking, or his body was trying to, dry heaves ransacking his empty stomach. He didn't remember falling, but his knees were grinding into the leaves and underbrush, his forearms barely strong enough to support his upper body against the base of the tree.

He was crying, too—probably had been for some time. His eyes felt raw; his throat felt like someone had him in a headlock.

And he was alone.

He put his forehead against the tree and choked on another breath. He clenched his damaged fist and slammed it into the bark of the tree. And again.

Alone.

A hand closed on his arm. "Gabriel. *Gabriel.*"

Nick. Gabriel turned his head and stared at his twin, wide-eyed and kneeling in the leaves like he'd been there for a while. His mirror image in a clean sweatshirt and cutoff sweatpants. No tears. No soot. No blood. Perfect.

Wind swirled through the trees to rustle the leaves. "What happened?"

Nick's expression was wary, as if he expected Gabriel to hit him, or snap. Or worse.

"I did it again," Gabriel said, and his voice sounded thick. He pressed the heels of his hands into his eyes and struggled to breathe. "I did it again, Nicky."

"What happened?" Nick's voice was softer now.

Gabriel shook his head. "Just go." His voice broke and he didn't care. Air swirled through the space between them, and the leaves rustled as Nick shifted to stand.

Good.

But then Nick had a hold of his sleeve, of his arm, and he was pulling. Hard. "Get up. Come on."

Gabriel fought his grip as anger pierced through the despair. "Leave me alone."

"Get up." Nick was still dragging at his arm. The air dropped ten degrees. "*Move.*"

"Let me go."

"Move."

"God*damn* it, Nick!" Gabriel wrenched his arm free. "I'm not going in the house!"

Another ten degrees. "Why not?"

"Because *I don't want to hurt anyone else.*"

Nick stared at him for a moment. Gabriel tried not to shiver.

Then Nick clocked him on the side of the head. "I don't care. Move."

When Gabriel didn't, Nick kicked him. First in the leg, then in the side. Right where that horse had gotten him with a hoof.

Gabriel swore and pushed to his feet, holding his side. "Stop."

"You stop." Nick got in his face. The air was colder now, thin and hard to breathe. "Stop being such an ass and come in the house."

Gabriel sucked in a breath to fight—but the air was frigid and snapped at his lungs. His ribs hurt. His hand ached. He felt like he'd been fighting for *so long*.

"I can't do this anymore," he said, so softly that he barely heard his own voice.

But the wind would carry the words to Nick, whose expression didn't soften. "Then don't. Come on."

And this time when he yanked at Gabriel's arm, he followed.

The house was quieter than the woods had been, filled with the hush of sleep and early morning. Still, the coffeepot was brewing when they came through the back door, though no one was in the kitchen. Chris's and Michael's doors were closed. Nick practically shoved Gabriel into the upstairs bathroom.

"Sit," he said, his tone clipped. He jerked at the faucet, turning the water on cold.

Gabriel sat on the closed toilet. He caught the edge of his reflection in the mirror, and just that edge was enough. Leaves and fire debris in his hair, tear-streaked soot on his cheeks.

"Nick," he said, and speaking still felt like talking around ground glass. "Just—"

"Shut up. Put your hand in the water."

When he hesitated, Nick sighed and grabbed his wrist, thrusting his raw knuckles under the faucet.

Gabriel hissed at the sudden pain, but Nick held fast. "I'll bet your hand is broken."

Probably. The skin was torn open across the back of each finger, and the side of his hand was swollen. The water felt fantastic and terrible at the same time.

Gabriel didn't say anything, just watched the water stream into the drain, dragging dirt and blood with it. Soon his hand would be clean, identical to Nick's again, except for the gaping wounds.

He sniffed and swiped his other sleeve across his face, but it didn't feel like it did much. "Nick."

"Yeah."

Gabriel glanced up and met his brother's eyes. *I'm sorry.*

But he couldn't make himself say it. There was just too much to be sorry for, as if two words couldn't contain it all.

Nick finally sighed and looked away, turning off the faucet. "I'll get you some ice. Think you can get out of those clothes?"

Gabriel nodded. He'd kicked off his shoes and wrestled out of his sweatshirt by the time his brother came back with an ice pack wrapped in a towel.

Nick didn't say anything, just set it on the counter and started to back out of the bathroom, pulling the door shut behind him.

But the door stopped with a few inches left. "You want me to bring you a cup of coffee?"

Coffee. The scent of it filled the house now, just like the guilt of his parents' deaths filled Gabriel's heart until he couldn't contain it all anymore. The raw emotion clawed at his chest, at his throat, at his eyes, spilling over until he was crying in earnest.

Then Nick had an arm around his back and Gabriel was crying into his brother's shoulder.

"I'm sorry," he said. "Nicky, I'm sorry."

And Nick just held him until he ran out of tears, and they were sitting on the bathroom floor, side by side. They'd used to hide in here, when they were younger, usually after pulling a prank on Michael. They'd lock the door and whisper with the lights off, crouching by the bathtub while Michael pounded on the door and yelled for Dad to get a screwdriver.

Now there was barely enough room to sit.

He didn't want to think about the past, anyway. Gabriel felt like he'd never have the strength to stand up again. To go to school.

To face Layne.

He wondered if she was okay, if the firefighters had put the fire out.

He wondered if she'd ever forgive him.

He wondered if he'd ever forgive himself.

"Want to know a secret?" said Nick, his voice almost casual, as if Gabriel hadn't just spent fifteen minutes sobbing on his shoulder—and spent days living like an outcast. As if nothing had changed, and they were as close as they'd been two weeks ago.

It reminded him of his conversation with Hunter, about how sometimes you were left with no choice but to move forward and do what you would have done anyway.

Still, Gabriel had to take a steadying breath to speak. "You're filming this for later blackmail?"

"That, and . . ." Nick paused, and his voice took on a new note. "When Becca's dad caught us and trapped us in that freezer, I was so glad I was in there, and you were out here."

Gabriel rolled that around in his head for a moment. "Why?"

"Because I knew you'd be strong enough to get us out."

Gabriel gave a humorless laugh. "Yeah, but not strong enough to keep you from getting caught in the first place."

"You were strong enough to get away."

"Jesus Christ, Nick, you don't think I feel bad enough about that already?"

Nick swung his head around. "Bad? Why do you feel *bad* about that? You don't think I feel *bad* being such a liability all the time? Like it's not humiliating enough that my brother has been saving my ass since middle school?"

"What are you even talking about?"

"I'm talking about Tyler. Seth. All of them. How every time they'd want to fight, you'd stand up to them and I'd run."

"Nick . . . you're crazy. You'd fight—"

"No. When the fighting got dirty, when they meant business, *you'd* fight." Nick was looking at the wall now. "You'd fight, and I'd run."

This was insane. "I'd tell you to run! I was usually running right behind you."

"Forget it. You're missing the point."

"Goddamn, Nick. What *is* the point?"

"Shhh." Nick glanced at the hallway. "You'll wake Michael, and he'll have an aneurysm if he sees you like this."

Gabriel shut up.

Nick looked down at his hands, rubbing at some of the soot that had come off his brother. "Sometimes I wonder if you didn't let me in on the fire stuff because you knew I wouldn't be able to handle it."

"That's not it at all." Gabriel swallowed. Somehow this was harder than telling Layne his secrets. "I knew you'd make me stop."

Now Nick was looking at him, hard. "Stop what?"

Gabriel took a deep breath.

And he told Nick everything.

Layne sat on the stretcher in the ER and hugged her arms across her chest. Her parents were right on the other side of the privacy curtain, having a whispered argument.

Like she was an idiot. Like she couldn't hear *every* word.

"Didn't you tell them?" her mother hissed. Layne could smell her Chanel perfume from here. "I can't believe they're not even *examining* her."

"Tell them *what*, Charlotte?" Her father's voice was tired. "She's fine."

"She's not fine, *David*." Her mother spat his name like it tasted bad. "She's already damaged enough, and now you're acting like nothing—"

"I'm not acting like anything. Why don't you get a handle on the histrionics. I'm sure you have a pill or something you can take."

Layne wanted to lie down on this stretcher and put the pillow over her face.

She's already damaged enough.

Thanks, Mom.

The paramedics had said they were taking her to the ER as a precaution, but a doctor had listened to her lungs and shined a light in her eyes and declared her perfectly well. He'd told her that normally people had breathing difficulties from smoke in-halation, coughing, shortness of breath. She didn't have any of those things. Now she was just waiting for a piece of paper so she could get out of here.

No one knew about Gabriel. No one *asked*.

She didn't start out keeping him a secret—she just didn't know what to say, or when to say it. People kept speaking over her head, never asking her anything more than whether she knew what day it was or how to contact her parents.

She'd found his lighter in the grass beside her, probably dropped when he'd grabbed his things and run. She'd shoved it into her pocket. Even now, she could slide her hand between the fabric panels and run her thumb along the slick metal casing.

I don't want you to hate me.

She thought about the recent arson attacks in the area. Was he telling her he was responsible?

Had he started the fire in the barn?

They'd lain together in the grass for at least fifteen minutes, maybe more. If he'd put this lighter to a bale of hay or some-thing, how long would it have taken the place to go up like that?

Surely faster than fifteen minutes, right?

And when would he have done it? Though she hadn't had her eyes on him every second they'd been together that morning, she couldn't see how he would have been able to climb into the hayloft and start a fire without her even noticing.

Beyond that, *why* would he have done it?

She kept running his words through her brain, as if they were a math problem, and all she had to do was find the right equation to solve for X.

The night I drove you home was the first night—

The first night that *what*?

Her mother yanked back the curtain, making the hangers rattle in the steel track. Though she was wearing a white tennis skirt and a pink trimmed sweater, her eyes were perfectly lined, her mascara unsmudged. Even her lipstick looked freshly applied.

Layne wondered how much time she'd spent getting ready to come see her daughter in the hospital.

She wondered if she'd actually been playing tennis.

"Baby? You okay?"

"I'm great," said Layne flatly. *Baby.* As if her mother gave a damn. She'd spent more time on the other side of the curtain than she had in here.

"I'm going to flag down the doctor," her mother said, her lips pursed. "Don't they know what I do for this hospital? I'm going to give these people a piece of my—"

"No," said Layne evenly. "There are sick people here. I can wait."

Her mom opened her mouth to protest, but then her cell phone started ringing, and she stuck a manicured hand into a designer bag to fetch it.

Layne sighed. She *was* ready to go home and get a shower. Her clothes smelled like horses and fire, the sweetness of alfalfa hay mixed with soot and ashes. She hadn't even unzipped her jacket, knowing the turtleneck underneath was soaked with sweat.

And she needed time alone.

She needed time to think.

A nurse came around the corner wearing pink scrubs with lollipops all over them. Some papers and a clipboard were in one hand, and she glanced between Layne's father—tapping away at his iPhone—and her mother, who was gushing about something to do with a celebrity polo match.

So concerned.

The nurse faltered.

Layne held out her hand. "Here. Can I just take it?"

"Your parents need to sign, sweetie."

Layne looked at her father. "Dad. Hey. Signature."

He put a hand out without looking up, hitting a few more keys on the phone.

Unbelievable. It reminded Layne of the day in Gabriel's driveway, when he'd been so dismissive of Michael.

Layne looked at the nurse. "I'm sorry. They usually act like they give a crap."

That got her dad's attention. "Watch it. I was supposed to be in court this morning."

Layne looked back at him in mock surprise. "I can't believe I forgot to add this to your schedule."

Her mom laughed into the phone and held up her hand. "Oh my goodness, that is *too much*. Let me step into the hallway. There's a lot of commotion here . . ."

Layne scooted off the stretcher. She wished Simon were here, but her father had sent him to school. "Let's just go," she said. "You can get back to court, Mom can get back to 'tennis,' and I can get back to school."

Her father had his head bent over the form—probably reading what he was signing. "You're not going to school. The doctor said for you to stay home and rest, make sure there aren't any delayed effects." His hand scribbled across the bottom of the form.

"He also said I was *fine*."

"End of discussion."

Of course it was. Layne sighed.

Her father handed the forms back to the nurse and looked at

Layne. "I rearranged my schedule. I'll stay with you until Simon gets home."

It should have made her feel better. It didn't.

It made her feel like an *obligation*.

She didn't even say good-bye to her mother—not out of any sense of spite or anger, but the woman had disappeared down some corridor to take her call, and there was no sign of her. Maybe she'd forgotten the whole reason they were at the hospital to begin with.

Layne just folded her legs into her father's BMW and stared out the window.

She wondered if Gabriel was all right. He'd been in that fire, too. And he hadn't had the luxury of medical attention.

He'd run when he'd seen fire trucks. That had to imply some sort of guilt.

But the look in his eyes after the fire—there'd been no guilt *there*. Only horror. Sadness. Regret, as he told her that some horses had been trapped.

The barn had been her sanctuary. She'd mourn its loss as much as she would the other horses. Gabriel had understood that. Respected it.

She *knew* he had.

My secret has to do with fire.

Layne wished she could call him. To demand answers.

But she was afraid to call him. She was afraid the truth would be more devastating than all these hypotheticals.

Her father disappeared into his study when they got home, making Layne wonder why he'd even bothered to stay with her. He'd tried to be supportive in the car, talking about how they'd find another place for her to ride, to move her horse to another facility, all concrete, easy things that should have been reassuring but weren't at all, really.

She stripped out of her clothes in the bathroom, clenching her eyes shut as usual, hating the sight of her naked body. She couldn't see, anyway; her eyes kept blurring with tears that she chased off. She kept her mind occupied by flinging her clothes into two piles by feel: keep or trash. The jacket was disgusting.

Trash. The boots were expensive and could use a good cleaning. Keep. Turtleneck, keep. Socks, keep. Riding breeches, trash.

Then the memory of that moment in the grass hit her, full force.

Your scars aren't all you are, Layne.

She gasped and pressed her hands to her eyes, letting her shoulders shake with emotion but refusing to let the tears fall.

Gabriel saw her. Really saw *her*, despite the scars, despite her imperfections. He'd kissed his way across her abdomen, saying all the right things and touching her in ways that had made her want to cash in her V card right there. She'd never felt like she could have a relationship with a boy, had never thought anyone would look past the destroyed flesh marking half her body.

That moment, *that* had been perfection.

And then it had all gone up in smoke. Literally.

She shivered and rubbed at her eyes. She was still standing in the middle of the bathroom, sniveling in her bra and underwear. All she could smell now was smoke and sweat.

But first, she wanted to see what he'd seen. She wanted to see just how bad the scars were, as if they'd changed since the last time she'd dared take a look in the mirror.

Quickly, before she could change her mind, she swiped the tears away, opened her eyes, and stared at her reflection.

And despite the chill in the air, she kept right on staring, not believing what she was seeing, despite the evidence right in front of her.

Her scars, every last one of them, were gone.

CHAPTER 33

Gabriel sat in math class, hating the empty chair beside him. He couldn't focus. Five hours ago, he'd been dragging Layne out of a burning barn.

Now he was listening to Anderson prattle on about negative numbers.

He'd been able to pull enough energy from the sun to ensure his hand wasn't broken, but when he went for his lighter to draw more power from a true fire, he didn't have it.

Whatever. The pain felt good.

He hadn't wanted to come to school. But Nick had a good point: If he was already a suspect—even an unofficial one—not showing up for school on the same day as a fire might raise a huge red flag. He'd spent most of first period fidgeting, watching the door, absolutely certain that cops were going to come storming into the classroom any minute to arrest him.

Absolutely certain that Layne would have turned him in.

But as time went on, as students went about their business, he realized that nothing had changed.

He hadn't seen Hunter yet, and the morning was too complicated to sum up in a text message. But when he hit the cafeteria, Calla was already sitting with Hunter.

Gabriel sighed and slung his backpack over his shoulder, heading for the gym.

The halogen lights were off, but sunlight streamed through the grated windows near the ceiling. The long stretch of beige floor was usually empty at this hour, but at the opposite end of the room, a kid was shooting free throws from the line. And from the looks of it, he was hitting every one.

Simon.

Gabriel stopped short. Would Layne have told her brother? Was Simon waiting here to confront him, to ask what exactly had happened this morning?

But that was crazy. He'd only just made the decision to come to the gym himself. And why would Simon be shooting free throws before a confrontation? Gabriel couldn't make it work out in his head.

Everything was making him paranoid today.

At the very least, if Simon was here, it meant Layne was okay.

He walked into Simon's line of sight, and the boy's expression brightened.

"Hey," said Gabriel. He held out a fist. Simon hit it.

But then the boy quickly gestured for Gabriel's phone.

There was a fire at the farm this morning. Layne was there. They took her to the hospital.

It answered a lot of questions—and created just as many. Gabriel stared at the words and wondered how to play this. He looked up and didn't have to fake concern. "Is she okay?"

Fine. Doctor says take it easy today. Precaution.

"Makes sense."

I emailed her from computer lab. She wanted to come to school. Dad said no.

Gabriel nodded. "Figures."

Can you stay for the game this afternoon?

This afternoon. He'd planned on it earlier this week, because he and Layne had fallen into the routine of watching Simon's practice. He'd just assumed they'd watch together.

"As long as I've got a ride, I'll stay," he said.

Simon's face broke into a grin.

Gabriel gestured for the ball. "Come on," he said. "I've got time. Let's play."

It felt good to lose himself in the sport, to have some distraction. His hand ached, but he played through it. Simon was getting *good*—practice was clearly paying off. Gabriel used the signs Layne had taught him, but he didn't need them much. When Simon ducked under Gabriel's guard to steal the ball and make a basket, Gabriel started to wonder if the kid shouldn't just be playing—he should be *starting*.

One of the gym doors slammed somewhere across the court, but Gabriel ignored it.

Until Ryan Stacey stepped onto the court and intercepted a pass.

His face was still bruised from Friday night, and the split lip hadn't healed, making his smirk look a little crazy. "Looks like the retard has a girlfriend."

"Looks like you didn't get the message last Friday." Gabriel could feel the anger coiling in his chest, ready to be let loose on this jerk.

But hands caught his arms, holding him back.

Ryan had brought friends.

At least four guys, but Gabriel couldn't see who else was behind him. Probably the same losers who'd been beating on Simon last week. Gabriel tried to fight them, but there were too many—and with the lights off, he couldn't pull any power from the electricity in the room.

Gabriel felt sure Ryan was going to take the chance to hit him—but the guy was going after Simon, who was backing away.

"Hey!" said Gabriel. "You touch him, I'll break your goddamn arms off."

Someone hit him in the back of the head, sending stars across his field of vision. Ryan caught up to Simon and gave him a solid shove in the chest, hard enough to knock him to the court.

Simon scrambled backward, but Ryan was leaning down, a hand drawn back, ready to slam a fist into Simon's face.

Gabriel redoubled his struggles, but he'd never be fast enough.

"Hey!" a new voice yelled from the corner by the bleachers. An authoritative voice.

The coach's voice.

The guys holding Gabriel scattered and ran. Ryan tried to follow, but he was under the net, and the coach beat him to it, even while dragging a full mesh bag of balls. Though he wasn't a big man, Coach Kanner could be plenty intimidating, and Gabriel enjoyed watching Ryan's face go pale under those bruises.

Until he realized Simon was just as pale, his breathing quick.

"Come on, Coach," said Ryan. "We were just messing around."

"You don't mess around on my court. You're out of the next two games."

Ryan's eyes just about bugged out of his head. "What? But that's not—"

"Want to make it three?"

"Whatever." Ryan turned away.

The coach called after him. "Stacey!"

Ryan looked like he was going to keep walking—but he must have wanted to stay on the team. He turned. "What?"

The coach raised an eyebrow.

Ryan sighed. "Yes. Sir."

"See you on the bench at four."

Ryan stormed through the doors into the locker room, shoving the door behind him to make the sound echo across the court. Gabriel would have mocked the dickhead, but he knew better. He was already on shaky ground with the coach. Instead, he put out a hand to pull Simon to his feet.

The coach looked at the younger boy. "You all right?"

Simon nodded. His face was red, his jaw clenched.

Gabriel felt for him. Simon could play—but he couldn't *play*, for real, in a game. He was small, and though a few years would probably take care of that, a year was an *eternity*. Especially a year spent getting your ass kicked.

And all that was on top of not being able to hear.

The coach rubbed at the back of his neck. "I caught some of your playing earlier. You've been working hard."

Simon nodded.

Then the coach gave Gabriel a good-natured shove in the arm. "Unless you're just getting lazy."

"Nah." Gabriel smiled. He'd forgotten how much he missed the easy camaraderie of a sport. Had it really only been a couple weeks? "It's all him."

Coach Kanner looked back at Simon. "Think you can play like that this afternoon?"

Simon's eyebrows went way up. He nodded vigorously.

"We'll give it a try," said the coach.

Simon nodded again.

The coach held up a finger. "One time." Then he slung the bag of balls over his shoulder and turned for his office at the back of the gym.

Simon turned wide eyes to Gabriel. He gestured for the phone.

Holy crap.

For the first time since the weekend, Layne fired up her computer.

She didn't even bother with her e-mail, rolling her eyes at the bolded number showing how many unread messages she had.

Seriously. Didn't they have anything better to do?

She couldn't stop thinking about fire. About arson. About Gabriel.

And her scars.

She'd stared at herself in the bathroom for what must have been a good twenty minutes. At first she'd wanted to yell for her father. She'd wanted someone else to see what she was seeing, to pinch her arm and prove she wasn't dreaming.

But her father would want explanations, and she sure didn't have one.

What had happened in that barn?

That night I drove you home was the first night—

A notebook sat open next to her laptop. She had to think back. The night her father had worked late. The night Gabriel had played basketball with Simon. Wednesday.

Wednesday, she wrote on the paper.

She went to the local news Web site and searched for the word *arson*.

Bingo. There'd been an article on Thursday about a fire Wednesday night. A family of four, though only three had gotten out. The reporter had interviewed the mother, a Mrs. Hulster, who said that the fire chief had declared the house too dangerous to search, that no one could be alive inside.

Yet somehow a firefighter had been in there. Somehow, her daughter had been pulled out.

Hulster. It sounded familiar.

Alan Hulster! Of course! Taylor had been talking about the fire the next day in class.

Had Gabriel seemed upset? Had he known about it?

Layne tapped her pencil on her paper. She couldn't remember.

She skipped to the next article. Another fire, another suspected arson. The firefighters had been ordered out, but one fell through the floor. He should have been trapped—he should have been killed.

But again, someone dragged him out.

So Wednesday, Thursday . . .

Friday was the night of the party. Layne had been with Gabriel, until late.

No arson.

Saturday. A day full of highs and lows. A day that ended with her father being a jerk in the Merrick driveway.

She scrolled to the next arson article and clicked on the link.

A day that ended with a fire in a townhome community. She'd already seen this article—Ryan Stacey had forwarded it to her with mocking comments.

This time she actually read it. A four-alarm fire, an entire row of homes completely consumed.

No fatalities. Only one serious injury.

She stared at the timeline she'd drawn on her paper.

One of those articles quoted a fireman as saying "this guy has a hero complex." That the arsonist was setting fires just so he could go in and save the victims.

That didn't match Gabriel at all.

Or did it? Had he done that exact thing this morning?

She remembered her question from the hillside. *Did you hurt someone?*

And the haunted look in his eyes. *No. Just the opposite.*

That seemed to point in both directions.

Her head hurt.

A knock sounded at her door, and Layne turned off the monitor before her father could see what she was looking at.

He leaned into her room, looking frustrated. "What time is Simon supposed to be home?"

She glanced at the clock. It was after four. "His first game is today. The activities bus drops us off around five-thirty."

"His first *game*?"

"Yeah. His first basketball game." She folded her arms on the back of her chair. "Though he's probably not playing."

"He was serious about that whole basketball thing?"

"Yeah, Dad." Layne stared at him, feeling sorry for him and wondering if he deserved it. She'd never sided with her mother, but maybe the woman was right about him working too much. He and Simon never talked, and she'd always thought it was because Simon resented his father.

She'd never really thought about her father making no effort to remedy the situation.

He came into the room and dropped onto the end of her bed. "Are you going to be all right?"

Layne thought about her scars disappearing. "Yes. I always am."

"I'm sorry if I seemed insensitive this morning. After hearing you were in a fire . . . after everything we went through when you were little . . ." He ran a hand through his hair, and now she could hear the emotion in his voice. "And then with your mother . . . It was . . . a lot."

Layne went and sat next to him. "It's okay."

"I never liked you going to that barn by yourself, but I always worried about you taking a fall—"

"Dad. It's fine."

He put an arm around her and kissed her on the top of the head. "I know it's not perfect right now. But I'm trying."

"I know." And she did. He was trying to keep doing what he'd always done—working himself too hard, forgetting to eat, leaving it to someone else to keep dinner on the table and the family in order.

At one time it had been her mother.

Now it was Layne.

"Want to go watch Simon sit on the bench?" she said.

He kissed her on the head again, giving her another squeeze. For a moment, she actually thought he might say yes.

But he stood. "I hate to leave you alone, but I need to head in to the office. My afternoon appointments were rescheduled for this evening, so . . ."

And she tuned him out.

She was back to square one. Familiar ground.

Alone.

The basketball game should have been dramatic, what with Ryan Stacey confined to the bench and Simon starting center. Poetic justice would have dictated that the stands be packed, with Simon making the winning shot in the last seconds.

But it was only JV, and the first game of the season, so the bleachers weren't crowded. The other team *sucked* and was barely organized enough to move the ball down the court.

But Simon was great. They were in the lead from the first shot.

And they won the game by twenty-two points.

"You said he can't hear?" said Hunter as they filed off the

stands. He'd stayed for the whole game. "You couldn't prove it by me."

Gabriel snorted and tossed his soda can into the recycling bin by the door. "Let's hope the coach feels the same way."

He'd been worried Hunter would judge him—for the fire at the barn, for telling Nick, for something else he couldn't quite identify. But Hunter had been steady as ever, listening as Gabriel rehashed his morning from a nearly empty section of the bleachers.

And then he'd said what he always did. "You want to stop?"

Gabriel didn't.

He couldn't. Even now, even after this morning, he could feel need burning under his skin, like a junkie going through withdrawal.

He wished he had his lighter.

They waited outside the gym to congratulate Simon, kicking at loose gravel as kids streamed through the doors around them. Mostly students first, finishing up after-school projects and clubs. Then the JV cheerleaders, arm in arm and giggling as they half danced across the parking lot to the activity busses. Then basketball kids, half damp from the showers, but high-fiving over the win.

When the flow of students dropped to a bare trickle, Gabriel wondered if he'd somehow missed Layne's little brother.

But he hadn't seen Ryan Stacey either.

Gabriel swore and went for the doors—but on this side of the school, the doors were locked to the outside. He pounded, but no one answered—of course, since he'd stood here like an idiot watching everyone leave.

"Come on," he said to Hunter, turning to sprint for the front entrance.

"What happened?"

"Ryan Stacey."

They tore through the halls, shoes squeaking on tile as they skidded around corners. A teacher yelled at them to stop running, but Gabriel didn't recognize her and they were well past before the words registered in his brain.

The gym: empty, aside from a few girls hanging a banner for a bake sale next week.

The locker room: empty. Boys' bathroom: empty.

Gabriel swore again. The school was huge—they could be anywhere.

"Wait." Hunter caught his arm. Gabriel froze and listened for a moment, but he didn't hear anything.

Hunter stepped across the narrow hallway and pushed on the door to the girls' locker room, opening it a few inches. The lights were off, revealing a well of shadowed tile and the edge of a trash can, but he yelled through the gap. "Anyone in here?"

Silence.

Hunter hit the light switch. Pink tile came to life, leading to pink steel lockers.

Empty—but Hunter strode forward anyway, rounding the corner into the girls' shower area. That's where they found Simon, shivering behind one of the pink shower curtains, sporting a black eye and a split lip.

And absolutely no clothes.

CHAPTER 34

Layne had never been a clock-watcher in class. Now it seemed every class took sixteen hours, the minutes ticking by until she could see Gabriel.

She still couldn't sort her feelings about him. Anger, at what had happened? She had no idea whether that was his fault. Curiosity? Absolutely. Intrigue, for certain.

Fury. Fear.

Desire. Longing.

All of it.

This morning had been torture. She'd woken before sunrise, as usual. Her hands had gone immediately to her side, seeking the familiar foreign texture, sure she'd dreamed that part.

Nope. The scars were still gone.

How?

She couldn't go to the farm—the surviving horses had already been trailered to another facility ten miles away for the time being. She couldn't call Gabriel, not with her father still monitoring her cell phone every minute. He was already on edge enough from Simon's black eye.

It had taken every ounce of Layne's restraint to keep her mouth shut—instead of reminding her father that she'd suggested they go to the game. That if they'd been there, Simon could have just walked out with them, instead of relying on some other kid to drop him at home after god-knew-what happened. Simon wouldn't have had a black eye—and he wouldn't have had a reason to lock himself in his room without explaining it.

But now, finally, the bell was ringing, signaling the end of second period.

Layne bolted for math class.

And Gabriel's seat, of course, was empty.

She stood there in the doorway, dismayed. Had he been hurt yesterday, and she just didn't know about it?

Or maybe this was intentional. Maybe he'd ditched class.

Maybe he didn't want to see her.

Her hands curled into fists. Disappointment felt just as crushing as the fury that had her pressing fingernails into her palms. As usual, she wanted to hit him and hug him at the same time.

If only he'd *show up*.

"Layne."

She spun around, hands still clenched, ready to swing.

Gabriel caught her wrists, his fingers gentle through the sleeves of her turtleneck.

But then he just held her there. He didn't push her away—or pull her closer. His voice was rough, low, just for her. "Don't hit me."

She stared up into his blue eyes, so close and full of emotion.

It took a minute to find her voice. Six billion questions had been rattling around her head all morning, and now all she could manage was, "Why?"

Gabriel winced, almost imperceptibly. "Well, at least wait until after school. Then you can beat the crap out of me if you want." His hands slipped free, releasing her. "Fighting in class is an automatic one-day suspension."

She swallowed. Now that he stood right in front of her, she was terrified to ask.

No, she was terrified of the answers.

Students were pushing through the doorway. Gabriel moved fractionally closer. "You all right?"

Layne kept flashing on that moment on the hill when the sunlight had danced along her skin, and Gabriel had kissed a path across her stomach, stealing her breath and her fears and making her feel perfect for the first time.

And then her sanctuary—*their* sanctuary—had gone up in smoke.

She pulled his lighter out of her pocket and held it out. "I think I need you to tell me."

A panicked look crossed his face. He snatched it out of her hand and slid it into his pocket. And then he was even closer, leaning in to speak right to her ear. "Getting caught with one of those is an automatic suspension, too."

His breath tickled her neck. She shivered.

Focus.

"Truth?" he whispered.

She nodded. "I want to know everything."

The second bell rang, and Layne jerked back. Her heart was in her throat.

"Free period?" he said.

"Yeah," she choked.

Then Ms. Anderson was coming through the door, urging them to their seats, calling the class to order.

Layne did the six questions of the warm-up automatically, grateful for the distraction, for the need to keep her eyes on her paper.

A folded piece of notebook paper landed in the crease of her textbook. Layne unfolded it under the edge of her desk.

Are you afraid of me?

The breath poured out of her lungs in a rush.

Then she put her pencil to the paper.

A little.

She watched his face as he unrolled her note. No regret, no disappointment. Just flat acceptance.

With a little spark of challenge.

Layne's palms were sweating on the pencil. She scraped them across her knees.

All of a sudden, she couldn't wait for that free period.

The intercom over the chalkboard crackled to life. "Ms. Anderson?"

"Yes?"

"Could you please send Gabriel Merrick to the guidance office?"

Just about everyone in the classroom turned to stare at him—including Layne.

"Are you in trouble?" she whispered.

He shrugged and shoved his math book into his backpack. "I have no idea."

Then he swung out of his chair and moved down the aisle. He was gone before she noticed the new fold of paper tucked beneath the corner of her notebook.

Truth: don't be.

Gabriel walked down the silent halls, his shoulders hunched, his backpack a dead weight.

The guidance office? If you were in trouble, they called you to the principal's office. He knew that routine by heart.

The guidance office called if there was a college recruiter here for an interview—and that had happened exactly zero times in Gabriel's high school career. The guidance office called if you were involved in an altercation with another student, and Vickers thought you could talk it out—but that wasn't something they'd call you out of class for.

Then he remembered the first week of school, when Allison Montgomery had been called to the guidance office during chemistry. Her father had been killed in a car crash.

Nick. His heart stopped in his chest.

But then it kicked back into action. Nick was *here*, at school. If something serious had happened, Gabriel would have heard about it. Same with Chris.

Michael.

But if something had happened to his older brother, wouldn't he be running into Chris and Nick in the halls, right this very second?

Then he remembered what had happened last night. Gabriel had no idea whether Ryan had made it to school today, but he remembered the way they'd found Simon in the girls' locker room. The way the poor kid had had the crap kicked out of him.

Maybe this had nothing to do with Gabriel at all.

He pushed through the double doors into the main office. Completely empty. No secretary behind the desk, no students waiting on the bench outside the principal's office.

Weird.

But he shoved through the swinging door into the guidance area. The school worked hard to make it look welcoming: a red and blue shag rug covered the tile, and four plush armchairs lined the back wall.

The five policemen standing there killed the welcoming vibe.

Gabriel stopped short. He actually felt the blood drain from his face. Didn't they send cops to tell you something bad had happened to your family?

He couldn't even remember the last words he'd said to his older brother.

And where were Chris and Nick?

Fear had his chest in a vise grip. He had no idea how his legs were holding him.

Ms. Vickers was standing in front of her closed office door. She looked as pale as he felt. "Gabriel?"

He'd *never* seen Vickers look rattled. His mouth was dry. "Yeah."

One of the cops stepped forward. He was the oldest of the five, probably in his late forties with salt-and-pepper hair. "Gabriel Merrick?"

"Yeah. Yes." His voice cracked. He could barely get the words out.

"Could you set the bag down, please?"

The backpack? It hit the floor with a *thunk*. "What happened?"

The officer took another step forward. "You're under arrest."

CHAPTER 35

Layne sat with her father and Simon, but she couldn't eat her dinner.

Really, she was amazed the food on the table was even edible, because she hadn't paid one bit of attention to cooking it.

Gabriel had been *arrested*.

He'd disappeared from math class, but she'd heard about it in the lunch line. It was all over school. The wild stories were completely unbelievable—Gabriel was wanted in three different states, he'd attacked the guidance counselor with an aerosol can and a lighter, he'd been caught running a meth lab. But the most common story was that he'd been arrested for arson, for starting the fires all over town.

The most popular story included the detail that someone had reported him for starting the fire at the farm.

Simon had found her, had demanded answers. Did she know? Did she believe it?

She didn't want to, but she couldn't forget that lighter tumbling out of Gabriel's sweatshirt. The haunted look in his eyes.

She also couldn't forget the note he'd left her, when she'd admitted she was afraid.

Truth: don't be.

She'd given Simon the only honest answer she had: *I don't know.*

Layne had gone looking for his brothers, but she didn't know their schedules and had no idea where to search. She'd looked up the number for the landscaping business as soon as she got home, but the phone went unanswered.

So she'd spent the last hour gathering her nerve.

If her imperfections had been enough to drive her mother away, what she had to tell her father might be enough to do the same to him.

As if sensing her gaze, her father glanced up from his iPhone. "You're quiet tonight."

She swallowed. "I have a hypothetical legal question."

He put the phone down. "In my experience, hypothetical questions usually aren't hypothetical at all."

She swiped her palms on her knees. "If you had a case where someone could give your client an alibi but that person would get in trouble for speaking up, would you still want the alibi?"

An eyebrow rose. "Define *trouble*."

She looked at her plate, pushing the beef in a circle. "Her father would disown her."

Now she had his full attention. Simon's too.

"Are we talking about you?" her father said. His eyes narrowed. "Who needs an alibi?"

"Gabriel Merrick," she whispered.

"For what exactly?"

"For arson." Her father's face looked like thunder now, so she rushed on, stumbling over her words, afraid she would cry before she got it all out. "They think he started the fires that have been in the paper, but I know—I know—"

"You know *what*, Layne?" Her father's voice was ice cold. "What do you know?"

"He didn't. I know he didn't. At least—"

"You don't know *anything*, Layne." Her father's fist was tight on the table. "Arson is a big deal. They don't just arrest someone on suspicion. There will be proof, and an investigation—"

"Apparently someone reported him for starting the fire at the farm. But he didn't do it. He couldn't have done it." Her hands were shaking. "Because he was with me."

Her father was staring at her. Simon, too.

Neither said anything.

She took a deep breath. "We were lying on the hill by the back paddock. He—"

"*Lying?* On the *hill?*"

"Talking!" she said. "Just talking! But the fire started while he was with me, so I know he couldn't have done it." Her father wasn't saying anything, so she rushed on, feeling tears prick her eyes with sudden emotion. "Can you call the police? Can you tell them? You can ground me forever. You can hate me. Just, please—"

"No."

Layne flinched. *"No?"*

"This arson case has been all over the news. Unless you can provide an alibi for all the fires—" His eyes narrowed. "You can't, can you?"

She shook her head quickly.

"It won't matter. And I'm not dragging you into some investigation just because you had a fling with the local bad boy."

"It's not like that! He's my friend—"

"Sure he is. Go to your room, Layne."

"But—"

"I said go!"

She backed away, feeling tears on her cheeks now. "I'm sorry," she whispered. "Please . . . just . . . we could help him . . ."

Her father's eyes flashed with anger. "He doesn't *deserve* your help."

Simon scraped his chair back from the table to stand. "*Yes,*" he said emphatically. "*He does.*"

Her father looked speechless with shock.

"He's my friend, too," said Simon, anger almost making the words unintelligible. He signed while he spoke, but even his hands were tight with rage. "You would know that if you ever bothered to talk to me."

Their father looked almost bewildered. "Simon . . . you don't—"

"Shut up! You wanted me to talk, so *listen*." Simon had to pause for an emotion-filled breath. "Gabriel Merrick deserves her help." He glanced at Layne and touched the bruising around his eye. "He deserves mine, too."

"Why?" she whispered.

Simon glanced at their father and scowled. "Are you sure you don't have to check your e-mail?"

"That's not fair, Simon." But her father put his phone in his pocket without even glancing at it.

"No," said Simon. "What's not fair is you treating us like we left with Mom."

Now her father flinched.

Layne caught Simon's wrist to stop his verbal assault and signed. *Please stop. He's all we have left.*

"Wait a minute," said her father. "What does that mean, I'm all you have left?"

Layne snapped her head around. "You . . . you followed that?"

"Of course I followed that. What does that mean?"

"But . . . you never sign—"

"Because I think Simon's going to have a challenging enough life without being entirely dependent on sign language. *Especially*," he emphasized, giving Simon a look, "when you can speak perfectly well."

Now it was Simon's turn to look shocked.

"I'm not going anywhere," said their father, his voice just a touch softer. "You have my full attention now. Tell me what I've missed."

They left Gabriel in an interrogation room.

A relief, really, since he'd gotten a glimpse of the holding cell, somewhere between fingerprinting and mug shots. Fifteen other guys, some sitting, some standing. Most were twice his size. One guy slumped against the back wall, and he'd puked on himself at some point. More than once, from the stains on his clothes.

He was the only one who didn't look up when Gabriel walked past.

The rest of them watched him. Especially a pale guy in his twenties with track marks down his forearms, who stared at Gabriel in a creepy, dreamy way.

Gabriel avoided eye contact with everyone.

He wished he could call Michael. He didn't even know if his brothers knew what had happened.

And he thought he'd been alone *before*.

He'd been holding it together, though. He'd had a brief burst of panic in the school—which blew out the lights in the guidance office. Suddenly, he'd been on the ground, with a knee in his back.

They had pinned him there until Vickers started babbling about recent electrical problems.

And then they'd searched him.

The cops had found the lighter in his pocket—and another one buried in his book bag. Had Layne turned him in for what had happened at the barn?

It made him remember the way she'd looked at him in the classroom this morning, breathless and wide-eyed and barely able to speak. Or her scripty handwriting on that piece of notepaper, when he'd asked if she was afraid.

A little.

Like he could blame her.

Just now, he could relate.

The interrogation room was just like on TV shows, barely twelve feet square with a table and four chairs. White walls, steel door with a tiny window. He got to sit, but they left him cuffed. And they left him alone, with the assurance that someone would be in to talk to him in a minute.

It was a long minute.

His stomach assured him it had been many hours since he'd eaten, though really, Gabriel had no idea how much time had passed. His shoulders were starting to hurt from being cuffed so long, but he didn't want to complain, because this was ten times better than that holding cell.

He wished he knew how long they could keep him here. Wasn't there something about seventy-two hours? Or was that just on cop shows?

So he sat. Waiting. Long enough that anxiety started to feel like something alive, consuming him from the inside out.

Maybe that was the whole point. A passive-aggressive mock-up of the clichéd good cop/bad cop routine. Maybe this could be called *no cop*.

He was under eighteen. What was the worst that could happen? Juvie?

He kept thinking of Michael's comments in the car, about how trouble with the law could lead to trouble with custody. The overhead light buzzed, flaring with power. Gabriel took a deep breath. The electricity evened out.

And then someone came in. No preamble, no knock. Just a twist of the doorknob, a slow entrance, a man with a stainless-steel mug and some papers. This was a new guy, in his late forties, though gray had just started to streak its way through his blond hair. He wasn't in uniform, just jeans and a sweater, though a badge clung to his belt. His eyes were narrow and blue and gave away absolutely nothing.

This guy had some authority; Gabriel could tell just from the way he carried himself.

"Gabriel Merrick?" He didn't wait for an answer, just sat down across the table and dropped some folders and a notepad in front of him. "I'm Jack Faulkner. The county fire marshal."

Faulkner. Hannah's father.

Gabriel didn't know what to say to him.

Marshal Faulkner leaned back in his chair and took a sip of coffee. "Been waiting long?"

The way he said it implied he knew *exactly* how long Gabriel had been waiting.

Maybe this was why he'd been left in handcuffs. So when someone deliberately acted like a tool, he couldn't punch the guy in the face.

"Is my brother coming?" he asked. His mouth was dry, and his voice sounded rough.

"Your brother?"

"You can't question me without a legal guardian or something, right?"

Marshal Faulkner leaned forward and lifted the cover of a manila folder. "You're seventeen?"

"Yeah."

The cover fell closed. "You're charged with first-degree arson. Right now, it's one count, but it'll likely be more, given the events of the past week. That's a felony, which means you're automatically charged as an adult. That's why you're here and not at the juvenile facility."

Gabriel couldn't move. The room suddenly felt smaller.

"You're allowed to have an attorney present." Marshal Faulkner clicked his pen. "Do you have an attorney?"

Gabriel shook his head. One of those other cops had read him his rights, something about an attorney being provided, but he had no idea how that worked. If he asked for a lawyer, that sounded like he was guilty.

"I didn't start those fires," he said.

Raised eyebrows. "You want to talk about it?"

"There's nothing to talk about. I didn't start them."

Except maybe that *one*. The one in the woods. But if he admitted he'd lied about that, it would make everything else sound like a lie. Gabriel looked away.

After a moment of silence, the marshal leaned forward in his chair. "Would you like me to remove the handcuffs?"

Gabriel's eyes flicked up. "Yes."

When he unlocked them, Gabriel rolled his shoulders to get the stiffness out, then wiped his palms on his jeans.

He hated that he felt like he owed this guy a thank-you or something.

Especially when Marshal Faulkner hesitated before sitting down and said, "How about some food?"

Gabriel would kill for some food, but he shook his head.

"You sure? If you're stuck here overnight, we have to feed you. Might as well be in here, where no one's going to take it away from you."

There were too many shocks in that sentence to process them all. *Overnight.* Gabriel thought of that pale freak in the holding cell and completely lost any appetite he might have had.

He shook his head again. "What time is it?"

"Just after six."

Six! Somehow it felt both earlier and later than he'd thought. Gabriel heard his breath hitch before he could stop it. His brothers would definitely know he was missing.

Marshal Faulkner reached into his back pocket and withdrew a pack of cigarettes. He held them out. "Smoke? No offense, kid, but you look like you need it."

"I don't smoke."

The marshal dropped the pack on the table and picked up his pen again. "Then why'd you have two lighters at school?"

Oh.

Gabriel scowled.

"And," said the marshal, "I understand there are a lot more at your house. Want to tell me about that?"

Gabriel froze. "At my house?"

"Officers are executing a search warrant right now."

At least it answered the question about whether Michael knew what was going on.

Thank god Hunter had the fireman's coat and helmet.

"I didn't start those fires," he said again.

"Is someone else in on it?"

A new note had entered the marshal's voice. Did they know about Hunter? Gabriel was wary after getting trapped by the lighter question.

He looked at the table, running his finger along the plastic stripping on the edge. "I don't know anything about it." His voice was nonchalant, but he felt in danger of choking on his heartbeat.

"You sure?"

Gabriel looked up, meeting the marshal's gaze evenly. "Pretty sure."

"Let me explain something." Marshal Faulkner dropped the pen on his folder and leaned forward. His voice gained an edge.

"You can jerk me around all night, but you're not doing yourself any favors. One count of first-degree arson carries a penalty of thirty years. That's *one*. We've got at least *four*. No matter what you tell me, we've got enough to keep you in the county detention center for a while."

Gabriel swallowed. His hands were sweating again. "I didn't start those fires."

"You know about the one on Linden Park Lane?"

The first one. Alan Hulster's house. The piercing fire alarms, the dead cat. The little girl. The anguished scream from the front lawn, the relieved, sobbing mother.

He gave half a shrug, feeling sweat under the collar of his shirt. "I don't know anything about it."

"Really?" Marshal Faulkner sat back. "You don't think if we asked Marybeth Hulster to come in here, she might not recognize you?" He paused. "She said she hugged the 'fireman' who saved her little girl."

Gabriel froze.

It had been dark. Soot had blackened his face.

But she'd stared straight into his eyes when she'd thanked him.

Would she recognize him? He had no idea.

He'd saved her child. Yes. She would recognize him.

Marshal Faulkner had that pen in his hand again. "I think maybe you know a little something."

Gabriel didn't say anything.

A pause, a glance in the folder. "Alan Hulster says you had an altercation in class that day."

Gabriel came halfway out of his chair. "He was being a dick! I didn't burn down his house!"

"Sit down."

"Damn it!" Gabriel's hands braced against the table. It took everything he had not to shove it across the room. "*I didn't start those fires!*"

"Sit. Now." The marshal hadn't moved. "Or the cuffs go back on."

Gabriel sat.

"I didn't start them," he said. "I didn't."

"Don't take this all on yourself, kid. Who else is in on it?"

"I don't know."

"You're lying to me."

"I don't know who's starting them."

"What *do* you know?"

"Nothing!"

"What are your brothers going to tell me?"

Gabriel felt like there wasn't enough air in the room. "They don't know anything, either."

"I have a report from a few weeks ago. You were caught with a few bags of fertilizer. Played it off as a prank, right? Was that supposed to be the first one?"

It *was* a prank. Tyler and Seth had beaten the crap out of Chris, so they were just going to screw with them. "What? No!"

"Your brother Christopher was with you. Is he the one starting the fires?"

"No."

"Did he help you?"

"No!" It was taking everything Gabriel had to stay in his chair.

"He's sixteen. We pull him in, he'll be treated as a minor. He'll be held in juvenile detention until we get around to questioning him. What's he going to tell—"

"You leave Chris alone! He had nothing to do with this!"

The lights blazed white hot and almost exploded, power pulsing in the air.

Gabriel reined it in, gasping from the effort.

The fire marshal had shoved back his chair, and he glanced between Gabriel and the lights overhead, which were settling back into a normal luminescence.

Gabriel swallowed. "Leave him alone," he ground out. "Chris doesn't know anything."

"What do *you* know?"

"I don't know who's starting them."

"Come on, kid—"

"I *don't*." Gabriel couldn't look at him. He was dangerously afraid he might cry if this guy kept pushing.

"We know you used lighter fluid to start them. How much of that are we going to find around your house?"

"None. I don't know." They might have some in the garage. Would that make him look guilty?

A pause, a tap of the pen against the folder. "Why don't you tell me about the pentagrams?"

Gabriel lifted his head. "The what?"

"Is it a cult thing? Some kind of initiation?"

Now a chill had hold of his heart. "What pentagrams?"

"Don't play stupid, kid. The pentagrams drawn in lighter fluid."

The door cracked open, and a uniformed officer stuck his head in. "Jack. Can you step out a sec?"

Gabriel glanced between them. "What pentagrams?"

The marshal was picking up his folder and his coffee mug.

"*What pentagrams?*" cried Gabriel.

But Marshal Faulkner was already stepping through the door, leaving Gabriel with all the questions.

Chapter 36

Gabriel wanted to pound on the door and demand answers. Unfortunately, that uniformed officer was standing there, obviously guarding him until the fire marshal returned.

Funny how being under guard made him feel *more* dangerous instead of less.

Gabriel chewed at his lip and stared at the floor, trying to reason it out. Pentagrams usually meant someone had called the Guides, had reported that Elementals were living in a specific house. Pentagrams were a target and a warning. Had there been pentagrams painted on the doors of the burned houses? He'd never gone in the front, so he had no idea. He and his brothers were the only full Elementals in town—well, until Hunter and Becca had shown up.

Right?

No, they had to be. Becca's father would have known about others.

Hell, Seth and Tyler would have known about others.

But why else would there be pentagrams?

The door opened, and he jerked his head up. Marshal Faulkner was in the doorway. He didn't look happy. "Someone is here to see you."

Gabriel straightened. Relief almost knocked him out of the chair. Michael had come. He'd figure out what to do.

He cleared his throat. "My brother?"

"I wish I were that lucky, kid."

"What does that mean?"

But the marshal was ignoring him, gesturing to the officer on guard. "Come on, Joe. I'll buy you a cup of coffee."

Then they were filing through the narrow doorway, the steel door falling closed behind them.

Only to be caught by a strong hand.

Belonging to Layne's father.

Gabriel stared up at him as he came through the doorway. The man had to be coming from work—or maybe he just wore a suit all the time. Even though it was after six on a Friday, his shirt looked pressed, his tie straight and tightly knotted.

His expression was all business. Gabriel had no idea how to take that.

He also had no idea what he was *doing here*.

Mr. Forrest set a briefcase on the table and unlocked the clasps. "You know," he said by way of greeting, "the night I caught you with Layne, I called you a future felon. I didn't realize you'd make good on that prediction so quickly."

"The night you dragged Layne out of my driveway, I called you an asshole. Guess we were both right."

A smile, but it looked a little vicious. "Normally I'd tell you to call me David, but given the circumstances, I think we can stick with Mr. Forrest."

"Don't tell me. You're the lawyer for the other side."

"That's not quite how this works."

Then Gabriel remembered her father's original threat from that first night, and realized this guy might be here to add more fuel to the fire. He shoved out of his chair. "Hey, I never did *anything* to Layne! If you told them I—"

"I'm glad to hear it. That's not why I'm here." Mr. Forrest eased into the opposite chair and pulled a legal pad out of his briefcase.

Gabriel watched him, perplexed. "Then what are you doing?"

A silver-plated pen came out of the briefcase next. "What

have you told them so far? Please tell me you haven't signed anything."

"Wait." After the news about the pentagrams, Gabriel's brain couldn't wrap itself around this. "What?"

An eyebrow rose. "What. Have. You. Told. Them—"

"Shut up. What are you *really* doing here?" Gabriel hesitated. "Did my brother *hire* you?"

"No. He didn't. He and I have spoken, however."

"So, what, you're just going to make sure I get locked up? I didn't start those fires."

That vicious smile again. "It doesn't really matter if you did or not."

"It sure seems to matter to everyone else."

"Not to me. I help people who 'didn't do it' all the time."

Wait a minute. "Are you saying you're here to help me?"

"I'm going to try."

Gabriel didn't trust him. "Maybe I don't want your help."

"They have several fires, a dead firefighter, and an eyewitness. Not to mention motive, a prior record, and a bedroom full of lighters. You want my help."

Gabriel frowned and looked away.

Mr. Forrest leaned back in his chair, spinning the pen between his fingers. "Did you really help Simon get a starting position on the basketball team?"

Gabriel couldn't get the fire marshal's threats out of his head, to say nothing of this mystery with the pentagrams, and Layne's dad wanted to talk *basketball*? "You want to talk about this now? Seriously?"

"If you want my help, yes. I want to talk about this now."

Gabriel glanced at the door. "Don't we have a time limit or something?"

"No."

"Fine. I gave Simon a few pointers. The coach made the decision. It wasn't a big deal."

"He came home with a black eye last night."

"Look, I didn't do that—"

"I know you didn't. He told me what happened." A pause. "Layne told me about the party, too."

"She did?" Layne had stood up for him? After everything that had happened? Then Gabriel felt his anger swell. "Why aren't you on *that* guy's case?"

"I will be. Don't worry." Mr. Forrest hesitated, and for the first time, his arrogance faltered. "She also told me you pulled her out of the barn yesterday morning."

Gabriel stared back at him. Talking about the fires felt like a trap.

"Anything you say to me is confidential. They can't use it against you."

Gabriel glanced at the corners of the room and dropped his voice. "What if they're recording what I tell you?"

"I hope they are. It's against the law, and then they'd never get a conviction."

Gabriel had to clear his throat. "I thought maybe Layne was the one to turn me in."

"No. From what I could find out, someone reported seeing you at the scene of the barn fire. Since you were already on their radar, they pulled you in." Mr. Forrest steepled his fingers. "Layne was ready to march down here and tell every officer she saw that you didn't start that fire. She said she was with you when it started. Is that not true?"

"It's true."

"She doesn't believe you started those other fires, either."

"I didn't."

Mr. Forrest nodded at the doorway. "They think you did. What have you told them?"

"Nothing." Gabriel paused. "Can they really keep me here overnight?"

"They can keep you a lot longer than that."

With every passing minute, the room seemed to feel smaller. Gabriel swallowed. "The guy told me I could go to jail for thirty years."

"He's right. Maybe longer if they can pin the dead firefighter on you."

Gabriel rubbed at his eyes. "Gee, I'm so glad you showed up."

"He's trying to scare you," Mr. Forrest said. "I'm going to work on it. If they're going to charge you, you'll get a bail hearing within twenty-four hours. Since it's a Friday night, it'll probably be tomorrow morning, and I imagine they'll set bail rather high."

The more this guy talked, the more it seemed like this was a hole Gabriel would never dig himself out of. "Fantastic."

"I'm going to see if we can avoid charges altogether."

"How the hell are you going to do that?"

"It sounds like they have a lot, but really, they don't have a thing on you. The lighters are suspicious, I'll grant, but no one actually saw you *start* a fire. No other incendiary devices have been found in your home. You have no record of starting fires. You're not a model student, but according to Layne, you're not a troublemaker around school, either. They can't even get you for impersonating a firefighter unless you did it to get money."

"They have an eyewitness."

"Sure they do. And you have a twin brother. Any eyewitness testimony is dead in the water."

Holy crap. Gabriel didn't have anything to say to that.

Mr. Forrest leaned in. "Layne says I was wrong about you."

Gabriel didn't know what to say to that, either.

"She has a whole timeline written out. She showed me some newspaper articles. Thinks you were the one to save the Hulster girl. Is that true?"

A timeline. That was so . . . so *Layne*. If he weren't knee-deep in drama, he'd smile. Instead, he just shrugged and looked away. "The little girl went down the laundry chute. They didn't think to check in the basement first."

"And the fireman who went through the floor?"

Another shrug.

"Are you crazy?"

Gabriel met his eyes. "Probably."

"They're going to want to question you some more. Think you can handle it if I stay?"

Gabriel narrowed his eyes. "Why would you do that for me?"

"You saved my daughter's life and protected my son. Why *wouldn't* I do that for you?" Mr. Forrest didn't wait for an answer, just glanced at his watch. "Let me make a few calls."

Before he was through the door, Gabriel said, "Do you really think they'll let me go?"

"I'll be honest. An hour ago, I wasn't too sure."

"So what's different now?"

Mr. Forrest gave him a grim look. "There's been another fire."

CHAPTER 37

Gabriel got to leave.

At five o'clock in the morning.

He hadn't eaten anything in almost twenty-four hours, and he sure as hell hadn't slept. Mr. Forrest was driving him home, the radio in his BMW playing some kind of light rock. The streets were deserted this early on a Saturday, especially with a cold front moving in, bringing rain to spit at the windshield.

Layne's father had stayed all night.

Gabriel cleared his throat. "Thanks." It felt woefully inadequate, but he wasn't sure what else to say.

"I don't mind driving you. Your brother has been dealing with the cops all night, too. No sense making him come out."

Michael was probably fit to be tied. "No . . . I meant, for all of it."

Mr. Forrest glanced over. "You know, they could still arrest you again. If you give them just cause."

Gabriel ran his finger along a seam in the leather upholstery and stared out at the darkness. "You're telling me to stay out of trouble."

"I'm telling you to stay away from fires. Don't even go out and buy a new lighter."

The cops had kept the ones they'd confiscated at school—and

they'd probably taken all the ones in his bedroom, too. Gabriel felt like he was missing a limb.

And he was already wondering about the fire he'd missed tonight.

"I'm serious," said Mr. Forrest. The car rolled to a stop at a traffic light, and he looked over. "I'm not a miracle worker. If they catch you at another fire, especially now, you'll be charged for sure."

Gabriel nodded. "I know." He wished he could text Hunter to let him know what was going on, but they'd kept his phone too. Thank god he'd been careful about deleting all the text messages relating to the fires.

"Look, I know I said it doesn't matter what you're doing, but I need to know. Is Layne doing this with you? She's been having a hard time since her mother left—"

"No." Gabriel shifted in his seat to look at him. "Layne's not . . . she's not doing anything wrong."

"I read once that children who've been injured by fire may experiment—"

"No! She's not. Experimenting." This felt more awkward than if Layne's father had asked if they were having sex. "She had nothing to do with this. I didn't even know about the scars until the party. No one did."

"What about the pentagrams? In there, you said you didn't know anything, but if she's wrapped up in some kind of cult—"

"Jesus, there's no *cult*, okay? I don't even know what the pentagrams mean."

And once he'd had a lawyer by his side, he hadn't been able to get any more information from the fire marshal.

Mr. Forrest glanced over. "What exactly *are* you doing?"

Gabriel stared out the window. How could he ever explain all of it?

The mist in the air turned to rain, forcing Mr. Forrest to switch on the wipers. "I said I'd help you, but I'm going to protect my daughter, too."

"From me. You think Layne needs protection from me."

"You tell me."

Gabriel gritted his teeth. "What happened to all that talk about saving your daughter and helping your son?"

"I'll help you stay out of prison. That doesn't mean I'm going to help you lead Layne into danger." He glanced over again. "You'll forgive me if I'd rather she date someone who *isn't* wanted by the police."

Gabriel reached into the backseat and grabbed his backpack, yanking it into his lap. "Let me out."

To his surprise, Mr. Forrest pulled over, right there on the side of Ritchie Highway. He hit the button to unlock the doors.

Gabriel stared at him. "I'd never hurt Layne."

"I'd like to keep it that way."

"So that's it?"

Mr. Forrest looked over. "Were you bluffing about getting out?"

Gabriel grabbed the door handle. When he was standing in the grit and rubble of the shoulder, feeling rain trail down his collar, he hesitated before closing the door. "You know I don't even have a phone."

"Would now be a bad time for a joke about smoke signals?"

"Fuck you." Gabriel slammed the door.

The BMW pulled back into traffic. Gabriel watched him drive, waiting for brake lights or some signal that this was just a bluff. Like his had been, really.

But then the car was cresting the hill, disappearing from sight.

Leaving Gabriel alone.

He pulled the hood of his sweatshirt up and shivered. He was only about a mile from home, but exhaustion added weight to his back while hunger clawed at his insides. The rain and darkness made him want to curl up here, by the side of the road, to wait for sunrise.

He forced his legs to move.

Again, he wished for a lighter, for flame to roll between his fingertips.

His foot kicked at a pile of roadside debris, sending dead

leaves and twigs and trash scattering across the dampening pavement.

He ducked and scooped a larger twig into his palm. The bark along the outside was dampened from the rain, but he snapped it in half easily. The inside was dry and jagged, a pale patch of exposed wood, barely identifiable in the darkness.

"Burn," he whispered.

At first, nothing.

But then, with a spark and a flicker, it flared to life.

He crushed the flame in his palm almost immediately, his heart pounding against his rib cage.

Control. He'd done it.

Another couple hundred feet down the road, he did it again, cradling the flame in his hands to protect it from the rain, breathing power into the fire until headlights appeared over the hill and he killed it.

Only to do it again once he was alone with the darkness.

This time, he let the fuel burn away until he held nothing but a lick of flame suspended between his palms.

It died quickly when a drop of rain slipped between his fingers, but Gabriel was more sure now. Another twig, another spark, another flame.

This one lasted until he made the turn onto his street, when he sent the fire slithering into smoke between his fingers.

After his night in the police station, after the argument with Layne's father, after his sheer inability to protect Layne or save Simon or identify an arsonist, this new control fed him some pride.

It made him long for the next fire, to test his abilities.

As soon as he had the thought, Gabriel smashed it as quickly as he'd crushed the fire in his hands. There couldn't be any more fires. He had to stop.

But there'd been a fire tonight. He should have been there. He could have helped.

By the time he reached his driveway, the misting rain had soaked through his hoodie and had probably done a number on the books in his backpack. Michael would be ready to raise hell, but Gabriel was so relieved to be home that he didn't care. He'd listen to whatever his brother wanted to dish out and then some. The lights on the lower level were on, and there was an unfamiliar car in the driveway. It didn't look like an unmarked police car, but anxiety grabbed Gabriel by the throat anyway.

He found the front door unlocked, and angry voices echoed from the back of the house. Michael was arguing with someone, loudly enough that he probably hadn't even heard the door opening. Tension was riding high in here, an almost tangible field Gabriel had to cross just to make it through the doorway. From what he could see, the house wasn't trashed—maybe the cops had just searched his room. He dropped his things in the foyer and headed for the kitchen.

The arguing stopped when he appeared in the doorway.

Michael was standing by the cooking island, his eyes furious—though his expression softened to something like relief when he saw Gabriel. Becca hunched close to Chris at one end of the table, their expressions tired and drawn. Hunter sat near them, his expression full of guilt and relief all at once.

And at the other end of the table stood the source of the arguing, Bill Chandler, Becca's father.

Michael ran a hand back through his hair. "Thank god. Mr. Forrest called and said you got out of the car—"

"Because he was being an ass." Gabriel cast another glance around the room, as if he could have missed his identical twin on the first pass. "Where's Nick?"

Bill took a step forward, pointing a finger at Gabriel though he was still arguing with Michael. "Just because he came home now doesn't mean there won't be more complications. I *told you* to lie low. I told you I would only be able to protect you for so long—"

"*Where's Nick?*"

"When the cops showed up, I told Nick and Chris not to come home," said Michael.

"But there was another fire," said Hunter. His voice was small.

It had almost been a relief, another fire occurring while Gabriel had a rock-solid alibi. But if Nick was involved—that feeling of anxiety turned into a noose. He couldn't breathe around it. Had Layne's father known? "Where is he?"

"In the hospital," said Chris.

"He was with Quinn," said Becca. "The fire was set at her house."

"Nick's okay," said Michael. "They wanted to keep him overnight for observation, and they won't let him leave without someone to sign him out. I asked Layne's father not to tell you."

"Quinn's okay, too," said Becca. "Nick got her out, then went back in for her little brother."

Gabriel remembered telling Nick about the fires, and his twin's comment about not being strong enough to go along.

Had Nick taken a risk just to prove himself?

Gabriel stared across at his older brother, feeling guilt and contempt steal some of the anxiety—but choking him just the same. "And you just left him in the hospital. Alone."

"What the hell did you want me to do?" Michael suddenly looked like he wanted to hit something, and his words slammed into Gabriel like a fist. "You were at the police station and Nick was in the hospital—and I couldn't help *either of you*, because the police were here all night, searching the house. I've spent weeks trying to help you, and you won't tell me the truth about what you're doing. Layne's father *keeps you out of jail*, and instead of trying to figure out how to repay him, you tell him off on the side of the road. We're all in danger here, and you're bringing it right to our doorstep. And *you're* going to get pissed at *me*?"

Gabriel flinched.

"I told you," Bill snapped. "I told you this would happen if you didn't keep your abilities in check—"

"We didn't start those fires," said Hunter. "We helped. People would have died otherwise." For the first time, Gabriel thought he understood the guilt in his expression.

It loosened something in Gabriel's chest, to know he wasn't alone here, that someone could carry the guilt along with him.

Then Becca's father said, "People *will* die. Everyone in this room. When the Guides find out—"

"They might already know," said Gabriel.

When everyone turned to him, he said, "When the police questioned me, they asked me about the pentagrams in the burned houses."

Hunter's eyebrows went up. "Pentagrams? You never said you saw—"

"I *didn't.*"

Bill turned to face Hunter, his expression fierce. "You told me you wanted to honor your father's position. You told me you wanted to know what to do."

Gabriel glanced at Hunter. His friend had never mentioned Becca's father, had never mentioned any discussion following their meeting in the food court.

Bill continued. "You wanted to *prove* yourself—am I right? And I said *watch Gabriel Merrick*, and you—"

Hunter was out of his chair. "That's exactly what I *was* doing!"

"What did you just say?" said Gabriel. A new feeling was coiling in his chest, something bitter and frightening.

But the room had fallen into a stricken silence.

Gabriel stared at Hunter. "That's why you were following me that night."

"Nice," said Becca. She was glaring at Hunter, too. "So you misled everyone around you, huh?"

Hunter shook his head. "No, it's not—it wasn't—"

But Gabriel was already storming back down the hallway, heading for the front door.

Michael caught him, grabbing him by the arm and shoving him up against the door before he could open it. "You are *not* leaving."

Gabriel struggled against him. "Let me go, goddamn it."

"No." Michael shook him, hard. "You're not leaving. Do you understand me? I will tie you up if I have to."

Gabriel stared into his brother's eyes, seeing the same exhaustion and fury he knew were reflected in his own.

He wanted to fight, but he was just too tired.

"Fine," he said. "I'll go to my room."

Michael let him go.

And Gabriel walked up the stairs.

Alone.

CHAPTER 38

Gabriel had thought people were talking about him when he couldn't try out for basketball.

That had nothing on walking through school the Monday morning following an arrest.

People actually went silent when he passed. Kids he didn't even *know* were staring at him.

"You want me to walk with you to first period?" said Nick.

"I'm not four," said Gabriel. He slammed books into his locker, pulling out the ones he needed for morning classes.

Like it mattered. Like he'd be able to concentrate.

He hadn't wanted to come to school, but he'd needed to get the hell out of the house. Michael had practically boarded his bedroom door shut. Trying to escape for a run had turned into a grand inquisition.

Probably for the best, really. He couldn't run without thinking of Layne, of the last time he'd tackled the four-mile trek to the horse farm.

How he'd saved her life.

How he had no idea if she was okay.

Nick was still standing there, watching him—the same way he'd been watching him since he'd gotten home from the hospital.

"Go," said Gabriel. "You'll be late, and I know you hate that."

His twin didn't move. Gabriel yanked the zipper closed on his backpack. "Go, Nicky. I'll be on my best behavior. I promise. I even did all my homework."

Because he'd had nothing else to do all weekend. He'd ridden the knife's edge of tension since getting home, waiting for *something* to happen. For the police to arrest him again. For the Guides to show up. For more information on the pentagrams.

Nothing.

Nick gave him a look. "You're not going to kill anyone in the hallways, are you?"

He meant Hunter. Gabriel hadn't heard from him, either—not like he was waiting around for a call.

Gabriel shook his head.

"Really?"

"Jesus, Nick!" Gabriel gave him a shove. "*Go.*"

All the students nearby went absolutely still. He could almost hear the collective gasp, like he was going to whip out a weapon. He wished he knew what stories were floating around. He could imagine, especially with the weekend to let people get really creative.

Gabriel slung the backpack on his shoulder and turned away from his brother. "Fine, then *I'll* go. I'll see you at lunch."

People cleared a path.

In first period, the teacher looked surprised to see him—and maybe a little afraid, too. Students left the seats surrounding him empty. No one spoke to him, but the focus of their attention fed his nerves like a shot of caffeine. It almost drove him to act, to live up to this violent criminal reputation he'd earned for himself. But he kept hearing Becca's father's voice in the kitchen.

People will die. Everyone in this room.

He slouched in his seat and pretended to be invisible.

People already had died—or come close. The pentagrams pointed to Elementals, but he couldn't reason it out in his head. Layne's barn had burned down—then Quinn's house. Were they being targeted somehow? But that didn't make sense, either. The Elementals in town knew where the Merricks lived—they'd marked the house with paint when Becca's dad first came to town. If they wanted to attack the Merrick brothers, they could just burn *their* house down.

And what about all the innocent people whose houses had been destroyed?

He watched the clock tick toward second period. Then third. When he'd see Layne.

He still had her note in his backpack, a little damp from his walk in the rain, but still legible.

Are you afraid of me?

A little.

She wasn't in the math classroom when he got there, but he yanked his homework from his binder and flung it into the basket on his way past Ms. Anderson's desk.

The teacher glanced up when he passed, and she was the first one who didn't look like she expected him to douse her desk in kerosene and flick a match.

"Mr. Merrick?"

He stopped, his fingers tight on the strap of his book bag. He didn't want to look at her, didn't want anything to interfere with the cord of tension holding him together.

"Yeah," he said.

She picked up the homework he'd tossed into the basket and glanced at it, then back at his face. "I understand you had a challenging weekend."

Challenging. Hilarious. He met her eyes, knowing his own were full of *don't-fuck-with-me*. "I've had better."

"Are you okay?"

The question caught him off guard, especially since her expression seemed genuinely concerned. She was the first person to ask how he was doing since the instant he'd been arrested.

His familiar defenses were clicking into place, ready to snap, to flip her off, to blame her for everything, because if she hadn't caught him cheating, he'd be on the basketball team. He never would have needed Layne's help, and he never would have gotten into that argument with her father. He never would have gone to that first fire.

And that little girl would be dead. Along with everyone else he'd pulled from a burning building.

He took a breath, feeling his shoulders drop. "Yeah."

Then, before she could say anything else, he pushed past her desk to drop into his seat.

Taylor Morrissey wasn't in front of him today, flashing her boobs and flipping her hair. Gabriel looked around—she was across the room, sitting at one of the spare desks, glaring at him like he was a serial killer.

He wanted to mock her, but he just didn't have the energy.

And then Layne walked into the classroom.

She was wearing jeans and those fuzzy boots girls seemed to like, along with a rich purple turtleneck. No makeup, same glasses.

Her hair was down, loose and straight and shining.

Perfectly average, probably, but Gabriel couldn't look away from her.

Especially when her eyes met his across the classroom and something inside him uncoiled.

He could read the relief in her expression, the longing and sadness and desperation he knew were mirrored in his own. He wished he could hold her, could press his lips against her skin and whisper promises that he'd never hurt her, that he'd always protect her, that he didn't care what anyone thought of him, that he'd do anything for her, always.

"Hey," called out Taylor. "Look who decided not to look like a total loser."

The girls around her snickered.

"That's enough," said Ms. Anderson.

Layne was blushing, pushing past the teacher's desk, her eyes down now. She dropped in the chair beside Gabriel.

"Hey," he whispered.

Her frenetic movement stilled. She peeked at him through the curtain of her hair. "Hey."

"Check it out," said Taylor, her voice loud again. "The burn victim and the pyro. Almost like Romeo and Juliet, right?"

Gabriel whipped his head around, but before he could get a word out, Layne's hand latched on to his wrist.

"Don't," she hissed. "Anything you say, they'll use it against you."

He bit back the words and faced forward.

"Ignore them," Layne murmured. Her hand softened, and she gave his forearm a gentle squeeze. "Just get out your notebook."

Gabriel turned his head to look at her. His entire life was going to shit, but seeing her here was like finding a little glimmer of light amid all the darkness. "Your hair is down."

She blushed a little and moved to pull her hand back.

He caught her fingers, trapping them beneath his own. "It's pretty."

"Thanks," she whispered.

And she left her hand there until Ms. Anderson started talking.

Gabriel still couldn't focus on class, but now his mind kept replaying the feel of Layne's hand on his wrist, instead of all the turmoil of the weekend.

A note appeared in the middle of his desk.

I'm glad you're okay.

He cast a glance right. Her cheeks were still pink, and he'd bet money that her heart was racing in her chest.

He wrote back.

I'm glad _you're_ okay. Thank you for having your dad help me.

Her blush deepened. He watched her put her pencil to the paper.

He doesn't want me to associate with you.

Like that was a surprise. But Ms. Anderson was looking at the class now instead of writing on the board, and he had to wait before he could write back.

What do <u>you</u> want?

Layne's expression sobered when she unfolded his note. Then she wrote quickly.

I want to understand how you can do what you did.

He stared at those words for a long time and wondered how much she knew. How much she'd figured out. She was staring at him now; he could feel it.

Finally, he nodded, then put his pen against the paper.

Free period? Library?

She didn't write back to that one, just unrolled it and nodded, then looked back at her work.

He'd caught up with the homework, but Gabriel couldn't understand a word Ms. Anderson was saying. He kept sneaking glances at Layne, fighting to keep his hands still, wanting to reach out and stroke her hair, to touch her arm, to hold her hand and feel her steady presence balance him out.

Then the bell was ringing and Layne was gathering her things.

"See you," she whispered. Her hand barely brushed his as she pushed past his desk.

"See you," he said, gathering his things to walk out of the classroom.

But Ms. Anderson stepped in front of him. "I'm pleased to see your work has improved."

"I have a tutor," he said. When her eyebrows went up, he shrugged and said, "I wanted to get back on the team."

Funny how basketball seemed so pointless now.

"Well," said Ms. Anderson, "I hope this means you'll do well on the makeup exam this afternoon."

"Wait, that's—"

"We agreed on today. You *are* free fifth period, correct?"

Christ, like he would have remembered a *math test* with everything going on. This lady couldn't cut him some slack? He glanced at the doorway, but Layne was long gone. He wouldn't even have a way to get a message to her. "I . . . look, I need to—"

"I want to give you more time," she said gently. "I know you're not focused today."

He breathed out a sigh. "Yes. More time would be great."

"I can't. I'm already giving you a free pass by letting you make up the test."

His hands balled into fists at his sides. "I don't give a crap about the team anymore."

"Do you care about graduating? Because right now you have a zero in the system. And with Friday's events, the principal asked me about it. I said you were scheduled to take a makeup exam today."

Gabriel wanted to hit something.

"Look," she said. "Just take the test. I've seen your work over the last few days. You'll do fine. And I can help you recover from a low score. I can't help you recover from *no* score."

"I can't," he said. "I need to be somewhere."

"Where?"

Somehow he didn't think *I need to meet a girl* would suffice here.

Her expression hardened. "I'm telling you that you will fail this class. You will not graduate. I know this might not matter to you right this instant, but I assure you, it will matter in the long run."

He snorted. The long run. Considering Bill Chandler's comments Saturday morning, he didn't even know if he *had* any chance of being around for the long run.

But then he realized he did have one last option.

Layne's voice was echoing in his head, the way she'd chastised him for cheating.

He shook it off. "Fifth period," he said. "Fine. I'll be here."

Now he just needed to find Nick.

CHAPTER 39

Layne sat in the back corner of the library, blocked by the stacks, yet with a crooked view of the entrance. The same table where she always sat. The same table where she'd stood up to Gabriel, two weeks ago. It felt like a lifetime ago.

The library wasn't crowded, but no one ever sat back here because the books were old and smelled musty. They must have cleaned the carpets over the weekend, because today it also smelled sweet yet acrid, a chemical scent that was giving her a headache.

Her palms were sweating, and she swiped them on her jeans, again reveling in the realization that there were no scars under the denim along her left thigh.

That was the only thing she'd left out of her confession to her father.

She just wasn't sure what to say. She was used to dealing with facts and numbers. Her father was used to dealing with truths and untruths. Neither had any experience dealing with the supernatural.

Because it had to be, right?

This morning, in math class, Gabriel had reminded her of the way he'd been that first morning on the trail, when she'd compared him to a land mine. Only this time it was more like a hand grenade after the pin had been pulled. It was just a matter of time before he went off.

"It's like every time I see you, you're sitting all by yourself."

Layne jerked and almost fell out of her chair. Ryan Stacey was behind her, leaning against the bookcase. He must have come around the side of the stacks.

"I didn't expect to find you here," he said. "But I like it. You will, too, I think."

Now her palms were sweating for an entirely new reason. "Go away. You're lucky I'm not having you arrested for assault."

"You kissed me, too, sweetheart."

"Don't call me that." She threw a glance at the doorway and prayed for Gabriel to appear.

He didn't.

"Besides," she said, making her voice hard even though her insides felt like jelly, "I'm not the only one you've assaulted."

"Yeah, like your baby brother is going to earn any friends by being a retard and a tattletale."

"Simon is *not* a retard."

"Whatever. I took care of him." He took a step toward her, and she scrambled out of the chair before she could stop herself. Her back hit a bookcase, and the metal shelves dug into her shoulders.

A smile lit his face, but not in a good way. "Too bad about the fire at the horse barn. Did that satisfy your little burn fetish? Add a new scar or two?"

She flinched, but then he looked at her crookedly. "Or is it Merrick who has the burn fetish? I guess you freaks all have to stay together—"

"Leave her alone."

Layne was choking on her breath, on her heartbeat, fear warring with relief. Gabriel was here, looking as fierce as ever. He'd protect her.

She just didn't want him to do it at his own expense.

She moved close to him, letting her hand close over his forearm like she had in class. "Don't fight," she said. "Let him say what he wants. It's not worth it—"

Gabriel glanced down at her hand, as if surprised to find it there. "I won't fight him." Then he made a face. "What is that smell?"

"Don't you know?" said Ryan. "I mean, they're going to find a bottle of it in your locker."

The forearm under her hand turned to steel, but Gabriel was absolutely still. "What are you talking about?"

Layne realized what Ryan had said. "You knew about the fire at the farm. You knew I was there."

"Of course I did. You told me where to find you." His eyes flicked to Gabriel. "Of course, I didn't realize you were riding more than just horses."

"Shut up!" she snapped, feeling tears grab at her throat.

"It was supposed to be a hay bale. I was just screwing with you," said Ryan. "I didn't realize the whole place would go up like that. When the cops found me in the woods, I had to say I was out running and saw who started it." A wicked smile at Gabriel. "Too bad for you it happened in the middle of an arson spree."

"You?" gasped Layne. "*You* . . . but Gabriel didn't—"

"Really, I hadn't planned on either of you being here, but it's kind of poetic justice." Ryan pulled a lighter out of his pocket.

Gabriel started forward. "It's you. You're the one starting the fires."

"Nope. You are." Ryan flicked the igniter.

And tossed it.

Layne didn't see where it went. She was just aware of the blast of heat, the roar of flames, and the feeling of her shoulders hitting the brick wall of the library. Gabriel's body trapped her there.

She couldn't see anything but fire and smoke and the side of Gabriel's face, all but pressed against hers.

"Lighter fluid," he said. "He sprayed the whole area with lighter fluid."

And the books were providing plenty of fuel. Layne coughed, her lungs trying to find oxygen through the smoke.

He pulled her down, against the ground, and suddenly it was easier to breathe.

"We have to move," he said.

She nodded. "But can't you"—she coughed—"can't you do something?"

He pulled her along the wall, to the corner, then swore. All the stacks in this back part of the library were blazing. The school's fire alarms were blaring now; one was right overhead.

He yelled over it. "I'm going to try to get us out of here."

"No—the fire. Like at the farm." Another cough. "In those houses. You can do something to stop it, can't you?"

"Not if you want to keep breathing."

She coughed again, and he pushed her closer to the floor. "What? I don't—"

"Wrong twin." His voice was grim. "I'm not Gabriel. I'm Nick."

When the fire alarms went off, Gabriel's pencil streaked across the paper. Students were suddenly flooding the hallways, laughing and roughhousing and carrying on, shouting over the alarms.

He looked at Ms. Anderson. "A drill?"

She was already slinging her purse over her shoulder, a grade book in her hands. "There wasn't one scheduled, but they don't always tell us." She sounded exasperated. She took the test and put it on her desk, even though he'd only finished the third question. "Come on."

He shouldered his backpack and headed for the hallway. His nerves were already shot, and the pulsing alarms weren't helping.

But as soon as he hit the hallway, he felt it.

Come play.

He stopped short in the middle of the flow of students. They were all heading right, toward the stairs at the end of the hallway that would lead outside. The fire was somewhere to his left—and that left a lot of school to search. He'd have to fight a sea of students to find the source.

He saw Ronald Coello, a guy he'd played soccer with, heading his way.

"Hey, Coello," he called. "What's going on?"

Drawing attention to himself was a mistake. Ronald stopped and stared at him. So did everyone else in the general vicinity.

Another guy from soccer, Jonathan Carroll, gave him an unfriendly up-and-down and got in his face. "The school's on fire, dickhead. You know something about it?"

Gabriel was ready to shove him back, but Ms. Anderson put a hand up in front of his face—and in front of Jonathan's, too. "We're evacuating, gentlemen. Keep moving."

Ronald and Jonathan kept moving.

"You, too, Mr. Merrick."

He hesitated. His element was calling him.

But his brain was warning him. If the school was on fire, being caught anywhere near it would be *bad*.

Then someone from behind him snorted and said, "Leave it to Merrick to find a way to set the library on fire."

The library.

Layne.

And Nick.

He shoved a hand into his bag for his phone—which wasn't there, of course.

"Mr. Merrick," said Ms. Anderson. "We need to move."

He moved all right—bolting left, fighting the surge of students, ignoring his teacher's protesting calls behind him.

CHAPTER 40

Layne and Nick were trapped.

They'd been able to crawl to the "Cozy Corner," an alcove the librarians had set up for casual reading. It was really just an old storage area, five feet high and four feet deep, and there was only enough room to sit on beanbag chairs. The back wall was painted cinder block with inch-wide openings that vented into the computer lab.

Which was deserted, of course, the door at the opposite side of the room closed. The library was at the dead center of the school. Any students would be heading *away*.

All the bookcases were engulfed in flames, completely blocking escape. The heat was *intense*. The carpet crawled with fire barely inches from where they crouched against the wall. She couldn't hear students screaming anymore and wondered if anyone even knew they were stuck here.

The fire alarms, however, were deafening.

Simon.

He'd been at lunch, and she knew he'd taken to shooting hoops in the gym instead of submitting to ridicule in the cafeteria.

Would he even know the fire alarms were going off?

"Stay close to the vents," called Nick. "I'm trying to create a gap in the oxygen so the fire stays out of here."

Staying close to the vents wasn't a problem. She practically had her face pressed against the cinder blocks, hyperventilating through the gaps. The air on the other side felt like it was coming out of a freezer. She was sweating through her clothes from the heat at her back.

She couldn't worry about her brother now. He hadn't been in the library, so he was probably in better shape than she was.

"How?" she gasped. "How are you doing that?"

"Maybe we can have that whole discussion another time." Nick glanced over and she watched the firelight flicker across his features. He was sweating, too. "You all right?"

"Is that a trick question?" But his efforts appeared to be working. The fire hadn't entered their little area yet. It gave her an idea. "Can you make a path through the fire that way?"

Nick grimaced. "I'd have to clear all the oxygen around us as we moved. It would take too much time."

"How much time?" God, she couldn't *think* with these fire alarms.

"Ten, twelve minutes maybe?"

Yeah, she couldn't hold her breath that long. She probably couldn't *survive* that long.

She was already starting to feel light-headed from whatever he was doing. She pressed her face to the gap again and inhaled. The air felt thin, and she took another deep breath. It felt like her lungs couldn't inflate all the way. Smoke was collecting along the opening to the alcove as if a pane of glass kept it out.

"How long can you keep that up?" she said.

"We're going to find out." His jaw was tight. "I should have just taken that stupid test for him."

"Gabriel was taking a *test*?"

"Yeah. The math teacher cornered him. He asked me to come tell you, but then Ryan Stacey showed up—"

He stopped talking. The fires went dark.

And all of a sudden, she was on the ground, looking up at Nick. His hand was patting her cheek, his eyes wide. "Layne? *Layne.*"

She sucked in a breath—a mistake, it was more smoke than oxygen. She coughed, hard. "What happened?"

"You passed out. You have to let me know if you feel light-headed again—"

Everything went dark.

This time, she came to with her face pressed against the narrow vent. The air was cool and rushed into her lungs. Fire still blazed at her back.

The fire alarms were silent.

She started to turn her head, but Nick held her there. "Don't," he said, and she heard strain in his voice. "I'm trying to keep the oxygen on *that* side of the wall, and it's no easy trick."

"How—" she gasped. The air was still thin. "How are you breathing?"

"The lack of oxygen won't bother me."

She tried to turn her head again, but he held fast until the edge of the cinder block was digging into her chin. "I'm not kidding," he said. "Don't even turn for a second."

She could barely see him from the corner of her eye, and she thought maybe the alcove was just too dark.

Then she realized it was full of smoke. He'd lost some ground to the fire.

She swallowed, and it hurt. "What happened to the alarms?"

"It must mean the school's been evacuated."

"Do you have a phone? Can you let someone know we're trapped here?"

"I already tried the first time you passed out. No signal."

Layne wanted to be brave. She wanted to be optimistic.

But she started crying anyway.

Nick's hand went over hers. "Gabriel will find us. He'll get us out."

"How?" she choked. "How do you know?"

"Because he always does."

Fighting through the crowds of students took a while. They packed the hallways, backed by teachers who did *not* want to let Gabriel run toward the library. He had to shove his way past them. Chris had chemistry this period, so he'd be on the opposite side of the school—and he wouldn't even know about Layne and Nick meeting in the library. He would have evacuated with everyone else.

Layne and Nick might have evacuated, too. Gabriel could be bolting for the library needlessly.

And the fire was calling him, full of fury and danger. He could smell smoke in the air.

By the time he rounded the corner to the Language Arts wing, the alarms went silent, only the warning lights were strobing. The halls were deserted, thick with smoke.

Come play.

He got low to the ground, putting a hand against the painted cinder block of the hallway. Two more turns and he'd find the library entrance.

But one more turn revealed bodies in the hallway.

Two girls, their faces red. Young, probably freshmen. He didn't recognize either of them. He hurried to the closest and put his cheek close to her mouth.

She was breathing, but barely. He needed to get her out of the smoke.

He jerked her into his arms and ran.

The front entrance to the school was the closest way out, but the halls were still dense with smoke. His sneakers squeaked against the floor as he bolted around turns, trying to stay as low as he could.

Just as he made the final turn into the front atrium, he almost ran smack into a group of firemen.

"Here!" he cried, shoving the girl at one of them. "There are more!"

And before they could stop him, he was running again.

He almost left the second girl. The firemen were coming, and they couldn't miss her in the middle of the hallway.

But this school was practically a maze. If they were trying to avoid the smoke, they might take a different route to the library and miss her altogether.

Before he even had it all reasoned out, the second girl was in his arms, and he was running for the front again.

This time the firemen tried to stop him. He heard shouts and felt a hand grab for the sleeve of his hoodie, but he ducked and bolted back into the smoke, running again for the library entrance.

He made it all the way to the hallway running parallel to the library before he found more bodies. The hall was so choked with smoke that he practically tripped over the first one. Two girls and a guy. He recognized the guy, Randy Sorenson. He played starting center for the football team.

He also outweighed Gabriel by a good fifty pounds.

Gabriel grabbed one of the girls first. She wasn't breathing at all.

The smoke was so thick that he had to drag her. He made it down two hallways before finding firemen.

Good. He dropped her and ran back, yelling behind him, "Down this way! There are two more!"

When he heard them behind him, he passed Randy and the other girl and dove through the smoke into the library.

Fire swirled around his feet to welcome him. It was happy he was here.

Because it wanted him to help *destroy*.

The rage caught him by the throat and held on. This fire wanted destruction just like the fires he'd found in the community. The carpet flamed around him, sending plumes of smoke into the air. Every bookcase was fully consumed to the point that he couldn't identify anything. He couldn't hear a thing over the roaring flames.

It didn't stop him from shouting. "Nick! Layne!"

Nothing. But he knew approximately where she would have waited, and he started forward.

Only to trip over another body.

This one was on fire, and he only knew it was a guy because of the shape. Not Nick—too big. Gabriel swept his hands across the clothes, sending the fire off to find other things to burn. Then he hooked his hands under the boy's arms and started to drag.

This guy was easily as heavy as Randy. Gabriel borrowed strength from his element, but it wasn't going to be enough.

Suddenly, hands were there, beside his, helping to drag. Gabriel looked up, expecting a fireman.

But finding Hunter.

"The firemen are waiting for hoses," Hunter yelled. "It's too hot. They can't—"

"Is this guy alive?" he shouted.

A pause. "Yes."

"Then shut the fuck up and pull."

They got him to the entrance. Gabriel didn't wait to see whether Hunter would follow him. He had more ground to cover.

Another girl was by the circulation desk, her skin red and blistered. Not breathing. He picked her up and carried her back to the entrance, pushing through when he didn't see firemen there.

They were just outside in the hallway, however, in full gear, masks on, radios crackling.

Gabriel shoved the girl at one of them and turned to bolt, but another fireman grabbed him. Gabriel fought, but a second fireman caught his free arm.

They were wrestling him back, pulling him away from the library entrance, shouting something, but he couldn't understand them through the masks and his fury.

Then Hunter was there, a gun in his hand.

And then he was pointing it at the fireman holding Gabriel.

They let him go real quick.

Gabriel didn't even *think* about the implications of this. He just ducked under Hunter's arm and ran back into the library.

Somehow, the smoke was thicker now. He crawled beneath it while flames snapped at his jeans and curled around his fingers.

He begged the fire to calm itself, to stop the rage.

It refused.

"Nick!" he yelled. "Layne!"

Nothing.

He crawled forward, around a row of bookcases, heading for the back of the library, where he knew Layne usually sat.

And all of a sudden, the smoke wasn't as dense. He could see flames billowing from the bookcases above him, but the smoke was moving away, toward the entrance.

Nick. Nick had to be doing that.

But fire was everywhere. Bookcases lined the walls, blazing like suns against the cinder block.

Except for the small alcove, where the carpet was on fire.

And Gabriel could see two figures there, just barely out of reach of the flames.

He surged forward, sprinting through the fire. He slid to his knees into the alcove and sent the fire away, creating a bigger space around them.

Layne was crumpled against the wall. Nick was crouched beside her, his eyes clenched shut, his hands in fists. The air here was freezing and thin, and all of a sudden, Gabriel almost couldn't breathe.

"Nick," he gasped. "I'll hold the fire. I need to—"

He didn't have to finish the sentence. Nick let go. A blast of cold air rushed through the vents. The fire rejoiced, flaring higher. Gabriel sent it away, toward the entrance, toward the ceiling, promising better things to burn.

And suddenly smoke billowed around them.

Only to retreat when Nick sent it away again.

Gabriel pulled Layne into his arms. She was limp, her skin clammy and warm. Her head flopped onto his shoulder.

But she was breathing.

"She's okay," said Nick. His voice was rough and worn. "I made sure she kept breathing. I just couldn't keep her conscious."

"Come on. We need to get out of here."

Gabriel cleared fire from their path, and Nick pushed the smoke ahead of them, working together wordlessly, the way they always had when they played with fire for fun. He headed for the north entrance to the library, knowing firemen would be waiting at the south side.

Layne made a small sound and shifted against him.

"You're all right," he said. "We're getting out."

Her eyes opened a crack. "Gabriel?"

The sound of her voice almost made him cry with relief. "Yeah. I've got you."

Her eyes fell closed again. "You're supposed to . . . math test."

"I thought maybe this was more important."

She pressed her face against his neck. Her skin was flushed and hot, but the whisper of her breath against his skin was the greatest feeling in the world—because it meant she was alive.

He ducked his head so he could speak into her ear. "Did you see who started the fire?"

She nodded—but Nick grabbed his arm and hauled him to a stop.

"Yeah," said Nick, an odd note in his voice. "It was him."

Gabriel looked up. They'd made it to the center of the library, an open space under a skylight. Ryan Stacey was lying in the middle of the floor.

Surrounded by a pattern blazing into the carpet.

A huge, flaming pentagram.

CHAPTER 41

Gabriel was still staring when Hunter appeared at his side. He looked surprised to see Layne and Nick—but then more surprised at the pentagram on the floor.

Not to mention the kid lying inside it.

"He's dead, isn't he?" said Gabriel.

"No. Not yet."

Gabriel glanced at him. "You didn't shoot the firefighters, did you?"

Hunter gave him a look. "No, but we don't have much time. They'll be blasting through here with hoses any minute."

"Too bad we can't just shoot *him*," said Nick.

"Why can't we?" said Gabriel. He walked forward, into the circle, scattering flames with every step. He kicked at Ryan's leg, but the other boy remained motionless. Layne shifted in his arms again, reminding him that he couldn't linger here. "This idiot can't be an Elemental—I've fought with the guy three times, and he's never called on anything."

"Then why's he lying in the middle of a pentagram?" said Hunter.

"And there's power here," said Gabriel. "If he wasn't feeding rage into the fire, then someone was." He paused, reading the flames around him. He felt eagerness. Expectation. "Someone still is."

Hunter had the gun in his hand again.

"Are you *always* armed?" said Gabriel.

"Since we started worrying about Guides, yeah."

Gabriel thought of all those fires, the focused fury that had made him wonder if he hid in the night with some other guy who shared his affinity for fire. Each fire had been a celebration of sorts. Nothing had been subtle.

Like the pentagram, those fires were a message.

He just couldn't figure it out.

And there wasn't time to stand here puzzling it through. "Can you two drag him out of here?"

"No!"

A female voice. They all turned.

Calla Dean stepped out from behind a flaming bookcase, easily as comfortable in the middle of all this fire as Gabriel was. "Leave him."

Hunter lowered the gun. His voice was full of shock. "Calla."

"You look surprised," she said.

"He's not the only one," said Gabriel.

She reached down and plucked a plume of fire from the carpet, letting it hover in her palm, feeding it power until it started to spiral off her hand. "You've been messing with all my pretty fires."

"You?" said Nick. He glanced between Calla and Ryan. "But . . ."

"Oh, he started all of them. I just helped them along." She rolled her fingertips through the flame she'd created. "The first one was an accident, I think. He and one of his idiot friends were goofing off at the house next door, putting lighter fluid in water guns. I just fed a little power into it, and the whole place went up like a match." She snapped her fingers. "He liked that. It got a little addictive. For both of us, I think."

Then she made a face, similar to the one she made when the broccoli was missing salt. "Though he was kind of a pain to follow around."

"You killed a fireman," said Hunter, his voice tight.

"I didn't kill anyone," she said. "He did."

"But you drove the fires," said Gabriel. "It was your rage I felt—"

"Oh yeah?" Her eyes flashed with the brightness of the flames in the room. She smiled and crushed the fire in her palm. "Prove it."

"You're drawing the Guides here," said Nick. "They were already watching this area, but—"

"That's the whole point," she said, and the flames around her grew. "We want them to come. That's why I drew pentagrams in the houses—"

"*You* drew them?" said Gabriel. "But why do you *want* the Guides to come?"

"So we can destroy them." Her gaze settled on Hunter. "I think you might know about the last two we killed? Convenient rock slide, huh?"

Hunter lifted the gun.

"Go ahead," she said. "Shoot me. We want a war."

He cocked the gun.

Then high-pressure water was blasting into them all, knocking them to the ground and soaking their clothes.

And putting out every last inch of flame.

CHAPTER 42

The holding cell was a lot easier to take the second time around.

Because this time Gabriel was sharing space with Nick and Hunter.

They sat against the back wall, their clothes still damp from the fire hoses. Gabriel was freezing, but he couldn't ask his twin to warm the air. Nick looked exhausted, as if it were a good thing the wall was there to hold him upright.

"You sure Layne will be all right?" Gabriel said.

Nick didn't even open his eyes. "For the fifteenth time, yes. I'm sure."

She'd been loaded onto a stretcher while cops were handcuffing them. Gabriel had tried to tell them Nick wasn't involved, but they'd ignored him. Calla Dean had disappeared.

And what would he say about her anyway?

He glanced at Nick. "I bet an arrest record will help the college search."

"I'll use it as my learning experience for the application essays." Nick looked over, and Gabriel could read the worry in his eyes. "What do you think's going to happen?"

"You'll be fine. I think *I'm* screwed." Gabriel considered what had happened in the hallway, the way Hunter had pulled a gun on a fireman—though he'd lost the weapon in the water. "I don't think I'm the only one, either."

Hunter sat a few feet down the wall, damp hair trailing into his eyes. He hadn't said a word since they'd been arrested.

"I can say it was me," said Nick. "We can switch—"

"No," said Gabriel. "I know what I did. I don't need you to cover for me anymore. I can take it."

But he kept thinking about Calla Dean. He should have been worried about other Elementals in town, about her threats of war, her purposeful attempts to draw the Guides near. He should have been worried about how she was the real arsonist, but he'd never be able to prove it.

Instead, he kept thinking about what she'd said to Hunter.

So we can destroy them. I think you might know about the last two we killed.

The last two. Hunter's father and uncle.

He opened his mouth to say something, but then remembered that Hunter had never been his friend. Not really.

Gabriel shut his mouth and faced forward.

A policeman came to the gate, a ring of keys jingling in his hand. "Hunter Garrity?"

Hunter got to his feet, his expression resigned. "Yeah."

"You're out. Your grandfather is here to pick you up."

Hunter's eyebrows went up. "I'm what?"

"Turns out the fireman who reported you with a gun changed his story. Said he made a mistake in all the smoke, and since we didn't find one at the scene . . ." The officer paused. "He also said you helped pull half a dozen kids out of that library."

Hunter stood there staring at him, like he wasn't sure if he should trust this stroke of luck.

"Go," said Gabriel. "Get out while you can."

But Hunter sat back down against the wall. "I'm not leaving until they do." He jerked his head toward Gabriel. "I didn't pull those kids out. He did."

Gabriel didn't look at him. He swore under his breath. "Don't do me any favors."

"Doesn't matter," said the officer. "You're all out."

Now Gabriel and Nick snapped their heads up at the same time. "What?"

"Your brother is here to take you home. Seems the librarian heard that Ryan Stacey boy admit the whole thing. Too bad the smoke got to him before he finished his little design."

The officer didn't sound like there was anything *too bad* about that at all.

"He's dead?" asked Nick.

"He's in the hospital." The officer didn't sound too broken up about that, either. "You kids coming or what? I've got real criminals to book."

Gabriel was ready to face Michael in the waiting room of the police station.

He wasn't ready for the firefighters.

More than a dozen men, plus Hannah and one other woman. Most of them, including Hannah, were wearing fire pants and suspenders, their faces smudged with soot, though a few just wore T-shirts with the fire house insignia and jeans.

Gabriel stopped short in the doorway and swallowed. He glanced at Michael, standing at the counter and signing a form. No answers there.

Then some of the firemen separated, revealing a guy in a matching T-shirt in a wheelchair, his leg in a Velcroed cast from ankle to thigh. He glanced between Nick and Gabriel. "Which one of you is the kid who pulled me out of the house on Winterbourne?"

Then Gabriel recognized him. This was the guy who'd fallen through the floor. Gabriel didn't know what to say.

Nick hit him in the shoulder, shoving him forward. "He is."

The guy held out a hand. "Thank you. I owe you a lot."

Gabriel couldn't move.

This time Hunter shoved him in the shoulder. "Shake his hand, you idiot."

Gabriel reached forward, not feeling like he deserved any

thanks at all. He hadn't been enough. He should have been able to stop the fire.

The man's hand closed around his. "I heard about today, too. How did you do it?"

Gabriel shrugged. "Just lucky, I guess." He glanced back at Hunter. "I had help."

"Luck doesn't last forever, kid."

Gabriel snorted. "No kidding."

The fireman didn't let go of his hand. "No more playing fireman. Promise?"

"Yeah," he said, thinking of Calla Dean and her vow to lure the Guides here. He wouldn't be able to stop if she kept this up. But he lied, because what else could he do? "I promise." He moved to pull his hand back.

The fireman held fast, surprisingly strong despite the fact that he was stuck in a wheelchair. "I'm serious. You want to walk into fires, go through school and do it for real."

"You know," said Hannah, "you can start fire school at sixteen."

Fire school? He'd never considered making a *career* out of his abilities. "I'll think about it," said Gabriel.

Nick clapped him on the shoulder again. "No, you'll do it."

Layne stared at the ceiling in the emergency room and listened to her parents bicker. For the second time in less than a week.

She was wearing a hospital gown, so they knew her scars were gone.

And unfortunately, it had turned into one more point of argument.

"Well, David," her mother snapped, "obviously you haven't been paying attention to the children if you weren't aware—"

"You weren't aware, either, Charlotte! Don't try to tell me about . . ."

Layne put the pillow over her face.

She hadn't known what to say.

Because she didn't know how it had happened, either.

The doctors had lots of theories, about growth spurts and skin regrowth, and healthy eating.

Really, they were grasping at straws. Layne let them grasp.

What was she going to say? *When I almost died in the barn, this guy saved my life . . .*

The pillow was pulled away from her face, and her mother's heavily made up face smiled down at her through a cloud of some expensive perfume. "Oh, Laynie, I wish you'd told me. Once we finish with this mess"—she waved a manicured hand to indicate the treatment room—"we can go to the mall. I saw the cutest dress the other day and thought, *If only Layne didn't have*—"

Layne sat up. The oxygen tube strung around her face pulled tight, but she didn't care. "No."

Her mother blinked. "No?"

"No. I like the way I dress. And it's too late to play mom."

More of the confused stare. "It's too late to play—"

"You heard me!" Layne snapped. "I get straight As, and you don't give a crap. I take care of Simon, and you don't give a crap. I spent the last ten years trying to *get your approval*, and you didn't give a crap. Now that I'm *perfect*, you want to play mom. Well, I'm not playing. I want you to leave."

"Layne, I am your *mother*—"

"Too late." Layne cut a glance at her father. "Can you make her leave?"

"I can't make your mother do much of anything."

Her mother folded her arms. "Layne, I am not listening to this—"

"Go," Layne hissed. "Or I'm asking the nurse to call a social worker. And I'm going to tell them all about how you ran off with some guy from the country club, and how you don't show up for visitations, and how you—"

"Layne!"

Layne jerked the oxygen tube away from her face. "Go. Or I will. How will that look to all your perfect friends?"

Her mother staggered back, her mouth working but no sound coming out.

Then she turned on her designer heels and walked out of the room.

Layne squinched her eyes shut and told herself not to cry.

She felt her father step in front of her. "I won't ask if you're okay," he said.

She opened her eyes. He was looking right at her, no sign of his iPhone.

"You can ask," she said, "because I am now."

Then she leaned forward to give him a hug.

CHAPTER 43

School was closed for the week.

It didn't stop Gabriel from waking at five the next morning. He wandered into the kitchen and flipped on the dim light over the sink, rinsing the coffee carafe to start a new pot. Then he found a package of chocolate chip cookies in the cabinet and dropped into a chair at the table.

A purse had been left on one of the other chairs, and Gabriel raised his eyebrows. Quinn or Becca had spent the night.

His brothers sure were getting daring.

Or maybe Michael was getting more lax.

It made Gabriel think of Layne.

He missed her.

Light footsteps crept down the hallway, and Gabriel grinned, wondering which girl he was going to catch doing the walk of shame.

When Hannah tiptoed into the kitchen with wet hair and wearing an oversized T-shirt with jeans, he almost choked on a cookie.

"Damn," she whispered, her cheeks pink, but a rueful smile on her lips. "I knew it was a mistake to leave my purse down here. Nick or Gabriel?"

"Gabriel." He pushed the cookies across the table. "Have a cookie. Is that my brother's shirt?"

Her cheeks turned redder and she grabbed her bag. "I think that's my cue to leave."

"Nah. Stay." Gabriel gestured at the counter. "I just made coffee. You want a cup? Where's Michael?"

She hesitated, then eased into a chair. "He's in the shower." She paused. "Look, I don't want you to get the wrong idea—"

"Don't worry, I already have." Gabriel pulled three mugs down from the cabinet. "How do you take it?"

"With an obscene amount of milk and sugar."

Déjà vu hit him in the chest, and he hesitated before pouring. "Me too." Then he joined her at the table.

She wrapped her hands around the cup and took a sip, just as Michael came through the doorway. Wet hair, clean shaven.

He stopped short upon seeing Gabriel. "I thought you'd be out for a run."

"Hey, Mike," he said innocently. "I thought girls weren't allowed to spend the night?"

"Watch it."

"At least you're not wearing *her* shirt."

"I think that's enough."

Gabriel opened his mouth to fire back, but then Michael stepped up to the table, ducked his head, and kissed Hannah on the cheek.

With enough tenderness that Gabriel didn't want to mock it.

Just checking up on the investigation, my ass, he thought.

He looked away. "I'm going out in a bit, so you two can have the house to yourselves." Then he smiled. "Except for Nick. And Chris."

"I've got to be at work at seven-thirty," said Hannah. "So I won't be here long." Then she jumped and pulled a vibrating cell phone out of her pocket. "It's my folks, so I've got to take this . . ."

But she was already walking down the hallway and stepping out the front door.

Michael turned from the counter with a cup of coffee in hand. "Don't start," he said to Gabriel.

"I didn't say anything. I'm just glad you weren't jerking her around." Gabriel paused. "So I guess you don't have too much baggage after all?"

Michael gave him a look. "Trust me. I do." He sat down at the table. "She just has enough to match."

"What does that mean?"

"It means she has a five-year-old son."

Gabriel went still. "Holy crap."

"So we're taking things really slowly."

"Looks like it."

This was quite possibly the first time Gabriel had ever seen his older brother blush. "It was late. She slept here. We did not—" Michael broke off. "I don't really think I need to explain myself to you."

Gabriel smiled and took a sip of coffee. "No, no, I'm enjoying this."

Michael ran a hand through his hair. "Not like it matters when I don't even know what the next few days will hold. You said you think this Calla girl is going to keep setting fires?"

"Yeah. I do."

The front door opened again, and Hannah whisper-shouted down the hallway. "Gabriel, someone is here to see you."

Michael raised his eyebrows. "It's five o'clock in the morning."

"Don't look at me." Gabriel walked down the hallway and out onto the front porch while Hannah walked back inside.

Layne stood there, in black yoga pants and tennis shoes, with a turquoise hoodie and her hair in a ponytail. Her face was flushed, her eyes shining in the porch light, tendrils of hair stuck to her forehead.

"When you said four miles," she said, "you weren't freaking kidding."

"You *ran* here?" he said. "In the *dark*?"

"Only the first two miles. Then I was dying." She shrugged a little. "I walked the rest. I'm sure I'm a mess."

"No," he said, feeling a bit dazed at finding her there. "You're beautiful."

"I'm sorry I just showed up," she said, looking shy. "I knew you'd be awake, and I need to ask you—"

"Ask me later," he said. And he kissed her.

CHAPTER 44

Layne's legs were ready to give out, but she didn't mind. Because Gabriel was walking her home.

"I should have driven you," he said, shaking his head. "This is nuts."

"This takes longer."

"Good point," he said, catching her waist in his hands and kissing her again.

And her back was against a tree and her fingers were tangled in his hair and she was forgetting what she'd even come to talk about in the first place.

But then his fingers slid under the hoodie.

She caught his wrists, and he drew back, his eyes dark in the early morning light.

"Are you still worried about your scars?" he said gently. "You know I think you're—"

"Wait." She blinked up at him in surprise. "You don't know?"

"I don't know what?"

She took his hand and slid it under her shirt. "My scars are gone."

His hand went still against her skin. "How?"

She gave a little laugh. "You tell me. They disappeared after the barn fire."

His fingers drifted higher, skimming along her rib cage. "All of them?"

"Yes, all of—" She gasped as his thumb went under the edge of her bra, then playfully smacked him. "Hey!"

"Sorry." He kissed her again. "Thought I should check thoroughly."

Then he pulled back. "We should walk. I don't want to get you in trouble. Your father hates me."

"Oh, you've saved my life twice now. I think he might give you the time of day."

"Really?"

She shrugged a little, smiling up at him. "Maybe. Give it time." Then she sobered. "But I want to know. About you."

He sighed, then bent to pick up a dead leaf from the path. He spun it by its stem. "Truth?"

She nodded.

The leaf sizzled and flared to life, catching flame that sparked light across his cheeks.

"Let's walk," he said. "And I'll tell you everything."

BEYOND
THE
STORY

Spark Playlist

"Blow" by Ke$ha

I probably listened to this song a hundred times while writing *Spark*. It's about a dance party, but the music is so penetrating that I'd turn off all the lights in the middle of the night, blast the song in my headphones, and write Gabriel's fire scenes. Something about the electronic music behind the lyrics reminded me of fire alarms, and the intensity of the song kept the adrenaline going.

"Stronger (What Doesn't Kill You)" by Kelly Clarkson

I'm a firm believer that what doesn't kill you makes you stronger, and Layne would feel the same way. This is totally a girl power song. Layne would love it.

"We Are Young" by fun

This song is all about being young and taking the world by storm. When I wrote the final scene between Gabriel and Layne, I imagined this song playing in the background.

"Stereo Hearts" by Gym Class Heroes, featuring Adam Levine

This is one of the sweetest songs I've ever heard, and I think it perfectly captures the romance between Layne and Gabriel.

"Everybody" by Ingrid Michaelson

This song is all about falling in love, and it's completely innocent and lighthearted and, believe it or not, this song was my backdrop for writing about Hannah and Michael. (Don't tell Michael. He'd be pissed.)

"Good Feeling" by Flo Rida

This song just makes me want to dance and gets my pulse going. Great backdrop for the action scenes.

"Without You" by David Guetta, featuring Usher

Another romantic song that makes me swoon for Layne and Gabriel.

"Love Bites" by Def Leppard

This is one of my favorite songs of all time, because it perfectly captures the pain of first love.

"Your Guardian Angel" by The Red Jumpsuit Apparatus

This song is a power ballad, and it works for both Layne and Gabriel. I think they'd both say that the other is their guardian angel, don't you think?

"Mean" by Taylor Swift

This song is all about standing up to bullies—and I must have listened to it on repeat about a hundred times, right along with "Blow."

"When She Turns 18" by Christian TV

If there's ever a perfect song for a boy telling off the father of his girlfriend, *this is it*.

"Start a Fire" by Ryan Star

This could be Gabriel's theme song.

"You're Gonna Go Far, Kid" by The Offspring

This song is angry and intense and challenging and is exactly the kind of thing I'd expect Gabriel to blast in his headphones.

"Something Beautiful" by NeedToBreathe

This song is the theme song for the Elemental Series. Any time I need inspiration for a book, I start with this song.

Read on for a sneak peek at

Spirit,

coming in June 2013.

CHAPTER 1

Hunter Garrity woke to the click of a gun.

His grandparents kept a night-light in the utility room, but either it wasn't working or someone had killed it—his basement bedroom was pitch-black. His breathing was a shallow whisper in the darkness. For an instant, he wondered if he'd dreamed the sound.

Then steel touched his jaw.

He stopped breathing.

A voice: soft, female, vaguely mocking. "I think you dropped this."

He recognized her voice, and it wasn't a relief. His arms were partially trapped by the sheet and the comforter; he couldn't even consider disarming her from this angle.

"Calla," he murmured, keeping his voice low so as not to spook her. He had no idea how much experience she had with guns, and this didn't seem like the right time for trial and error.

"Hunter." The barrel pressed harder into the soft flesh under his chin.

He needed her to move, to shift her weight. Right now, she was just a voice and a weapon in the darkness.

He let out a long breath. "How did you get in here?"

"I drugged your dog and picked the lock."

It took monumental effort to keep still. He had a knife under his pillow, but going for it would take about three hours in comparison to the amount of time it would take her to pull a trigger. "You *drugged* my *dog*?"

"Benadryl in a New York strip." Her voice turned disdainful. "I can't believe you let the dog out of the house without watching him."

His grandparents lived on an old farm. Like he should have considered that psycho teenage girls might be leaving tainted steaks for his dog to find. "If you hurt him, I'll kill you."

"You know," she said, ignoring him, "I thought about burning this place down. Kerosene, match, *whoosh*."

"What stopped you?" He slid his hand beneath the blanket, just a few inches to see if she would notice.

She didn't. "Nothing. There's still time."

"I don't believe you," he said. "If you wanted to start a fire, you wouldn't be here right now."

"We want you to get a message to the other Guides."

"I don't *know* any other Guides," he hissed.

Well, he knew one, but Becca's father was just as far off the grid as Hunter was.

His hand slid another few inches, clearing the blanket.

"Come on, Hunter," she said sweetly. "Aren't you your father's son?"

Her voice had grown closer. She was leaning in. The gun moved a fraction of an inch.

All he needed was a fraction.

He swung for her wrist, going for deflection, ducking under the movement. His other hand was free, flinging the blankets at her while he slid to the ground. He threw a punch where her knee should be, but she was gone already, somewhere back in the darkness.

He tried to slow his breathing, his heart, trying to convince his body that he needed to *hear*.

"Nice try," she said.

He focused on the air in the room, asking the element to reveal her location more precisely, but it was never something he could force. He had to wait.

And the air wasn't talking.

At least the darkness was working to his advantage. If he couldn't see her, she sure couldn't see him.

He slid a hand under his pillow, and the knife found his fingers, the hilt a reassuring feel in his palm. He'd never cut anyone with it, but he knew how to throw.

Then he heard her breath—or maybe he felt it. Close, too close. He lifted a hand to throw.

A board cracked him across the side of the head. Now the room was full of light—stars danced in his field of vision. He went sprawling, and for a painful moment, he didn't even know if he was lying faceup.

Then she kicked him, rolling him onto his back. "Idiot," she said. "You think I'd come alone?"

Rolling sent the back of his head into the carpet. It hurt. A lot.

His knife was gone.

"I should shoot you right now," she said. "But we *need* you."

"Go to hell." He could taste blood when he talked. He slid his hand against the carpet, looking for his knife, but a booted foot stomped down on his fingers.

God, how could they *see* him?

The gun went against his forehead. "A message," said Calla. "Are you listening?"

"Yeah," he ground out. He still had a free hand, but he had no idea whether her "helper" had an extra weapon.

"We're going to burn a house every day," she said. "Until they come."

She was nuts. "They'll destroy you," he said.

"I don't think so," she said. "Tell them to come and see. You have a week."

"You'll kill ordinary people—"

"No. Until they come, that's on you." She shifted the gun. "You like piercings, right?" The hard steel pressed into his bare shoulder. "How about a little bullet hole to convince you?"

Hunter whipped his free hand out to deflect again, this time rolling into the motion and trying to break her wrist.

She shrieked and dropped the gun.

He didn't let it distract him—he kept moving and drove his fist into the leg of whoever pinned his other hand.

This time, he connected. He heard a male grunt of pain. His other hand was free. Movement filled the darkness around him, and he knew they were getting ready to retaliate.

And then Hunter found the gun.

He didn't wait.

He pointed at motion, then pulled the trigger.